THE
GINGER
MAN

J. P. DONLEAVY

THE ATLANTIC MONTHLY PRESS
NEW YORK

Published simultaneously in Canada
Printed in the United States of America

Library of Congress Cataloging-in-Publication Data
Donleavy, J. P. (James Patrick), 1926–
    The ginger man.
    I. Title.
PS3507.0686G56   1988   813'.54   88-3417
ISBN 0-87113-199-4

Atlantic Monthly Press
841 Broadway
New York, NY 10003

98 99 00 01 20 19 18 17 16 15 14 13 12 11 10

THE
GINGER
MAN

1

Today a rare sun of spring. And horse carts clanging to the quays down Tara Street and the shoeless white faced kids screaming.

O'Keefe comes in and climbs up on a stool. Wags his knapsack around on his back and looks at Sebastian Dangerfield.

"Those tubs are huge over there. First bath for two months. I'm getting more like the Irish every day. Like going on the subway in the States, you go through a turnstile."

"Did you go first or third class, Kenneth?"

"First. I broke my ass washing my underwear and in those damn rooms in Trinity nothing will dry. In the end I sent my towel to the laundry. Back at Harvard I could nip into a tiled shower and dive into nice clean underwear."

"What will you have to drink, Kenneth?"

"Who's paying?"

"Just been to visit my broker with an electric fire."

"Then buy me a cider. Does Marion know you've hocked the fire?"

"She's away. Took Felicity with her to visit her parents. On the moors in Scotland. I think the Balscaddoon was getting her down. Scrabbling on the ceiling and groans from under the floor."

"What's it like out there? Does it freeze your balls?"

"Come out. Stay for the weekend. Not much in the way of food but you're welcome to whatever I've got."

"Which is nothing."

"I wouldn't put it that way."

"I would. Since I've arrived here everything has been down and these guys at Trinity think I'm loaded with dough. They think the G.I. Bill means I crap dollars or a diarrhea of dimes. You get your check?"

"Going to see about it Monday."

"If mine doesn't come, I'll croak. And you're saddled with a wife and child. Wow. But at least you get it steady. And I've never got it at all. Any loose women out there on Howth?"

"I'll keep a watch."

"Look I've got to go and see my tutor and see if I can find out where they hold my Greek lectures. Nobody knows, everything is secret. No more drink for me. I'll come out over the weekend."

"Kenneth, I might have your first woman waiting for you."

"Yeah."

2

It was a steep hill up to Balscaddoon. Winding close to the houses and the neighbor's eyes having a look. Fog over the flat water. And the figure hunched up the road. On top it leveled and set in a concrete wall was a green door.

Within the doorway, smiles, wearing white golfing shoes and tan trousers suspended with bits of wire.

"By all means come in, Kenneth."

"Some place. What holds it up?"

"Faith."

O'Keefe went through the house. Opening doors, drawers, closets, flushing the toilet, lifting its lid, flushing it again. Stuck his head in the hall.

"Say this thing really works. If we had something to eat we'd be able to use it. They've got one of those big shops down there in the town, why don't you pop down with that English accent of yours and get some credit. As much as I like your company, Dangerfield, I'd prefer it on a full stomach."

"I'm up to my eyes already."

"And you don't look so hot in those clothes."

O'Keefe jumped on the floor of the drawing room. Pulled open the conservatory door, pinched the leaves of a dying plant and went out into the garden. Standing on the shaggy grass he gave a shrill whistle as he looked down precipitous rocks to the swells of sea many feet below. He went round the narrow back of the house, looking in the windows. In a bedroom he saw Dangerfield on his knees chopping a large blue blanket with an axe. He rushed back into the house.

"Jesus Christ, Dangerfield, what are you doing? Have you gone Asiatic?"

"Patience."

"But that's a good blanket. Give it to me if you're going to chop it up."

"Now, Kenneth, watch me. See? Put this round the neck like this, tuck in the ragged edges and presto. I'm now wearing Trinity's rowing blue. Always best to provide a flippant subtlety when using class power. Now we'll see about a little credit."

"You shrewd bastard. I must admit it looks good."

"Make a fire in the stove. I'll be back."

"Get us a chicken."

"We'll see."

Dangerfield stepped out into a deserted Balscaddoon Road.

The counter was covered with rich sides of bacon and wicker baskets of bright eggs. Assistants, white aproned, behind the long counter. Bananas, green from the Canary Isles, blooming from the ceiling. Dangerfield stopping in front of a gray haired assistant who leans forward eagerly.

"Good day, sir. Can I be of any help?"

Dangerfield hesitating with pursed lips.

"Good day, yes. I would like to open up an account with you."

"Very good, sir. Will you please come this way."

The assistant opening a large ledger across the counter. Asking Dangerfield's name and address.

"Shall I bill you monthly or quarterly, sir?"

"I think quarterly."

"Would you like to take anything with you today, sir?"

Dangerfield caressing his teeth together, his eyes darting among the shelves.

"Do you have any Cork Gin?"

"Certainly, sir. Large or small size?"

"I think the large."

"And anything else, sir?"

"Do you have any Haig and Haig?"

Assistant calling to the end of the shop. A small boy goes behind the scenes and comes out with a bottle. Dangerfield points to a ham.

"And how many pounds, sir?"

"I'll take it all. And two pounds of cheese and a chicken."

Assistant all smiles and remarks. O it's the weather. Shocking fog. No day for them ones at sea or the others either. And clapping his hands to the little boy.

"Come here and carry the parcels for the gentleman. And a very good day to you, sir."

Up the hill, O'Keefe waiting and sweeping the packages into his arms. In the kitchen, laying them out on the table.

"How you do it, Dangerfield, I don't know. The first time I went looking for credit they told me to come back with a letter from a bank manager."

"It's the blue blood, Kenneth. Now I'll cut off a little piece of this cheese and give it to the little boy."

Dangerfield returns to the kitchen smiling and rubbing his hands.

"What made you get all this damn booze?"

"Warm us up. I think a cold front is on the way from the Arctic."

"What will Marion say when she gets back?"

"Not a word. These English wives are great. Know their proper place. Ought to marry one yourself."

"All I want is my first piece of arse. Plenty of time to get snowed under with a wife and kids. Give me some of that Scotch and out of my way now while I rustle up this food. Cooking is the only work I sometimes think I'm fitted for. One summer when I was working in Newport I thought of giving up Harvard. There was this Greek chef who thought I was wonderful because I could speak aristocratic Greek but they fired me because I invited some of the boys from Harvard into the club's bar for a drink and the manager came over and fired me on the spot. Said the staff weren't to mix with guests."

"Quite rightly so."

"And now I've got a degree in classics and still have to cook."

"A noble calling."

O'Keefe flipping pots and bouncing from sink to table.

"Kenneth, do you think you're sexually frustrated and maladjusted?"

"I do."

"You'll find opportunities in this fine land."

"Yeah, lots, for unnatural connections with farm animals. Jesus, the only time I can forget about it is when I'm hungry. When I eat I go mad. I sat down and read every book on sex in the Widener Library to see how I could get it. Did me no damn good. I must repel women and there's no cure for that."

"Hasn't anyone ever been attracted?"

"Once. At Black Mountain College in North Carolina. Asked me to come up to her room to listen to some music. She started to press up against me and I ran out of the room."

"What for?"

"She must have been too ugly. That's another thing against me. I'm attracted to beautiful women. Only thing for me is to grow old and not want it anymore."

"You'll want it more than ever."

"Jesus, that isn't true, is it? If that's what I've got to look forward to I may as well flip myself off the end of the back garden out there. Tell me, what's it like to have it steady?"

"Get used to it like most things."

"I could never get used to it."

"You will."

"But what's this little visit of Marion's to mama and papa? Friction? Drinking?"

"She and the baby need a little rest."

"I think her old man must be wise to you. How did he ever screw you out of two hundred and fifty notes? It's no wonder you never got it."

"He just took me into his study and said sorry son, things are just a little tight at the moment."

"Should have said dowry or no marriage. He must have dough, an admiral. Give him the stuff, like to provide for Marion the way she's accustomed to. Could have touched him with a few of those rosy ideas of yours."

14

"Too late. This was the night before the wedding. I even refused a drink for strategy. However, he waited a good five minutes after the butler left before pleading poverty."

O'Keefe spins holding the chicken by the leg.

"See, he's shrewd. Saved himself two hundred and fifty nicker notes. If you had been on your toes you could have told him you had Marion up the pole and with a birth imminent you needed a little nest egg. Now look at you. All you need to do now is flunk your law exams and bingo."

"I'm all right, Kenneth. Little money and everything's all right. Got a house, wife, daughter."

"You mean you pay rent for a house. Stop paying rent, no house."

"Let me pour you another drink, Kenneth. I think you need it."

O'Keefe filling a bowl with bread crumbs. Night outside and the boom of the sea. Angelus bells. Pause that refreshes.

"This, Dangerfield, is your blood for which your family will starve and which will finally send you all to the poor house. Should have played it cozy and married strictly for cash. Come in drunk, have a quick one and whoops, another mouth to feed. You'll be eating spaghetti as I had to as a kid till it comes out of your eyes or else you'll have to take your English wife and English kids and screw back to America."

The chicken, trussed, was laid reverently in the pan. O'Keefe with a smack of the lips pushed it in the oven.

"When that's ready, Dangerfield, we'll have chicken à la Balscaddoon. You know, this is a pretty spooky house when it gets dark. But I don't hear anything yet except the sea."

"Wait."

"Well, ghosts won't bother me on a full stomach and certainly never if I had a full sex life. Do you know, at Harvard I finally got Constance Kelly in my power. There was a girl who strung me along for two years till I found out what a fraud American womanhood was and I squeezed her right under my thumb. But I can't figure it out. I never could get it. She'd do anything but let me in. Holding out for wealth

15

on Beacon Hill. I would have married her but she didn't want to get stuck at the bottom of the social ladder with me. One of her own kind. Jesus, she's right. But do you know what I'm going to do? When I go back to the States when I'm fat with dough, wearing my Saville Row suits, with black briar, M.G. and my man driving, I'm going to turn on my English accent full blast. Pull up to some suburban house where she's married a mick, turned down by all the old Bostonians, and leave my man at the wheel. I'll walk up the front path knocking the kid's toys out of the way with my walking stick and give the door a few impatient raps. She comes out. A smudge of flour on her cheek and the reek of boiled cabbage coming from the kitchen. I look at her with shocked surprise. I recover slowly and then in my best accent, delivered with devastating resonance, I say Constance . . . you've turned out . . . just as I thought you would. Then I spin on my heel, give her a good look at my tailoring, knock another toy aside with my cane and roar away."

Dangerfield swinging back in the green rocking chair with a wiggle of joy, head shaking in a hundred yesses. O'Keefe striding the red tiles of the kitchen floor, waving a fork, his one live eye glistening in his head, a mad mick for sure. Perhaps he'll slip on one of the toys and break an arse bone.

"And Constance's mother hated my guts. Thought I'd suck her down socially. Would open all the letters I'd write to her daughter, and I'd sit in Widener Library thinking up the dirtiest stuff I could imagine, I think the old slut loved them. Used to make me laugh thinking she'd read them and then have to burn them. Jesus, I repel women, damn it. Even this winter down in Connemara visiting the old folks, my cousin, who looked like a cow's arse wouldn't even come across. I'd wait for her to go out and get the milk at night and go with her. At the end of the field I'd try to nudge her into the ditch. I'd get her all breathless and saying she'd do anything if I'd take her to the States and marry her. I tried that for three nights running, standing out there in the rain up to our ankles in mud and cow flop, me trying to get her

16

in the ditch, knock her down, but she was too strong. So I told her she was a tub of lard and I wouldn't take her to East Jesus. Have to get them a visa before you can touch an arm."

"Marry her, Kenneth."

"Get tangled with that beast of burden for the rest of me days? Be all right if I could chain her to the stove to cook but to marry the Irish is to look for poverty. I'd marry Constance Kelly out of spite."

"I suggest the matrimonial column of the *Evening Mail* for you. Put no encumbrance. Man of means, extensive estates in West. Prefers women of stout build, with own capital and car for travel on Continent. No others need apply."

"Let's eat. I want to leave my problem uncomplicated."

"Kenneth, this is most cordial."

The toasted bird was put on the green table. O'Keefe driving a fork into the dripping breast and ripping off the legs. Pot gives a tremble on the shelf. Little curtains with the red spots flutter. A gale outside. When you think of it, O'Keefe can cook. And this is my first chicken since the night I left New York and the waiter asked me if I wanted to keep the menu as a memory and I sat there in the blue carpeted room and said yes. And around the corner in a bar a man in a brown suit offers to buy a drink. Comes and feels my leg. Says he loves New York and could we go somewhere away from the crowd and talk, be together, nice boy, high class boy. I left him hanging from his seat, a splash of red, white and blue tie coming out of his coat and I went up to Yorktown and danced with a girl in a flower print dress who said there was no fun and nobody around. Named Jean with remarkable breasts and I was dreaming of Marion's, my own tall thin blond with teeth fashionably bucked. On my way after the war to marry her. Ready to take the big plane across the sea. I first met her wearing a sky blue sweater and I knew they were pears. What better than ripe pears. In London in the Antelope, sitting in the back with a fine pot of gin enjoying these indubitable people. She sat only inches

17

away, a long cigarette in her white fingers. While the bombs were landing in London. I heard her ask for cigarettes and they had none. And leaning forward in my naval uniform, handsome and strong, please, do have some of mine. O I couldn't, really, thank you, no. But please do, I insist. It's very good of you. Not at all. And she dropped one and I reached down and touched her ankle with my finger. My, what rich, lovely big feet.

"What's the matter, Kenneth? You're as white as a sheet."

O'Keefe staring at the ceiling with a half chewed chicken leg hanging in his fist.

"Didn't you hear that? Whatever that scrabbling in the ceiling is, it's alive."

"My dear Kenneth, you're welcome to search the premises. It moves all over the house. Even wails and has a rather disconcerting way of following one from room to room."

"Jesus, stop it. That scares me. Why don't you look up there?"

"Rather not."

"That noise is real."

"Perhaps you'd like to look, Kenneth. Trap door in the hall. I'll give you an axe and flashlight."

"Wait till I digest my meal. I was just beginning to enjoy all this. I thought you were kidding."

O'Keefe at one end, carrying the ladder to the hall.

With axe cocked, O'Keefe advancing slowly towards the trap door. Dangerfield encouraging him on. O'Keefe pushing up the door, peering along the beam of light. No noise. Not a sound. Bravery becoming general again.

"You look frightened to death, Dangerfield. Think you were the one up here. Probably just some loose papers blowing across the floor."

"Suit yourself, Kenneth. Just give me a whistle when it gets you around the neck. Go in."

O'Keefe disappeared. Dangerfield looking up into the descending dust. O'Keefe's footfalls going towards the drawing room. A wail. A scream from O'Keefe.

18

"Christ, hold the ladder, I'm coming down."

Trap door down with a slam.

"For God's sake, what is it, Kenneth?"

"A cat. With one eye. The other a great gaping hole. What a sight. How the hell did it get up there?"

"No idea. Must have been up there all the time. Might have belonged to a Mr. Gilhooley who lived here only he fell off the cliff out there one night and was washed up three months later on the Isle of Man. Would you say, Kenneth, that maybe this house has a history of death?"

"Where are you putting me to sleep?"

"Cheer up, Kenneth. You look terrified. No need to let a little thing like a cat get you down. You can sleep wherever you like."

"This house gives me the creeps. Let's build a fire or something."

"Come into the drawing room and play a little tune on the piano for me."

They walked along the red tiled hall to the drawing room. Set on a tripod before the baywindows, a large brass telescope pointing out to sea. In the corner an ancient upright piano, its top covered with opened tins and rinds of cheese. Three fat armchairs distorted with lumps of stuffing and poking springs. Dangerfield fell back in one and O'Keefe bounded to the piano, struck a chord and began to sing.

> In this sad room
> In this dark gloom
> We live like beasts.

The windows rattling on the rotten sills. O'Keefe's twisted notes. There you are, Kenneth, sitting on that stool, all the way from Cambridge, Massachusetts, freckled and fed on spaghetti. And me, from St. Louis, Missouri, because that night in the Antelope I took Marion to dinner and she paid. And a weekend after to a hotel. And I pulled down her green pajamas and she said she couldn't and I said you can. And other weekends till the war was over. Bye bye bombs

19

and back to America where I can only say I was tragic and lonely, feeling Britain was made for me. All I got out of old man Wilton was a free taxi to our honeymoon. We arrived and I bought a cane to walk the dales of Yorkshire. Our room was over a stream at this late summertime. And the maid was mad and put flowers in the bed and that night Marion put them in her hair, which she let down over her blue night gown. O the pears. Cigarettes and gin. Abandoned bodies until Marion lost her false front teeth behind the dresser and then she wept, wrapped in a sheet, slumped in a chair. I told her not to worry for things like that happened on honeymoons and soon we would be off for Ireland where there was bacon and butter and long evenings by the fire while I studied law and maybe even a quick love make on a woolly rug on the floor.

This Boston voice squeaking out its song. The yellow light goes out the window on the stubs of windy grass and black rocks. And down the wet steps by gorse stumps and rusty heather to the high water mark and diving pool. Where the seaweeds rise and fall at night in Balscaddoon Bay.

3

The sun of Sunday morning up out of the sleepless sea from black Liverpool. Sitting on the rocks over the water with a jug of coffee. Down there along the harbor pier, trippers in bright colors. Sails moving out to sea. Young couples climbing the Balscaddoon Road to the top of Kilrock to search out grass and lie between the furze. A cold green sea breaking whitely along the granite coast. A day on which all things are born, like uncovered stars.

A wet salty wind. And tomorrow Marion comes back. And the two of us sit here wagging our American legs. Marion, stay away a little longer, please. Don't want the pincers on me just yet. Greasy dishes or baby's dirty bottom, I just want to watch them sailing. We need a nurse for baby to wheel her around some public park where I can't hear the squeals. Or maybe the two of you will get killed in a train wreck and your father foot the bill for burial. Well-bred people never fight over the price of death. And it's not cheap these days. Just look a bit glassy eyed for a month and take off for Paris. Some nice quiet hotel in Rue de Seine and float fresh fruit in a basin of cool water. Your long winter body lying naked on the slate and what would I be thinking if I touched your dead breast. Must get a half crown out of O'Keefe before he goes. I wonder what makes him so tight with money.

Late afternoon, the two of them walking down the hill to the bus stop. Fishermen in with their chugging boats unloading catches on the quay. Old women watching on thick chilblained ankles with heavy breasts wallowing.

"Kenneth, is this not a fine country?"

"Look at that woman."

"I say, Kenneth, is this not a fine country?"

"Size of watermelons."

"Kenneth, you poor bastard."

"Do you know, Constance had a good figure. She must have loved me. How could she help it. But wouldn't let it stand in the way of marriage into some old Yankee family. Many are the days I sat on my cold arse on the steps of Widener just to watch her go by and follow her to where she was meeting some jerk with not an ounce of joy in him."

"Kenneth, you wretched man."

"Don't worry, I'll manage."

Sunday. Day set aside for emptiness and defeat. Dublin city closed, a great gray trap. Only churches doing business, sacred with music, red candles and crucified Christs. And the afternoons, long lines of them waiting in the rain outside cinemas.

"I say, Kenneth, could you see your way clear to lending me half a crown repayable Monday at three thirty one o'clock? Check tomorrow and I could pay you at the Consulate."

"No."

"Two shillings?"

"No."

"One and six?"

"No. Nothing."

"A shilling is nothing."

"God damn it, Dangerfield, don't drag me down with you. For Christ's sake, my back's to the wall. Look at me. My fingers are like wet spaghetti. Get off my back. Don't doom us both."

"Relax, Kenneth. Don't take things so seriously."

"Seriously? This is a matter of life and death. What do you want me to do? Shout with joy?"

"You're upset."

"I'm not upset, I'm prudent. I want to eat tomorrow. Do you honestly think these checks are going to be there?"

"Quite."

"When you're sitting on your arse in the poor house screaming for drink I don't want to be next to you. Let one of us go down, that's enough. Not both. I want to eat tonight."

"I want some cigarettes."

"Look, here's my bus, I'll give you three pence and have it for me tomorrow."

"Kenneth, I want to tell you one thing before you go. You're a jewel among men."

"Look, don't bother me, if you don't want the three pence, I'll take it back. It'll pay half my fare."

"Kenneth, you lack love."

"Ass and money."

Bus pulling away. O'Keefe's head vanishing on the top deck and over a green sign, Guinness is good for you. How true.

Turning up the hill. Sunday on the desert of Edar. Great to know the old names. Do a bit of deep breathing. Lately been having the dreams of arrest. Come up from behind and grab me for committing a public nuisance. So long as it isn't indecency. Go over to this shop and have this good man fetch me up some cigarettes.

"A fine day, sir."

"Aye."

"Forgive the impertinence, sir, but are you the new gentleman living up on the rock?"

"O aye."

"I thought so, sir. And is it to your liking?"

"Splendid."

"That's fine, sir."

"Bye, bye now."

O I tell you. I tell you, names and numbers. Want to wear a sack over the face. Why don't you come up and watch me eat? Steam open my letters and see if I wear a truss. And I like to have my wife in bare feet. Good for a woman. They say it's great for the frigidity. I'm all for wiping that out. Come watch me through any window.

Walking up to the Summit and down there is Gaskin's Leap, Fox Hole and Piper's Gut. And the Casana Rock which is great for the sea birds. Bit of warmth in the air. How I like it. Lonely and Sunday. Faced with the cat. Should have locked O'Keefe up there with it. Take the ladder away. Give him a lesson in courage.

A girl approached.

"Mister, could I have a light?"

"Certainly."

Dangerfield striking a match, holding it to her cigarette.

"Thank you very much."

"You're welcome on a lovely evening like this."

"Yes, it is lovely."

"Quite breathtaking."

"Yes, it is breathtaking."

"Are you out for a walk?"

"Yes, my girl friend and I are walking."

"Around the head?"

"Yes, we like it. We've come out from Dublin."

"What do you do for a living?"

"Well, I guess I work."

"At what?"

"My girl friend and I work in Jacob's."

"Biscuit factory?"

"We label tins."

"You like it?"

"It's all right. Gets boring."

"Walk along with me."

"All right. I'll get my girl friend."

Three of them walking along. Some trivia. Names, Alma and Thelma. And telling of the steamship Queen Victoria, wrecked off here at 3 o'clock on the morning of February 15th, 1853. Tragic disaster. And there is the quarry. See the stones. Built the harbor with this rock. Oh I tell you Alma and Thelma, Howth's the great place for the history. And I might say I'm adding to it meself. In my own little way. And they thought he was having them on and they were Catholics and giggled at this Protestant face.

Little dark now. Just let me take your hands now. O a

24

dangerous place, this Howth at night. Young women want
protection. And I'll hold your hand Alma and it's a nice
hand in spite of the work. Thelma walking ahead. Mind
Alma? Thelma away in the dark. Stop here now, like this.
It's better, a little arm around you. Keep you. You like that?
Well, you're a fast worker, and kissing a stranger, what will
my girl friend think? Tell her I'm such a lonely gent and you
couldn't resist a little innocent embrace. My house is here,
come in? O no. A drink? I'm a member of the Pioneers. Have
a glass of water then. I could come next Sunday. I'll be in
Africa in the middle of the Congo. You have a nice bosom,
Alma. You shouldn't make me do those things. Now Alma,
come in for a little while and I'll show you my telescope.
Don't be rude, besides I can't leave my friend. Honesty never
gets me anywhere. Let me kiss you goodbye, Alma. Don't
think I didn't like it but my girl friend would go back with
a tale to my sister. Bye.

Alma running away through the evening. With her new-
warmed heart touched by a stranger and I know you are
thinking I would have seen your nice new underwear. Go
in the drawer tomorrow for a week. And for a nice Protestant like him and there would have been chocolate and
taxi rides and dances. Torturing chances, may not ever come
again. Thelma, wasn't he a smasher.

Through my green haunted door. Into this house of
sounds. Must be the sea. Might even come up through the
floor. The cat. Just like O'Keefe with one eye. Says he can't
catch a ball. And when they took him to the hospital and
took it out they never told him he had only one left.
Kenneth, I love you all the same. And even more if you
could have buried the axe in the cat, just behind the ears. I
think the drawing room the safest tonight. Don't want to
crowd the demons. And have a little nightcap. And read my
nice fat American business magazine. No one will ever know
what it's done for me in my sad moments. My bible of happiness every month. Open it up and I'm making sixty three
thousand big bucks a year. Odd three thousand makes it more

authentic. And must drive into my office from Connecticut. I insist upon that. And repair evenings to my club. Difficult in New York with the Irish getting into everything. Imitating the Protestants. And I'll have a nice little family of two children. Use the best in contraception. Never should let the lust sneak up on one. Passion of the moment, a disaster over the years. Must not bungle more than twice. Could be fatal. Marion making that sucking noise with those front teeth. Sucking them in and out, surely it's not done. Just not done, that sort of thing. On and off her gums. Little circle of hair round her nipples, tickle the baba's mouth. O she'll live a long time. They'll put me to rest. But not before I've seen a bit of the corporation law and maybe later a bit of investment banking. Sebastian Bullion Dangerfield, chairman of Quids Inc., largest banking firm in the world. Then I would act. Change the interest rates in the pawn shops. Lower them? No, make them higher. People shouldn't be pawning anyway. And send O'Keefe to the Sudan so he can run naked.

Dangerfield settled with feet up and back against the wall. Wind shaking the windows. A sudden long haunted wail from the ceiling.

"God's teeth."

Must keep a grip. Won't do to lose courage. And moaning under the floor. For the love of Jesus.

Fetching the axe, going into his room. The sea air, a great wet ghost, coming in the open window. Slamming it shut. Tearing the covers back from the bed. Make sure of no rattlesnakes. Go flush the toilet now, take the edge off the fear. And straighten out the room, make the bed. And another sup of the good Cork Gin. Wallop a little freshness into this pillow. Good grief. The room filling with floating feathers. Well God damn it. For the love of Jesus, if that's the way you want it. Off with this damn mattress.

And Dangerfield lifting the axe above a wild head, driving it again and again through the pillow. Screams of money, money. Dragging the mattress out the door, along the hall to the kitchen. Up on the table with it. And the axe is right

26

here ready to cleave the first imposter who sets foot in this room. One more good swig of this. I'm sure it's good for the bowels and at least hurry me to bye byes. Left my soul sitting on a wall and walked away, watching me and grew cold because souls are like hearts, sort of red and warm, all like a heart.

4

There was a tugging at his leg. Slowly opening eyes to see the irate face of Marion looming over him on this Monday morn of chaos.

"Good God, what's happened to the house? Why weren't you at the station to meet me? Look at you. Gin. This is horrid. I had to take a taxi out here, do you hear me? A taxi, fifteen shillings."

"Now, now, for Christ's sake have some patience and let me explain everything."

"I say, explain? Explain what? There's nothing to explain, it's all quite evident."

Marion holding aloft the gin.

"All right, I'm not blind, I see it."

'O dear, this is frightful. Why you honestly are a cad. If Mommy and Daddy could only see what I've got to come back to. What are you doing on the table?"

"Shut up."

"I won't shut up and don't look at me like that. What are these feathers doing all over the place? Dishes broken on the floor. What were you doing?"

"Goat dance."

"How frightfully sordid it all is. Disgusting. Feathers in everything. You damn, damn drinker. Where did you get the money? Didn't meet me at the train. Why? Answer me."

"Shut up. Be quiet for the love of Jesus. The alarm didn't work."

"You're a liar. You were drinking, drinking, drinking. Look at the grease, the mess, the filth. And what's this?"

"A sea bird."

"Who paid for all this? You had smelly O'Keefe out here. I know you did, I can smell him."

"Just leave me alone."

28

"Did you pay the milk?"

"Yes, now sweet Jesus shut up, my head."

"So you paid it, did you? Here it is. Here it is. Exactly where I left it and the money gone. Lies. You blighter. You nasty blighter."

"Call me a bugger, I can't stand the gentility on top of the yelling."

"O stop it, stop it. I don't intend to go on living like this, do you hear me? Your brazen lies, one after the other and I was trying to get Father to do something for us and I come back to this."

"Your father. Your father is a sack of excrement, genteel excrement, as tight as they come. What has he been doing, playing battleship in the tub?"

Marion lunged, her slap landing across his jaw. The child began to scream in the nursery. Sebastian up off the table. He drove his fist into Marion's face. She fell backward against the cupboard. Dishes crashing to the floor. In tattered underwear he stood at the nursery door. He kicked his foot through and tore off the lock to open it. Took the child's pillow from under its head and pressed it hard on the screaming mouth.

"I'll kill it, God damn it, I'll kill it, if it doesn't shut up."

Marion behind him, digging her nails into his back.

"You madman, leave the child alone, I'll get the police. I'll divorce you, you blackguard, coward, coward, coward."

Marion clasping the child to her breast. Sobbing, she lay her long English body and child across the bed. The room echoing the hesitations of her wailing voice. Sebastian walked white faced from the room, slamming the broken door, cutting off the sound of suffering from a guilty heart.

Dangerfield took a late morning bus to Dublin. Sat up the top side in front, clicking the teeth. Out there the mud flats and that windy golf course. North Bull Island shimmering in the sun. Cost money to leave Marion. Vulgar blood in her somewhere, may be from the mother. Mother's father kept a shop. Bad blood leaks out. I know it leaks out. And I ought to get out. One way on the boat. She doesn't have the nerve for divorce. I know her too well for that. Never gave me a lousy chance to explain the account. Let her rot out there. I don't care. Got to face the facts of this life. The facts, the facts. Could square things with her. She's good with the cheese dishes. Few days without food will weaken her. Maybe I'll come back with a tin of peaches and cream. She's always airing the house. Opening up the windows at every little fart. Tells me she never farts. At least mine come out with a bang.

Fairview Park looks like a wet moldy blanket. Feel a little better. O'Keefe broke a toilet bowl in that house. Fell into it when he was trying to sneak a look behind a woman's medicine chest. Long suffering O'Keefe, bent over tomes in the National Library studying Irish and dreaming of seduction.

Amiens Street Station, Dangerfield stepping down from the bus, crossing and using the ostrich step up the Talbot Street. My God, I think I see prostitutes with squinting eyes and toothless mouths. Don't relish a trip up an alley with one without wearing impenetrable armour and there is no armour at all in Dublin. I asked one how much it was and she said I had an evil mind. Invited her for a drink and she said the American sailors were rough and beat her up in the backs of taxicabs and told her to take a bath. She said she liked chewing gum. And when she had a few drinks she got frightfully crude. I was shocked. Asked me how big it was. I almost slapped her face. With it. Provocation I calls it. And told her to confess. Dublin has more than a hundred churches. I bought a map and counted them. Must be a nice thing to have faith. But I think a pot of Gold Label run from the barrel in the house of the aspidistras. Settle the nerves. No time to be nervous now. With youth on my side. I'm still a young man in the late twenties, although the Lord knows I've been through some trying times. A lot of people tell you, caution you. Now young man, don't get married without money, without a good job, without a degree. E. E. E. They are right.

Into the pub with stuffed foxes behind the potted plants.

And the snug stained brown. Reach over and press this buzzer for action.

A young man's raw face flicked around the door.

"Good morning, Mr. Dangerfield."

"A fine spring morning, a double and some Woodbines."

"Certainly, sir. Early today?"

"Little business to attend to."

"It's always business isn't it."

"O aye."

Some fine cliches there. Should be encouraged. Too many damn people trying to be different. Coining phrases when a good platitude would do and save anxiety. If Marion wants to make the barbarous accusation that I took the milk money, it's just as well I took it.

A tray comes in the discreet door.

"On your bill, Mr. Dangerfield?"

"If you will, please."

"Grand to be having some decent weather and I think you're looking very well."

"Thank you. Yes, feel fine."

I think moments like sitting here should be preserved. I'd like friends to visit me at my house and maybe have a cocktail cabinet, but nothing vulgar. And Marion could make nice little bits. Olives. And kids playing on the lawn. Wouldn't mind a room a bit on the lines of this. Fox on the mantelpiece and funereal fittings. Outside, the world, I think is driven. And I'm right out in front. To keep friends, photographs and letters. Me too. And women stealing alimony for young lovers. Wrinkled buttocks astride rose wood chairs, weeping signing each check. Become a lover of women over fifty. They're the ones that's looking for it. Good for O'Keefe. But he might balk. A knowledgeable man but a botcher. And now get that check. I want to see dollars. Thousands of them. Want them all over me to pave the streets of me choosey little soul.

"Bye, bye."

"Bye now, Mr. Dangerfield. Good luck."

Across the Butt Bridge. Covered with torn newspapers and hulking toothless old men watching out the last years. They're bored. I know you've been in apprenticeships and that there was a moment when you were briefly respected for an opinion. Be in the sight of God soon. He'll be shocked. But there's happiness up there, gentlemen. All white and gold. Acetylene lighted sky. And when you go, go third class. You damn bastards.

And walking along Merrion Square. Rich up this way. Wriggle the fingers a bit. American flag hanging out there. That's my flag. Means money, cars and cigars. And I won't hear a word said against it.

Spinning up the steps. Big black door. With aplomb, approaching the receptionist's desk. Unfallow Irishwomen of middle age and misery. Belaboring poor micks headed for that land across the seas. Giving them the first taste of being pushed around. And ingratiating to the middle western college boy who bounces by.

"Could you tell me if the checks have arrived?"

"You're Mr. Dangerfield, aren't you?"

"I am."

"Yes the checks have arrived. I think yours is here somewhere. However, isn't there some arrangement with your wife? I don't think I can give it to you without her consent."

Dangerfield warming to irritated erection.

"I say, if you don't mind I will take that check immediately."

"I'm sorry, Mr. Dangerfield but I have had instructions not to give it to you without the permission of your wife."

"I say, I will take that check immediately."

Dangerfield's mouth a guillotine. This woman a little upset. Insolent bitch.

"I'm very sorry but I will have to ask Mr. Morgue."

"You will ask no one."

"I'm terribly sorry, but I will have to ask Mr. Morgue."

"What?"

32

"You must remember that I am in charge of handling these checks."

Dangerfield's fist swished through the air, landing with a bang on the desk. Receptionist jumped. And her jaw came down with a touch of obedience.

"You'll ask no one and unless that check is given me this instant I'll have you charged with theft. Do you understand me? Am I clear? I will not have an Irish serf interfering in my affairs. This irregularity will be reported to the proper authorities. I will take that check and no more nonsense."

Receptionist with mouth open. Trickle of spittle twisted on her jaw. An instant's hesitation and fear forced a nervous hand to deliver the white envelope. Dangerfield burning her with red eyes. A door opening in the hall. Several bog men, watching from the staircase, slipped hurriedly back to seats, caps over folded hands. A final announcement from Dangerfield.

"Now, God damn it, when I come in here again I want that check handed to me instantly."

From the door, a middle western accent.

"Say buddy, what's going on here?"

"Twiddle twat."

"What?"

Dangerfield suddenly convulsed with laughter. Spinning on his heel, he pushed open this Georgian door and hopped down the steps. The rich green of the park across the street. And through the tops of the trees, red brick buildings on the other side. Look at these great slabs of granite to walk on. How very nice and solid. Celtic lout. I'm all for Christianity but insolence must be put down. With violence if necessary. People in their place, neater that way. Eke. Visit my broker later and buy a French Horn and play it up the Balscaddoon road. About four a.m. And I think I'll step into this fine house here with ye oldish windows.

This public house is dark and comforting with a feeling of scholarship. With the back gate of Trinity College just outside. Makes me feel I'm close to learning and to you students who don't take the odd malt. Maybe I put too much faith in atmosphere.

Put the money away safely. A bright world ahead. Of old streets and houses, screams of the newly born and grinning happy faces escorting the lately dead. American cars speeding down Nassau Street and tweedy bodies of ex-Indian Army officers stuttering into the well-mannered gloom of the Kildare Street Club for a morning whiskey. The whole world's here. Women from Foxrock with less thick ankles and trim buttocks shod closely and cleanly with the badge of prosperity, strutting because they owned the world and on their way to coffee and an exhibition of paintings. I can't get enough. More. See Marion like that. Going to make money. Me. A sun out. With Jesus for birth control. This great iron fence around Trinity serves a good purpose. World in resurrection. Yellow banners in the sky, all for me, Sebastian Bullion Dangerfield.

> And dear God
> Give me strength
> To put my shoulder
> To the wheel
> And push
> Like the rest.

5

Spring warmed into summer. In Stephen's Green, actors were sitting in three penny chairs getting a bit of tan. Here there are great rings of flowers and ducks sliding around the sky. And citizens riding the late trams to Dalkey for a swim. On this June morning, Dangerfield came in the front gate of Trinity and went up the dusty rickety stairs of No. 3 where he stood by the dripping rust-stained sink and banged on O'Keefe's door.

A minute passed and then the sound of padding feet and latches being undone and the appearance of a bearded, dreary face and one empty eye.

"It's you."

The door was swung open and O'Keefe plodded back to his bedroom. A smell of stale sperm and rancid butter. Mouldering on the table, a loaf of bread, a corner bitten from it with marks of teeth. The fireplace filled with newspapers, old socks, spittle stains and products of self pollution.

"Christ, Kenneth, don't you think you ought to have this place cleaned up?"

"What for? Does it make you sick? Vomit in the fireplace."

"Don't you have a skip?"

"I've better things to spend my money for than having a footman. I'm leaving."

"What?"

"Leaving. Getting out. Do you want some ties? Bow ties."

"Yes. Where are you going?"

"France. Got a job."

"Doing what?"

"Teaching English in a Lycée. Besançon, where Paul Klee's mother was born."

"You lucky bastard, you're telling the truth?"

"I'm leaving in exactly an hour from now. If you watch me very, very carefully, you'll see me fill this sack with four packs of cigarettes, a pair of socks, two shirts, a bar of soap and a towel. Then I put on my cap, spit on my shoes and give them a wipe with my sleeve. I'm out that door, drop my keys off at the front gate and I'm into Bewley's for a cup of coffee, alone I might add, unless you have money to pay for yourself. Then if you're still watching, I'll saunter down O'Connell Street past the Gresham and take a sharp right at the corner and you will see my slender form disappear into a green bus marked airport and finis. Do you see what I mean?"

"I can only say I'm delighted, Kenneth."

"See? System. The well ordered life."

Dangerfield waving a hand around the room.

"Is this what you call ordered? Hate to see you in disorder."

O'Keefe tapping his skull.

"Up here, Jack, up here."

"What are you going to do with that jug on the dresser? Still has the price on it."

"That? It's yours. Do you know what that is? I'll tell you. A year ago when I got into this hole I was full of big ideas. Things like rugs and easy chairs and maybe a few paintings on the wall, have some of these pukka public school boys up to tea to have a look at my objets d'art. I thought things would be like Harvard only I'd be able to crack into a few of the clubs as I was never able to do in Harvard. I felt it would be best to start the furnishing with a few bedroom items, so I bought that jug for one and four as you can plainly see, and that was that. Needless to say I never cracked or rubbed shoulders with these public school boys. They talk to me but think I'm a little coarse."

"Pity."

"Yeah, pity. I'll give you the jug to remember me when I'm gone from the ould sod, sacked in with some lovely French doll. Jesus, if I had your accent I'd be set here. That's the whole thing, accent. I'm beat even before I get my nose in. Anyway it won't stop me in France."

"I say, Kenneth, I don't want to be personal—"

"Yeah, I know. Where did I get the money. That my friend is an affair of state which is top secret."

"Pity."

"Come on, let's go. Take the ties if you want them and the jug, anything that's left for that matter. This is the last I'll ever see of this dreary setup. Never even had a fire in my fireplace. I'm twenty-seven years old and I feel like sixty. I don't know, I think I'd die before I'd go through this again. Wasted time. No degree. I think I got to four Greek lectures and two in Latin in the last six months. This place is tough, not like Harvard. These boys work day and night."

"How about these used razors?"

"Take anything. I'll be as poor as a church mouse for the rest of me days."

Sebastian gathered the bow ties in his fist and stuffed them in his pockets. Filled a wash cloth with razor blades and several slivers of soap. On the table, a pile of penny notebooks.

"What are these, Kenneth?"

"Those are the fruits, rotten ones I might add, of my efforts to become a great writer."

"You're not leaving them behind?"

"Certainly. What do you want me to do?"

"Never know."

"I happen to know. One thing I'm sure of, I'm no writer. I'm nothing but a hungry, sexstarved son of a bitch."

Dangerfield turning the pages of the notebook. Reading aloud.

"In the ordinary Irish American family this would have been a very happy occasion of hypocritical and genuine gaiety, but the O'Lacey's were not the ordinary Irish American family and the atmosphere was almost sacrilegiously tense—"

"Cut it out. If you want to read it, take it. Don't remind

37

me of that crap. I'm finished writing. Cooking is my trade."

Two of them passing out of the bedroom with newspapers spread on the mattress springs. Imprint of the body. January in here and June outside. Sad rat, O'Keefe, the hunk of bread gnawed. And the scullery a blackened vestibule of grease. Under the gas ring lie bacon rinds the color green and a broken cup half full of dripping; O'Keefe's first move, no doubt, to open up a highbrow restaurant. Lives punctuated with shrewd business deals, quick flashes of happiness ending in dismal abortion. Keeps one awake at night and poor as well.

They tripped and bounced down the worn stairs. Walked across the cobbles. O'Keefe leading, hands plunged in pockets, lilting, a caterpillar walk. Followed austerely, nervously, by the twitching Dangerfield on his bird feet. Into No. 4 to urinate.

"Pissing always gives me a chance to think. It's all the good this thing has ever done me. But I'm out. On the move again. Best feeling in the world. How does it feel to be loaded with wife and child, Dangerfield? It's a problem for you even to get out the door."

"One manages, Kenneth. Be better days. I promise you that."

"Be Grangegorman."

"Did you know, Kenneth, that Trinity graduates get preferential treatment in the Gorman?"

"Good, you'll be murdered. But you know, Dangerfield, I don't dislike you as you might think. I've got a soft spot somewhere. Come on, I'll buy you a cup of coffee even though it's bad to encourage tenderness."

O'Keefe disappearing into the porter's lodge with his keys. Porter looking at him with a grin.

"Leaving us, sir?"

"Yup, for the sunny Continent, yours truly."

"The very best of luck, always, Mr. O'Keefe. We'll all miss you."

38

"So long."

"Goodbye, Mr. O'Keefe."

Prancing out to Dangerfield waiting under the great granite arch, and swinging around the front gate to Westmoreland Street. They entered the smoke and coffee scented air and sat in a cozy booth. O'Keefe rubbing his hands.

"I can't wait to get to Paris. Maybe I'll make a rich contact on the plane. Rich Yankee girl coming to Europe for culture who wants to see the points of interest."

"And perhaps your own, Kenneth."

"Yeah, if she saw that I'd make sure she saw nothing else. Why is it that I can't have something like that happen to me? That guy who came around to my rooms who was over from Paris, a nice guy, told me once you cracked a clique in Paris you were set. Like the theatrical crowd that he knocked around with, a lot of beautiful women looking for guys like me who haven't got looks but brains and wit. Only one drawback he says, they like to ride in taxis."

Waitress comes over and takes their order. Two cups of coffee.

"Do you want a cream cake, Dangerfield?"

"Most cordial suggestion, Kenneth, if you're sure it's all right."

"And waitress, I want mine black with two, two remember, full jugs of cream and heat the rolls a little."

"Yes, sir."

Waitress giggling, remembering a morning when this short madman with glasses came in and sat down with his big book. All the waitresses afraid to serve him because he was so gruff and had a funny look in his eyes. Sitting alone all morning turning page after page. And then at eleven he looked up, grabbed a fork and started banging it against the table screaming for service. And never took his cap off.

"Well, Dangerfield, in less than an hour I'm off in search of me fortune. Jesus, I'm excited, like I was going to lose my cherry. Woke up this morning with an erection that almost touched the ceiling."

"And they're twenty feet high, Kenneth."

"With spiders crawling all over them. Jesus, a couple of weeks ago I was desperate. Jake Lowell came to see me, pukka Boston from Harvard but he's colored. Gets women like flies but having a slack period at the moment. Said I ought to go queer. Said it was more intellectual and more down my alley. So he gave me my debut one night. It was just like going to a dance at Harvard. I got shaky all over and my stomach in a panic. And we went to a pub where they hang out. He gave me all the coy dope to let them know you're on the make. Said all the invitations that mean anything come when you're in the jacks."

"All rather risqué, Kenneth."

"A wild goose chase. We finally get an invitation to a party and here I am getting all excited thinking of how a woman must feel and then they say it's off because Jake's colored and there'd be too many fights over him at the party. Note. No one fighting over me."

"Kenneth, it's hard but it's fair. Always remember that."

"Jesus, what do I do."

"Animals left, or make a public exposure with indecent intent and have a placard with your name and address."

"I've got charm. Make a magnificent husband. And I've been beaten, beaten. But maybe I only wanted to marry Constance Kelly because I knew she would never consent. If she came up and said O Kenny, dear, I surrender, I'm yours, I'd be on her like a shot and away twice as fast. I think, looking back, that the only time I've ever been happy was in the army. Except for the South, stationed down there with those miserable crackers. But I had it damn good. Got fat. Company commander was a Harvard man so needless to say I was put behind a big desk with some one to make coffee for me. And I'd hear all these bastards groaning about the lousy food and gee I miss mom's cooking and I told them my mother could never cook this good. They wanted to beat me up. The food almost made me weaken to the point of an army career

40

until I discovered you could get this food outside if you made money."

"Talking about money, Kenneth."

O'Keefe's jaw clamping. He reached quickly for a bun.

"Look, Kenneth, I know this is rather an impromptu request, but could you possibly let me have ten quid?"

O'Keefe looked around with his one eye for the waitress and beckoned her over.

"Give me my bill, two coffees, two rolls and this bun. I'm getting out of here."

O'Keefe, hands fore and aft, pulling his cap squarely in place. Picking up his sack he swung it over his shoulders. Dangerfield up, a faithful dog following the precious bone.

"Kenneth, ten quid, promise to have it to you in four days, be there when you arrive. No question about that. Air tight loan. My father's sending me a hundred quid Tuesday. I say, Kenneth, air tight, your money is safer with me than in your pocket, may get killed on the plane."

"Thoughtful of you."

"Make it eight."

"You're making it eight, I'm not making it anything, I haven't got it. I'm hounded fuckless through the streets, beaten to the wall, scratching up pennies and for the first time in months I've got a few beans to have a bath and haircut and get out and you come and push me to the wall again. Jesus, why do I know poor people."

They were walking out between the chairs and tables with their glass tops and the waitresses lined along the counter, arms folded over black breasts, clink of cups and butter balls, and smell of roasted coffee beans. Standing by the high cash desk, O'Keefe fumbling in his pocket. Dangerfield waiting.

"All right, all right, watch me, go ahead. Yeah, you're right, I've got money. You've put me up, fed me, all right, all right but now you're beating me."

"I've said nothing, Kenneth."

"Here then, God damn it, here, take it for Christ's sake and get drunk, throw it away, tear it up, do anything but

41

there's one Goddamn thing, I want that money there when I arrive. You've beaten me."

"Now, Kenneth, no need to feel this way."

"I'm a fool. If I were rich I could tell you to go to hell. Poor crippling the poor."

"Poverty is temporary, Kenneth."

"With you it may be, but I'm not fooling myself, I know damn well that I can go down for ever and stay. This whole damn setup exists to keep me in penury. And I can't stand any more. I had to break my ass to get this dough. Work. Use my head."

"Tell me how."

"Here, read this."

O'Keefe pulling several penny notebook sheets from his pocket. Scribbled torn and dirty.

"Rather scruffy, Kenneth."

"Read it."

This is my position. I haven't got any clothes to wear nor have I eaten in two days. I have to have my fare to France where I have a job. In my present condition I have absolutely no scruples or any regard for the respectable name of O'Keefe. I am therefore going to present myself to the U.S. Consulate for deportation and see that it gets an ample airing in the "Irish Press" and "Irish Independent" who would find it extremely amusing and good gas that an American is in the ould country without a penny, ignored by his relatives. If I get money by the end of the week I will leave for France immediately where you won't hear of me again. Quite frankly either alternative would suit me however I must think of my relatives and what the neighbors would say. I think it would kill my mother with shame.

Yours truly,
K. O'Keefe.

O'Keefe drew another letter from his pocket.

"Here's the reply from Father Moynihan. He's the one

my mother gave me the shoes for and I told the customs man that if I had to pay a penny of duty on them I'd fling them into the sea. He let them through. Jesus, will I ever forget this bastard."

Dangerfield holding the blue notepaper between his hands.

I find myself incapable of even addressing you since this is the most despicable letter I have ever had the displeasure to receive and it amounts to blackmail. It is difficult to believe that you are the product of a good Catholic home or, for that matter, my nephew. You are an insult to the American people. However, there seems to always be an element, the scum and evil minds bred in the gutter, who are a threat to those decent people who have devoted their lives and sweat to rearing ungrateful blackguards. How dare you threaten me with such insolence. It is only that you are my sister's son that I have not brought your filthy correspondence to the attention of the police. Enclosed are your thirty pieces of silver and let it be understood that I shall not tolerate hearing from you again. While here as my guest you violated my hospitality and also the dignity to which I am accustomed in this parish. I am also aware of your efforts to corrupt the purity of one of Mrs. Casey's daughters. Let me warn you, should I again hear anything of you, I shall send the details of this execrable outrage to your mother.

J. MOYNIHAN P.P.

"Kenneth, this is fantastic. What did you do down there?"

"O me. I don't want to remember. I told the girl who worked in the library she ought to liberate herself. She was fascinated. No doubt had remorse when I left and told the old bastard in the confessional I had touched her on the arm, same old thing. Nothing new. Same old pattern, despair, frustration, misery. And that sneaky old bastard with his bottles of whiskey and dignity neatly misered away. I was never so damn cold in my life. Damn house was like a morgue. Wouldn't put an extra piece of turf on the fire.

43

Soon as he found out I hadn't a bean and I'm living on his charity, there's no fire at all and the cigarettes that were lying around the house disappear and the housekeeper watches the kitchen like a hawk. However, no cause to be bitter, that letter of abuse arrived with ten quid in it. When I asked him before for money, he sent me a half crown."

"One thing can be said for you, Kenneth, you're resourceful. If you ever go back to America you'll be rich."

"I want money here. Stay here till my last breath if I had the necessary nicker. But what tight bastards. Stay out of the country. After my visit with the Reverend Moynihan I thought I'd see what could be had in the way of hospitality on my father's side. A bunch of damn phonies. But when I first arrived they gave me the best of what they had but it was embarrassing. I'd be sitting at the other end of the table with a table cloth and napkin and they'd be gobbling off the bare boards. I'd say, look why can't I be the same as you and eat off the bare boards and they'd tell me, O no, you're from America and we want you to feel at home. They even kept the pigs and chickens outside which I didn't mind. But then they wondered when I'd be going and like a jerk I said I was broke. Bingo. The chickens and pigs in the house, table cloth and napkin gone. But I hung on till Christmas Eve when my uncle says now let's all kneel down and say the rosary. And there I was, on hard cold stone mumbling hail marys and thinking of ass I was missing in Dublin. I beat it the next day after Christmas dinner. I thought it was the least I could do was to eat the dinner."

"A fine concession."

They crossed the street and O'Keefe bought an "Irish Times" and moved jauntily over the bridge, both filled with a torrent of words bled from O'Keefe's excitement and memories of Dublin. They looked a curious pair and a group of small boys called after them, Jews, Jews, and O'Keefe spun back with an accusing finger, Irish, Irish, and they stood barefooted in silence.

"That's what I like about Ireland, so open about hatreds.

I guess all I want out of this life is a decent fire in the grate, a rug on the floor and a comfortable chair to sit in and read. And just a few quid I don't have to slave for and mix with people with money, not, I may add, in your exact circumstances, Dangerfield. But Jesus, when you don't have any money, the problem is food. When you have money, it's sex. When you have both it's health, you worry about getting rupture or something. If everything is simply jake then you're frightened of death. And look at these faces, all stuck with the first problem and will be for the rest of their days."

"And what's mine, Kenneth?"

"You just sail dream boats. You think because you were born rich you're going to stay that way. Too many guys like me around waiting for a slip up. Get your degree, passport to security, and use contraceptives. If you get snowed by kids you're whipped."

"Touch of truth there."

"Keep in with these rich Trinity students. They all like you. I'm crippled by my accent but as soon as I have my phonetics taped, watch my smoke. I'll come back from France a new man."

At Cathal Brugha Street, they turned and O'Keefe bought the Paris edition of the *Herald Tribune* and *The Western People*. He shoved the papers in his sack and faced Dangerfield.

"This is where I leave you. It's against my principles to have people see me off."

"As you wish, Kenneth. I'd like to thank you for the money."

"Don't make it painful. Just send it to me. I'm counting on it. Let there be no bungling."

"No bungling."

"So long."

"Take care of yourself, Kenneth, and wear armour."

"I want nothing between me and flesh the first time. God bless."

Dangerfield stood adjusting the strands of wire which held

his trousers. Clenched fist of notes. O'Keefe loose, lost and sinned upon. Bought a green army surplus shirt to keep him in the running longer.

Kenneth O'Keefe turned and sallied forth this sunny morning. Cuffless trousers wrapping round the legs Constance Kelly had said were so smooth. Cap set square to deceive beggars and his one eye, a wet gem seeking out the sign which pointed the road to the limbo of the living, the deep carpeted womb of the idle rich.

6

O summer and soft wind. Relieves the heart and makes living cheaper. Get that fire out in the grate. Get it out. That's better.

There's the butcher a few houses up the street. A tram line goes by the window. And across the road is the most fantastic laundry with forty girls and great steaming vats. O I think they are a bunch for using just the little touch of acid.

Mr. and Mrs. Sebastian Dangerfield and their daughter, Felicity Wilton, late of Howth, are now residing at 1 Mohammed Road, The Rock, Co. Dublin.

It was decided to get out of the haunted house of Howth. But there were hesitations till the morning after the storm when Marion opened the kitchen door to get the milk and she screamed and Sebastian came running and they looked down into a mud stained sea into which had fallen the back garden and turf shed. They moved.

The new house was not new. And you didn't want to walk too fast in the front door or you'd find yourself going out the back. Mr. Egbert Skully took Mr. Dangerfield aside and said he was glad he could rent to an American because he and his wife had worked for twenty years in Macy's Department Store and loved New York and was pleased he could find tenants like themselves. And I hope you, your wife and little one will be happy here. I know it's a little small but I think you'll like the cozy quality, ha, you look like a gentleman, Mr. Dangerfield as likes his cozy comforts, and do you play golf? O aye. But my clubs are indisposed. Having them looked over by a professional for flaws, particular about alignment, you know. A very good idea, Mr. Dangerfield and perhaps my wife can give yours some recipes. Great.

Walls newly papered with brown flowers even feel soggy

47

to the touch. And a nice brown, fourth-hand Axminster rug on the sitting room floor and a scabrous, blue settee. The kitchen was fine but the tap and sink were out the door. Up steep narrow stairs, a closet with plate sized skylight, the conservatory. And a toilet bowl wedged between two walls, the lavatory. Tory was a great suffix in this house. And the sitting room window two feet off the sidewalk was perfect for the neighbors passing by, so don't want to get caught with the pants down. But the tram rumbling by keeps one on one's guard.

A visit to the fuel merchant for coal to keep piled under the stairs. Marion got crates and covered them with table cloths for color and respectability. And my special maps one or two of which are rare and old. The one I have of a cemetery I keep under thick glass. And got the card table for a desk under the window. The laundry girls will take me mind off the awful grind of studying. They come out twice a day, hair in curlers and breasts like needles in these American uplift bras. Think the Bishop had something to say about that and rightly too. Then watch them line up for the tram, a row of steamed white faces. And some of them giving a giggle in this direction at the madman behind the curtain.

Facing the summer ahead. Living in this little house was calm. No drinking and minding the baba when Marion was off to shop. Had a cup of beef tea in the morning. Also see a rather pleasant creature up there in the window. Catch her looking in here with rather large brown eyes, no smiles or giggles. A little disdain, her dark hair straight and thick. And I think I see intelligence, a little embarrassing that look. Retreat into the kitchen. Most exciting.

Made a little case and filled it with books of law, a short life of Blessed Oliver Plunket and others on birds. Bottom shelf for business magazines for the big days ahead. And then a section for my extensive collection, which, God forgive me, I stole from Catholic Churches. But I did it because I needed strength in paupery. My favorites are, "This Thing

Called Love," "Drink Is A Curse," and "Happiness In Death."

The first morning tram almost shakes one to the floor and Felicity gives the twisted cry from the conservatory. Growl back to sleep. Pull the legs up in the foetal crouch. Marion wearing my underwear. Sometimes the sun would sneak in. Then Marion beating barefoot on the linoleum. Entreaties. O do get up. Don't leave me to do everything every morning. In my heart where no one else can hear me, I was saying, now for God's sake, Marion, be a good Britisher and get down there in that little nest of a kitchen and buzz on the coffee like a good girl and would you, while you're at it, kind of brown up a few pieces of bread and I wouldn't mind if maybe there was just the suggestion of bacon on it, only a suggestion, and have it all ready on the table and then I'll come down and act the good husband with, ah darling good morning, how are you, you're looking lovely this morning darling and younger every morning. A great one that last. But I come down martyred and mussed, feeble and fussed, heart and soul covered in cement.

But later in the morning great things were to be seen. Sound of horses on the cobble stones. Then up to the bedroom to look down in the street. These sleek black animals glistening in soft rain. Heads high, driving slits of steam in the morning air. Sometimes I see through the little glass windows, a lily on a pine box. Take me with you too. And I can't help murmuring from memory poems I read in the *Evening Mail*:

> Sleep thy last sleep,
> Free from care and sorrow.
> Rest where none weep,
> And we too, shall follow.

And I see the grinning faces popping out the windows of the cab, radiant with the importance of the dead. Hats being tipped along the road and hands moving in a quick sign of the cross. Whiskey passed from hand to hand. Green, greedy mouth is dead. A fiddle across the fields. Mushrooms fatten in the warm September rain. Gone away.

Then time to go for the paper. And back with it to the lavatory. Between the green peeling walls. Always feel I'm going to get stuck. One morning there was sunshine and I was feeling great. Sitting in there grunting and groaning, looking over the news, and then reach up and pull the chain. Downstairs in the kitchen, Marion screamed.

"I say, Marion, what is it?"

"For God's sake, stop it, stop it, Sebastian, you fool. What have you done?"

Moving with swift irritability down the narrow stairs, stumbling into the kitchen at the bottom. Perhaps things have gotten too much for Marion and she's gone mad.

"You idiot, Sebastian, look at me, look at the baby's things."

Marion trembling in the middle of the kitchen floor covered with strands of wet toilet paper and fecal matter. From a gaping patch in the ceiling poured water, plaster and excrement.

"God's miserable teeth."

"Oh damnable, damnable. Do something, you fool."

"For the love of Jesus."

Sebastian stalking away.

"How dare you walk away, you damnable rotter. This is horrible and I can't bear any more."

Marion broke into sobs, slammed into silence with the front door.

Walking past the parking lot, down the little hill to the station. Stand by this wall here and watch the trains go by. Just take a crap and look what happens. This damn Skully probably put in rubber pipes. Three pounds a week for a rat hole, with brown swamp grass on the walls and cardboard furniture. And Marion has to be standing right under it. Couldn't she hear it coming? And the sun's gone in and it looks like rain. Better get back to the house or it'll weaken

50

my position. Get her a little present, a fashion magazine filled with richery.

Marion sitting in the easy chair sewing. Pausing at the door, testing the silence.

"I'm sorry, Marion."

Marion head bent. Sebastian tendering his gift.

"I really am sorry. Look at me, I've got a present for you. It's hot tamale with ink dressing, see."

"O."

"Nice?"

"Yes."

"Like the gold teeth of God?"

"Don't spoil it now."

"My little Marion. I'm such a bastard. I tell you the whole thing up there is just a bunch of roots."

"I'll have something to read in bed."

"I'm an incredible pig, Marion."

"Aren't these suits nice."

"Don't you hear me, Marion? I'm a pig."

"Yes, but I wish we were rich and had money. I want to travel. If we could only travel."

"Let me kiss you, Marion, at least."

Marion arose, embracing him with blond arms, driving her long groin against his and her tongue deep into his mouth.

Marion you're good underneath it all and not a bad feel. just irritable at times. Now go in there and cook the dinner. And I'll relax here in the chair and read my *Evening Mail*. I see listed conscience money. Great thing, the conscience. And letters about emigration and women who marry for quids. And here's a letter about Blessed Oliver Plunket. Went up to see him there in the St. Peter's Church, Drogheda. A decapitated, two hundred and sixty year old head. Made me feel hushed. Gray, pink and battered and a glint of dead, bared teeth in the candle light. Charwomen told me to touch it, touch it now, sir, for it's great for luck. I put my finger,

51

afeared, in the mouldy nose hole, for you can't have too much luck these days.

Now I see them across the street coming out of the laundry. Pouring into the road, faces lining up for the tram. There's the girl with the brown eyes and dark hair, her face colorless but for handsome lips. Her legs in lisle stockings and feet in army surplus boots. Hatless and hair in a bun. Goes to the newsboy, calves knotting softly on the backs of her legs. Tucks the paper under her arm and waits in the queue.

In my heart I know she isn't a virgin, but perhaps childless with pink buds for nipples or even if they're sucked and dark I don't mind. Wears a green scarf around her nice neck. Necks should be white and long with a blue nervous vein twitching with the nervousness of life in general. My good gracious savior, she's looking over here. Hide? What am I? A scoundrel, a sneak? Not a bit. Face her. You're lovely. Absolutely lovely. Put my face on your spring breasts. Take you to Paris and tie your hair in knots with summer leaves.

"Sebastian, it's ready, do bring in the chair."

In the kitchen cutting a thick slice off the loaf, scraping butter out of a cup.

"Sebastian, what about the toilet?"

"What about it?"

"Who's going to fix it?"

"Marion, I beg of you, this is dinner time. Do you want to give me ulcers?"

"Why won't you take some responsibility?"

"After dinner. Don't drive me up the wall over Irish plumbing, it's new to the country and the pipes got mixed."

"But who'll pay?"

"Skully out of his little gold egg."

"And the smell, Sebastian. What can we do about the smell."

"It's just healthy shit."

"How dare you use that ugly word."

"Shit's shit, Marion, even on judgement day."

52

"It's foul and I won't have it said in the same house as Felicity."

"She'll hear it and also in the matter of foulness I'll see to it she's laid before she's fifteen."

Marion silently seized. Putting egg shell in the coffee to make it settle. Notice her fingers bitten. She moves through the mess.

"All right, Marion, take it easy. It's just adjustment. Got to get used to it here."

"Why must you be so raw?"

"The mean meat in me."

"Be sincere. You weren't like this before we came to Ireland. This vulgar filthy country."

"Easy now."

"Children running barefoot in the streets in the middle of winter and men wagging their things at you from doorways. Disgusting."

"Untruths. Lies."

"They're a foul lot. I understand now why they're only fit to be servants."

"I say, Marion, a little bitterness?"

"You know it's true. Look at that frightful O'Keefe and his dirty ideas. America doesn't seem to help. Brings the worst out in them. He's not even fit to be a servant."

"I think Kenneth's a gentleman in every respect. Have you ever heard him fart? Now, have you?"

"Absolute frightful rot. One has only to watch him leering over the cat when it's in heat to see he's dreadfully base. When he comes into the room I feel he's criminally assaulting me in his mind."

"It's legal."

"It's the revolting lechery of an Irish peasant. And he tries to give the impression of good breeding. Watch him eating. It's infuriating. Grabs everything. That first time we had him to dinner he just came in as if we were servants and proceeded to eat before I even had time to sit down. And

53

pulling hunks out of the bread, how can you be blind to these things."

"Now, now, a little patience with the people who have given your country a Garden of Eden to play in, make your fires and serve your tea."

"I wished we had stayed in England. You could have waited for Oxford or Cambridge. And we could have at least maintained a measure of dignity."

"I'll admit there's not much of that."

Long limbed Marion settled in the chair. What makes you so tall and slender. You raise your eyelids and cross your legs with something I like and wear sexless shoes with sexiness. And Marion I'll say this for you, you're not blatant. And when we get our house in the West with Kerry cattle out on the hills sucking up the grass and I'm Dangerfield K.C., things will be fine again.

A tram pounding by the window, grinding, swaying and rattling on its tracks to Dalkey. A comforting sound. Maps shaking on the wall. Ireland a country of toys. And maybe I ought to go over to Marion on the couch. We're experimenting with marriage. Got to find the contraceptives or else another screaming mouth for milk. The brown-eyed girl in the laundry is about twenty-five. Marion sucking on her false teeth again, I think it must be a sign of wanting it.

In the bedroom, Dangerfield rubbing stockinged feet on the cold linoleum. And the sound of Marion using the piss pot behind Skully's genuine Ming dynasty screen. And a little tug at these tattered shades for the privacy. Even in this great Catholic country you've got to keep covered, you know, or they watch you undress, but mind you, the Protestants use a field glass.

And Marion clutching the hem of her dress and drawing it over her shifting shoulders. She said there was only thirty shillings left.

"Our good accents and manners will see us right. Didn't you know, Marion, they can't put Protestants in jail?"

"You've no responsibility and to have my child raised

among a lot of savage Irish and be branded with a brogue for the rest of her life. Pass me my cream, please."

Sebastian passing the cream, smiling and waving his feet from the edge of the bed. Letting his body fall with a squeal of springs and looking at the patches of pink in the ceiling. Marion a bit upset and confused. Difficult for her. She was breaking. Isn't as strong as me, led a sheltered life. Maybe shouldn't have married me. Matter, all of it, of time. Pumping it around and around and around, air in, air out and then it all goes like the shutters of a collapsing house. Starts and ends in antiseptic smell. Like to feel the end would be like closing leaves of honeysuckle, pressing out a last fragrance in the night but that only happens to holy men. Find them in the morning with a smile across the lips and bury them in plain boxes. But I want a rich tomb of Vermont marble in Woodlawn Cemetery, with automatic sprinkler and evergreens. If they get you in the medical school they hang you up by the ears. Never leave me unclaimed, I beg of you. Don't hang me all swollen, knees pressing the red nates of others where they come in to see if I'm fat or lean and all of us stabbed to death on the Bowery. Kill you in the tenement streets and cover you in flowers and put in the juice. By God, you hulking idiots, keep the juice away from me. Because I'm a mortician and too busy to die.

"Marion, do you ever think of death?"

"No."

"Marion, do you ever think you're going to die?"

"I say, Sebastian, would you mind awfully stopping that sort of talk. You're in that nasty mood."

"Not at all."

"You are. Coming up here every morning to watch the funerals of these wretched people. Dreadful and sordid. I think you get a perverse pleasure out of it."

"Beyond this vale of tears, there is a life above, unmeasured by the flight of years and all that life is love."

"You think you're frightening me with these sinister airs

55

of yours. I find them only boring and they tend to make you repulsive."

"What?"

"Yes, they do."

"For the love of Jesus, look at me. Look at my eyes. Go ahead, come on."

"I don't want to look in your eyes."

"Honest globes they are."

"You can't talk seriously about anything."

"I just asked you about death. Want to know how you feel, really get to know you. Or maybe you think this is forever."

"Rubbish. You think it's forever, I know you do. You're not as flippant as this in the mornings, I notice."

"Takes me a few hours to adapt. Snap out of the dream."

"And you scream."

"What?"

"You were yelling a few nights ago, how do I get out of this. And another time you were screaming, what's that white thing in the corner, take it away."

Dangerfield holding his belly, laughing on the squeaking springs.

"You can laugh, but I think there's something serious at the root of it."

"What's at the root? Can't you see I'm mad. Can't you see? Look. See. Madness. E. I'm mad."

Sebastian ogled and wagged his tongue.

"Stop it. Always willing to clown but never to do anything useful."

Dangerfield watched from the bed as she flexed her long arms behind her back and her breasts fell from the cups of her brassiere, tan nipples hardening in the cold air. Red line on her shoulder left by the strap. Stepping wearily out of her underpants, facing the mirror and rubbing white cream into her hands and face. Little brown strands growing round the nipples. You've often said, Marion, about giving it the wax treatment but I like them that way after all.

56

Sebastian quietly stepping from the bed approaching the naked body. Pressing his fists against her buttocks and she pushes his hands away.

"I don't like you touching me there."

And kissing her on the back of the neck. Wet the skin with the tongue and the long blond hair gets in the mouth. Marion taking the blue nightdress from the nail. Sebastian stripping and sitting naked on the edge of the bed, taking white fluff out of the navel, and doubling himself, plucking the congealed dirt from between his toes.

"Sebastian, I wish you'd take a bath."

"Kills the personality."

"You were so clean when I first knew you."

"Given up the cleanliness for a life of the spirit. Preparation for another and better world. Hardly take offence at a little scruffiness. Clean soul's my motto. Take off your nightie."

"Where are they?"

"Under my shirts."

"And the vaseline?"

"Behind the books on the box."

Marion ripping the silver paper. Americans great for packages. Wrap anything up. And she draws the opening of her nightdress back from her shoulders, letting it fall to her feet and folding it carefully across the books. She kneels on the bed. What are other men like, do they grunt and groan, are they all curved and circumcised, with or without. She climbs into bed, a soft voice.

"Let's do it the way we used to in Yorkshire."

"Umn."

"Do you still like my breasts the way they are?"

"Umn."

"Tell me things, Sebastian, talk to me. I want to know."

Sebastian rolled near, pressing the long, blond body to his, thinking of a world outside beating drums below the window in the rain. All slipping on the cobble stones. And standing aside as a tram full of Bishops rumbles past, who hold up sacred hands in blessing. Marion's hand tightening and touching in my groin. Ginny Cupper took me in her car out to the spread fields of Indiana. Parking near the edge of woods and walking out into the sunny rows of corn, waving seeds to a yellow horizon. She wore a white blouse and a gray patch of sweat under her arms and the shadow of her nipples was gray. We were rich. So rich we could never die. Ginny laughed and laughed, white saliva on her teeth lighting up the deep red of her mouth, fed the finest food in the world. Ginny was afraid of nothing. She was young and old. Her brown arms and legs swinging in wild optimism, beautiful in all their parts. She danced on the long hood of her crimson Cadillac, and watching her, I thought that God must be female. She leaped into my arms and knocked me to the ground and screamed into my mouth. Heads pressed in the hot Indiana soil and pinned me in a cross. A crow cawed into the white sun and my sperm spurted into the world. Ginny had driven her long Cadillac through the guard rails of a St. Louis bridge and her car shone like a clot of blood in the mud and murk of the Mississippi. We were all there in the summer silence of Suffolk, Virginia, when the copper casket was gently placed in the cool marble vault. I smoked a cigarette and crushed it out on the black and white squares of the tomb. In the stagnant emptiness of the train station after the cars were gone, I walked into the women's toilet and saw the phallic obscenities on the wooden doors and gray walls. I wonder if people will think I'm a lecher. Ginny had gardenias in her lovely brown hair. I hear the train, Marion's breath in my ear. My stomach's shaking, my last strength. The world's silent. Crops have stopped growing. Now they grow again.

7

"Marion, I think I'll go and study in the park this morning."

"Take the baby with you."

"The pram is broken."

"Carry her."

"She'll piss on my shirt."

"Take the rubber sheet."

"How am I going to study, watching her? She'll crawl into the pond."

"I say, can't you see? I've got my hands full with all this, the mess. Look at the ceiling. And there you are, and you're wearing my sweater. I don't want you wearing my sweater. What do I have."

"Jesus."

"And why don't you go to see Mr. Skully and have this loathsome toilet fixed? I know why. You're afraid of him, that's why."

"Not a bit of it."

"You are. All I have to do is say Skully and you're off up the stairs like a frightened rabbit, and don't think I can't hear you crawling under the bed either."

"Just tell me where my sun glasses are, that's all."

"I didn't have them last."

"I must have them. I absolutely refuse to go out of this house without them."

"Well look."

"Do you want me to be recognized? Do you?"

"Yes, I do."

"God damn this house. It's the size of a closet and I can't even find my own foot in it. I'll break something in a minute."

"Don't you dare. And here, a revolting post-card from your friend O'Keefe."

59

Marion flicked it across the room.

"Watch my correspondence. I don't want to have it thrown about."

"Your correspondence, indeed. Read it."

Scrawled in large capitals:

WE HAVE THE FANGS OF ANIMALS

"E. O aye."

"That's what he is, a detestable animal."

"What else?"

"Bills of course."

"Well don't blame me."

"I will blame you. Who started the account in Howth? Who was the one who bought whisky and gin? Who was?"

"Where are my sun glasses?"

"And who pawned the fire irons? And who pawned the electric kettle—"

"Now look Marion, can't we be friends for this morning? The sun's out. Christians at least."

"See? You immediately get sarcastic. Why do we have to live like this?"

"My glasses, damn it. British hide everything. Can't hide the toilet now, anyway."

"I won't have this talk."

"Have this then."

"Someday you will regret all this. Vulgar."

"Do you want bird calls all your life, the B.B.C.? I'll do a series of programs for you called 'My Bottom was Green'."

"Your nasty mind."

"I'm cultured."

"Yes, from your chromium plated life in America."

"I'm distinguished-looking. Speak the King's English. Impeccably tailored."

"What rot. I don't know how I ever let you meet Mommy and Daddy."

"Your Mommy and Daddy thought I had lots of money.

And I, for that matter, thought that they had lots of money. Neither had nicker, no notes, no love."

"That's a lie. You know it's a lie. There never was a question of money until you started it."

"All right. Get the baby. I can't stand it any more. I need a long trolley ride in the womb, to take me out of this."

"Take you out? I'm the one who ought to be taken out and it may be any day now."

"All right. Let's be friends."

"Yes, it's easy isn't it. Just like that, after being so horrid."

"I'll take the baby."

"And you can do some shopping too. Get me some bones from the butcher and don't bring back one of those revolting sheep's heads, and don't let Felicity fall in the pond."

"I insist on a sheep's head."

"Be careful shutting the door. It fell on the mailman this morning."

"Suffering saints and sick sinners. I'll be god damn well sued on top of everything."

Out on Mohammed road wild with traffic and thundering trams. The laundry a hive of activity. See them in there beating sheets and that's the way it ought to be. Warm yellow sun. Most beautiful country in the world, full of weeds and weeds are people. Stay here to die and never die. Look at the butcher shop. Look at the hooks, groaning with the meat. He has his sleeves rolled way up with the chopper. A bunch of them behind the counter.

Entering the park. Green, green grass, soft and sweet from the night rain. The flower beds. Circles and crosses and nice little fences. Pick that bench. Newly painted. If my father dies by Autumn I'll be very rich, golden udder. And sit on a park bench for the rest of my life. What a warm, lovely day. I'd like to take off my shirt and let a sup of sun to me chest but they'd be hounding me out of the place for indecency. Help my hairs to grow, give them a fashionable tinge of blond. Dear child, stop kicking me in the back. Here, now get on this blanket and play and I don't want any nonsense

61

from you. Jesus, let go of the blanket, think I was going to kill you. Papa's got to study his law and become a big big K.C. and make lots of money. A great big golden udder. A tan on my chest means wealth and superiority. But I'm proud of my humility. And here, reading the dead language, my little book of Roman Law. For parricide, flung off the cliff in a bag with a viper. Fat ugliness writhing in the crotch. And little daughter, gurgling on the grass, have fun now. Because papa is finished. Getting it from all sides. Even in dreams. And last night I dreamt I was carrying a bundle of newspapers under my arm and climbed on a bus and went racing across the Curragh with massive horses galloping beside. In the bus, a man studying butterflies with a magnifying glass. And we were going to the West. Then a bullock leaped from behind a hedge and the bus cut him up and left him hanging on a huge hook in front of a village butcher shop. Then suddenly I was in Cashel. Streets filled with goats and gutters brown with dried blood. And in the hot sun's stillness, a crowd of men and women in thick black overcoats walking down the middle of a winter road, summer's hesitating heat on every side. The funeral of the gombeen man. He caught her, lips bubbling, eyes spinning, sitting on the shop assistant on a crate from Chicago and he heard it collapse and was after them with a hatchet. And they conspired between hot wet lips, clutching at each other's clothes to put poison in the tea, trembling hands to the till and each other's flesh, to wind a cocoon of sin between the pineapple and peaches. The box was closed. Summer. The long line shuffling. Through Cashel. A song:

> Shuffling through Cashel
> A box in the sun
> Through Cashel, through Cashel
> The gombeen man's dead.
> The gombeen man's dead
> In a box in the sun.

The assistant got the wife
And the gombeen man got done.
Poor mercy on the gombeen man.
There's a hand in the till,
There's a box in the sun,
God's mercy on the gombeen man.

Someone talking to Felicity. Good God. Wow.

She was kneeling on one knee and crouched over her tight legs, Felicity tugging at her outstretched finger. She wagged her head. Hello, little girl, hello. Wearing a green skirt, matched on the grass and her lisle stockings, slim slender ankles. Her gleaming round bottom poked up her heels.

"Hello."

She didn't turn around. Prodding the baby belly. Fading magic moment. That bun of black hair.

"Hello."

Looking over her shoulder, direct dark eyes. Mellow voice.

"Hello. Admiring your child. What's her name?"

"Felicity."

"Really. Hello, Felicity, aren't you a pretty little girl? Aren't you now?"

What lips across what white teeth. The shoulders of her suit, arms through small circles. I'd like to get my hands on you.

"You work in the laundry, don't you?"

"Yes. And you live in the house across the street."

"Yes."

"I suppose you've seen me looking in your windows."

"What do you do in that room?"

"That's my office."

"I see you drink a lot of tea."

"Coffee."

"Pleasant."

"She's got such lovely hair. Haven't you, haven't you, little girl? I must go. Bye bye now, Felicity, bye bye."

Waving long fingers. A little smile and she walks away

on the asphalt path. Chevrons dividing across her calves and wider over her thighs. She waves again. She smiles once more. Please come back and play with me. Your sensible clothing is sexy.

Throw this damn law in the sea. I can't learn a thing. Children are good advertising. Shows them the end product, the thing you do it for. I think she has hair on her legs. That's what I like, slight suggestion of the male. I'm in love with that girl. The way she walks, a twist of the hips. The neck tells everything, slight gangle. Certainly I'm not homosexual or an elf's child. I want to know where she lives and what she does at night. I must know. O I think things are beginning to straighten out. If I get that toilet fixed. Anything. Block it up, run it into the street, just anything. But there is so little that Egbert and I have in common, especially money. How does one make this approach about impaired function of the drain. I feel I am moving to a different level of experience. Get my dark suit out of pawn and take Marion to the Dolphin for a grilled steak and Beaujolais. She needs a little recreation. Poor girl. I'm such a hard bastard to live with. And I'll come to the park tomorrow.

There was a sheep's head simmering in the big black pot. Marion washing her bottom in a pan on the floor. Fine thing for sixpence. The baby quietly to bed upstairs, the afternoon over, the evening begun. They are coming into their houses all over Dublin city with their arms light with a few sausages, old butter and little bags of tea.

"Sebastian, give me my talcum powder on the window sill."

"Certainly."

"How was the park?"

"Very nice."

"That's such an odor."

"I tell you, it's the finest thing in the world. I need it for my brains. Sheep's head gives brain food."

Sebastian picked up a movie magazine and sank in the easy chair, waiting for the sheep. Red brash brightness of

64

these faces. I was once approached by a talent scout in summer stock. He said, how would you like to come to Hollywood. I told him they'd have to feed me brandy day and night. He said he was serious and wanted me to think the offer over. I told him my allowance from home was as much as that. But kid, you just wait till after your first picture. This man's name was Bill Kelly. Call me Bender Kelly. He said his mother and father were born in Ireland and someday he thought he would take a trip over there looking for talent, and maybe find some real talent. Mr. Kelly said they got a lot of girls from Ireland. But, you see, these Irish girls don't get far in Hollywood. Got to drop the drawers at the strategic moment. You see, you got to realize there's compromise wherever you go in this world, get screwed or sacked. Some hold out but not for long. But a guy with your stuff could go places. Where'd you pick up acting? I beg your pardon, Mr. Kelly, I was born an actor. Well, that's what they all say. Mr. Kelly had a few more drinks and said Hollywood killed you like these Aztec guys used to get one of these girls and dress her all up, big star, then put her up there on the altar and tear her heart out. But Mr. Kelly, how sordid. It's sordid all right, that's why you've got to be tough. But I'm just a frond, I just know I couldn't bear it. Well, Mr. Sebastian Beef. Sebastian Balfe Dangerfield. Jesus. Well, anyway, I'd like to get married and have some kids. I've knocked up some high school girls. Maybe that's not so good but isn't that the way life is, all squeeze and tease? I've handled some big stars in my time. Big. Really big. And Mr. Kelly got drunk and vomited all over the bar. It is well to remember there's a village called Hollywood in the Wicklow mountains.

Marion humming in the kitchen. Not often that happened.

"Make some toast, baby."

"Slice the bread."

"I'm studying."

"I see that silly movie magazine."

"Marion, do you like men with hairy chests?"

"Yes."

"Biceps?"

"A bit."

"How about the shoulders?"

"So that he can wear a suit."

"Would you say now, that I'm your man?"

"Don't like men with pots."

"I beg your pardon. Pot? Not a bit—just look. Will you look in here a minute. See. Nothing there at all. You might even say I was wasted."

"Come and deal with this wretched head."

"Delighted. O I tell you, it's coming along a jolly treat. What ho and bang on and wizard whip. Sound the horn you buggers."

"Cut the bread."

"Of course, darling."

"Don't say that if you don't mean it."

"I mean it."

"You don't mean it."

"All right, I don't mean it. Why don't we buy a radio? I think we need a radio."

"With what?"

"Hire purchase. A system for people like us."

"Yes, and that could pay our milk bill."

"We can have milk too. Few shillings a week."

"Why don't you take a part time job then?"

"Must study."

"Of course. Yes of course, you must study."

"O now, now, now, give me a little kiss. Come on, on the lips, one."

"Get away from me."

"Not cricket."

"Bring in the chair, please."

"Then, let's go to the cinema."

"Have you forgotten? We have a child you know."

"Shit."

"Stop it, stop it. Stop using that ugly word to me."

"Shit."

66

"If you say that word once more I'll leave this house. You may use that sort of language with your working class friends but I shan't stand for it."

"Leave."

"Every meal is like this, every meal."

"Meals? What meals?"

"My God, what did I marry."

"You certainly didn't have to marry me."

"Well, I wish I hadn't now. Father was right. You're a wastrel. Done nothing but drink with your wretched friends, all useless people. Will they help you to get on?"

"British rubbish. Get on where? Where to?"

"Make something of yourself. You think it's so easy, don't you. I don't even think you'll get your degree. Cheat on your exams. Don't think everything you do escapes attention. Don't look shocked, and I know how you go and butter up your professors. How long do you expect to get away with it?"

"Absurd."

"You've insulted every friend I have. People who could help you. Do you think they'll help a rotter, an absolute rotter?"

"Rotter? Rotter? Me, a rotter?"

"And a liar."

"Liar?"

"You needn't smirk. My friends could help us. Lord Gawk could have introduced you to a firm in London."

"What's stopping him?"

"You. Your insulting manner. You've ruined me socially."

"Not at all. Why blame me if your pukka friends ignore you?"

"Blame you? My God, how can you say that I can't blame you, when you called Lady Gawk a whore, ruined her whole party and shamed me. Blame you?"

"The woman is stupid. Moral decadent."

"It's a lie. You sit there and you haven't had a bath for a month, your feet smell and your fingernails are filthy."

"Quite."

"And I have had to suffer the humiliation of having my family involved. What do you think? Daddy was so right."

"Daddy was so right. Right. God's teeth, let me for Christ's sake eat my dinner. Daddy, daddy. Sterile bastard, that daddy of yours is merely a leech on the Admiralty's bottom and a pompous lot of shit."

Marion ran from the room, she tripped up the narrow stairs. He heard her slamming the bedroom door and the creak of the bed springs as she fell. Silence and then her choked sobs. He reached for the salt, shook it over the plate. Nothing came out. He raised his arm. The salt cellar crashed through the window and smashed to little pieces on the gray concrete wall outside. He kicked his chair over, picked up his jacket. He went behind the clock where he knew Marion had been saving change for weeks. He took it all and let it slip, clinking, into his pocket.

A very red face. Guilt. Grinding the teeth. Soul trying to get out of the mouth, swallowing it back into the body. Shut out the sobs.

He ordered a bottle of stout and a Gold Label, telling the boy to bring him another stout and Gold Label. Boy didn't understand. Sebastian stamping his foot, shouting.

"Do as I say."

Boy, short sleeved, mumbling.

"I don't think you should talk to me that way, sir."

"Sorry, I'm upset. Bring me some cigarettes too."

What a sorry sad day. I want company. A morass of black coats, coughing and spitting. Get out of here.

He went across the street. Had a nickelodeon there. He played "That Old Black Magic," and "Jim Never Brings Me Any Pretty Flowers." Like Chicago. A man in Chicago accused me of having a Harvard accent. What are you, from Evanston? Don't talk to guys like me. The bruised and dumb, the snotty and sniffling. Her stinking hairy tits. I'm not blaming her for hair around her nipples. That's all right. I just don't like the British, a sterile genital-less race. Only

68

their animals are interesting. Thank God they have dogs. She wants her life sitting on her fanny in India, whipping the natives. Wants Bond Street. Afternoon tea at Claridges. Lady Gawk tickling her twat with a Chinese fan. I'll break something over that woman's face. The way I lose my dignity is dreadful. Worrying about silly misunderstandings. She can leave. I'll tell her to get out. Stay out.

The end of the song. Outside, standing in front of the cinema waiting for the roaring tram. It's so noisy, coming down the hill out of the night, mad teetering vehicle. Seems to work like a coffee grinder. But I love the color and the seats, all green and warm, orange, pink and passionate. Like to run up the spiral stairs to the top and see the schoolchildren sitting on the outside platform. I like it because I can see into all the gardens and some of the evening windows. I was impressed by trams when I first set foot in this country. From the top deck you can see into some personal windows. Women wearing slips only. I often saw a great deal of chromium plate in the bedrooms and electric fires glaring from the walls. Also the beds were covered with satin eiderdowns, big, thick and puce.

He got off at College Street. Swarms of people. A girl pipers' band was rounding the front of Trinity College, all green and tassels and drumming. La, de da deda la de. Followed by gurriers. This English amusement park. Must get into a public house. Where? I owe money in every one. That's one thing about me anyway, I can run up credit in a public house and that's saying a whole lot. Go up the Grafton Street, cheer me up with its wealth. But where are the rich. Just poor miserable bastards like me, have nowhere to go. Invited nowhere. Why doesn't someone invite me. Come on, invite me. You're all afraid.

At Duke Street. Just about to cross. Foot half down from the curb. Hold on.

On the opposite side, looking in the shoe shop. I mustn't panic. No bungle. Get to her before she starts walking again. She's staying. Stay still. Rebuffed. I'll not be rebuffed. Whoa.

She sees me. She's confused. Optimum moment. Show slight surprise. I am surprised. Don't have to show it. Be natural. Brave and noble. And a gentleman, of course. A quick greeting.

"Good evening."

"Hello."

"Are you window shopping?"

"Yes, it passes the time."

Mate in one move.

"Come and have a drink with me."

"Well."

"Come along."

"Well, there's nothing stopping me. All right."

"Where do you live?"

"South Circular Road."

"You're not Irish."

"What makes you say that? My voice?"

"No, your teeth. All the Irish's teeth are rotting. You have good teeth."

"Ha, ha."

They walked to the bottom of Grafton Street.

"We'll go in that pub. Nice soft seats upstairs."

"All right."

They wait on the curb. Two beetle American cars go by. A breeze. Cool sky. Taking her hand an instant, warm knuckles of her long fingers. Just guiding you safely across. She went up the stairs before him, curious climber. White petticoat. Slight pigeon toe. The voices around the corner and in the door. Slight hush as they enter, and sit. She crosses her legs and smooths her skirt over her nice knee.

"My name is Christine."

"Mine—"

"I know yours."

"How?"

"One of the girls in the laundry. She has a friend who works in the grocers where your wife shops."

"Fantastic."

70

"I agree."

"Must know what I eat too."

"Yes."

"What?"

"Sheep's head."

"O aye."

What a good-looking girl you are. White. Your body must be very white. Let me eat the lotus. I came out tonight feeling badly. How weak are our hearts. Because now I can jump with joy. The world obeys a law. Large and brown black. Eyes.

"Do you like working in the laundry?"

"I hate it."

"Why?"

"O the heat and steam and noise."

"And what's it like where you live?"

"O I don't know. Don't know how I can describe it. There are trees down the street anyway. That's always something. Just one of those terraced houses on South Circular Road. I live in the basement. It's quite nice though, compared to what I might have to live in."

"Alone?"

"Alone. I can't bear sharing."

"What would you like?"

"Stout, please."

"How long have you been working in the laundry?"

"A few months."

"Money?"

"Not much. Four pounds ten."

"Now, Christine, I think you are a most pleasant girl."

"What do you study?"

"Law. This is most pleasant. I was in despair. Wretched. Beat. A walk up Grafton Street sometimes kills it. But everyone looked beat like me."

"Wrong time. Just people looking for somewhere to go."

"You?"

"Just looking. I often just look. I like to feel there is something in the shops I want. I get off the bus at the top of Stephen's Green and walk through the park. I like that best and watch the ducks from the bridge and go down Grafton Street. Sometimes I have a coffee in one of those icecream parlors. Then I go home. That's all there is to my life."

"No culture?"

"Cinema, and sometimes I go sit in the back of the Gate for a shilling."

Sitting there and then lighting up cigarettes. I don't usually approve of smoking. I find now that things seem good. That suddenly out of the darkness the light. That's Christian. The light showing the way. When I've thought of it, I've stepped into Clarendon Street Church, to pray and sometimes to see if it was warmer and after sitting awhile, to relax a bit from the tension. I have awful tensions and in that Catholic gloom and the Erse that is in it, I grew slightly sad and pitiful, considering the after and before and I often got the feeling there that I was really going to haul down some quids. I don't know why quids get rid of gloom. But they get rid of it. O Christine. What are you like underneath?

They had one more round of stout and she turned and smiled and said that she must be going home. And may I take you? That's all right. I insist. It's really not necessary. For the joy that's in it then. O.K.

They set off along Suffolk Street, into the Wicklow Street and up the Great George's. And over there Thomas Moore was born. Come in and see it, a nice public house indeed. But I must go home and wash my hair. But just a quick one.

In they went. The embarrassed figures looking at them and bird whispering. The man showed them to a booth, but Mr. Dangerfield said that they were just in for a fast one.

O surely, sir and it's a grand evening. 'Tis that.

And passing the Bleeding Horse he tried to steer her in there. But she said she could go on alone just around the corner. But I must come.

The house she lived in was one at the end of a long row.

72

Went through an iron gate, just a speck of garden with a bush and bars over her window. And her door just at the bottom of three steps with a drain to run the water off that would surely be going under the door. Only that I must wash my hair I'd ask you in. That's quite all right. And thank you for walking me home. Not at all, and may I see you again? Yes.

She went down the steps. Paused, turned, smiled. Key. Green door. Few seconds. A light goes on. Shadow moves across the window. Hers. What sweet stuff, sweeter than all the roses. Come down God and settle in my heart on this triangular Friday.

8

July. Be over in another week. See awnings up in Grafton Street with such a bunch of healthy people going underneath. Everything looks good with the sun out. Even my affairs.

But mornings in the bed with the sheet well up over the eyes, when you hear them downstairs when Marion's out to shop, knocking hard on the door. And it can't stand it. And they never stop the damn knocking and some try to push it in. O the fear of them coming up and naked, my dignity wilts and it's a poor enough weapon defending debts. And they yell up the stairs, not wanting someone to be home, embarrassed to have penetrated so far into the house.

Marion not standing up to it very well. Worry. Couldn't control herself any longer, shaking and crying, tired of it all. Mousy blonde hair, hanging over her head like sauerkraut. Silence got her. If she breaks a blood vessel, the doctors and expense will be something terrible.

And slide from the bed and press warm feet into cold golfing shoes. Pull the blankets around me and crouch and shuffle to the cracked basin. Step on the tube of toothpaste, catch one more speck and vigorously brush the teeth. The pain of morning. Hulk over the gas, wordless and hungering. No coffee but piss-tinted tea. Nothing to do but sing:

> Come Holy Ghost
> And fill my
> Faithful belly.

And riding in this tram to the bottom of Dawson Street my heart thumps to see Chris in Jury's lounge tonight. By compressing the lips, erase guilt. Take a look in the window of this fashionable men's shop. I think a bowler hat with my next check. Simply must. Keep the dignity. Dignity in debt,

74

a personal motto. In fact a coat of arms. Bowler hat crossed by a walking stick.

In the front gate of Trinity. At least this is a bit professional with all these notices tacked up here. Must admit to an overwhelming fear when I think of exams. I hear these students say they haven't done a scrap of work when their eyes are bloodshot. But me. I just see a massive vista of my total ignorance. The weeks left before the little white paper. A man like me has to get through. Can't afford failure. Must have my offices of law where I come in at ten o'clock and hang my hat. And when they come in to see me I smile with reassurance. A great thing, that, in the law.

Sebastian Dangerfield crossing the cobble stones. Looking up at O'Keefe's rainstained windows. His little dusty dungeon. Up the steps of the reading room. A strange building indeed. These people standing on the steps smoking cigarettes. They call that a break from work. Inside they have the names of the glorious dead in gold and red wreaths on the white marble. And then down these steps through the swing door and the faces come up from their books. Get back you damn thugs. Because you frighten the life out of me. Especially the few of you I see from my class dug right into the bindings. As for me, I think I'll read a bit in the encyclopedia Loosen up the brain. Up there around the balcony are eligible young things watching the door, hoping for a husband. Not a spark of joy anywhere except from a few lechers I know personally. Otherwise a rogues' gallery of Calvinists.

An evening sky so very blue. Light wind, south by south east. I'm just a little weather station, really. Nice openness of Dame Street this time of day. And sprinkles of people rounding the round corners. And in this little cul-de-sac at the back of the bank with all the lovely green leaves brightening up the granite. There is nothing more pleasant than this on the summer evening.

In the side door to Jury's. There she is, all dark hair, all white skin and dark lips and mouth, heart and sound. Sitting sedately. And near by, a sly-eyed business man, licking his mouth for her. I know them. I know them all right. In this nook of utter respectability. But this a nice lounge with palm fronds and wicker chairs. Flexing her legs, recrossing. Pale nails, long, tender fingers and moisture on her eyes. What do you have underneath, my dear Chris. Tell me.

And they sat drinking coffee for she said how much better than spirits and perhaps a ham sandwich too. And all about exams. All about this place. And the Erse.

They walked home. Holding her happy hand. And he paused at the top step, leaving. But she said do come in. Green carpet on the floor, faded and beat. Square wash basin in the corner and a red screen. The fireplace neatly covered with a copy of the *Evening Mail*. A boarded-up door out to the back garden. She said in heavy rain, water came in on the floor. And another door into the hall. Out there I take my baths and late at night for leisure. I will scrub your back. That would be nice. I'm a great man for the risky conversation. A battered wardrobe, half open and a green coat, and three pairs of shoes. On the window sill next to the front door, a gas ring, and a few pans hanging on the wall.

I am lost in love with this room. Because it's an oasis of hiding with no door knocks for me. And the building looks sound. Want to have something solid to put the back to. When your back goes to the wall it is sensible to see that the wall is well founded and not given to collapse.

Sebastian lying on her bed while she told him. All about her year at London University. I didn't like it there and after a year I found Psychology drab and empty but I had to give it up anyway because my money was gone. There was money in Ireland left to my father and that's why I'm here. My father was Irish and my mother a Russian. Strange combination, isn't it, both killed in the beginning of the war and so I got to England. But I needn't tell you that I got less than half the money left to my father. Well, obviously I had to find work. So. See. The result? The laundry. I hate it and I hate Ireland. I'm lonely and bored. Thirty five shillings for this. Horrid little room, really.

76

My dear Chris, don't worry now. I'm here. I think it's a fine room, safe, nest of love. And you won't be lonely again. I tell you there are good things and pints of the best and pineapples too and fields and guts and lust, soil and bull. Sebastian, do you really think that way? I do. But I'm a woman and I can't. I hate these Irishmen. Seedy bodies, their drunken smirks. I hate them. To listen to their snide remarks and their tight sneaky little nasty jokes. I hate this country.

My dear Chris, don't worry now.

She got up with her lovely legs, and poured the milk into the pot. For Ovaltine and biscuits.

At one a.m. just before he left he said he liked her so much. Gentle girl. And my dear Chris, I have my problems too. I think I am being choked to death by paper. Bills before breakfast and I do so want to have my breakfast first. And Sebastian, how did you ever get into such a mess. Miscalculation, my dear Chris and misunderstanding.

He kissed her hand as he left. And walked through the night by the canal, counting the locks and bulging waterfalls.

The story was, Marion, I missed the last tram. Just going down Nassau Street at a ferocious clip. Couldn't possibly get it. I'm in poor condition for running so I went back to Whitington's rooms in college. Smart bloke that, great help with the law of contract. You're a liar, I know when you're lying.

Marion, what is there left for me to say then?

On other evenings, Chris and he went for long walks and one Friday on her payday they went to the Grafton Cinema Cafe where on the top floor they dined mid shaded lamps and open medieval windows. It was so comfortable and full of rest and peace and better than home. Chris so insisted on paying. But I did not want to make a bad impression by appearing to be unconcerned. And after, we walked down along the quays and across the canal locks to Ringsend, the emptying mouth of Dublin. All black.

He had taken the tram home at eleven. Chris left him at the stop. Marion in the scabrous seat. Looking up from a copy of *Woman's Home Companion* that a barber had given him. There was a sign of gladness in her. But padded conversation out of my mouth. And she asked him would he like some warm milk with sugar in it. All right. They talked about America and mansions.

When they were going upstairs he noticed flowers on the box beside the bed. Marion undressing before the little mirror. Brushing her hair. His name in her plaintive voice.

"Sebastian?"

"What?"

"Sebastian."

Pausing, looking at the dresser, wrinkling the cloth with the brush.

"Sebastian, what do you think is happening to us?"

A shock ran through his body, rigid for a second and he drew his knees up in the bed. Slow rising sheet.

"How do you mean?"

"I don't know. Just happening. We don't talk to each other. I hardly see you."

"See me? Of course you do."

"You know what I mean."

"What?"

"Be with me, sort of. I feel cut off."

"It's only till my exam."

"I know, but you come home so late."

Marion poking the cloth in little hills. His lungs light.

"You may have to study but there's no response when I do see you."

"What do you mean?"

"Response—it's as if you didn't love me."

"Absurd."

"Don't mock me, please, Sebastian, I've got feelings just as you have. I can't help being English. Nor can I help feeling desperate left alone here and then at night too. I don't want to fight or argue any more. What's going to become of us and Felicity? Won't your father help us?"

"I can't ask him till we're really desperate."

"But he's rich."

"I can't."

"But you must. I won't mind if every once in a while you go out and even if you drink. But I'd rather you studied at home. You have every evening after six. You used to. And if we could only be a little happier when we're together. That's all I'm asking. Just that."

"There's great strain."

"But who has to bear it all. I stay in this dreary house day after day, seeing nothing but these damp horrid walls. If we could only get out into the country for a few days, see some green fields and feel free instead of hiding behind the kitchen door in mortal fear of that frightful Mr. Skully. He called last night."

"What did you tell him."

"To see you."

"O."

"How can I put him off? I think he was drinking too. Even had the nerve to say the front knocker could be polished. He has an excuse to walk in here any time he wants. It's such a hideous feeling. I don't like his eyes. He has no character. I even wrote to Father. But you know how hard things are for them now."

"Quite."

"They really are. I know you don't understand. They would help us if they were able."

He rolled over on his side and pushed his head into the pillow. Marion turned off the light. Her hand pulling back the sheet. A groan of rusty springs. Darkness like the sea come for him. A bed of pain. Asking the dark tide to take me away. And I went out with the sea and knelt praying in the deep.

Suddenly he was awake. In sweat and fear. Marion clinging to him sobbing. Hear the thunder of her heart and wailing. I'm smitten with remorse and calculating in my heart. Dublin looming a Swiss Cheese of streets and running through them screaming in tears. Children shrinking in the doorways. Gutters running pig's blood. Cold and winter.

79

In the morning all silence between them. Sebastian heating soup jelly, dipping bread in it and drinking a cup of tea. How I hate the fear of it. Hate my own hatred. Get out of all this with escape and murder. Poor Marion. I have never felt so sad or pained. Because I feel it all seems so useless and impossible. I want to own something. I want to get us out of this. Get out of this goddamn country which I hate with all my blood and which has ruined me. Crush Skully's head with a poker. A green Jesus around my neck and this damn leaking ceiling and this foul linoleum and Marion and her wretched shoes and her stockings and panties and her tits and goddamn skinny back and orange boxes. And the black smell of grease and germ and spermy towels. All the rot behind the walls. Two years in Ireland, shrunken teat on the chest of the cold Atlantic. Land of crut. And the drunk falling screaming into the ditches at night, blowing shrill whistles across the fields and brown buggered bogs. Out there they watch between the nettles, counting the blades of grass, waiting for each other to die, with the eyes of cows and the brains of snakes. Monsters growling from their chains and wailing in the dark pits at night. And me. I think I am their father. Roaming the laneways, giving comfort, telling them to lead better lives, and not to let the children see the bull serving the cow. I anoint their silver streams, sing laments from the round towers. I bring seed from Iowa and reblood their pastures. I am. I know I am Custodian of the Book of Kells. Ringer of the Great Bell, Lord King of Tara, "Prince of the West and Heir to the Arran Islands." I tell you, you silly bunch of bastards, that I'm the father who sweetens the hay and lays the moist earth and potash to the roots and story teller of all the mouths. I'm out of the Viking ships. I am the fertilizer of royalty everywhere. And Tinker King who dances the goat dance on the Sugar Loaf and fox-trots in the streets of Chirciveen. Sebastian, the eternal tourist, Dangerfield.

For two days he sat in the little room. Out twice to buy a tin of spaghetti and pig's trotters. On the third day, remorse hardening with idleness. Reading letters of those with problems in the back of a women's magazine and a few proverbs from the Bible, for the Christianity that was in it. And suddenly the sound of mail. On the hallway floor a letter from O'Keefe.

Dear Phony,

I'm up to my teeth. I'm a hungry son of a bitch, enough to eat dog. I bought a tin of peas and I ration myself twelve after every meal. This place is the dullest I've ever been. I put an ad in the local paper to give English instruction to girls that wanted to take posts in England with families. Two showed up. One as ugly as an old man's sin and knew what I was after and didn't mind at all but as hard up as I am I couldn't get myself to seduce her, even for academic purposes. I am destined to love beautiful women and to inspire in them a desire to lay for someone else. But things are more complicated than that. The other girl complained to the head master and I was scared I was going to get the kaput. But the head master is a good skin and he laughed and sympathized but told me to lay off because it wasn't so hot for the school. So much for my heterosexual life from which I have officially retired.

My homosexual personality is complete. I have been reading André Gide in French, the Marquis de Sade and Casanova. It's just like they say it is, being in love with a boy. I'm afraid of getting caught or that he might report me. He comes to my room at night and teases me by turning off my light and then wrestling with me in the dark. Jesus Christ, I think it will drive me crazy. I'm sure he must know, these French kids know everything, but he's teasing me just like Constance used to do in my rooms at Harvard. If I were in America the class would have reported me long ago. They notice I always ask him questions and that I never yell at him when he comes up to my desk but treat him like a bowl of cream. Being in love with a boy is an experience everyone should have but it's break-

81

ing my balls, but I must say that for me it is more exciting than chasing women who never gave me a tumble. Everyone does that. I'm dying for the want of a smell of the ould sod. Eire is in my blood, veins and jowls. I'm thinking of joining the Jews to fight the Arabs or the Arabs to fight the Jews. What the hell. I'm sick of it all. I'm raising a beard among other things. No more women—I've discovered I'm impotent, ejaculatio præcox.

Now what about the money? You've let me down badly. You've got to realize that I'm up against it. I'm depending on you. Nothing else except that I hope to get up to Paris soon. I'm saving a hundred francs from my pay every week and I'm going to lose my cherry once and for all to a pro. My best to Marion.

> God bless you,
> Kenneth O'KEEFE,
> *Duke of Serutan.*

Will I ever see time of largess. Say with a bit of butler. With O'Keefe at the front door blasting his way in with a pukka accent. Kenneth must have money troubles but he'll be all right. Nice little job. Quite a pleasant life that. He doesn't know that he has it good now. But I do think that Kenneth needs a menopause.

This is the month of August. Football season, a sunny New England afternoon. An indifferent summer air blowing sweetly softly across the grass. There is that word enthusiasm. And watch these people running out of locker rooms full of pep and zip and of course, enthusiasm. To see a ball spiral lazily down the field, plunging into the brute arms of a gentle idiot who charges through this so strange indifferent summertime. I could get down on my knees in this wretched little room and weep for things like that. I don't play football, however, but it wrings my heart for that dry wistful air. O the aching pangs of it. And the wholesome girls. Like bread, good enough to eat. Eat me. And brandy, rugs and cars. What have I now? The G.I. Bill. Of Rights

82

too. And when you get as old as I am now I can only feel I need preferential treatment. Preference of the veteran. I had a dream that these veterans were looking for me. They were arriving in Battery Park. Thousands of them off the Staten Island ferry. More out of the subway from Brooklyn. Beating great drums with leather-thonged fists, holding aloft torches of liberty. Going to get me. And a dreadful feeling it is. Get me for lechery and cheating. For not being at the front. I tell you, you oafs, I was behind the book. The man behind the book. They had a statue of the Blessed Virgin. But I beg of you, I'm just an ordinary guy. Say, bub, you're a moral leper, and degenerate. We're the Catholic war veterans and we're going to purify lousy bastards like you by hanging. But I tell you I'm rich. You're not rich bub. They were marching through Wall Street, coming up through the city to get me. Sleeping in my booze-stained room with someone's crying sister. Finding my room, picking out my brown fireproof door from a million others. I was in the Washington Heights for the anonymity that was in it. They were at 125th Street, a rumble of drums. Please, protection. None. Me an example. A mile away with placards, "Wipe Out Degenerates." But I tell you, I'm not degenerating. My God, they have dogs too. This sister of somebody, sobbing. Gentlemen, I put it to you that I am a Protestant and above this nonsense. Look, bub, we know what you are. But, gentlemen, I'm an Irish Catholic. Bub, we're going to hang you for sure for saying that. Mercy. Pounding feet up the stairs. I must say it was all most distasteful. The door was down. A football player plunging into the room. Bub, I'm from Fordham and we make short work of perverts like you. What are you Bub, crazy or something? Needless to say, I winced in terror and they pushed a flag pole out the window and dragged me from my corner, punching me in the ribs and twisting my balls and hanged me. I woke up with the bed sheet in shreds. Marion thought I had a touch of distemper, or papaphobia.

In this little room. I can only smile. A tram rumbling by. And twiddle my thumbs. And take some of these newspapers

83

and just squash them up and wee, into the grate. Little match. My room is orange. Must see me Chris tomorrow, maybe at the night time. I can only think of standing in the Glen of the Downs smelling the garlic or on the banks of the Barrow, a summer evening out on the lark sprinkled air, and last songs and salmon leaping. Fingers of the night touching me. Honeysuckle sorrow. Humming. I must weep.

9

Eight o'clock. The streets were wet, puddles of water on the granite blocks. Western clouds swarming soundlessly catching up the turf smell from the steaming chimney pots on this chill Saturday night. Bird feet moving his soul through this Danish city. The hoarse voices of newsboys punctuating the corners of streets behind. Up here in White Friar Street I can hear them saying rosaries. And in the hospital window, the light goes on and a nurse pulls down the shade. Hospital morgue where they were looking upon dead strangers with love and the white beauty of those dead young. Candles flickering in the carriage lamps in the alleyways of the funeral furnishers. He felt a hand on his arm, staying him, an ould one asking for a copper to spare, put wild joy in the heart and gently saying to her, that it wasn't since the mother. And she laughed at the English gentleman, fangs in the mist. Bought her a drink in the pub. Had small ones and she was proud of the company of this Protestant gentleman, telling him that her old man had spilled boiling water on his foot and that he had been laid up this year since. He filled her with lies and left the whole pub in tears when he sang "O Danny Boy."

This city of all these changeling streets, old windows and bleeding hearts, and boiling black pots of tea. Her warm little room, and neat possessions, patchwork quilt and people moving in the hall. And the soft bits of rain. Going in the houses with loaves of bread and butter with maybe a touch of cheese and the chattering chilled children awake everywhere.

The yellow light was in slits around the window. Tripping down the concrete steps. He knocked D in morse code on the green door. A smile of welcome.

"Come in. I had a strange intuition you would come tonight."

"Bright. A new light?"

"Yes."

"Fine. And frying."

"Would you like to have some bacon with me? It's the best I can do. And I'll also give you a nice piece of fried bread. Would you like that?"

"I think fried bread is the most delicious thing in the world. My dear Chris, may I sit here?"

"Yes. I stayed in Thursday night thinking you might call and take me to see Christ Church."

"Marion a bit upset. A little confusion."

"What was the trouble?"

"General misunderstanding. Absence of dignity in our lives. I think that damn house is going to fall down. Do you know, that one day I think the whole thing will just go prostrate into the street with me under it. Damn place trembles when I'm brushing my teeth. I think the trams have undermined the foundations, if there are any."

"And what upsets your wife?"

"Money. And I certainly don't blame her for that. O me. I like you Chris. I think you're very nice. What sort of men have you known."

"Harmless mostly. And mother-bound ones. Even little dark men who follow one around London. When you want to walk in the park it seems that none of them will believe you that you want to be alone and that you don't want to talk or be taken somewhere but just left alone. And a medical student and various students. Lots of students."

"In Ireland?"

"None that I've wanted to know."

"Me?"

"Silly. I wanted to know you. I knew I was going to meet you somehow. Well, I'm almost responsible for it. Aren't I? I must admit I was dreadfully curious. So when I saw you on the bench with your baby. Brazen of me."

"It's a bold one you are."

"I'm glad."

"Good."

"And your bacon."

Chris in her long fingers. A white plate of browned bacon. I like your arm and sweater. My God, how are you underneath? Nipples soft pattern and green swell of breast. Quiet room in the city. Lovely dark girl. Out there is the largest brewery in the world beating up the foaming pints over on the Watling Street and Stephen's Lane and the lovely blue trucks bringing it around the city so that at any time, any place, I'm never more than twenty paces from a pint. I am certain that stout is good joy, reblooder of the veins, brain feeder, and a great faggot for when one is walking in the wet. These people wear chains around their heads. These Celts. But I have sneaked into the churches, saw them at the altar, music in their voices, gold in their hearts and there was the sound of frequent pennies down the brass chute to build them bigger, better and more. My dear Chris, my very precious Chris, how can I take out my heart and put it in your hand.

Poking the fried bread with her fork, breaking it. Putting it in her mouth and looking at him. His child had his hair and eyes. His child a lovely child. Nice not to be alone. And Saturday and Sunday to stay in bed.

Mr. Dangerfield took the crust of his bread and wiped up the grease. Into his mouth with it.

"Very good. I'll say this, Chris, it's a fine country for the bacon."

"Yes."

"And now, may I suggest something?"

"Yes."

"Shall we have some refreshment?"

"Yes."

"I know of a very fine house."

"I'm going to get out my nylons. Precious. Get out of these drab things."

"Sensible."

"Drab. But as drabness goes, the least drab."

She unfolds the diaphanous things. Facing me. O but fully fashioned.

"My dear Chris, you do have a lovely pair of legs. Strong. You hide them."

"My dear Sebastian, I do thank you. I'm not hiding them. Does that make men follow one?"

"It's the hair that does that."

"Not the legs?"

"The hair and the eyes."

"So you're the man out of that tattered little house."

"It's me."

"Do you mind if I say something?"

"Not at all."

"You look like a bank clerk or perhaps someone who works in a coal office. Except for that funny tie."

"I stole that from an American friend."

"I must say you're the most curious American I've ever met. I don't like them as a rule."

"They're a fine, fleshy race."

"And you live in that house with brown torn shades. You know, the walls and roof are in a terrible state."

"My landlord doesn't see it that way."

"None do. I'm ready. I'm glad you asked me to go and have a drink."

Chris suggested a bottle of gin. Mr. Dangerfield up importantly to deal with the transaction.

"Let's not stay here. It depresses me. Look how drunk they get and I always feel that one of them is going to lurch over here and start to talk to us. Let's go for a walk. I like that so much better."

"I like you, Chris."

"Do you mean that?"

"Yes."

"You know, I don't know quite where I stand with you."

88

And on the Saturday night street with the old women going in to look for them ones wasting the money and have a quick malt hidden in their hands and the frolic of high-skirted girls pecking the pavements on their way in this fantastic poverty. They walked along the canal. The moon came out and shadows leaping on the water. Tightly she held his hand. Thinking happiness. The windows low down beneath the grates. People collected in the cellars around red specks of fire, gray heads on gray chests. Most of Dublin dead. A fresh wet air from the West. Turning down Clanbrassil Street. That canal goes across Ireland to the Atlantic. The Jewish shops. She pulled his arm against her breast. A few freckles on her upper lip.

"I wonder if it's possible, Sebastian."

"What?"

"If we are possible."

"Yes."

"Do you know what I'm talking about?"

"I think so."

The West's taken the rain out of the sky. They walked slowly. His feet in nervous restraint. Her soft voice speaking, pushing at the night.

"What about your wife?"

"Marion?"

"Yes."

"What about her?"

"Well, she's your wife. And you have a child."

"That's so."

"You're not helping me, you know."

"I can't, I don't know myself."

"Do you care for them, for Marion?"

"I'm fond of Marion, at times extremely fond of both her and the child, but I've made them both unhappy."

"What about us?"

"Us?"

"Yes."

"I think we're good for one another."

"Do you?"

"Yes."

"For how long are we good for one another?"

"That's impossible to tell. I feel very strongly about you." She stopped and turned to him.

"I like you. It's so much harder for a woman if love means anything and it does to all women and I want it to mean something to me."

"I like you too, very much."

"Let's go back to the room."

Gentle tugging of her hand.

They returned through three narrow streets. Feet hesitant on the steps. Lock turning. Into the little room and its new bright light. Chris pulled the curtains closed. Sebastian pouring gin, his back to the fire place. She stood on the green carpet, unbuttoning her jacket. Watching her, the long dark-haired girl. Drinking my gin with a shaking hand. She stood silently in the center of the room, facing him. He sat down. Crossing her narrow wrists upon the hem of her sweater she drew the wool garment over her head and pulled it from her arms. Folding it gently on the bed. Hands reversed behind her back, her hair, her hint. I know how you are underneath. Walking over to his chair, stooped over his head. You've pushed your breast against my face. And the solid tip on my mouth and between my teeth. Up in your eyes you're crying and tears collecting on your chin. She pushes his head back over the chair and touches his eyes with her fingers. Softly telling him.

"I'll light two candles. And they're Italian and scented. I knew this was going to happen. Till tonight I was going to the zoo. Thinking about it all week and you. Can I watch you?"

"Yes."

Warmed in candle light. Her dark eyes big.

"Now turn around. I thought you were thinner. A businessman's paunch. You don't exercise."

90

"My hands refuse to labor."

"Help me put the mattress on the floor. On the papers. You look so funny. Both of us. How strange a man is. I feel absent and naked there."

"Sweet suffering Christ."

"What's happened?"

"I've stubbed my toe. Cut it."

"I'll fix it. We'll bathe it."

Water running in the pan, swilling on the sides and she puts his feet in.

"Better?"

"Much."

"Now we'll dry them and put some talc on. Nice? It's so funny and curious, men and women and everything, it must have something to do with the meaning of positive and negative. Aren't the veins blue. I read somewhere that it's the smoothest part of the body, there's no part of a woman so smooth."

Her fingers rubbing up through the hair of his leg. Dumping the pan. Waiting secret and shy, loosening her skirt.

"My nylons now. I'm embarrassed now. Horrid garter belts."

She held each breast in each hand, squeezing the blood, veins full, and the dark lip flesh a long cylinder and eyes syrup of cool white and warm gray. Moving against him. Telling him it was her expression and tears of soundless happiness and I want to dance for you. She stood and pressed her breasts together and then her hands above her head and swung her chest and flesh. And touch his skin again with her. Slide her body into his and said she was ready and she somehow knew, I'll tell you, that each day she stood waiting for the tram so cold, intolerable, alone, hungry for love for weeks, damp body and Sebastian and tonight all the laundry steam has come out of my heart, I'm ready and juices in my groin. Dear Chris you're full of soft love spilling on your dark lips. Outside and down that road by St. Patrick's Cathedral I hear the Gregorian chant. It's not far away. She furrowed her tongue and blew a warm moist air into his ear. I feel that the warm air you blow into my ear is like the still sultry summer air that was in the afternoon of a Westchester day in America, in Pondfield Road and I lay on my back listening to music coming in the window from a back garden. I was young and lonely. Are you cold Sebastian, I like it slower, we fit so well, keep you from coming out so much like a disappearing sun, so much my female pumping body milking gold. See the olive trees and rivers, a thousand O Sebastian a thousand, I feel and feed and push and heart and pump. Because, dear Chris your neck lies in my arm. Hear the bells of Christ. O Sebastian now, good gracious God, now O now, tighten me taste me O good gracious God I love it. Her head hanging back, words moving her chin in his nook of shoulder, have you come, I can't care but you're so funny, could I have a cigarette. Sweat drying on their skins, and blowing smoke to watch it winding on the ceiling.

"Funny man."

"Me?"

"Yes. And what do you feel now?"

"The good things."

"As?"

"Joy. Relief."

"Some men feel disgusted."

"Pity."

"Yes. And I feel better. I need it. What's she like?"

"Marion?"

"Yes."

"An enigma, not getting what she expects."

"And what does she expect?"

"She wants it both ways. Dignity and me. She's got me. One way, you know. But she's not to blame."

"What's she like when you're—"

"Making love?"

"Yes."

"Likes it. Not as creative as you. She has great latent sexuality."

"And don't you make use of it?"

"It comes out. Worry doesn't help."

"I wonder if there is any such thing as a perfect sex life among married people."

"Waxes and wanes."

"Yes. It's such a complicated thing. Always frightened me. You feel funny there. Does it tickle. Gets me thinking and it's so smooth. Must be an instinct to kiss smooth things. When I was fifteen I thought my nipples were like the skin on lips and I kissed them and when my mother knocked on the bathroom door I was terrified that she would ask me what happened to them. I got a thing about it. Parents' sex is so different. At seventeen I got an awful shock seeing my mother and father making love."

"For God's sake, tell me what happened."

"I had the flu and I was going to the bathroom and I saw them from the stairs. I was just beginning to learn then and I never knew a woman could sit on a man. I told this to my girl friend and she wouldn't speak to me for a month afterwards."

"I tell you Chris, there's no end to it. You are an intelligent girl."

"And you must be intelligent to tell me."

"Exactly. I like it here. Little comforts, little joys."

"You don't want much."

"I don't. And you?"

"Married, I guess. Most women want to."

"Then what?"

"Children. I'm not looking for a picket fence around the house and a loving husband struggling away in the local bank. I want a certain contentment. What are you laughing at?"

"Just thinking of myself."

Turning on her shoulder, facing him.

"Tell me, did you know I was going to sleep with you?"

"Never thought of it."

"Did you want to?"

"Instantly, the first time I saw you."

"I knew we were. How do you feel now that we have?"

"I don't know. I feel I know you."

"Hold my hand."

"You'll be able to breast-feed your children. Let me see under your arm."

"I refuse to shave them for anyone."

"Smell of Russia."

"How dare you."

"Rich. And your navel."

"England?"

"No but interesting. If I have to work for a living I'm going to tell people's fortunes by their navels."

"A woman doesn't want you to see more than her own. Funny that before tonight I was prepared to accept coming back to this dreary room. Turn on the radio and listen to some silly people. Cooking myself dreary meals. It makes all the difference to have someone to cook for. How curious and sudden it all is. One expects it to happen. It happens. Now I know what you look like without clothes. I won't be able to look at you from the laundry. I'll be mentally undressing you. It's ridiculous when you consider a man's genitals and the way he dresses. They ought to wear kilts or cod pieces."

"I'd have mine tailored in Savile Row."

"Priests would have to wear black ones. Let me bite you. I want to bite you. O you've got something in your navel. Fluff."

"Ekke."

"My navel's sexless and flat and doesn't collect. And these are funny little things to kiss. Do you like it?"

"More. I tell you, more's the more."

"And in your navel too."

"For God's sake, yes."

"And there? It's got a funny smell. It's tiny."

It's such a long pleasant night. I hope I can remember this

when I am suffering. Her gentle fingers. Sweet substance of girl, alone and damp and loving me and moving over me, over me and over, covered safe with her heart and each other's thighs, my head gone away, tickling teasing, curling hairs and hood of smells and flesh and salt taste like swimming. I live in such a house of cracked concrete. I ride to town on a crazy trolley to Trinity with the rest of them and now bury my head in the round white pincers of a stranger's thighs. Her hands are going down my legs. Tear the cartilage islands from my knees and I'll wobble forever after in the streets. Her dark head bouncing on the yellow candle air. This threnody in my scarlet skull. The laundry girls are standing on pots of steaming clothes, pounding them with thick Celtic ankles and doing a strip tease. I see them all out there and we laugh, he ho ha, the pulse of it and the country girls, naked for the first time in their lives, falling into the tubs and suds, slipping, flapping, slapping their obese bodies. It's holiday. The bestial bedlam. And he, me, raised his holy hand and told them to shut up for a minute so as to arrange them in ranks and give each a green garter of shamrocks to wear on the left thigh so as not to be criticized by the Bishops for nudity. Out now, the kip of ye. Into the streets, Dublin's fair city where the nude are so pretty. You look like the oblate and your rumps too. Strike up the band. He led them through the streets. At the Butt Bridge they stopped and the nice gentleman led them through the line, "I Left my Heart In An English Garden." The word spread quickly through the city that there was a touch of the nakedness on the roads. Pubs emptied. And the million farmers' sons and others too, on bicycles to see these fine shapes of girls who were of stout build.

Chris's willowy fingers dug into his thighs and hers closed over his ears and he stopped hearing the soup sound of her mouth and felt the brief pain of her teeth nipping the drawn foreskin and the throb of his groin pumping the teeming fluid into her throat, stopping her gentle voice and dripping from

95

her chords that sung the music of her lonely heart. Her hair lay athwart in clean strands on his body and for the next silent minute he was the sanest man on earth, bled of his seed, rid of his mind.

10

With two tomes under the arm walking out the back gate of Trinity College. Bright warm evening to catch the train. These business people are bent for their summer gardens and maybe a swim by Booterstown. On these evenings Dublin is such an empty city. But not around the parks or pubs. It would be a good idea to pop onto the Peace Street and buy a bit of meat. I'm looking forward to a nice dinner and bottle of stout and then I'll go out and walk along the strand and see some fine builds. For such a puritan country as this, there is a great deal to be seen in the way of flesh if one is aware and watching when some of them are changing on the beach.

"Good evening, sir."

"Good evening."

"And how can I help you, sir?"

"To be quite honest with you, I think I would like a nice piece of calf's liver."

"Now, sir, I think I can see you with a lovely bit, fresh and steaming. Now I'll only be a minute."

"Bang on. Wizard."

"Now here we are, sir. It's a fine bit. On a bit of a holiday, sir? Nice to have a bit of fresh meat."

"Yes, a holiday."

"Ah England's a great country, now isn't it sir?"

"Fine little country you have here."

"Ah it's got its points. Good and bad. And hasn't everything now. And here we are, sir, enjoy your holiday. It's a nice evening, now."

"A great evening."

"I see you're a man of learning and good-sized books they are too."

"They're that. Bye bye, now."

"Grand evening. Good luck, sir."

Wow, what conversation. Doctor of Platitudes. Holiday, my painful arse. But a nice bit of liver.

Into the gloom of Westland Row Station. He bought the papers, rolled them and beat his thigh up the stairs. Sitting on the iron bench, could see the people pouring in the gate. Where are the slim ankles on you women. None of you. All drays. Well what's in the paper. Dreariness. The Adventures of Felix the Cat. Put it away. I must to the lavatory. So big in here. Dribbling water. Good God, the train.

Rumbling, pounding, black dirty toy. Whistling by with the whole gang of these evening faces peeking and pouting out the windows. Must find a first class compartment. Jesus jammed, the whole damn train. O me, try the third. Pulling himself up. Pushing his meat onto the rack, squeezing around, sitting down.

Across from him the people who lived in the semi-detached houses of Glenageary and Sandycove, all buried in the paper reading madly. Why don't some of you look out the window at the nice sights. See the canal and gardens and flowers. It's free, you know. No use getting meself upset by the crut. I say there, you, you little pinched bastard, what are you staring at. That little man staring at me. Go away, please.

Chug, chug, chug.
Choo, choo, choo.
Woo, woo, woo.

We're away. Mustn't mind these damn people. Getting me upset. Mustn't get upset. Still staring at me. If he keeps it up I swear by Christ I'll lash his head right through that window. Expect rudeness like this in the third class.

The girl sitting across from him gave a startled gasp. What is this. Must be I've gotten in a train going to Grangegorman. What's the matter with her. That pinched bastard must be up to something, feeling her thigh. Lecher. Perhaps it's my place to take measures against this sneak. O but mind my own business. Things bad enough as they are already. Well look at them all. Whole seat is writhing, wriggling. What

98

are they looking at. This is the end. I look forward to a nice evening of my liver and a walk and what's that girl pressing the book up to her face for. Is she blind. Get a pair of glasses you silly bitch. Maybe that bastard is embarrassing her, she's blushing. The damn sexual privation in this city. That's it. Root of it all. Distraction. I need distraction. Read the In Memoriams.

Donoghue—(Second Anniversary)—In sad and loving memory of our dear father, Alex (Rexy) Donoghue, taken away July 25, 1946, late of Fitzwilliam Square (Butcher's porter in the Dublin abattoir) on whose soul, sweet Jesus, have mercy.
Masses offered. R.I.P.

Gone forever, the smiling face,
The kindly, cheerful heart
Loved so dearly through the years
Whose memory shall never depart.

Coming upon his ears like goblets of hot lead.
"I say, I say there. There are women present."
Absolute silence in the compartment as the little train clicked past the Grand Canal and the slovenly back gardens of Ringsend. Sebastian glued to the print, paper pressed up to his eyes. Again, like an obscenity uttered in church.
"Sir. I say. There are ladies present in the carriage."
Who would be the first to jump on him. Must let someone else make the first move, I'll grab his legs when trouble starts. O this so worries me. I hate this kind of thing. Why in the name of the suffering Jesus did I have to get into this damn car. Will I ever be delivered. No doubt about it, this man was a sexual maniac. Start using obscene language any second. There's just so much I can take. It's like that old woman saying her rosary and after every decade screaming out a mouthful of utter, horrible foulness. And I can't bear foulness. Look at them, all behaving as if nothing had happened. Better keep my eyes up, he may try to level me with a surprise blow. That man in the corner with the red nose.

99

He's laughing, holding his stomach. For hell, deliver me. Never again ride third class.

"I say there. Must I repeat. There are ladies present."

Sebastian levelled his face at him, lips shearing the words from his mouth.

"I beg your pardon."

"Well, I say, haven't you forgotten something?"

"I beg your pardon."

"I repeat, there are ladies present. You ought to inspect yourself."

"Are you addressing me?"

"Yes."

This conversation is too much. Should have ignored the fool. This is most embarrassing. I ought to take a clout at that bastard in the corner who seems to be enjoying it so much. He'll enjoy it if I break his jaw for him. Why don't they lock these people up in Ireland. The whole city full of them. If I'm attacked, by God, I'll sue the corporation for selling this madman a ticket. Those two girls are very upset. This damn train an express all the way to the Rock. My God. Sit and bear it. Control. Absolute and complete control at all costs.

"Sir, this is abdominable hehavior. I must caution you. Frightfully serious matter, this. Shocking on a public convey-ance. Part of you, sir, is showing."

"I beg your pardon, but would you please mind your own business or I'll break your jaw."

"It is my business to discourage this sort of thing when there are ladies present. Shameful. There are other people in the car you know."

No hope. Don't let him suck me into conversation like that. Must employ me brain. We're coming into the Booters-town. Get out in a minute. Showing? Yes. My fingers are out. Holy Catholic Ireland, have to wear gloves. Don't want to be indecent with uncovered fingers. And my face too. This is the last time positively that I appear without wearing

100

a mask. There's a breaking point. But I'll not break not for any of them and certainly not for this insane lout.

Avoiding the red, pinched, insistent, maniacal face. Look out the window. There's the park and where I first saw my dear Chris to speak to me. O deliverance. That laughing monster in the corner, I'll drag him out of the car and belt him from one end of the station to the other. What's he doing. Pointing into his lap. Me? Lap? Good Christ. It's out. Every inch of it.

Leaping for the door. Get out. Fast. Behind him, a voice.

"Haven't you forgotten something else?"

Wheeling, wrenching the blood-stained parcel from the rack.

Behind him.

"You can't remember your meat at all today."

11

Turning the glass around and around, swill, swallow, more. At his elbow the parcel of trusty liver, brown and blood. Over the tops of the houses across the street, the sun going down. It's late and Marion will be fit to be tied. I've tried to reason over this. It's not a matter of courage or grief or what, but I find it impossible to come to grips with that dreadful embarrassing situation. If only I'd buttoned my fly. If only that.

"My very good man, would you fill me up again."

"And certainly, Mr. Dangerfield."

Can I not be spared this misery. I thought I was over things like that. Well thank God I didn't walk through the Rock with it out. I need people to talk to. I have nobody to talk to. Go back is the only thing for it. Buy a head on the way.

He pushed through the broken, green door and wearily flung himself into the tattered chair. Marion in the kitchen, staring dumbly at her. Up on the wall behind her is the gas meter. I would like to point out that the meter is green, the penny slot is made of brass, and this meter measures my gas for me to cook my pitiful grub. I just can't stand any more.

Marion quavered at the door.

"I can't go on, Sebastian."

Sebastian looking up with interest.

"I really mean it. It's too much. You've been drinking."

"My dear Marion. I really mean it. It's too much. You've been drinking"

"I'm going to leave you."

"You're going to leave me."

"I mean that."

"O you mean it."

102

"Yes."

"Marion. I'm upset. Now do you know what upset means? It means that I'm capable of doing anything. I'll kill you here and now unless I'm given some peace. I want peace. Now, Marion, you know what I want. Peace, God damn it."

"Don't shout at me. I'm not afraid of you."

"You're afraid of me, Marion. It's better that way. You'll keep away from my hands."

"You don't frighten me in the least. O you're so wretched."

"My dear Marion, you're upset. O you're really upset. Blinking your eyes. Now you lie down and I'll get you a little prussic acid to soothe your nerves."

"You'll regret every bit of this. How dare you say a thing like that? Staying out all night drinking, guttering. You've come to this house the last time drunk. Just how far can you go? How low? Tell me, how low?"

"There was a man from Calcutta, who lived a life in the gutter."

"My child's name is ruined. How much you care for her. You were studying weren't you? You even had the gall to take the money I had saved behind the clock and you sit there with that horrid grin on your face telling me you're going to kill me. Well, try it. That's all I can say, try it. And there is one more thing I would like you to know. I've written to your father and I've told him everything. Every blessed thing you've done."

In the greasy chair, Sebastian, silent, still, his hands tightening on the arms. Looking at her and looking at her, a face blank with fear.

Sebastian speaking quietly, slowly.

"You've made a big mistake, Marion. A very big mistake."

"Don't."

"A big mistake, Marion. You're forcing decisions."

"Don't for God's sake go on like this. I can't bear it."

"You had absolutely no right. Do you understand me? No right, I say."

"Stop it."

"What did you tell him?"

Marion, hands to face, weeping.

"I repeat, what did you tell him? Answer me."

"You're horrid. Horrid and hideous."

"What did you tell him, God damn it?"

"Everything."

"What?"

"I said everything."

"What, God damn it, did you tell him?"

"The truth. That we've been starving. That the baby has rickets. And because you're drinking every penny we get. And this house too and that you slapped and punched me when I was pregnant, threw me out of bed and pushed me down the stairs. That we're in debt, owe hundreds of pounds, the whole loathsome truth."

"You shouldn't have done that, Marion. Do you hear me?"

Marion, her voice pumping out in pauses.

"How can you say that. What do you want me to do? Go on like this forever? Until there is no hope. Live on your dreams of becoming a great barrister when you never work and cheat on your exams. And you never intend to work. I know you don't, and spend your times in the slums. Out all night. I hate this house. I hate it all, Ireland, everything in it. Leave me to cope with this wretched hole."

"Shut your damn mouth."

"I won't."

"Shut it."

"I won't."

He slowly reached out and took the shade off the lamp. He placed it on his little table.

"Are you going to shut up?"

"No."

He took the lamp by the neck and smashed it to pieces on the wall.

"Now shut up."

Marion quiet, wild eyed and tearful, watching the man in the rickety chair who held the end of the smashed lamp in his loose pink fingers. Sinister man. Staring at her and she couldn't get her feet to bring her out of the room, listening to his voice tearing at her.

"You're rotten. Bloody British blood. Damn stupidity. Hear me? Cry. Cry. You've done the one thing for which I would kill any man. You're a scheming slut. Did you hear what I said? I said you were a scheming slut."

"Don't say that to me, please."

"That letter cost you a great deal of money. Do you hear me? Money. If you ever write to my father again I'll strangle you."

"O for God's sake stop it."

"I'm driven mad. Jesus to come home to this. This on top of every damn thing. I want to tear this house down. Everything in it. I'll smash every God damn thing in it. You won't have a house then. You'll be in the gutter. You belong in the gutter. Your God damn vulgar father and your smutty mother and that sniveling sneak of a titled uncle. Do you hear what they are? Human garbage and rubbish, not fit to be alive."

"Please, I beg of you to stop it."

"Get out."

"Please, Sebastian."

"Get out God damn it. Do as I say. Get out or I'll strangle you here and now."

"What's made you like this?"

"You've made me like this. That's what made me the way I am now. You."

"I haven't. You can't blame me. I'm sorry I wrote your father. I'm sorry for it."

"Get out."

"Can't you see I'm sorry. Can't you see anything?"

"I can't see a goddamn thing. I'm mad and I'm blind. I'm mad."

"Please stop it. I beg of you, Sebastian to stop it."

Marion walked half across the room towards the man wagging his body in the chair, showing his teeth, shaking his fists around his head.

"Stay away. Get away from me. Jesus, what ever made me come to this God damn country? I'm finished. I'm finished. Finished. Not a hope. A God damn snake can't live here. Nothing can live here. Every Christ botched thing on top of me. Every side. Every minute. What are you trying to do to me? Finish me forever? Do I actually have to suffer this now? Do I? Will you shut up about work, study, work. I'm not going to work. Never. That letter cost you thousands. Damn you."

"Can't you see, even for a second, that I'm sorry for it? I didn't mean to do it. Can't you see I've been driven to it?"

"Twenty thousand pounds. Jesus."

"You've left me here day after day in this sordidness. No gas, no hot water and the toilet and the roof's leaking. I'm the one to be angry and get upset. But have I?"

"Mother of Christ, all right. I don't want to hear it. Just stop that right now. I don't want to hear it. You've disinherited me."

"It won't be for years and years."

"Shut up, I know when it will be."

"It will. You'll wait for years."

"So what. You're alive. You're not dead. You're not sick. Can't you wait a year?"

"I'm not well either. We may be dead by then. And Felicity. She's yours too. Think of her."

"I just don't want any more of this. Take it all away. Take it away. I'm so damn fed up that I swear to Christ I'll just demolish this whole house. Poke the windows out. I'll beat it to the ground. Out of my way. Where's my damn head. Where is it?"

"It's on the floor there."

"I want no more. Just nothing. Nothing. O Jesus.

Honestly, I need distraction. I can't do with this any longer. Just forget it and leave me in peace for tonight because if I don't get peace—that's all."

"The pot's under the table."

"Thanks."

"There are two onions and a carrot if you want to put them in."

"Thanks."

"I put five pence in the gas."

"O.K."

"I'll help if you like."

"It's O.K. .... Is there any of my garlic left?"

"I saw a clove in the table drawer."

Marion standing holding her hands. Intense, despaired. She moves around and goes to the chair, puts her hands on the arms and looks out the window with the sky darkening with clouds and rain drops hitting the panes. Sound of him juggling pots in the kitchen. Knife striking the table top and the head drowning in the water. I see so many old vegetables, wrinkled and dry at the bottom of so many drawers. A little peace. Just a little. I would like very much to have a few days in the country, watching the cows sucking up the grass.

"I'm going out a minute, Marion. Anything you want? Don't cry. For heaven's sake, don't cry. What are you crying for? Please. I'll be back in a minute, now don't cry. You don't want anything?"

"No."

God rest ye merry gentlemen. It's just a matter of time. Raining again. And cold now. One more pint. I'd like to have something to soothe my nerves. I ought to be a chemist —nervebalm, new product of Dangerfield, largest dispensing chemists in the world. Big signs all over Ireland. Nervebalm. Undignified. Keep the dignity and to hell with the money.

He moved swiftly down the street. And stands at the bar drinking down a foaming pint of porter. Orders another and goes with it to sit by the fire. Crossing his legs, studying the hole in a heel. Sole of the feet warming deliciously and the brown gargle as they say was putting the mind afloat. Poor Marion. Not such a bad person. But what fantastic notion put that into her head. Was there any love left. I think that the best thing I can do under the circumstances is to just lie low until it blows over. O the weapons by which we the tender hearted, live. The father will be upon me.

But now I'll get back to that sheep's head. Eyes. I love the eyes. I'll give a clear soup to Marion. She ought to darn my socks and clean my shirts. Things could be different. Must control myself hereafter. Might break a blood vessel in my brain and die wiggling. Everybody wants it both ways. Money and love. Get it one way, and I'm just completely screwed. Two ounces of butter. Pushing in the door of a tiny shop.

"Good evening, sir."

"Good evening."

"Fine evening. Looks as if it will hold."

"Yes."

"Blow over. Best you can expect."

"Best you can expect."

"Could you give me two ounces of butter?"

"Two ounces did you say, sir?"

"Yes."

"Well, I don't know. We sell butter usually by the weight —half pound or a pound."

"Do you sell quarter pounds?"

"Well, I think so."

"Could you give me half a quarter pound?"

"Yes."

"Half a quarter pound then."

Sebastian watching him. O you sly gombeen man. The backs of these stores, most sordid places in the world. In there with his big-busted wife, two barrels banging. You stupid, intolerable oaf.

Man handing him the little package, carefully tied, with a loop for his finger.

Out into the air. A contrast. Bit of turf smell. Things not so bad. Wait and see what happens. Have to take what comes. Good with the bad. Lot in these old sayings. How one can tell lies in times of stress. My God, it's absolutely awful. Be made for the world. But the world was made for me. Here long before I arrived and they spent years getting it ready. Something got mixed up about my assets.

He shoved the green door in with his toe and kicked it closed with his heel. Marion sitting in the chair. I won't ask her to get out of it this evening. Suffer a little discomfort for the sake of peace. Have her terrified and keep her that way. Makes her very quiet. O I smell it. O me. Am I a cook. Wee. Make O'Keefe swoon with envy. Must write him. Have a flair for cooking. I have, I have. Now a nice bowl of clear for Marion. Put a little of the butter to be floating majestically around in it, bit of richness. Be calm, use Nervebalm.

"Marion."

She looks up, hesitant. Reaches out her two hands and clasps the white bowl. The glass has been cleaned up, pieces of my anger.

"Thank you."

"Here's bread and a bit of butter."

"Thanks."

"Taste it."

"Good. Thanks."

"Enough salt? Don't cry anymore now. It's all right. It's just that this evening I came home on the train with my penis out."

"What do you mean?"

"Forgot to button my fly."

"And did people see you?"

"Yes."

"O no."

"O yes. Most exasperating thing that ever happened in my life. It was out from Dublin to the Rock."

"You poor darling. I'm sorry for everything."

Life's much better that way. Patch things up. Renewed sense of security. If we could get out of this house. Skully has us by the balls. The lease is a noose. O'Keefe was right, never pay rent. Cramped between these damp walls. The child gets me right in the ear. Must find a bigger house. Just get the hell out of here. Explain to the father. But it's impossible to undo the damage with a new set of lies.

Filling the bowl. Spooning out the eyes, sliding them into the mouth. Wag them around. Sit down and rest. This is very nice.

"Where are you going, Sebastian?"

"Just thought of something. Need a little fire for cheer."

Out in the hall a second. Back and has it in the center of the floor a raised foot goes crash, splintered and cracked. One genuine antique, Louis the cat torts.

"O Sebastian, you mustn't."

"O I think so, for the fire that's in it. My Dear Egbert, you see, we were at the cinema, having left our dear child with an aunt and a rogue or rogues. Front door's broken. His responsibility. A little matter of theft in this great Catholic country."

"He won't believe it."

"He has no alternative. If he accuses me of anything, I'll have him know I'm being slandered. Student of the law you know. Must have him understand that I know the law."

Sebastian stood on the couch, lifts his foot again over the chair, crashing through the center.

"Now that's a case of engineering. Puts a general weakness in the structure."

He turned the chair upside down and broke the legs off one by one.

"A little paper in the grate, Marion. I'll be back in a second."

He walked out of the house, a small bag with him. Marion put the pieces of chair on the fire. Sebastian back, opening his little bag proudly, bearing forth seven lumps of coal.

"Sebastian, what in the name of God have you done? Where did you get that coal?"

"Now, now, never question these good things."

"But it's really stealing."

"Theft is only in the heart."

"O dear."

"Marion, Land of hope and glory, mother of the free."

"You're nice like this."

Sitting in the little room, doors shut and window too. Glow, coal and merits of marriage. Full of sheep's eyes. Juice of the skull. I take up my pen.

My dear Kenneth,

There is a word for it all; funt. Now if you say this word upon rising in the morning and before each meal, you will see things change. To get the best out of it one must place one's incisors on the lips and exhale till there is a hissing noise and then the word. It is also good for fertility. And I may add that I am a great believer in fertility. Things here are a little desperate. There are items like rent. You see, a man gives you a key and you go into this house and start to carry on your life and at the end of the week you give this man three slips of paper with redeemable in London written on them and the man lets you stay where you are. If you don't give this man these little pieces of paper you find that he is outside the window watching you scratch your balls and as you may well realize, to have impersonal eyes upon you while dealing with testicular itch is a most awkward state of affairs. So I look to you, Holy Duke, to allow me to stay on payment of ten desperate papers redeemable in London. By the way, London is a very fine city, largest in the world. There is something in the back of my head which makes me think I will be there one of these days.

About this boy. A most shocking state of affairs. It is not, my dear Kenneth, that I am prude. Far from it. But really, do you think it wise to give up the joys of the heterosexual world without first considering all its possibilities. Grant you, there is no question but that it can be trying and even devastating to endure the celibacy but once you have achieved success, presto, little O'Keefes, just like you. But if you have despaired, if you have the heteroghost, then there is nothing for it but to give yourself with abandon. But with this boy. Let him get to know you better. Show your interest in others. Unfortunately, it is difficult for me to advise you in these matters and I can only depend upon knowledge, which at best, is merely general. But it will take time, Kenneth, time, for all these things we want so much. We must be prepared to wait for them. But they will come, on one bright and sunny morning. About ejaculatio præcox; this will right itself in time with practice. I assume that your present method of fulfillment is by hand. I therefore suggest to you that you take things easier. It is a matter of degrees, degrees of misery, perhaps, but do you know that I find the tougher things get, I become more immune, must be the development of a natural defense, you know the sort of business, to every action an equal and opposite reaction. I should suppose that these things are so.

I haven't seen anyone since you left, indeed for several months, because I must keep off the main streets but my courage is developing and I feel that I may see a day or two of the good life with some of these people I have not seen for some time. Dublin is a curious city. It is a city which is full of the good things but somehow one is too busy thinking about things like bread and tea, peace and a place to sleep where the rain dripping in does not give one the dream of the Titanic. I spend a lot of my time walking along the canal and having coffee, when I can afford, in Jury's. When you come back to the ould sod I will be very happy to take you there. One sits under palm trees, with legs crossed and one talks and comes to all sorts of conclusions some of which are valuable, others merely interesting. But we expect all these things. They are still taking them out to the Grange every morning. I find it most stimulating but much more so since I have bought myself a second hand bicycle and have painted it black and put a little black flag on the handle bars and I take up the rear of all funerals going to the Grange. I have found that some people laugh at me for doing this and think that perhaps this man is a little mad but I say o aye and go on about my little tortured business. I have discovered one of the great ailments of Ireland, 67% of the population have never been completely naked in their lives. Now don't you, as a man of broad classical experience, find this a little strange and perhaps even a bit unhygienic. I think it is certainly both of these things. I am bound to say that this must cause a great deal of the passive agony one sees in the streets. There are other things wrong with this country but I must leave them wait for they are just developing in my mind. But you must try not to take your problem too seriously. You see, sex is something that we have to make new and better babas. If you can make a baba then you are all right. I feel that it is a selfish world that wants this cheap thrill that one comes by in making a baba. Forget it.

Tonight I am nestled up in my little drawing room. I have had a hard day of it. Some say that it will always be this hard for me but they are mostly bastards. I committed an act of indecency on the train out to the Rock, about which I will tell you when you are back in the ould sod. There are some other things too, also left to tell you when you come. I take it you are a little desperate and would like to get back to the ould country. Why not come back? You should be able to find something to do here without much trouble, especially speaking French. I'll be very happy to put you up here and feed you with what we have and in closing my dear Kenneth I hope you will find use for this, below, in one of your operas. Perhaps a little chorus after each act.

> Down in Dingle
> Where the men are single
> Pigwidgeon in the closet
> Banshee in the bed
> An antichrist is suffering
> While the Gombeen man's dead.
> Down in Dingle.

Your friend,
S. D.

12

Raining outside. Cold morning. Felicity in her pram in the kitchen, wiggling a toothbrush in a jam jar. Marion standing against the mantelpiece in front of the black empty grate. Wearing slippers, wrapped in a blanket, her shanks showing. Just finished reading the letter, folding it carefully and slipping it back into its envelope.

I could tell there was trouble. I came down the stairs with my usual innocence and pain right smack into her silence which is the sign that she has a weapon. She stood there as if she were watching the groom saddle her horse. There was a smear of lipstick at the corner of her mouth, gave her a twisted smile. I thought for a second she was an Inca. She was quite polite when I asked her who the letter was from. She said simply, from your father.

"I'll get my glasses."

"I'm afraid the letter is addressed to me."

"What do you mean, you're afraid?"

"Just that. You're not going to read it."

"Now just a minute, that letter is from my father and I intend to know what's in it."

"And I intend you shan't."

"Don't get snotty."

"I'll be as snotty as I want. I no longer have to tolerate your nastiness."

"What's this mumbo jumbo. Don't act as if you have a secret file on me."

"I assure you it's not mumbo jumbo. I'm leaving this house."

"Now look, Marion, I don't feel well. I'm not up to farting about at this godforsaken hour of the morning. Now just what the hell do you mean you're leaving this house?"

"Leaving this house."

"There's a lease."

"I know there's a lease."

"For three years."

"I know it's for three years."

Marion's eyebrows raised. She kept reaching over her shoulder, pulling the blanket up. Sebastian stood in the doorway wearing a pair of purple pajamas, bright red slippers and a gray turtle necked sweater, its yarn unravelling, the string suspended behind him and disappearing up the stairs.

"Ah for Jesus sake, now let's not get started. I only want to know what you're talking about. You know, just for the sake of making things clear, I'll never get this damned exam if I have to face more misunderstanding. Now what is it? Has my father made you an offer of money or something?"

"You're not reading the letter."

"All right. I'm not reading the letter. Now tell me, what the hell is this all about?"

"Your father is on my side."

"Look Marion, all right. Now we know that you have everything your way. I know the drivel in that letter. Probably sent you a check."

"As a matter of fact, he did."

"Told you that I've always been a bastard."

"Quite."

"Expelled from schools."

"Yes."

"All right. What are you going to do?"

"Move from here, instantly."

"Where?"

"I'm going to see an agent this morning."

"What about the lease?"

"That's your doing."

"You stupid bitch."

"Go right ahead. Say anything you want. It matters nothing to me. By the way, you've left half my sweater on the stairs."

"Now, Marion, let's understand each other. I don't feel that this fighting is going to get us anywhere."

"It's certainly not going to get you anywhere."

"Now look, how much is the check."

"That's my business."

"I've got to get my typewriter out of the pawn. I must have it for my notes."

"Ha. Ha. Ha."

Marion's mocking head back, disdainfully shutting eyes. The blue vein, handsome and large on the blonde throat. Pink slip and her shanks shifting the slippers, grinding the coal dust on the floor.

"Supposing I admit to a few indiscretions."

"Indiscretions? That really is amusing you know."

"Now that we have a chance to start over again."

"We do, do we? O we. It's we now."

"I'm thinking about the lease."

"You signed it."

Sebastian turned and went quietly up the stairs. Tip toe, tip toe. Dragging the wool string behind. Into the bedroom. Dropping the purples, pulling on the trousers. Tied a knot in the sweater. Put his sockless feet into shoes. A jacket for the respect that was in it. And my dear pair of golfing shoes. Pity, but must to the pawn. Ten and six for sure. Now my dear Marion, I'll give you a little something to think about.

In the toilet, Sebastian forced a board up from the floor. He hammered a nail through the lead pipe with the heel of his golfing shoe. He went quietly down the stairs. Marion saw him pass out the hall. The door squeaked shut.

I'll say one thing. She's not going to pull this stuff much longer. This is final. If she wants it this way, this way it shall be.

In this bitterness and hazy hatred. No cozy road to the swelled udders. This is at the midnight of everything. Because when I was living in America I had a lot of good things. I never had to think about hot water. I went to my club where it was running rampant. Stand under a shower and let it beat the head. Soothed me. Ease and comfort and quiet is all I want. And on this damn tram I'm riding into the face of debt and other things as well. I'm a college student standing on the chapel steps with the white paper which says I know the law of Contract and can be paid starvation wages for a year. My certificate that I won't steal from the open till but I'm a gentleman and I'll close the till after rifling it.

Four o'clock on this oblong Tuesday. Sebastian pushing through the door of a secret public house, moved cautiously to an empty space at the bar. Bartender suspiciously approaching him.

"I want a triple Irish, Gold Label. Quickly please."

"Sir, I'm afraid I can't serve you."

"You what?"

"Can't serve you, sir, rules of the house, you've had enough to drink."

"I've had enough to drink? What on earth do you mean?"

"I think, sir, you've had sufficient unto your needs now. I think you've had enough now."

"This is contemptible."

"Peacefully sir, now. Keep the peace. When you're sober sir, now, be very glad to serve you. Little sleep. You'll be fine."

"Frightful outrage. Are you sure you're not drunk yourself?"

"Now sir, a place and time for everything."

"Well for Jesus sake."

Sebastian turned from the bar pushed out through the door and along the street. In dazed condition. Along the pavement by shop windows with pens and pencils and stone steps to Georgian doors and black spokes of fences and by a tea shop with gray women clustered at the tables. So I'm drunk. Strangled Christ. Drunk. Nothing to do but suffer this insult as I have suffered so many others. It will die away in a few years, no worry about that. I'm going on a tram ride. Dalkey. That nice little town out there on the rocks

118

with pretty castles and everything. A place where I will move when the quids are upon me. I hate this country. I think I hate this country more than anything else I know. Drunk. That son of a bitch, take him up by the ears from behind that bar and beat him against the ceiling. But must forget the whole thing. I'm at the bottom of the pile. Admit that I'm in such a state that I can barely think. But I won't be insulted. Incredible outrage.

He passed in front of the Kildare Street Club, crossed over the street and waited for the tram, leaning against the railings of Trinity College.

Isn't that a beautiful place. In spite of all rejections and refusals. But I remember a pitiful time in there, too. During the first week in the dining hall. Autumn's October and I was so very chilly that year because the weather was bad. But it was nice to get in there because there is a thick pipe that goes all around the walls and it is filled with hot water. And it's such a big room, with enormous portraits high up on the wall which kept me well in the center in case one fell on my head. But it is such a very pleasant experience to go into this dining hall on a Dublin cold day and say, how do, to the lovely woman at the door taking gowns and move along in the academic line with a tin tray. On magic days with half crown, it is so delicious to take a Chelsea bun and a little white dish. Further along the line on the top tables there are nice little balls of butter. All balls are bells. Then there is the woman with the white hair who serves out the potatoes. How are you now? And on these days with that ever ready half crown I'd get a rabbit pie from the delightful lady with the red hair who got younger every day and then say, ever so quietly, because these were magic words—and some sprouts too, please. Not the last. No. Further along the line. Trays covered with trifle. Had to get there early to get the trifle because it was so good that it was gone fast. Next table, a jug of sugar because I was going to get some cream to put on a banana, all slices and mixed in the cup and then at last to the cash desk. My tragic two and six. And this day I was so very hungry. I went through the line gathering all the food, arranging it with care. And my head was hard and thick from thinking and tired eyes. My tray skidded from my fingers and fell on the floor. My orange jelly mixed with broken glass on this day when I bought a glass of milk to have with my Chelsea bun. They told me I was clumsy and asked why did I do it. And at times in my heart there is a music that plays for me. Tuneless threnody. They called me names. I was so afraid of them. And they could never look inside me and see a whole world of tenderness or leave me alone because I was so sad and suffering. Why did you do it. And hearts. And why was love so round.

Tram swaying down the flat street. Squealing and stopping. Sitting all the way and dreaming. Even passing 1 Mohammed. Perhaps I was a bastard to lay foul the pipes again. Make her know she needs me. And I need that money. Out in Dalkey I'll be all alone. No fear of meeting anyone.

He arrived in the main street. Twisted with people. Into a public house. Two lovely, laughing girls behind the bar.

"Good day, sir."

"Double Gold Label, please."

She reached under the bar. Always hiding the stuff. Damn girl with her gold, cheap bracelets, earrings, damn pair of gold tits, squirting out money.

"And twenty Woodbines."

Under the bar again. Out with them smiling and wagging her eyes. Rows of bottles of wine and minerals and port and sherry there for years. As decorations for drinking stout. A lot of rich people live out here in Dalkey. Big houses on the sea. I like it. And take a walk along the Vico Road and see across Killiney Bay to Bray. A change of scene is good for a change of mind. And the mortification of being treated like a drunkard is dreadful for me as stark and stone sober as I am.

"I wonder could I have a pint of porter, please."

"Certainly, sir."

Lot of work pumping that out. I like this pretty girl. I have a passion for her. I know I have passion. Through that window the yellow sun is coming in. Those men down there are talking about me. I don't get along with men.

"And another small one."

"Gold Label?"

"Please."

I was a curious little boy. Sent to the proper places. And went to most improper ones. Secret and sinful and I even worked once. I think it is quite a common thing, start at the bottom. He, ha, haw, eke. But when you have so many problems it's not easy to be distracted into the past. I was a spoiled child I should suppose. Quickly given to lies. And gross falsehoods to teachers, mostly out of fear I guess. But what would I have done without the odd lie these days. I remember a teacher telling me I pouted and was ugly. Which wasn't true. I was an extremely handsome, curious child. Teachers are insensitive to true beauty.

"What's your name?"

"Gertrude."

"May I call you Gertrude?"

"Yes."

"Gertrude, will you give me another Gold Label and a pint of porter?"

"Yes."

I went to a proper preparatory school, preparing for college. I never felt that these schools were good enough for me. I was aloof. Never seeking friends. But my silence was noticed by the teachers and they thought that I was a shifty article and once I heard them telling very rich boys to stay away from me because I wasn't a good influence. Then I got older and bolder. A wanton girl who had pock marks on her face and stubs of hair all up her legs when I thought girls' legs were always nice and smooth, took me into the city from the suburbs where I lived and we drank in bars. When she felt all pally and possessive and sensing my reserve and fright she said that I ought not to wear a striped tie with a striped shirt and I kept saying to myself, hiding the hurt, that I just

121

put on the shirt quickly and the tie in a rush. And when we went home together on the subway train she slept with her head on my shoulder. I felt embarrassed because she looked old and tough. A girl who ran away, was expelled from schools and smoked when she was twelve. And me, I was always somehow getting to know these girls, not out of sex or sin, but because their souls were fetched up out of them by dismal sodas and dances and they would see me with my big, shrewdless eyes and come and invite me to sneak a cigarette or drink.

"Gertrude, you're very good behind the bar. I want a really big lash of Gold Label."

Gertrude smiled at Kathleen.

I was nineteen and older and in a sailor suit and back in Virginia and Norfolk. On leave I would go to the libraries because in behind the stacks I could escape. Sunny days meant nothing to me. And I made a trip to Baltimore. Into a strange boarding house on a dry cold New Year's Eve. The wind blowing. My room had no windows. Just an open transom. All the time I was in that part of America I felt the closeness of the Great Dismal Swamp and broken boards and peeling signs and road houses isolated with greed and silence, drink and snakes. I walked about the city, lost and trying to get it. Put it in one spot and look at it and stand there with all Baltimore around me where I could pick it up in my hand and take it away. But move on and up and down and around each street and find it blank and unimportant without the rest. I went into a bar, crowded and dark, tripping over people's legs. Voices, sighs and laughs and lies and lips and teeth and whites of eyes. Secrets of shaved armpits and the thin, small hair on women's upper lips showing through tan powders. All these breasts slung in rayon cradles. I pushed through elbows to the bar and sat on a red and chromium stool. Sitting beside me, a girl in a black, ungainly dress. Down on her leg I saw net stockings. Curious girl with large brown eyes in her round face of rough skin and thin lips. Here in Baltimore. Sitting, searching at a bar. There was a dreadful fight. And the abuse. Cheapskate, tough and wise. And bastard. There are babes present, buddy. I'd like to see you do it, who's pushing who, come outside, say, watch your language, no cheap son of a bitch, hit him for Christ's sake, hit him. In the middle of all this tiresome behavior she turned to me and said hello, smiled slightly, weakly and said you look so much more peaceful. I asked her to have a drink and she said yes, but she didn't need a dozen drinks to have a good time, or drink all evening because I'm here because I wanted to do something different, and really, you don't mind me picking you up. Her black hair combed straight down around her head and I listened to her talking in her rich, pleasant and kindly voice. I just walked in here alone and now I'm talking to a sailor—yes, I'd like to share a bottle of champagne with you, I would like it—I've never had it before—is it nice? And why did you come in here? I hope you'll forgive my conduct, but I'm just curious. She was a girl who was soft and clean. And she said am I being presumptuous and forward. I don't intend to be—I'm just a little groggy, I bought myself three whiskies. I've been promising myself to just someday walk into a bar by myself and sit up and drink with other people, but it took New Year's Eve to make me do it—no one is being themselves on New Year's are they? Or don't you care? I told her she was very likeable. And saw her eyes light. Is that why you're buying a bottle of champagne, because I'm likeable? I hope you are. I feel rather good—giggly and silly and you're quiet and reserved, aren't you? And I'm just sitting here talking to you, an utter stranger and just going on and on—well I'll tell you about me. I'm at college and I don't really like it because I don't have any time to enjoy it because I have to work and I don't get dated, never been to a nightclub—I'm curious, naturally, but it's contrary to everything I believe, I mean the frivolous, sophisticated life of society people. I don't hold that sort of thing important—and I'll tell you the truth—that really I came in here because I didn't have a date on this night of nights and I told myself that anyway I would buy myself a drink and if anyone talked to me I would talk to them but I talked to you first because you looked as if I could talk to you and you would be nice and you're alone too, aren't you? And I'm not a brave girl so much as a frustrated one. I've just walked into a bar, and I was frightened to death that the barman would tell me that women without escorts couldn't come in. Now that I'm here it all seemed so very simple and easy and I'm glad I did. And I'm beginning to see that that is the way to do a lot of things in life—just to go ahead and do them. I saw you coming in and I just thought to myself that you looked rather nice and then you were next to me and I just felt like talking to you—so I did—and now where are we? She told me she had only one request to make—that she didn't want me to know her name because she might regret everything, and not to spend so much money on her, a stranger, that they would probably never see each other again, anyway. She was warm. I pressed my nose through her straight black hair and my lips behind her ear, whispering I liked her and please stay with me. She put her face in front of mine and said distinctly, if that means you want to go to bed with me or if you want me to come to bed with you, I'll be blunt, I will. Whole hearted. Blunt. And I'm not trying to be whorish. But I suppose I am. Am I? Or what. What do you expect of a girl like me? And I don't suppose after that remark you would believe I don't have any idea of how to go to bed with a man. But where and how and when? There's a whole lot to it, isn't there?

Sebastian stood up, taking his glass to this bar in Dalkey, waiting behind the figures.

"A double Gold Label."

Returning to his seat. Sitting slowly and putting out his legs, crossing his knees, shaking his foot and placing his glass within the circle movement of his arm. The public house was filling with the seven o'clock after work after dinner faces.

I brought her to a room in a large, prominent hotel in

124

Baltimore and we passed by the mobbed streets and a girl dancing on top of a taxi, sailors and soldiers clutching at her ankles. Pulling at her clothes until they were ripping them from her body. Hands taking her apart. In the room she said she was a little frightened. We had more champagne. On one twin bed I sat down, excited. I talked to her. Twister that I was. Heart of hoax. Bluffing my way into her hands. Carrying her down beside me. Heard her in my ear. I'm frightened. I'm scared. Don't force me to do anything, will you? But I think you're kind. And I'm just a little blasé and not caring, but I worry very much what's going to happen to me, really. But after a while you get to hate everyone and everybody and you get very bitter inside because you haven't money and clothes and wealthy boyfriends asking you out to smart places and even though you know that really all of it is false, it somehow manages to seep in and you find yourself resenting the fact that all you have is a good brain and you're smarter than they are but would like to wear false breasts because your own are flat but you feel it's such a horrid lie and yet they do it and get away with it and then in the end you're faced with the blunt truth that they will get married and you won't and that they are going to hate their marriages but then they will have tea parties and cocktails and bridge while their husbands are sleeping with other men. She was a girl gone away. And I put my finger in her sad, tight, little hole, feeling lost and crying and wandering in rain and trees, a world too big, and lost and her dark head was so dark and her eyes shut.

He brought his glass back to the bar, and walked out. Get on the tram. On to the tram because we are all going to East Geenga. I'm a man for getting off at the end of the line. I've had more than I can bear. Take me on the ship, away. To Florida. I drove my big car right through The Everglades. A little wet and soggy. I used to walk around Fort Lauderdale drunk and diving in the canals at night killing alligators. And drive along Miami Beach steering with my toes. What do you want me to do. Stay on this dreary stage of church-bound hopelessness? This country is foreign to me. I want to go back to Baltimore. I've never had a chance to see everything, or ride the trains, or see all the little towns. Pick up girls in amusement parks. Or smell them with the peanuts in Suffolk, Virginia. I want to go back.

Quick feet up the street. Seeing nothing on either side. No houses or stairs or iron spokes of fences. Half running, tripping, pounding, pulling the air aside.

Slow down. Nonchalant, and careful too, while going in, possessed with reserve and other things as well and we will see about this.

The bar was filled with old men. Spitting secrets in each other's ears. Smoke coming over the top of all the snugs. Faces turning as Dangerfield comes in. The sound of corks ripped pop. Ends of bottles bang on the bar. Seaweedy foam rising in the wet glasses. Rudeness must be dealt with. Swiftly. Put them down, I say, not up, down and don't spare the clubs.

Sebastian stepped to the bar, stood dignified and quiet. Bartender removing bottles. Comes along up to him. His eyes meeting the red ones and he nods his head to this tall customer.

"Yes?"

"A double Gold Label."

Bartender turns a few steps and back with the bottle, tense and pouring.

"Water?"

"Soda."

Bartender goes, gets the soda bottle. Squirt, squirt. A blast coming out of it. Whoops. The whiskey shot up the sides of the glass, splashing on the bar.

"Sorry, sir."

"Yes."

"It's a new bottle."

"Quite."

Bartender puts away the bottle and comes back for the money. Stands embarrassed in front of Dangerfield. Licking

126

his lips, ready to speak, but waits, says nothing. Dangerfield looking at him. The old men sensing disaster, turning on their stools to watch.

"Two shillings."

"I was in this public house this afternoon about four o'clock. Do you remember?"

"I do."

"And you refused to serve me."

"Yes."

"On the grounds that I was drunk. Is that correct?"

"That's correct."

"Do you think I am drunk now?"

"That's not for me to decide."

"You decided that this afternoon. I repeat. Do you think I am drunk now?"

"I want no trouble."

"Half my whiskey is on the bar."

"No trouble now."

"Would you mind bringing me the bottle to replace the amount splashed in my face."

Bartender in his white shirt and sleeves rolled up brings back the bottle. Sebastian taking out the cork and filling his glass to the brim.

"You can't do that. We don't have much of that."

"I repeat. Do you think I'm drunk now."

"Now peacefully, no trouble, no trouble, we don't want any trouble here. No, I don't think you're drunk. Not drunk. Little excited. No."

"I'm a sensitive person. I hate abuse. Let them all hear."

"Quietly now, peace."

"Shut up while I'm talking."

All the figures spinning about on their stools and flat feet.

"No trouble now, no trouble."

"Shut up. Am I drunk? Am I drunk?"

"No."

"Why you Celtic lout. I am. I'm drunk. Hear me, I'm

127

drunk and I'm going to level this kip, level it to the ground, and anyone who doesn't want his neck broken get out."

The whiskey bottle whistled past the bartender's head, splattering in a mass of glass and gin. Dangerfield drank off the whiskey in a gulp and a man up behind him with a stout bottle which he broke on Dangerfield's head, stout dripping over his ears and down his face, reflectively licking it from around his mouth. The man in horror ran from the building. The bartender went down the trap door in the floor. Sebastian over the bar standing on it. Selecting a bottle of brandy for further reference. Three brave figures at the door peering in upon the chaos and saying stop him, as this Danger made for the door and one man's hand reached out to grab him and it was quickly twisted till the fingers broke with his squeal of agony and the other two lay back to attack from behind and he jumped phoof on Dangerfield's shoulders and was flipped neatly on his arse five paces down the street. The rest had gone to doorways or posing that they were just out walking their dogs.

Dangerfield was running like a madman down the middle of the road with the cry get the guards pushing him faster. Into a laneway, bottle stuffed under his arm. More yells as they caught sight as he went round and down another street. Must for the love of God get hidden. Up these steps and got to get through this door somehow and out of sight quick.

Heart pounding, leaning on the wall for breath. A bicycle against the wall. Dark and racy for sure. Hope. Wait till they are by the house. Feet. I hear the heavy heels of a peeler. Pray for me. If they get me I'll be disgraced. Must avoid capture for the sake of the undesirable publicity it will produce. Or they may take clubs to me. Suffering shit.

The door opens slowly. Light shining in through the dark. Dangerfield moves cautiously behind the door as it widens against him. A small head peers in, hesitates. I must be upon him for the sake of safety. Sebastian drove his shoulder against the door pulling the figure in by the neck.

"If you so much as breathe I'll belt you to death."

"No. Jesus, Mary and Joseph I won't make a peep."

"Shut up. Give me that hat. And the coat."

"O none of that, I'm a man of God. You don't know where to stop."

"I'll stop you living if you don't shut up and give me that coat."

"Yes sir. Anything you want sir, anything, but don't harm an old man, sir. I'm a cripple from birth, sir and I'll help ye get away. All I can."

"Get up the stairs."

"What are ye going to do with me at all. I've got a Friday to go out of the nine first Fridays."

"You won't have a minute to go if you don't get up the stairs. Up to the top and stay there. If you utter a sound I'll come back and disembowel you."

The little blue-eyed man stepped backwards up the stairs, stopping at the first landing and ran tripping up the rest. Sebastian getting into the coat. Shoulders get in, sleeves at the elbows. He bends over to pick up the brandy. The coat parts down the back. Peers out the door. No one in sight. Take all care, proceed with caution. How did I ever get into this frightful mess. How fantastically undesirable.

Down the three granite steps. Which way? From around the corner, a blue uniform and helmet. God's unmerciful teeth. The Guard stops, looks, starts forward up the street. Dangerfield setting his vehicle firmly in the gutter, straddling it, pushes off pumping fearfully followed by the voice of the little man out the top window of the building.

"That's him all right. He's got me coat and hat. That's him."

The bike moves off speedily up the narrow road and around the corner into a screaming of horns and the bottle slides, bangs his knee and breaks with a wet pop on the street. Policeman in the middle of the road directing traffic. Putting his hand up to stop. Couldn't know it was me. Can't take the chance, onward you crazy christian soldier, peddling off to doom.

"Hey you, stop there. Stop there you. You hear me, stop. Hey."

Helter skelter for St. Stephen's Green. Bike wiggling on the cobbles, skidding on the tram tracks. Dangerfield bent double over the handlebars. Licking his lips. Eyes wet with the wind, blinking and blind. They'll have the patrol car, if they have one, after me or maybe motor bikes or the whole force on roller skates. Traffic lights ahead. Whoa. Red for stop.

The bike making a wide arc in front of the oncoming traffic. More horns and screech of brakes. And on down the street aswarm with children until one small boy dodging right and left in front of the wiggling machine found himself beneath the panting Dangerfield.

"Are you hurt?"

"No I'm not."

"Are you sure?"

"No I'm not hurt."

"I'm very sorry, little boy. Must rush. Here, you can have this damn bike as a present, before I get killed on it."

The child left standing in the middle of the street, staring after the man who took off his hat and flung it behind the railings and bundled up his coat which followed it, opening, fluttering down.

Through this Cuffe Street. Up Aungier. Flat out. I'll keep up the pace. Get down this alley here and get through all these backyards. Walking between the white walls and piss smells. Don't want to be trapped either.

Dangerfield walked swiftly through the labyrinth of lanes into a little square with a lamp standard and more children. Stepped into a doorway and waited. No one behind. A little girl dragging a boy by the hair in the gutter. Kid screaming and kicking his legs. Bare feet swollen and cut. Another boy comes out of the house with a bundle of newspapers yelling for her to leave him alone and he gives her a punch on the arm and she kicks him in the knee and he grabs her and throws her down. She claws and scratches at his eyes and he bends her arms back and she spits in his face.

Sebastian leaves his doorway and walks slowly out the lane. Navigating widely and back and around and coming out along these terraced, red brick houses each with a polished knocker and curtains and little precious things at the first floor windows. Straight out this road I can see the Dublin Mountains with evening sun on them and I wish I were away out there with a massive wall built all round me. Into the tree lined street. Crossing over smartly. Slamming the little gate. Down the steps. Rap, rap. Wait. Silence, rap, rap. My God, my dear Chris, don't leave me out here for them to get me.

"Hello."

Voice behind him.

"Jesus."

"What's happened to you?"

Chris carrying packages, her face wreathed with concern as she came down the steps behind him.

"Let me in."

"Hold these. There's blood all down the back of your neck."

"A little misunderstanding."

"O dear. Have you been in a fight?"

"Little upset."

"Now tell me. Just what did happen?"

"All right. I'll go."

"Now don't be such a fool. Come in, sit down. Of course, you won't go: But you can't expect me to be all complacent when you just suddenly appear all covered in blood. How did this happen?"

"It happened."

"Don't talk nonsense. Hold still. I'll have to boil a kettle and wash it. You've had too much to drink. Does it hurt?"

"No."

Chris in her drawer. Picking out the bottles. Iodine. Water in the kettle.

131

"Chris, I want you to tell me how I can get away from evil in this world. How to put down the sinners and raise the doers of good. I've been through a frightful evening. Indeed, my suffering has been acute and more. More than sin or evil or anything. I have arrived at the conclusion that these people on this island are bogus."

"You had a fight, didn't you?"

"Most ungentlemanly incident I think I've ever experienced."

"In a bar?"

"In a bar. The rudeness on this island is overwhelming."

"Well? How? Why?"

"I went into this public house for a quiet drink. Stone cold sober. Man seizes me by the arm and twists it—says get out —you're drunk. I said, I beg your pardon but I'm stone. Naturally I left under the maltreatment that was in it. Now I'm not an evil person, nor do I ever encourage any type of trouble. However I returned to this bar later, ordered another drink and they attacked me brutally. Disgraceful behavior. All on me like a pack of wolves. Trying to put me down and jump on me. It was only by employing the most elusive tactics that I succeeded in escaping with my very life. I have no doubts but that they are searching the city to visit me with more abuse."

"Now really."

"Come sit by me, Chris."

"No."

"Sit by me. I'm most upset."

"I'll do your head."

"Can I stay here tonight."

"Yes. I think you ought to have a bath."

"I've got to get out of this damn country. Honest to Christ."

"Any pennies?"

"None."

"You'll have to have a threepenny bath."

Helping him to take off his clothes. Out into this damp

132

bathroom with the bathtub up on lion's paws and the cold sticky floor. In blub, gurgle slub dub glub. Foamy white face, no one to recognize me. Forever to walk backwards in the streets. The yellow light and green cracked ceiling. All last year you were in here in the tub while I was haunted and sad on Howth.

"Come away with me, Chris."

"You've had too much to drink. Say that when you're less confused."

"What? I say, confused."

"Turn around and let me dry your back."

"I want you to."

"I just can't suddenly decide something like that."

"You want to?"

"Where? And your wife and child?"

"We'll all manage."

"And your degree?"

"Have to wait till I can regain my senses. I am in an awkward position."

"You are."

"You're giving me the evil treatment. Now I don't deserve that."

"Pull the light. I'll make you some chocolate."

No way out except the big way. I have put myself into a most unfortunate position. I hope to God that they don't catch me and put me in prison. They saw me ride madly through all the streets of Dublin. Please don't put me in Mountjoy prison, unless I'm given charge of the library. To be married to you, my dear Chris. But what has confounded me is blood. I was such a believer in blood, establishing the dynasty of Dangerfield, honorable kings of kingdoms and I have gotten as far as 1 Mohammed where the shit falls from the ceiling in a most sickening way and the bread is a week old and the tea like iron filings. I desire to be away in a more civilized country. What's to happen to me when I am old. And bent and busted.

Chris bringing two white cups to the table. She is all un-

133

dressed wearing a robe. My head feels better. And she fills the hot water bottle. I can only say roll up the carpet of the earth and put it away till next summer, things will be better then. We two in the bed together. I think this is the only peace I have had for years. My dear Chris, to put my hand on your bare arse is such a pleasure. And to touch and feel you're near, for both of us are protection. All together in here. And we are, aren't we? Let us pray. To St. Jude for the impossible or is it allowed to pray for an orgasm?

13

I can't bear to get out into the chill air with my legs all stiff and head hard with some of the things that have been on my mind all night.

Sound of Chris dressing. She put a tray beside his bed before leaving. Of toast and one piece dipped in dripping, a slice of bacon and cup of coffee. She kissed him on the head, tucked him in, whispered his breakfast was there and was gone.

Spending the afternoon reading and worrying. A look, now and again, out the window to see what was to be seen. Police or informers. But just casual persons. Mostly bent and carrying. But it would terrify the life out of me were I to see the squad cars out there. My only hope is to lie low and maybe grow a moustache.

The bed is pleasant. With my head resting. If I had the things which are in this room. Lust brought us together. But a horrid word. I think love. But what puts us apart in the bed at night. I turn over on my shoulder away from her and her back and go to bye byes trying to be alone. I can't even remember what I do with Marion. Being the sort of person I am, I make life pleasant for everybody. I'm not hard to live with. No bad breath or secret vulgarities. My dear Chris, I hear your feet.

"Hello, Chris."

"You're an awful liar."

"What?"

"Here in the paper."

Chris hands him the paper. Center and fat and black with the size of print and reading:

MAN AMUCK IN PUBLIC HOUSE
Chase through streets

What was reported by a witness to police as a most savage attack took place in Kelly's Garden Paradise, licensed premises, yesterday evening.

A man described as "foreign looking" with an English accent was reported to have entered above premises in a threatening mood and to have set upon the occupants in a wild way.

Witness to the attack told police that he was having a quiet drink with friends when there was shouting and commotion. He turned to see a man throwing a bottle of whiskey at the head of the bartender who ducked and went down through a trap door in the floor. The man then vaulted over the bar and smashed everything in sight. He turned upon occupants who had no alternative but to escape to the street.

The accused then ran away and was followed by witness who alerted Guards. He found the man hiding in a hallway but was threatened with violence and told to give up his hat and coat. Culprit then escaped on a bicycle. Several Guards and citizens gave chase to the top of Stephen's Green but all trace was lost in Cuffe Street where it is thought he may still be in hiding.

Guard Ball, who returned to the scene of attack for evidence, stated that the general condition of the premises gave every indication of being that of a battlefield.

Witness, whose four fingers were broken in the attack, was treated at St. Patrick Dunn's Hospital and allowed to go home. The search for the culprit, described by police as being tall, of light complexion, wearing tan trousers and sports coat, is being continued as it is thought that he may be insane. His eyes were given as very wild.

"Libel."

"Sound as if you were attacked."

"I was, and set upon viciously."

Chris silent, bending over the gas ring. Dangerfield sits strained and pitiful on the edge of the bed. The *Evening Mail* hangs open between his knees, eyes tearfully seeing that big print. O there was a man amuck.

Sebastian stands and walks to Chris's side. He puts his hand on her rump, taking up flesh in his fingers. Her head turns away from his mouth and pushes down a hand from her breast.

"If that's the way you want to be, Chris."

"It is."

"All right."

He goes to the door, opens it quickly, closes it quietly, steps into the drizzle and street, bleak and black.

Dear Blessed Oliver, martyred, quartered and generally chopped up, I'll tell you one thing, see me right out to the Rock without a horde hounding me and I'll publish thanksgiving in the *Evening Mail*.

On the empty evening bus coming down the curving hill into the Rock. Neon lights. Little line of figures waiting at the cinema. A delightful little place.

Stepping off the bus, walking swiftly to the green door of 1 Mohammed. Knocking. Nothing. A few knuckles on window. No sound, no light inside. He went back to the door. Pushed it and pulled. Locked and stuck. He withdrew a pace and lunged. The door fell down. Gingerly into the hall, he picked it up and pushed it back in place. He yelled. Nothing. Up the stairs, the bedroom empty. Nobody home.

And the weather was so dreary and dark. All night now. The only thing the rain does is to keep down the dust and me. Now Marion, you blue blood from Geek, wife and washer, slave to all me dirty little wants, where and what have you done and gone.

He came downstairs into a barren sitting room and kitchen. A white paper on the stove held down under a tin of beans.

> As you can see, I have moved.
> 11 Golden Vale Park
> The Geary
> Co. Dublin.

I don't know what to do except this sounds like a house with running water and I could do with a bath. Perhaps it's nice. Get the hell out of here before Skully sticks his thick skull in for rent or·some other repulsive request. The Geary. A rather posh area I gather. Golden Vale Park. O lovely. Say that again. Golden Vale Park.

There was one last house in the road of houses squat, semi and detached with concrete blocks dividing off front gardens of tiny lawns and flower beds. Passing number seven and nine, houses of caution and saving and iron gates to stop dogs' befoulment. People who lived here owned cars. My God has she only taken a room and maybe nowhere for me.

He paused in front of the little green gate to examine the latch which was quite tricky. In the garden were choice rhododendrons and the odd laurel. At the side a garage attached to the house. What in heaven's name have you done this for or why and you didn't tell me. I won't have it. The rain running off the leaves and bing in puddles. I'll just walk up this concrete path and make believe I've come to the wrong house. Looks like a garden in the back, a path around the side. This calls for indignation. I won't have it, I say, I just will not stand for this.

Could hear the bell ringing inside. And the steps coming. Can't see a thing through this frosted glass.

Door comes ajar.

"Let me in for God's sake, Marion."

Door slams.

"I say, Marion, are you alone? Really, this is ridiculous behavior. You can't do this."

Circling the house with great care looking for flaws. The lavatory window open. Sebastian scrabbled up the wall, knees knocking out the stuccoed stones and he fell, head first into the washbasin. Marion was in the door.

"Why don't you leave me alone. You desperate bastard."

"Don't call me a bastard when I'm breaking my damn neck trying to get in this house. For Christ's sake help me on to the floor. Why didn't you let me in the door?"

138

"Because I don't want you in the house. This is my house and I can call the police and have you thrown out."

"For the love of God, Marion, have you no mercy? Look at me, I'm soaked to the skin."

"And you weren't home last night."

"Delayed."

"What happened to your head."

"A frightfully decent chap asked me to play squash and I busted my head on the wall. A damn good player, but I just managed to beat him."

"O get out why don't you."

"Just for playing squash? I say, let's play the game. A most influential chap. His father owns—"

"Get out. I spent all day packing and moving and I'm not going to listen to you lie."

"Forgive me. It's such a nice house. Just let me look around. Are you here alone. All this?"

"Yes."

"How much?"

"My business."

"But Skully."

"You can still live there."

"O Jesus. Come on. Look, just five minutes' peace. It's got a hall. This is very nice, Marion. Can I see in here?"

Sebastian moving around the house followed by Marion, teeth clenched and silent. A sitting room with these divan beds, one of them along the wall and a definitely pre-war radio. Three chairs to sit in and a carpet and some pictures of horses and hounds racing across the wall.

"Wow."

"I'm not going to let you ruin this for me."

"Not at all. I'll leave. Just let me have a quick bath. I'll die with a case of death."

"Die, but this is my house."

Sebastian bent with inquiry looked in the rooms. A morning room with a desk and table and fire. A pleasant wooden statue with a cross on the belly on the mantelpiece. A window overlooking the back garden with rows of good things. Must get in here at all costs.

"Where do you sleep?"

"In there."

Marion pointed to the door.

"Let me stay, Marion. Please. I promise to abide by anything you say but I've just got to get a little security—"

"Ha. Ha."

"That's true. Just because I'm big and strong. Just look at this muscle. But it doesn't mean that I can't be stricken by the insecurity that's in it. Please."

"If there is even the suspicion of drink I'm having you put out."

"You're wonderful, Marion. This is frightfully good of you—"

"That's enough of that."

"Anything you say, Marion."

"And be quiet, Felicity is asleep next to the bathroom."

"Mum's the word."

Great splashing in the suds. And after a pot of tea. Marion with arms folded, hiding her breasts from his beast's eyes and watching the disappearance of a loaf of bread and package of margarine. He put his arm around her shoulders, a hand over her wrist. Naked in a blanket, he pointed to the garden, a gray weird wave of leaves.

"Marion, there's food out there for sure."

> On the land
> A plant.
> On the plant
> A leaf.
> This man
> Ate
> The leaf.

14

By the use of delusive enticements, Sebastian dug in at 11, Golden Vale Park. Several nights after ten thirty, he went by circuitous routes to 1, Mohammed Road to quietly pilfer divers articles. These were carried in gray bags for parcelling stout. One large mirror was traded for a bowler hat at his broker, a ruse to avoid recognition. And arrangements made with the *Evening Mail* for publication of thanksgiving to Blessed Oliver.

The landladies called to tea. An elderly Protestant couple, sisters, of a class living on investments. They hoped that Sebastian and Marion would keep up the garden, because they had several rare Himalayan plants given by a cousin, a member of the Royal Horticultural Society. And they would leave their Wedgwood, finding them such a delightful couple, Mr. Dangerfield a student at Trinity, well, it really made them feel secure right from the start. And we were so upset about renting at first, the sort of people one might get these days, Dublin isn't as it used to be of course, people making money with shops and these people running the country.

Sebastian with votive eyes, their loyalist words, tender drops of balm. I am deeply delighted to be dealing with these people of Protestant stock. Their spinster eyes glistening with honesty. Yes, the front gate, clumsy boors moving their things had broken it, careless bounders indeed, have a reliable man deal with it forthwith, it's been such a pleasure to have you both. Do čome again. And I'm having a load of manure laid on the garden. Bye, bye.

This house was in a dead end. It was both secret and trapped. Can't have everything. And I prefer to have the coal bin out of doors. Doesn't do to hang suits over the coal. I can breathe again, grow flowers and eat for nothing. Almost.

Marion said they ought to let the sitting room and it would pay half the rent. She wasn't going to slip back into poverty again and be hounded day in and out by lecherous moneymongers. Sebastian volunteered putting in the ad, on condition that they rent to a Catholic.

"I won't have a Catholic living in my house. They can't be trusted. Nor do they bathe."

"Marion. That's absolutely preposterous. Let's have a little democracy here, I say."

"I hate Catholics."

"Must forgive a little spiritual scruffiness."

Marion gave in. Sebastian sat down at the desk in the morning room and on a clean piece of paper composed:

Bed-sittingroom. The Geary. Quiet and select. Conveniences. Business girl preferred, N.D., R.C., T.T.

Simplicity. Non-dancer weeds out the fancy and flippant. T.T. is always good for the respectability. However, have it understood that this is a house of freedom.

Saturday evening both notices appeared. Under Thanksgiving:

Grateful thanks to Blessed Oliver for deliverance. Publication Promised.

Monday afternoon, Sebastian collected the answers. They were good gas. Three with enclosed photographs, one rather risqué. But I shall not tolerate indecency. God forgive the Catholics.

It was a matter of selecting a good name. There was a Miss Frost. Lilly Frost. A straightforward inquiry. Send a letter and ask her to come see the room.

Miss Frost arrived wearing a tweed coat and hat. A botanist for a seed company. Of medium build and suggestion of the middle thirties. Sebastian offered that if Miss Frost were interested, the back garden was available for her work. The curtains of the morning room were parted and Miss Frost said the ground looked to be in good heart.

Can see her out there after work with the spade. Wouldn't

142

mind seeing a few bits of the food coming free. They say that gardening is good for you.

Miss Frost agreed to take the room and said she would like to move in immediately as she would be glad to be out of the place where she was. Miss Frost seemed an interesting person. Showing the first signs of age, slight belly under the chin, nervous smile, mouth thin and bit drawn, living out the last years of fertility. And respectability.

After she had gone, Sebastian sat in a chair he called his own with an adjustable back. Could lie supine and watch the ceiling. After awhile it moved. Time to take stock. Look at things in retrospect. Come a long way. From Rock to Geary, from low to the middle, from coal in the closet to coal in the bin, from the tap outside to the tap inside, from cold to the hot. Away from the broken doors and walls to carpets and Wedgewood. My broker will be surprised. I only miss the trams, lovely trolley that took me by stiff track to Dublin and back. No doubt Mr. Skully will be a little upset to find us gone due perhaps to the lease and maybe the odd pound outstanding. O dear, it's a selfish world. But I'd say Skully will have his hands full to find me now. It's so pleasant here. And I think I'm going to enjoy having little talks with Miss Frost about the garden.

On Wednesday evening Miss Frost arrived in a taxi with her things. Sebastian came smiling to the door. The room was ready. A lamp engineered by the bed for reading. It was grand. Furniture dusted and polished with lavander wax. A runner fixed on the curtain. It was a fine room. Plenty of shrubbery outside the window keeping out the light. My favorite room. Darkness gives a sense of security but nothing's too good for the boarder.

Me and Marion have twin beds. Better that way. Don't want lust and fecund congress. I went into chemists for those things when I first came to Ireland. I said, may I have a dozen. The man said to me, how dare you ask for such a thing and he hid behind the counter till I left. Naturally I thought he was mad. I went further up the street. Man with a great grin, how do and what not, I let me teeth out for second. I noticed his were a little black. I put it to him pleasantly, asking for the American tips if possible. I saw his face go down, slouch of the jaw, hands twitch and a bottle break on the floor. The woman waiting behind me indignantly swept out of the shop. The man in a hoarse whisper said he didn't deal in things like that. Also to please go away because the priests would put him out of business. I thought the gentleman must have something against the American tips which I prefer. I entered another shop and bought a bar of Imperial Leather for the class standing that was in it. Quietly I put it to him for a half dozen with English tips. I heard this man utter a low prayer, sweet mother of Jesus, save us from the licentious. He then blessed himself and opened the door for me to leave. I left thinking Ireland a most peculiar country.

I took to studying again and found having that splendid beverage made from the cacoa bean, most pleasant with Miss Frost. Marion said she had to get her sleep, so Miss Frost and I would sit for an hour talking of an evening.

"Miss Frost, forgive me my question, but I'm intensely interested in Irish boarding houses. You did stay in one?"

"I did, Mr. Dangerfield. It doesn't bear repeating, but one gets used to them."

"Now, how is that Miss Frost?"

"Well, Mr. Dangerfield, some of them are nice enough people but it was hard to get a proper night's rest with the goings on."

"Now what sort of goings on, Miss Frost?"

"It would be embarrassing to tell you, Mr. Dangerfield."

Miss Frost with her slight, shy smile and pale lids dropping over her eyes. I think her lashes were gray. She had worked in England as a land girl. Saved money. Wanted to go into business for herself. She said she was go-ahead.

Miss Frost would sit across from him at the kitchen table. At first they had their drink in the morning room but as they got to know each other a little better, the air relaxed and they sat around the kitchen table. One evening she said she hoped Mrs. Dangerfield would not object to her talking with her husband alone, the way they were.

There were a few weeks like this. Weeks with a sunny security. Until one morning. Alone in the house. Chilly and clouds stuffing the sky, squeezing out the rain. There came a suspicious knock on the front door. Action stations. Sebastian quickly to Miss Frost's room for a hasty look out on the steps. My God, I am indeed a cooked geek. Surveying sullenly, hands angelically twisted, the rain dripping from his black hat, stood the malcontent, ingrate, Egbert Skully. Suck in my breath so as not to make a sound. Use the tip toe. I hope desperately that the front bloody door is locked. Take a chance and get to the back fast.

Sebastian turned the key in the kitchen door. He pulled the curtains of the morning room. There was another knock at the front door, then steps down and steps coming round the side of the house. Sebastian went to the front door. Locked. Returning to Miss Frost's room, drawing the curtains tightly across with an inch to see out from and wait. A rapping on the back door. That nosey bastard. I have been tracked down. I have been found out. Travel only at night, under heavy disguise with trinkets and trash and crippled and otherwise incapacitated. The pity.

Sebastian gave a squeal.

"Eeeeeee."

Skully rapping on the window just on the other side of those curtains and they were vibrating with the awful concussion of it. I'm a fool. I pulled the curtains. Skully has noticed it. You dirty little bastard. Thank the Jesus the doors are locked. Must be calm. Fear a state and condition of the mind, maybe. In theory I'm here but really I'm gone. Use the mental telepathy, as good as anything in a situation like this. Mr. Skully. Mr. Egbert Everad Skully. Listen to me. Mr. Dangerfield, Mr. Sebastian Balfe Dangerfield, has gone to Greece. I tell you he's in Athens playing a drum. He left a month ago on the Holyhead boat because he didn't want that tiresome trip to the Liverpool. He's not behind this green curtain with the red flowers as you think he is, terrified and ready to cough up a few quid to get rid of you. Go away from this house and forget him. What's fifty quid anyway. It's nothing. You're well rid of this bastard, Dangerfield. Mr. Skully, can't you hear me? I tell you, I'm in Greece.

More raps on the window. Telepathy having no effect. This Irish animal can't have any brain to receive the message. How long can this pig keep it up. Boor. Philistine most odious. Right now I would like to become a particular Percival Buttermere O.B.E. and come to the door complete with walking stick and pajamas, look out, see Skully, step back and with a great deal of British nasality, I say my good man, are you mad? What, just what are you trying to do. Would you mind awfully not rapping on my windows and getting off my front porch. Are you the coal man? Then go around to the back, my cook will deal with you, if you're not, would you mind frightfully removing yourself, you're most suspicious looking.

Suddenly Skully turned. He fiddled with the front gate. Closing it carefully behind. Giving it that unopened look.

Jittery, Sebastian went for a rest in the supine chair. Please, God, don't let Skully meet Marion or my goose will be cooked beyond recognition. I'm a man sitting here discovered. Only thing for it is to get a few quid to him. Mail them from East Jake. That black beast will be here, morning, noon, night and the hereafter and times between. O tis a world filled with woe and misunderstanding. Get the rent from Miss Frost and send off a few bob. Must now take precautions and everything organized for the siege.

And the fear. It's coming up from my toes and makes me feel empty and sick. I feel I'm standing before a blackness. Have to jump it and I won't make the other side. Blessed Oliver I put it to you again, get me through these exams. You may think me only a conceited Prod but there is more to me than that. And they judge me. Just with a paper with those little questions. And I can just see myself coming

146

to the notice board. O dreadful day. Looking at the paper with the names neatly on it. Naturally I start with the first honors and then second and the last names of the third honors. No Sebastian Dangerfield. And the small note of damnation at the bottom of the white paper. One candidate unsuccessful. What do I know about law. Can't park in the middle of the street or make too much noise or present a state of undress to the public. And I know no man would ravish a maiden within age, neither by her own consent, nor without her consent, nor a wife or maiden of full age, nor other woman, against her will on penalty of fine and imprisonment, either at the suit of a party or of the King.

O there are a few things I know all right. And make up the odd case, never check up. Geek versus Gook. Why do you hound me so, Skully.

Marion arrived in through the garage with an armful of groceries.

"Sebastian?"

"What?"

"I thought you were going to do these dishes?"

"Couldn't."

"Why not?"

"Skully."

"What do you mean?"

"He was groping around the house all morning."

"O no."

"O yes. I told you."

"I knew it wouldn't last."

"Nothing, my good Marion, lasts."

"O dear."

"Quite."

"Will our lives ever be free."

"Cheer up, the worst's over."

"O shut up—we're back where we started."

"Not at all. At the end, Marion."

"And you tell me how we're going to explain all this

147

hiding and not answering the door and things, to Miss Frost?"

"You're forgetting Miss Frost is Catholic. How do you think they survive in Ireland?"

"And when he's snooping about?"

"I'll send him a money order from the North of Dublin. Enclose a note telling him I'm staying there with friends."

"He won't be fooled."

"But must try. Any and every ruse. We must warn Miss Frost."

"Don't for heaven's sake."

"We've got to."

"Why?"

"Suppose Skully comes around some evening, pulling at doors and rapping on the windows. We can't sit here and do nothing. I'll just explain to Miss Frost that I met one of those people who go on outings from Grangegorman, mad as a hatter, bought him a drink and he's been after me ever since. She'll understand. This city's full of them."

"What a dreadful business it all is."

"Now Marion, cheer up. Have heart. Everything is going to be all right. Just leave it to me."

"I've made that mistake before. Why did we have to sign that lease. We'll have to pay the rent till it's up."

"A custom of the country. Just relax. Change our schedule of living. Tell Miss Frost about this crazy man—Catholics have great respect for the insane—and tell her we have to have the front of the house blacked out."

"O God, we can't suggest such a thing."

"We've got to. Now if we do that I'll build a mobile barricade at the side of the house so Skully can't get to the back and then we can have the light on. Now I'll even deal with Miss Frost. There is a measure of rapport there."

"So I've noticed."

Marion went into the kitchen. Strained and pained. Hear her putting away the groceries, a good sound. I will not be beaten nor put down. Few more weeks of holding out and be out of it all. Be in a position to give Skully his blood money. I will campaign in such a manner as to totally bring about an unconditional collapse of Egbert, the blood man. And the rest of them in the Rock could wait for theirs too. Peace is gone. No more of the sunny sessions with me *Irish Times* of a morning, looking over the mad growth in my little garden. But O aye, take the sun while ye may and when we pull the damp curtains over the soul of day, rest secure for we will see the light of day another time.

Over bread, tea, pot of blackcurrant jam rife with vitamin C, sausages and a bit of margarine, Sebastian faced the gray face of Miss Frost. A bit of lip paint on and pencil around the eyes. She moved for the bread with reserve. I pushed the margarine over because I cannot tolerate bad table manners although I'm a great one for toleration generally.

"Miss Frost. I have a rather weird thing to tell you. Ridiculous really. I hope it won't upset you. But there's been a man about here. Harmless sort but mad as a hatter. Foolish of me, but just by accident one night I loaned this man a cigarette in a public house not realizing the implications. I found him a rather interesting sort. However, I was taken aback by his eyes. It turned out that he had an afternoon off from the Grangegorman. From there the whole situation developed in a most fantastic way. This man has got it into his head that he was a former landlord of mine and that I owe him money."

"Isn't that the limit, though, Mr. Dangerfield?"

"It is rather. And now he's been at the house. Well, I've had no alternative but to ignore him. Lock the doors and things and pull the curtains. But I thought it wise just to tell you. Nothing serious. But I wouldn't want you to have someone tapping on your window. Perfectly harmless type. Wouldn't be let out otherwise. So just ignore him."

"Couldn't you tell the police, Mr. Dangerfield?"

"O I'd rather not, Miss Frost. Unfair to subject this poor unfortunate to abuse and he'd be kept in after that. I think it best to ignore him and I'm sure he'll stop. If you happen

149

to be outside and he starts on about this rent and money just tell him I'm not home and to go away."

"Yes, I'll do that. Thanks for telling me. I imagine I would be a bit frightened by a strange man, Mr. Dangerfield."

"Quite."

"I'll do these dishes, Mr. Dangerfield. Now you stay there and finish your tea."

"O no, Miss Frost."

"Only take me a minute, Mr. Dangerfield."

"Very good of you, Miss Frost."

Sebastian licked his mouth. Miss Frost running the tap. Sebastian pulls up the table cloth. A quick wipe of the lips. Marion reading in the bedroom. Nice evening. Think I'll just slip in there and tell Marion the good news.

"I say. Marion."

"O what."

"Everything's all right. I told you Miss Frost would understand."

"All right."

"Move over."

"Get in your own bed."

"It's cold. Don't you want a bit of arse?"

"Go talk to Miss Frost, foul mouth."

"Like to get you right here."

"Take your hands away."

"Weeeeeee."

"You're revolting."

"This is the way to live. The light. Bing. Let there be electricity. Let there be gas for continuous hot water and cooking. Let there be a hot bedlam for those needing it. We've come a long way, Marion. A long way."

"And you had nothing to do with it."

"Bend over."

"Get away."

From Miss Frost's room there came the sound of music. And the laurels rubbing outside. The air smelling of green, fresh in from the branches. When I was little, a colored maid

150

pinched my penis. Her name was Matilda, and I watched her through the key hole, powdering her pudenda. She did a lot of things to me. Worried about my physiology. Little colored boys have bigger ones. O they feed you up for the teeth and the weight and clean out the ears and other things and cut the fingernails and brush the hair but there's no organ orgy. I think Marion thinks mine too small.

> But I know
> It's bigger
> Than most.

15

These days I can sneak away to the bathroom and perform my toilet with dignity.

Miss Frost has to go by my door. Marion leaves it open in the fuss to feed the kid. I lie looking out at Miss Frost passing in various stages of titillating undress. In her red kimono, gray shanks, shapely with the type of thin ankle I prefer. Indeed, Miss Frost is well put together. And this morning she saw me. I smiled as one does. Her neck went scarlet. It's all right to blush in the face but watch out for those given to the neck blush.

I went in to get my breakfast. Dear daughter shut your lousy yap. Close it. Or I'll jam it. And it won't be the black-currant either.

"Daaaa, da."

"What is it?"

"Ahhh, da pooh-pooh."

"Will you let da-da eat his breakfast. Da-da's hungry. Now shut your hole."

"Stop it. She has a perfect right to make noise."

"Well lock her in the garage—I can't understand why they don't have chains for children. I'm going to Trinity."

"Go ahead, I'm not stopping you."

"Thought you might like to know."

"Well I don't."

"Now, now. I'm coming right back. I think perhaps we ought to pay off a pound on the electricity bill. Marion, are you listening?"

"I heard you."

"Good idea to clear up part of this little matter."

Marion pouring milk into a pan.

"I say, Marion, are you ill? Now for the teeth of Jesus—"

152

"Stop using that language in front of the child. And Miss Frost too. And I'm sick of it. Go if you're going."

"Now, Marion, let's be reasonable. This bill must be paid sooner or later or they'll be out here to cut it off. What will the Miss Smiths think? I say—"

"O for God's sake, stop whining. Since when have you been concerned with what people will think?"

"I've always been that way."

"What rot."

Sebastian got up from the table and walked into the kitchen and put his arm across Marion's shoulders.

"Take your hands off me, please."

"Marion."

"I thought you were going to Trinity. Well go."

"I don't want to waste the trip in."

"O you are a liar."

"Little severe, Marion."

"And you come back drunk."

"I beg your pardon. I'll give you a shot in the mouth."

"Why don't you fight a man. I'm not giving you one penny."

"I have a proposition—"

"I don't intend to change my mind."

"All right, Marion. If you wish it that way. Be Protestant and miserable. If you'll excuse me. I'll go."

Out of the kitchen stony faced. He took a bag from the morning room and went into Miss Frost's room. Two decanters. Into the bag. And bowler placed neatly on his skull. Quickly out the front door, skipping down the steps and whoops. He stumbled headlong into a choice laurel, face in the rotting leaves. Decanters held high for safety. A few foul words of abuse. Tugging at the little green gate. Stuck. A lash with the boot. The gate slumped open. The lower hinge wagging by its spring.

He arrived in Dublin on the top of the tram. And slid through the fashionable throng of the Grafton Street. He walked under the three gold balls and to the counter.

153

Plunked down the two decanters. A funereal man hunched whispering over them.

"Well, Mr. Dangerfield."

"Heirlooms. Fine Waterford."

"I see, Mr. Dangerfield. Not much of a market these days. Seems people don't set much of a value."

"Wine's becoming very popular."

"Ah yes, Mr. Dangerfield. Ha."

"Americans are mad for them."

"Ten shillings."

"Make it a pound."

"Fifteen and we won't argue."

Sebastian turned with his money. He bumped into a man coming in the door. A man with a rotund skull and shoulders streamlined against the weather.

"Jesus Christ come home to roost. Sebastian."

"How do you do, Percy."

"I hose shit off the toilet seats in Iveagh House. Drink anything that's going and hump when I can."

"Jolly good show."

"And I'm in to pawn five pounds of steak."

"Eeeek, you're not."

"Here it is."

"Percy, incredible."

"Will you have a drink. Wait for a second while I flog the meat, and I'll tell you the whole story."

Sebastian waited under the three balls. Percy, grinning, came out and they set off down the street. Percy Clocklan, a short bull man. So strong he could collapse the walls of a room with a deep breath. But only did this in people's houses he didn't like.

They sat in the corner of a tiny public house. Few hags beating gums in each other's deaf ears. Saying the dirtiest imaginable things. Absolutely shocking. Percy Clocklan's face was all grin and laughter.

"Sebastian, I've had everything. My father was a bank manager. My sister's a member of the Purgatorial Society,

154

my brother's a company director and I reside in the Iveagh
House over the Bride Street, a hostel for the poor and dying."

"Better days coming."

"But let me tell you. Here I am, educated with the best of
them at Clongowes. Nine years in the textile trade taking
guff from these awful eejits and not even a raise. I told the
manager to stuff his kip up his hole. Jesus, I shouldn't have
done it. Now look at me. Every morning I have to take a hose
and go around cleaning after these ould bastards who come
in at night full of red biddy and do their business all over the
floors. Last night I caught an old bugger pissing into the
drinking fountain. But it's only a shilling for a good feed and
two and six for a cubicle for a night. I'm a porter there.
That's the big cheese. And I get my pay and into the red
biddy lounge where I get laggards for eight pence."

"What would you like out of life, Percy?"

"Know what I want? I'll tell you. And you can listen to
these bloody eejits who sit around talking bull shit for hours
and they don't get anywhere. I'll tell you what I want and
it's all I want. I want a woman with awful big tits and arse.
Biggest tits and arse in whoredom. Get up on her—o the tits,
the tits. Whoever thought of them. God knows a good thing.
Just tits, a big arse so's I can come home of an evening and
lash a sup of steak on the grill and fill me gut and then get
up on her. I want some kids. Something to work for. Incen-
tive is what I want. I sit around an oul' bleedy pub wasting
me time. I'm coming to forty and maybe I could have been a
big fella with cars and maids but I don't give two tuppenny
turds. It's over now and no use shouting about. But if I had
a woman with an awful big pair of tits you'd see me for the
last time in a pub. Be as happy as sin. I'm married once but
I'll never make the same mistake again. Wanting to drink
every night and terrified of having some kids."

"Pregnancy first, Percy. Then the drink to recover from
the insecurity that's in it."

"I know, I know. I was an awful eejit. But she wouldn't

hear of it. Said she was too young to be slaving after children. I know better now. She wouldn't give up her job. Didn't have any power over her. I don't care now, any old whore will do now and lots of biddy to forget about food and rent."

"And where did you get that meat?"

"Sebastian, don't breathe a word of this. Now I'm telling you, it's confidential. I had this bird who worked in the butchers. She'd get me as much as eight pounds of the finest steak of an evening. I'd flog three or four pounds and have enough to see me crawling from biddy and lash the rest raw into me gut. See me right for days. I'd give old Tony Malarkey a few pounds now and again for his kids. I was living with him for a while but he's like an oul' hen, clucking around and jealous when I'd come in of an evening laggards. Can't stand to see anyone else enjoying themselves. I bloody well moved out. But my woman got caught."

"Where did you get the meat today?"

"Wait till I tell you. They caught her stealing the bloody stuff and she was fired on the spot. And she wanted me to get up on her of an evening for nothing, and I told her did she think I was a stud bull wasting me energy humping her ould carcass. Imagine that, expecting me to act the bloody bull for nothing and her ould flat tits without a sup of meat behind them. There's no decency in some of these people. You're the only decent person I know, Sebastian. You buy a man a drink when you have the money and you don't do all this yelling about it. I should have been a priest and have Morgan's van calling every week with lashings of drink and a housekeeper with boobs like pyramids. Then you'd hear some sermons. I'd lash some bloody decency into these people. But when I got no more meat from this ould whore, I looked up another bird in a butchers. Went in every day buying bones for a week and it wasn't long before she was sneaking the meat out to me."

"You're an awful man."

"And I've got an ould maid in the Iveagh House who's

156

taken a shine to me. She says a pair of decent balls in the
hand is worth a cock in the bush."

"You'd make a fine husband, Percy."

"Don't come the hound."

"You would."

"Look at me. Losing me hair. Sleeping next to a bunch of
newsboys at night and the bunch of them saying hello to me
on Grafton Street. Me from Clongowes Wood College."

"Look at me, Percy."

"Look at you. More money than the president with that
G. I. Grant."

"The expense, Percy, is dreadful. And must keep my
dignity."

"Ould whore's dignity. Do you want to come to a party?"

"Not tonight."

"Have you gone mad, Sebastian? It's in Tony's house, the
Catacombs. Tony wants to see you. I hear O'Keefe's gone to
Paris and went queer as well."

"True. He's in a little town after anything that moves."

"Jesus, come to the party."

"Can't."

"Have a drink then."

"Percy, I've been put down a great deal since I saw you
last. A Mr. Skully, a former landlord, is after me for money.
Then there are a few business houses."

"You ought to go in for betting, Sebastian. That's what
your trouble is. A bet changes my whole day. Jesus, let's go
for some red biddy."

Red biddy is sweet and thick, dried dead blood. All running through the streets. I can only imagine that I would
like to be between thighs. I knew a girl who wore an orange
sweater. I put my hands on her naked waist of slim belly.
She was a milkmaid. I was a gentleman. We stood in an
erotic embrace.

They were gone down the street through the kids and
granite gutters talking about the money made in raising
sheep.

"Sebastian, did you ever get up on one?"
"I say, really, Percy."

> In
> Algeria
> There is a town
> Called
> Tit.

16

Sebastian sat hunched over his belly, transfused with joy. A night of a party. They were sitting in the Scotch House between two big barrels. Outside the Guinness boats going chug chug. Clocklan bellowing laughter.

I think I will see a great night of it. All manner of men invited. Sick and infirm, the bogus and bitchy. Those unclean and disgraced. Daily communicants and members in good standing of the Legion of Mary. The failed and about to fail. Dublin is great for minor clerks and officials. Nine in the office till six o'clock at home. The wracked and choked bodies. The wife will not put her hand on it or have a painful pump. A party of the anguished and underling. Mr. Dangerfield, alias Danger, Bullion, Balfe, Boom and Beast, will tell you how to get out of it. But well to remember it's hard but it's fair. These little buggerings showed people you could take it. The pain as well as the pleasure.

And I think there ought to be a table in the middle of the floor for a demonstration of the animal. Penny notebooks for notes, please. Tell you anything you want to know. I might not look like much now, but in five years. Wow. And don't forget that I'm at Trinity either. No end to where I am. To close the evening I'll do a Spanish dance and catch olives in the mouth and a few other things as well. And songs of course, led by Mr. Dangerfield and the tea and cakes served by genuine North of Dublin whores for those of you who are repressed.

"Clocklan, I'm suffering from a woeful case of blackdog."

"Get the bloody stout and never mind the blackdog. This is going to be a great party."

"I ought to go home, Percy."

"Go on out of that. Can't miss this bash."

They were walking up Grafton Street carrying gray parcels of stout. Dangerfield singing:

> My heart is like
> A squeezed grape
> Only the pip
> Is left.
> Only the pip.

"I'll be thrown out of the house."

"Jesus, what kind of a house do you keep. Give your woman a good boot in the hole. Throw you out? Nonsense. This is Ireland."

They pushed through an iron gate and down the black, steep steps. Tony Malarkey, host, grinning, a pleased bull smelling the hot rump of a cow in heat, counting the parcels of stout. Eyes on the corks. Through a scullery there was a huge kitchen. Drink was put on the table. Clocklan brought his to a corner of the room, hiding the bottles under some rags. Malarkey watching him.

"Where are you going with that drink, Clocklan, you stingy ould whore?"

"Not wasting it on your ould guts."

The air filled with the popping of corks. A smell of damp walls and cavities. A feeling of long corridors and hidden rooms, tunnels in the earth, black pits and wine cellars filled with mouldy mattresses. A bulb burning in the center of the kitchen. The floor, stained, red tiles. Whitewashed walls and scabby buttresses crossing the ceiling. And more people bursting in the door laden with bags of stout.

Sebastian putting bottles in his pockets. Arming. He crossed over the room. A short, stocky girl standing alone. Smoldering green eyes and long black hair. Perhaps her father is a casket maker. Or she is a servant.

Sebastian next to her. She raised an eyebrow. Wow, this is no servant or serf either. What green, animal eyes. He took the bottle, holding it between his knees, a quick spin of the corkscrew. Then straighten the body. Bop. The brown foam dripped over the sides of his mouth. He smiled at the girl.

"What's your name?"

"That's a funny question to be asking me right off."

"What would you like me to ask you?"

"I don't know. It's just funny asking my name right away."

"My name is Sebastian."

"My name is Mary."

"You look Italian, Mary."

"Are you being fresh?"

"Boooobebo. Danggigigeegi. That's African for, certainly not beautiful maiden."

"You're making fun of me. I don't like it. You're queer."

"Have a bottle of stout, Mary. I want to tell you a few things. First a little bit about sin."

"What do you know about sin?"

"I can forgive sin."

"That's a sin you're saying. I won't talk to you if you say things like that."

Assuming the role of gentleman, Sebastian gave Mary a glass of stout. He brought her to where they could sit on a bench and talk. She said she minded the house. Her father had not been able to move his bowels for three weeks and they had to call the doctor and the doctor couldn't do anything for him and they thought he would die of the poison. She said he would just lie in bed and wouldn't go out to look for a day's work. Been there for months and the smell was too much and she had to take care of the house and her two small brothers.

Clocklan across the room, paying court to a smooth skinned blonde. The party distilling overtones of boredom and discontent. Suddenly a stout bottle whistled across the room, smashing an effeminate man's head. There was a quavering word of admonition and a chorus of encouragement. A chair broke, a girl twisting and yelling that she would not be handled. Sebastian retreating down his bench with Mary, giving her an account of what was going on. Something brewing across the room. Clocklan had turned from his blonde woman and was talking to a tiny man who someone said was a jeweler by trade and disposition. Suddenly, Clocklan raised his fist and drove it into the little man's face. He fell on the floor, crawling desperately towards safety under a bench and away from the bellow of Clocklan, to receive a kick in the face from a girl who thought he was trying to look up her dress.

A cellar of the damned for sure. I cannot tolerate economic cripples and I do not like those who were once rich. In it all to get away from it all. Perhaps I cannot bear to ever finish waiting. Those few left in the center of the room. The others beaten in battle had retreated to the corners of the room and did not have any opinions, standing glassy eyed and drunk.

Mary looking up out of her green eyes.

"O the things that are happening here."

"An awful bunch, Mary."

"Where are you from in England?"

"I'm not lime, Mary."

"What are you then."

"I'm American."

"Are you. Really?"

"And you're Irish."

"Yes."

"And do you like Ireland?"

"I like it. I wouldn't live anywhere else."

"Have you lived anywhere else?"

"No."

"And do you like your father?"

"That's a funny question. Why do you ask me these funny questions?"

"I like you. I want to know if you like your father."

"No. I don't like him."

"Why?"

"Because he doesn't like me."

"Why doesn't he like you?"

162

"I don't know but he's never liked me."

"How do you know he doesn't like you?"

"Because he punches and beats me."

"Good God, Mary. I say, he beats you?"

"Yes, he beats me."

"What for?"

"For nothing."

"Must be for something."

"No. If I come home late he asks me why I'm late and no matter what I say he finds some excuse to start punching me and he gets me in the hall so I can't get away and just punches me. He hates me."

"He does?"

"Yes. And there's no reason for it. As soon as I come in the house, he's sitting listening to the wireless and I go to put my coat away and he calls me into the sitting room and then asks me where I've been and accuses me of seeing men in parks and going off with them. And I haven't seen any men. Then he calls me a liar and awful names and then if I say I'm telling the truth, he comes after me."

"What about your mother?"

"She's dead."

"And you take care of your father and brothers?"

"Yes."

"Why don't you leave? Go to England and get a job."

"I don't want to leave my little brothers. They are only small."

"He can't beat you up now."

"He tries to sometimes but I'm stronger than he is now."

I can look at Mary. What's this thing? She's easy to look at. Are you easy to feel, too? Sleeves of her sweater stuffed up around her elbows, slender smooth wrists and a fine set of shoulders. Wouldn't want to come to grips, 'cept in mutual passion.

There was suddenly a crash at the door, the center boards giving way and a huge head came through singing.

Mary Maloney's beautiful arse
Is a sweet apple of sin.
Give me Mary's beautiful arse
And a full bottle of gin.

A man, his hair congealed by stout and human grease, a
red chest blazing from his black coat, stumpy fists rotating
around his rocky skull, plunged into the room of tortured
souls with a flood of song.

Did your mother come from Jesus
With her hair as white as snow
And the greatest pair of titties
The world did ever know.

Mary tugged at Sebastian.
"Who's that? It's a shocking song he's singing."
"That's the son of the rightful Lord Mayor of Dublin. And
his uncle wrote the national anthem."
Mary appreciative, smiling.
This man swept across the red tiles wildly greeting people
on all sides, telling the room.
"I loved the British prisons. And you lovely women. The
fine builds of ye. I'd love to do you all and your young
brothers."
He saw Sebastian.
"For the love of our Holy Father, the Pope, may he get
himself another gold typewriter. Give me your hand Sebas-
tian before I beat you to death with bound copies of the
Catholic Herald. How are you for Jesus' sake?"
"Barney, I want you to meet Mary. Mary, this is Barney
Berry."
"Pleased to know you, Barney."
"Why you lovely woman, Mary. How are you? I'd love
to do you. Don't let this whore touch or pluck your flower.
How are you again, Mary?"
"I'm fine."

Barney leaped away and up on the table and did a quick goat dance.

Mary turned to Sebastian.

"He's good gas."

"A fine build of a man, Mary."

"Did his uncle write the song?"

"Mary, when I say something, it's the truth. I speak nothing but the truth. And tell me, Mary, what are you going to do with yourself?"

"What do you mean?"

"In life."

"You mean what am I going to be? I don't know. I don't know what I want to be. When I was little I wanted to be a dancer. I wouldn't mind going to the art school. I like to draw."

"What do you draw?"

"All sorts of things. I like to draw women."

"Why not men?"

"I like women better. I like men too."

"But women most?"

"Yes. No one has ever asked me these questions before. I've never met a nice man."

"None?"

"I don't mean you. I don't know you. Perhaps you're all right. Women are kind."

"Do you like women's bodies?"

"These are funny questions. Why do you want to know these things anyway?"

"Because you have a nice build."

"How do you know?"

"By your teeth."

"How?"

"Good teeth a good body. God's teeth are great teeth. Mary you must come with me for a drink."

"Everything is closed."

"O there are places."

The room thick with smoke. Bobbing skulls. Those beaten

into silence, glued to the white peeling walls and the beaters, a great bunch. Barney singing, swaying on the tiles. Sweating. Clocklan had left the blonde to drag the little jeweler to the black rear of the catacombs for further discipline. Busting him in the head with the bottom of his fist. I tell you, the place is writhing, simply writhing. Malarkey shouting he was high bloody king and if they all didn't cheer up he would break their faces. Clocklan's woman got up on the table to dance. Wiggling wang, she called it. And Percy came back with a grand grin which he wiped when he saw his woman on the table and he said she was a disgusting tramp and didn't she have any pride at all to be dancing like that in front of a whole bunch of people.

I think Mary's father an uncouth, constipated boor. Things in the North of Dublin have nothing to recommend them. But I think Mary has great charm and sensibility. Take her with me into my personal garden of sunshine which I do not call Eden for obvious reasons. Madam, may I touch your nipples with my eyes. I think these people here are mostly against each other. They think nothing of living between dirty sheets and carrying on indiscriminately. With nary a thought of the consequences stored up with God.

Malarkey grabbed Dangerfield by the arm.

"Sebastian, do you want to see the most amazing thing in your life?"

"I do."

"Come back into the wine cellar."

Sebastian and Mary following Tony.

"Now for the love of Jesus, don't make a sound or old Clocklan will have a fit. Just take a look inside."

At the end of the long black hall, they paused before a half-open window. Leaning over the sill, peering into the black hole. In the center of the room, two figures on a narrow canvas camp bed, reeling on four twisted legs. Writhing. There was a great squeak. And then a squeal. The camp bed collapsing, bare bums slapping the stone. A naked Clocklan clinging desperately to the smooth nude. She said O my God

166

what's happened and groaned. Clocklan grunting, ignoring the laughs in the hall, glued to the bleating blonde.

"Have you ever seen anything like it in your life before, Sebastian?"

"Tony, I must say that Clocklan is full of spirit."

"Ould dirty whore. He'd get up on his mother in her coffin."

Mary had run back to the kitchen. A jammed place. Floor covered with broken bottles. A girl standing in the corner, drunk, pissing down her nylon leg. A nice pool. A voice declaring.

"Say what you want about me, but by God, don't insult my King."

"Hump your old King."

"Who said that?"

"Hump your old King."

"I say, I say there, out with it. Who said that?"

"The King is a shit."

"Look here, I won't stand for it."

"Up Ireland."

"God save the King."

"Bollocks the King."

"God save all here. And the others as well."

O thread my way back into this Catholic blood. And there's something about slaughter. Fists in the smoke and smell. What a tiresome scene. A decibel of this is enough. Moral decadence. And an agreeable lack of fibre. But decency, not a bit of it anywhere. I must put a stop to it.

Dangerfield taking a chair, and stepping on to the table, wound his fingers around the electric light and yanked it from the ceiling. There was a blue roar of flame. Layers of plaster crashing to the floor. Screams all over the black room.

"Mary and Joseph we're being murdered."

"Get your filthy hands off me."

"Who did that?"

"I've been robbed."

"I've been goosed. Wow."

Through the dark Sebastian led Mary and together they pounded up the iron steps to the street. A horse cab was passing.

"I say, my good man."

The cab stopped.

"Tell me where can the lady and I get a drink?"

"Certainly sir, certainly."

They climbed into the mouldy interior. Sitting on a mass of torn upholstery and damp rugs.

"Isn't this great, Mary?"

"What did you pull the light out of the ceiling for? You could have killed somebody."

"I was appalled by the depravity and the general slump in morals. Does your father ever hit you in the chest, Mary?"

"He hits me everywhere. But I can defend myself."

"I'm going to take you to The Head, Mary. Where we can drink with a better class of people."

"I think I better go home."

"Why?"

"I have to. You go to Trinity."

"How do you know?"

"One of the girls told me. All these Trinity students are the same. The only nice ones are the black ones. They're gentlemen. They don't get personal or fresh."

"Mary, I may not be black but I'm not bad."

"You just laughed at those people in the back room without any clothes."

"They were having congress."

"Fancy names."

Under the train trestle went the horse cab. Past the monument makers. And a shop where I used to keep my rations. A milky, cold smell. I often bought two eggs and one slice of bacon. From a bowl-breasted girl. She eyed me. And once I bought oatmeal and went out and got dreadfully drunk across the street. Invited the pensioners in for a pint. They all came

168

in adjusting scarves, coughing graciously. They all told me stories. About men and their daughters. I heard them before but once is never enough—got to have them more often. Later I spilled my bag of oatmeal all over.

Sebastian kissed Mary. She put her elbows over her breasts. But she's opening her mouth. And she's got a hard little back and thick thighs but I can't get my hand to her bosom. Can't squeeze it in under here. Not an inch. Say, Mary, how about you and me going where the olives grow? Or at least where it isn't so goddamn damp. Boy, your lips are narrow.

Now that we are going along the quays, it reminds me of how much I would like to see a bit of largess. This grabbing Mary is a little embarrassing because she's as hard as a rock and is almost trying to fight me. I get that impression. She had hold of my hand then and without question gave it a twist. I'll twist it right back and take it off altogether.

"Mary, I've got something to show you."

Sebastion took a match box out of his pocket. Pulled it open and showed Mary a replica of the Blessed Oliver Plunket.

"Are you a Catholic? Sure you're not?"

"Mary, I'm everything. Especially a Catholic."

"You can't be Catholic and something else as well."

"Mary, I'm a big wind from East Jesus, a geek from Gaul."

"You're just trying to kid me. And I have to go home. I live over the Capel Street Bridge."

"Now, Mary, I want you to see this fine old inn. Finest of its type in Europe. And I'll sing you a song."

> O the Winetavern Street is the silliest
> Of the streets full of fury,
> O the very, very best
> For this moo from Missouri.

"Like it?"

"You're a gas man."

"When all the world is funt, Mary. That's the time."

"You're crazy."

Sebastian whipped his head out of the window and had a polite word with the driver.

"Mary, we are going into a nice warm room with a fire. And I'll buy you a few nice drinks and we can sit and talk. I'd like to talk with you about Papish things. We would never get along without the Pope. He keeps a little dignity on this earth. If we had a few more like him there wouldn't be all this lechery and deceit. Mary, there are a lot of bad people in this world."

Mary rolled her head on his shoulder and whispered:

"I want you to kiss me again."

Sebastian bolted, eyebrows raised.

"I say, Mary, really!"

"Don't embarrass me."

I can see the Courts of Justice across the river. O the pleas of trespass against the peace of the King in the kingdom of England, made with force and arms, ought not, by the law and custom of England, to be pleaded without the King's writ. O these little things of law. I know them all. And a river is a natural stream of water of greater volume than a creek or rivulet. And the Liffey is a river. And the dome of the four courts is like a prostrate bub. But never mind. This Mary, her spatulate rump, twisting on her tough, tight body. Sit on my knee, now while I learn off the laws of sewers. A lot of strange things happen to one, of an uncanny nature. Perhaps if I had a fish, dead and slime and if I kept Miss Frost's window open and the curtains closed and wait for nosy Skully to stick his head in and give him a violent lash in the face. Splosh. Right in the eyes, too. Slish. Take that, cad.

There was a bump as the cab passed over the sidewalk making the turn into Winetavern Street. The scruffy vehicle pulled up to a closed iron gate. Horse snorting nervously. Case of fleas. Sebastian stepped out gingerly and the man asked him for a pound.

Two of them waiting in the silence. This was to be a case of slight misunderstanding. A time for measuring one's words. Sebastian began quietly.

"I say, old boy, how would you like to spend Christmas in the 'Joy,' with your teeth dropping out of your Catholic arse?"

"It's a pound this time of night."

The man looking through lethargic eyes full of shillings. Looking down into the wild, bloody eyes, all gray round the red globes.

"Perhaps you'd rather that I kick this rolling rat trap to pieces and give you a Celtic baptizing in the Liffey, you vulgar thug."

"I'll call the Guards."

"What?"

"I'll call the Guards."

"What? God damn it."

Sebastian's hand shot out and caught the man by the coat until his face was plunging towards the street and his feet were caught in his seat.

"God damn it, another bit of insolence out of you and I'll ram this horse and casket up your hole. Do you understand me?"

"I'll call the Guards."

"You won't be able to call your god damned mother when I'm finished with you. Lout. Hear me? Lout. A pound you bastard. Festering sneak. No decency in you. No love. Do you know what love is? Where's your love, you bastard? Why I'll throttle you to death if you don't show some love. Show me some love or I'll strangle you."

A vague smile came to the man's mouth. His eyes, two holes of terror. Little scene on the Winetavern Street. Mary came out, tugging at his fingers around the silent man's throat.

"Leave him alone. What did he do to you? Why don't you pay the man his money and leave him alone."

"Shut up."

"You're a terrible person."

"Shut up. We're all going for a drink."

A glimmer of hope in the man's eyes, and guilt. Sebastian, still holding him by the throat.

"Will you come in for a drink?"

"All right, I'll come in for a drink."

"I want to go home."

"It's all over now, Mary. This gentleman will come and have a drink. You'll come and have a drink too."

"I want to go home. You're an awful person."

"Not at all. This gentleman knows he was taking advantage of me. I know how much it is to Winetavern Street."

Man's evasive eyes.

Sebastian went to the iron gate and reached in and pressed a bell behind the wall. Waiting. Sebastian rattling the gate. A suspicious whisper came up out of the black alley.

"Who's up there? Stop that racket. Go home to bed—there's nothing down here."

Sebastian put his face between the bars.

"Travelers from the West. Just ten minutes. We're friends of the man with the beard."

"Go on with you. Get out of here. What do you think this is?"

"We're sent by the man with the beard. Friend of the corpse."

The voice came nearer.

"Let me look at you in the light and stop the noise. A man couldn't be dead down here with the likes of you carrying on. Let me see the faces. Who's the woman? No women allowed here. What do you think this is?"

"Now, now—she's a Dawn Beauty."

"Dawn Beauty, my virgin bub. I can't have this sort of going on—you've been here before—what's all this racket? —you ought to know better. Don't make any noise coming in and get out fast."

"O you're a fine woman with a build of a woman of thirty."

"Go on out of that. Where's the man with the beard?"

"He's in Maynooth. He said the price of drink was scandalous and for a few prayers he could get it for nothing."

"Don't be blasphemous now and watch those barrels. You're a troublemaker you are—have my hands full with the lot of you."

"Now, now, Madam—"

"Don't call me madam—I know what you're up to."

Group moving slowly. Down the alley. Through a door. Along the black hall. And into the yellow light of the medieval room. This is the pineal eye of the world.

"Where's Catherine, the girl? Send her with two scalding malts and spot of gin for the lady and anything for yourself. And I wouldn't be past a bit of bed with you."

"O go on out of that and no noise, mind."

In this semi-circle of expectation. Twisted bulgin' sofas. Not much British fellowship here in spite of the sportiness of the room, with hunts racing everywhere. Catherine is a beauty and so's Mary around the nose and eyes. But this is a horsehair sofa. Say after me, Mary.

Sebastian
Thou art blessed,
And Sebastian,
Also the true song.
A tinder of night together
With being
A bargain basement
Of kisses.

Get astride me.
Touch, whoops, tender
Me,
Mr. big tree of love.

Catherine, the maid, pushed through the door with a tray of drinks. Regarding Sebastian with a sly, shy grin. Blue-eyed, and a bit of the Celtic bovinity around the ankles. The horse-cab man wiping his mouth with his sleeve and the lip of glass with his hand to purify it. Mary sitting still, smoothing out her skirt and watching Sebastian.

"Now, isn't this nice, Mary?"

"It's all right."

"It's a good bit of malt, sir."

"Rather."

"It's been showery weather."

"For sure."

I don't think I'm getting far with this conversation or with Mary. Play on her sympathy for being outside the church and grace. Might be the thread needle hole to her own. I've got a cloacal grip on life. Lot of people have said that. Nor am I going to let go. If there is illusion, live it with a flourish. I'll get you, Mary. Just like Marion. In the good old days I had Marion wrapped around. My finger. Up to get the tea. And toast. That was love. But I killed it. Things just don't last. They change. And sometimes they multiply, like babas.

The woman of the establishment came in.

"Now that was the last round. I have to get my sleep."

"One for the road and for yourself. Weary travelers we are."

"Do you want to have me arrested?"

"For fear we get killed on the highways."

"Go on out of that. You're a fine one. Once you get in here I can't get you out. Just one more. Catherine, two whiskies and a gin, and get a move on. Can't get an ounce of work out of them these days with all their fancy clothes and going out to dances. A while back I'd take the arse out of the likes of her and her men friends. They don't want to work these days."

"They don't know their place."

"Don't I know it. Up from the country and you'd think they was from society. Take that out of them."

"Catch them in the first-class."

"The likes of them should walk—never mind riding in the first-class."

"Discipline. More discipline."

"Out with black men every night of the week. I'll pound that out of them."

"There'll be a day of reckoning for all their laziness. That's for sure."

"And it won't be too soon."

"I'm a great believer in the fairness."

"It's all right."

"Now if you'll excuse me a moment, I must make wee wee."

"That's thirteen and six."

"My driver will see to that."

Sebastian felt his way through the hall and out a door under the sky. He pissed indiscriminately. He met Catherine coming back in the darkness. They locked. And she put her hand between his legs. And dropped the tray with a clang. The hall suddenly alight.

"What's going on? Now I won't have any of this going on with my girls. Stop it. Catherine, take your arms from around that gentleman, you dirty little slut."

"Now, now, everything's all right. Catherine and I were lost in the hall."

"I've had enough of your carrying on, Romeo. And get back into that kitchen you, the very nerve of you. Slut."

Sebastian gave madam a pinch in the bottom as he waltzed by and she slapped his hand. O good O. We'll all go and sit under the shittah tree. Something that no one knows is that I pawned a mirror of a public toilet. One of those modern jobs, just screwed in. I had the end of a fork to take them out and went to my broker. Then I went to the Grafton Cinema to have a supper in the pseudy tudy interior. Sitting by the window from where I could see Dawson Lounge written up on a high wall. Happiness can be uncomfortable. And waiting for food it was great but I called on a few fears to temper the glow of conservative mellowness. The waitress, a lovely black build of a girl, full mouth and white teeth and healthy breasts full of opulent undulation as she came with plates of stuff. O the hunger of it.

Madam stood at the door, huge bosom coming out the hall.

"Now that's all, the lot of you out of here now, before the Guards come breaking down the door."

"And let me thank you for a fine evening."

"Just get out."

"Am I becoming the hound?"

The lady of the house laughed. Ushered them through the long dark hall and out up the alley of barrels. And drunks lurking in doorways, reeling and pissing. Sebastian told the driver to let them off at the Metal Bridge and that there would be a day coming when he would repay him for his great kindness.

They went up the flat steps. Stopped, watching gulls and swans. Mary took Sebastian's arm.

"It's a lovely view."

"Quite."

"All the seagulls."

"Yes."

"I like to do this sort of thing."

"Do you?"

"Yes. It gives me a nice feeling."

"True."

"As if you were floating or something."

"Yes, floating."

"What's the matter, don't you like it?"

"Love it, Mary."

"You just go on and on and then you get a queer notion and don't say much."

It was the meal at the Grafton Cinema that took my mind

176

away. Because the waitress was so kind. A plate full of fine, fat sausages, lashings of rashers and a mountain of golden chips. I heard the waitress saying down the hatch would they ever hurry up because this fine gentleman was starving. And the tea was so good that I'd giggle with the impossible joy of it all. And a gentle Grafton Street breeze, tempting me to stay alive forever. But I know when to be pushing up the mushrooms, flavorful and frequent. And just as I was laying knife to a sausage there was a scream. The pantry curtain flew open. The waitress scurrying out, a white plate breaking on her head, and chased by a steamy faced girl, her hair, congealed tresses scattered round her head. She was yelling that she would commit murder, that she couldn't stand it any more in this hot hole. Crying and telling them all to leave her alone. She went on breaking dishes. And selfishly, I worried for fear she would destroy my sweet. I did feel that my supper had been ruined with the indignity that was in it. But she calmed down and they gave her five minutes off to be getting this rebellion out of her head. Only for my meal, I was all tenderness for her working skin and the red blotches on her legs. But there must be discipline. However, I'm all for that moment of reverie at time of crackup.

Sebastian leaned on Mary's blunt shoulder, kissing the corner of her mouth as she twisted away.

"Don't do it where everybody can see us. Let's go look in the window of the woolen shop."

They crossed the bridge, holding hands. They looked at the pieces of cloth. Mary said she was saving to have a suit for Spring. She said her father would never let her buy any new clothes and accused her of wanting to wear them to dances.

She told Sebastian she had friends who colored photographs and some of the pictures weren't very nice. Perhaps she would do that soon because her uncle might be able to take her brothers and then she would be free. The only thing she didn't like about living in Phibsboro was that Mountjoy prison. Coming by one day she saw a man hanging between the bars and he had a funny beard and he asked me to bring him some champagne and smoked salmon. I just ran away and it's just the same with that Grangegorman, the lot of them running around in there without a brain in their heads.

They walked along the old torn houses of Dominick Street. Mary showed him a house where she lived before they moved up the Cabra Road. Saying it was an awful street with drink and them beating each other to death with bicycle chains. She was frightened out of her wits to go out at night. But in Cabra she walked in the Botanic Gardens and liked to read all the funny names in Latin on the plants, and along the Tolka, a nice river.

"I live here."

They stood in front of a red brick house.

"When can I see you again, Mary?"

"I don't know. Talk quiet and we can go in the hall. We live upstairs."

"You're a nice girl, Mary."

"You tell them all that."

"Let me kiss your hand."

"All right, if you want."

"Lovely green eyes, and black hair."

"You think I'm too fat?"

"Not at all. Are you mad, Mary?"

"Well, I'm going on a diet."

"Let me feel you. O not at all, just makes you ripe. This, just the way you want them."

"O you really are bold."

Her back against the wall, standing in front of her, arms cocked, holding her by the elbows in her plum colored coat. He kissed her and she bent her head back.

"Do you like it, Mary?"

"I shouldn't tell you that."

"You can tell me."

"But you don't kiss like the rest of them."

"Them?"

"Yes."

"But, Mary, I'm a man of refinement."

"But they don't do that."

"And they're not refined."

"It isn't that."

"I'll give you another one."

She put her arms around his back, tight and tied.

"It isn't the way they do it."

"Do you like it?"

"Why do you want to know?"

"I want to take you away."

A noise came through the ceiling. Mary stiffened, holding her head back, listening. She whispered.

"Give me your hand."

She led him to the back of the hall and down two steps behind the stairs. They waited and then she put her hand up into his hair and scratched. Good for dandruff. O the tenor of it in this hall. The safety of it. Mary, your mouth and tomato sauce.

"Sebastian is a funny name."

"Venerable."

"What?"

"That's what it means. Deserving of honor and respect."

"You're funny."

"Eeeee and eeeee and eak."

"You're a gas man."

"And you're a great build of girl."

"You're just saying that."

"O you are. Right here. Lovely. And there, too. You're just great all round."

"It isn't safe here."

"Where?"

"We could go in the back. We must be quiet."

Some light at the end of the passage. Passing a line of

broken prams, great for transport to the pawn. Could pass by any landlord. Must have the wits these days. I'm starved for love. Not ordinary love but real love. The love that's like music or something. Mary's a good strong girl for heavy work. Scrub floors and things. Get her and a house that's a box for the soul. And I'm fed up with the cardboard type. If I got Mary as the maid, Chris as the boarder, Miss Frost as secretary and Marion to run the whole lot, we'd be a great bunch. Then take my proper place in society, suits over-hauled and the rest. O there'll be changes made. I won't take any nonsense either, or concede carelessness. At least I have rules. And I know society respects a man for his discipline.

She was holding his hand, leading him. At this early hour in the morning. I must get home. And out of these dung smells. Mary pushed open the half broken door of a shed.

"Mind the bicycles. In here."

"What's that?"

"Coal."

"For the love of Jesus."

"What's the matter?"

"What's this, Mary?"

"A mattress."

The clatter of a falling broom. Mary whispering with fright:

"Jesus, Mary and Joseph."

And Sebastian, to be helpful.

"Pray for us, Blessed Oliver."

"It'll be all right. Would you like a bottle of stout?"

"Mary, I'll love you till your dying day. Where is it?"

Mary reached behind boxes and turf.

"It's the landlord's. He hides it back here for when the pubs shut. His wife raises holy murder if he brings it in the house."

"This is good of you, Mary."

"Do you say a lot of things you don't mean?"

"What?"

"What you said."

"What did I say?"

"When I said I had the stout."

"Come here and sit beside me while I open this bottle."

She came and sat on the mattress beside him, leaning against the wall, watching him with a flourish of wrist, pop the cork. We lay in the remnants of coal. And a pile of turf. I happen to know that dogs and cats prefer coal and turf. And I don't relish finding myself sitting in it.

"This is peace, Mary."

"It's quiet here."

"I need this, Mary."

"Why?"

"Lot of reasons. Little difficulties here and there. Misunderstanding mostly. A girl like you is a great comfort."

"It's not very clean or nice here."

"Come closer."

"I don't know what to say to you."

"I'm married."

"I know you are."

"I say, Good God, Jude, Joseph and a general variety of the blessed and saintly."

"But I don't care if you are. I don't think I'll ever get married."

"Don't."

"Why?"

"Might marry an Irishman."

"What's the matter with an Irishman?"

"They come home drunk and beat your head off. Jump on your arse every Saturday night and prod you to death with it. Other nights too. Pigs. You don't want that Mary."

"I might."

"Far be it, then, for me to give you advice. Get me another bottle of stout."

"You drink fast."

"Got to with the lack of decency around us, Mary."

"What do you do?"

"Read law."

"Outside that?"

"Gardening. Collect stamps, horse brasses. I'm very interested in bird watching. I refuse to gamble. Absolutely refuse to bet on a horse."

Mary's eyes broody. Sebastian leaned over and pressed his lips to her ear. Mary came down on top of him. And I put my hands up under her sweater. These two mountains up out of the sea.

"Mary, would you like to come to England with me?"

"Yes. I'll go anywhere you want me to."

"We'll need a little money."

"I have thirty pounds in the bank."

"That'll do nicely."

"But I'm not sure I can get it out."

"It's in your name?"

"Yes."

"Bob's your rudd."

Dangerfield grunting for she was no lightweight. But here was a girl good and strong, not afraid of work, I don't think. Willing to get her shoulder to the wheel. That's the trouble with the world, not enough of these people with shoulders to the wheel, letting others do the work. Kick some of the laziness out of them, out on Sundays, taking senseless rides in the country. It's painful to see them looking for something to do on a day off. I must roll Mary over on her back because lumps of coal are pressing through this mattress into my spine. Whee. Like turning turtle. Over you go. I don't think I'm quite up to this exertion. Circus, clowning, her sweater pulled up. Wow what a wench and puffing heavily. Do my most penetrating thinking just slopping around with someone else's body, penetrating to the root. How many more interesting things can be done with thirty pounds than keeping it in the bank. Her breasts are all over her chest. I haven't met with nipples like these before. A breast feeder for sure.

182

There is a restaurant in Grafton Street called the Udder Shop served by hefty wenches from the country. Teat lunch a specialty. Stop this deprivation of the breast. Because in my own case I can't get enough of them and even though I am a little tired tonight I'm enjoying playing with this strange pair.

"I've never felt this way before, Sebastian. Purple inside. Do everything to me, all the things. I want you to do everything."

"Easy, Mary. You don't want to have a baby, do you?"

"I don't care. I want everything, all of it."

"Ruin your life."

"I want it anyhow."

"Some other night when I'm prepared."

"I don't want you to use those things anyway. I want it the way it is. Go ahead."

"For Jesus sake, take it easy, Mary. Don't break it off altogether. You don't want to be a fool."

"I'm not a fool, I know what I want."

"Ruin both our lives. These babas want to eat, I can't let you, Mary. Not tonight."

"Please do it to me. I want everything. I've never felt this way before."

"You'll get this way again."

Mary ground her lips down on him. Locking her thighs on his knee, forcing him over on his back and knocking over a bottle of stout. Jesus, Mary, I can't get involved. Don't do this to me. There's enough misunderstanding in my life already without a case of illegitimacy. She's trying to force me to submit. I absolutely refuse to be taken by force. The indignity. She's quite mad. Also without any reserves. Stop at nothing.

"Someone's sure to hear us, Mary."

"Everyone's in bed. I like it."

"Mary !"

"I like it."

"Mary, really."

"You're sweet."

"Mary, we'll get caught."

"You're so sweet."

"Mary, stop."

"I like the feel of it. I've never felt it before. Is it poison?"

"It's great for sore throats."

"Cod."

"It is."

"I've touched myself with it."

"My back's killing me, Mary. Move over."

"There. Is that better?"

"Mary, my bottle of stout has leaked all over the floor."

"I've kissed it."

"My stout."

"It's not poison, sure?"

"Easy, Mary. That can hurt."

"You're sweet. I like you. I'll go away with you if you want me to."

"Be nice for a little trip. Can you save any money? Money's important, Mary."

"I only have this thirty pounds. I'm not able to save any."

"With a little care. Eke is the operative word, Mary."

"Kiss me, please."

His hand desperately clutching a bottle of stout, he kissed Mary's feverish mouth and she opened his shirt and kissed his chest. Rolling around with the flesh of it. My problems come with me wherever I go, even on detours. At least Mary and I would have enough to live on in London. A holiday for me. A job for her. Shake off a few of these Erse chains. So long as I keep out of Wales and jail. Because there I'd have cover. Eight million others. From this forlorn back cellar with Mary's bare backside pumping all over me. A time to make decisions. Set up a trip wire for Skully with a sack of you know what waiting to flop on his head. And secrecy, more silently and at night. With experimental Mary. The vision of it is almost too much. A belly of joy. Anyway, you, Mary, take what you want from me so's you won't have to be asking for more. A sexual feast if need be, anything I can give you, because I'm getting out. Let me at them. With my new tongue. I'm going to be a reality.

"I love you, Sebastian."

"Your nice little eyes, Mary."

"I want to go away with you."

"Need money for both of us."

"I have four pounds saved for my suit too."

"Better bring it."

"When am I going to see you again?"

"Not for awhile, Mary."

"Why not?"

"I've got to make plans."

"But why can't I see you?"

"My wife."

"She doesn't have to know."

"Must take precautions, Mary."

"But I want to stay with you."

"All right but we must be careful and not rush things. I can go to London first and then you can come. I'll need a little money."

"I'll give you some."

"I might need quite a bit."

"I can give you half."

"Won't need that much but we'll see."

"I want to go with you."

"I'll write to you. Care of the post office."

"All right. You will?"

"Trust me, Mary. Don't want your father to know. We want to avoid anything unpleasant."

"He's a bastard."

"Mustn't say that, Mary. He's a man who's a little confused. A lot confused like him. But never be bitter. Just remember, it's hard but it's fair. The way things are meant to be. And I don't want you to make a mistake, Mary. I'm going to give you a week or two to think it over and if, at the end

185

of that time, you still want to come, send me ten pounds. It might be difficult at first."

"I don't care, so long as you let me stay with you."

"Mary, just see if there's another bottle of stout before I go. A little sup to see me right on the long journey. See if there isn't one or two I could be carrying. Makes me think better."

"You're very fond of stout."

"Fond, Mary, is not the word. It's in me blood and a few other things as well. I want you to write to me care of The Geary Post Office. But don't use my name. I want you to use Percivil Buttermere. The spelling's important. P-e-r-c-i-v-i-l B-u-t-t-e-r-m-e-r-e."

"This is fun."

"This, Mary, is a matter of playing who lives the longest."

"You're sweet. And will we have a room together and you'll do all of it? Will we?"

"We will."

"I don't care if we die."

"Don't say that. Give God ideas. We must discourage that attitude. Just put these bottles in some paper."

"Kiss me once more."

"And don't forget Percivil Buttermere. That's very important. And I'll tell you when to send the money. And not a word to anyone."

"I won't tell anyone. I don't have anyone to tell anyway."

"Got to go."

"Once more with your tongue."

There was yelling going on in Mary's house and no screams from her. I got out of the street fast. Passed by the cattle market. And men growling at the bullocks. Which is which. They were prodding moaning beef through the gates and they'll shoot them in the head or put them on the ship. This night's over. Means waiting for another.

A fresh, new morning. A few souls in the streets. He went into a public house where old men sat, hands around pints of cider, spitting narrowly in the sawdust. Conversation ceased as Dangerfield came in. Each took a turn to look around.

> There was a man
> Who made a boat
> To sail away
> And it sank.

17

My eyes are glued together. Feet blistered. What have I
done?

At least I'm not in jail. Lay a bit to get the latitude and
longitude. I'll never do this again. Seems I had something to
do with cattle. And with drink. And with several parties.
And pints of cider. Claws the brain apart. I don't like this
when I don't even know what month it is. Who's been
meddling with the dresser and pulling out the drawers? And
I've only got a sheet and coat over me. Marion? Just a mattress on her springs.

He sat up. Rubbed the flakes out of the eyes. The door
bell ringing. Close the watertight compartments. Latch the
hatches. Seal up, we're going down you mad bastards. The
back door.

Sebastian crawled naked through the morning room into
the kitchen. Turned the key and scrabbling back to the
morning room, waiting under the table. Through the mirror
on the opposite wall he saw the cap of the mailman pass by.
I've got to see the postman. Get a blanket off Miss Frost's bed.

The mailman coming around the side. Dangerfield opening
the door.

"I say there."

"I was just around the back. Thought you might not hear
the bell. I have a registered letter for you, sir. There was no
one in yesterday."

"Been out. I was just taking a bath."

"Will you sign here, please? Sorry to disturb you, sir. Be
a bit warmer today."

"I sincerely hope so. Thank you very much. If ever you
don't find me in, just put it under the door."

"And there's one more."

"Right."

"Thank you, sir."

"Good day"

Good mailman that. Write to the Minister of Posts and Telegraphs and have that man moved up. Just get a knife and slit these.

Dear Mr. Dangerfield,

I have tried, without success, to get in touch with you at your present address. I am sending this letter by registered post in the hope that it will finally reach you. I have a great number of things to do and I find it hard to spare time trying to get in touch with you.

As you know you were fifty-four pounds in arrears with your rent and also that you have violated your lease which is not up until November next year, leaving fourteen months and one week and four days. I will gladly cut off one week four days if you would be considerate and send me all or part of the sum this week. My wife is not feeling too well since we have had so much trouble dealing with this property. And when we went to see the house I was sorry to find it in such a condition as to make my wife feel sick to her stomach.

I want you to know, Mr. Dangerfield, that I did not disturb anything nor look in anything that appeared to be your property. But I feel that you should know that there is a large frying pan and boiling pot missing out of the kitchen. There is only one cup left of the four supplied and two dishes, one badly cracked and needing repair, of the four supplied. The sofa is needing repair and the old, antique chair with the round knobs is gone completely from the drawing room. The Axminster rug is covered in soup stains and other stains which my wife, thinking of your wife, wishes me not to disclose. I had the plumber in at considerable expense to myself to see the lavatory and he claims the lead pipe was hacked apart with an object which may have been an axe, and found other holes of a suspicious nature.

It is not for me to advise concerning your living methods, Mr. Dangerfield, but it causes my wife great grief that an American gentleman such as yourself should perhaps not keep up the standards we mutually know as Americans, but my wife and I are still proud of the citizenship we acquired in that land across the seas.

Before closing, I will mention that the ceiling in the bedroom has fallen down to a great extent which would be such a blow to my wife that I did not let her go upstairs in the house. The two mirrors are gone, one which was antique and hard to come by and a lace curtain from the front room and nine pieces of assorted cutlery. I would be glad to overlook such minor things as stains on the rug and of grease on the stove if I got satisfaction in the way of some payment this week. My wife has been making a number of visits to the doctor since she has been feeling so ill over the breaking of the lease and I have been put in the way of a great deal of expense. I know, Mr. Dangerfield, that you will come through and I would appreciate it if you would let me know when you are in, as it is a long drive when I don't get satisfaction. I do not want to get in touch with my solicitor yet as I feel perhaps you have just been a little busy with your little baby and have happened to overlook the little debt now outstanding between us. My regards to your wife, who both my wife and I hope is enjoying her good health.

Respectfully yours,
Egbert SKULLY.

Dear Mr. Skully,
I have caught my neck in a mangle and will be indisposed for eternity.

Yours in death,
S. D.

Why can't we all be little friends. Friends of Jesus. Not a sound in the house, must be made of rubber.

He put on the gas, filling the teapot. Miss Frost was always good for a shilling in the meter. Now what's this from O'Keefe? Kenneth, what news? What fearful news have you? Don't tell me anything unpleasant, will you now, nothing unpleasant. Just nice things. I think I'm going to go bye bye. All alone in this house. And afraid of getting that last and final chill, the one to be avoided at all costs. This world which has caused me so much distress and indignity. I'm heartbroken and frightened. But before I go down, pack up, dry up or waste away, a few people are going to know about it. Kenneth, don't be unkind.

Dear Phony,
    No money. As I expected. Right. I know your affairs are in a mess. I can't stick it here any longer—as you say, funt. Now I would like to make this arrangement with you. Don't send any money here to me because I am coming back to the ould sod, arriving next Monday. Three weeks ago I wrote to the *Irish Times* to send a paper. And I got a job. Ever hear of Lady Eclair, Roundwood, Co. Wicklow? Well evidently Lady Eclair wants to do the thing properly and wants a French Chef. You can gather the rest. For all practical purposes, I am now a frog.
    I feel that there may be opportunities in the kitchens of Lady Eclair for romance with the scullery maids who will be under my lascivious thumb. Now I don't know for sure whether I have this job but Lady Eclair says she will pay my fare to Ireland and this is where you play the lead. I want you to arrange to have seven (7) pounds waiting for me so that I won't starve in that agricultural country.
    I find that hunger puts one at a disadvantage when dealing with people who eat three times a day. I'm depending on you.
    I have abandoned homosexuality for it has only succeeded in complicating my life further. I have been satisfying myself by hand as usual but find it very boring. However, I had written what I called "A Beginners Guide to Masturbation" in Greek to add sophistication, but gave

it up in despair. That was when I decided to try to get back to the ould sod. If I must be celibate I may as well live where celibacy is a virtue. I speak French enough to be phony. I've told Lady Eclair I was educated in England and have travelled extensively in America.

Have that seven quid. Or else I'll be kaput and at the conversational mercy of Lady Eclair whom I want to impress with my command of the English language and also any items of interest I should spot around the house. I also want to appear temperamental as this will give me a certain amount of leeway and perhaps I can meet some of her rich guests after they have feasted on the food from my well run kitchen. If things go wrong I can always suggest that Lady Eclair sail a nate in a sauce boat. Don't let me down.

God bless you,
Kenneth O'KEEFE
Acting Duke of Serutan.

Kenneth, we all want wampum. And as you must know, if only I had some I would be only too willing to share. But the only thing I have here is a pile of business magazines which I am going to burn for a fire.

Day is covered in clouds, high gray sea and white horses. Be wild and fretful all along the coast. A day like this when I used to watch the brave men out on the grave water. And seals popping up. If a yellow light bobs on the end of land that means a fearful thing. Out there, death and disaster.

Sebastian went looking for aspirin. The house looks unusually empty. The closet. Marion's clothes are gone. Just my broken rubbers on the floor. The nursery. Cleaned out. Bare. Take that white cold hand off my heart.

Feverishly around the house again. Pulling out all the drawers, tearing through the closets. Sewing kit gone, and balls of yarn. No message, no sign. Into the desk. Locked. He took the poker and smashed it through the smooth veneer. Curled his fingers round the side and ripped off the cover.

Inside, neat and clean, and empty. But for a few of my calling cards. Through the kitchen. Looking in the garage. Gray puddle of water coming in under the door. No pram. An empty shell of concrete blocks.

Back to the pot boiling on the stove. Tea and aspirin. Auburn is tea. And tea is about all there is. This is a day when they put the clods on the pine box. Jesus, where are the warm moist winds from the Atlantic and the tropical plants in profusion. I'll die of cold. Do something. Shave. Is it true that women are frigid because men don't have beards? Marion, you've taken your hairy tits away. For butchered Christ, I'm finished. No blades. Shave with the edge of the tub. Miss Frost, I must borrow your towel, criminal, but these are desperate times. I'm going to sprinkle nitric acid on Mr. Skully's Axminster rug.

On the mantelpiece is one of my treasured possessions, my stoical statue which has a cross on the belly. I must now lie without movement, eyeballs frozen in my head. Absolute zero. So Marion has left me holding the bag in which there are two leases. There's a game called cricket. And this is a wet wicket.

Sebastian went to sleep in the supine chair. At five forty five, Miss Frost came in. In my dream I had just given orders to lower lifeboats, to start singing and a few other things and I went to the bow to lower myself into an unsinkable rubber raft. This was April 14th, 1912. And the sea was icy. The light on. Miss Frost standing in the doorway. Looking. Embarrassed.

"O, Mr. Dangerfield."

"Excuse me, Miss Frost, I'm afraid I fell asleep."

"O."

Dangerfield sweeps the rug around, covering his exposed parts.

"I'm sorry for all this mess, Miss Frost."

"That's all right, Mr. Dangerfield."

"I hate to ask for such a thing, Miss Frost, but I wonder, could you ever let me have a cigarette?"

"Certainly, Mr. Dangerfield, I'd be glad to, here."

"I really am very grateful—very grateful indeed."

"I don't know how to say this, Mr. Dangerfield, but Mrs. Dangerfield told me to tell you that she's not coming back."

"Can you tell me where she has gone?"

"She was very upset and she left without saying exactly, although I understood that she was taking the Liverpool boat and she had a ticket on the train to Edinburgh."

"Rash."

"She was disturbed."

"Couldn't have gotten my gram."

"I don't think she got a telegram."

"No. More's the pity. Avoid this misunderstanding. Rash."

"I'll clean up a little here, Mr. Dangerfield."

"O don't bother, Miss Frost. Leave it to me. I'll take care of it. Desk was a little stuck."

"O no, Mr. Dangerfield, you look so tired. I'll do it. It will only take a minute. I bought some bread and sausages. I think there are a few tomatoes in the cupboard. Would you like to share them with me, Mr. Dangerfield? You must be very hungry."

"I couldn't, Miss Frost, it's not fair."

"Please do, Mr. Dangerfield."

"Well, it's extremely kind of you, Miss Frost."

"O it's nothing at all, really."

"God damn, arse hole, bitch."

"Is something the matter, Mr. Dangerfield?"

"O no, Miss Frost—my leg a little itchy. If you'll excuse me, I think I'll change for dinner."

"Certainly, Mr. Dangerfield."

Swathed in blanket, Sebastian crept from the room. I'm an Iroquois for sure.

He put on his corduroy trousers, kept hidden and damp in a drawer. And difficulty buttoning the fly. Don't want any pink penis showing or Miss Frost will think I'm being suggestive for sure. And I could never bear another night-

194

mare due to exposure of part or parts. Must be careful of my approach to Miss Frost. Rather nice. Fine. And there weren't many of them these days. All after foul wampum. O where is the dignity? Old families and estates? Carriages and footmen? The vulgarity that has come to pass. Put them back down. Back down. And Marion with them. Sneak off, go ahead. Get out, stay out. Wouldn't give me a chance. Some day you'll show up when I'm back where I belong in this world. When I have what I ought to have. My due. And when you do. My gamekeepers will drive you out and away for good. Out. Away. Out.

He was yelling.

"Is there anything wrong in there, Mr. Dangerfield?"

"Quite all right. Everything's all right."

"Whenever you're ready, Mr. Dangerfield."

"Thank you, Miss Frost."

Finish joining this piece of copper wire around my waist. And a bit of this curtain for the scarf that's in it. Just cut it off. Cut. Cut. Cut. Fold. Like that. Hide a few of the ragged edges. Little comb of the hair. See how my teeth are. Spread the lips. Look rusty. But I have fine flared nostrils on a fine straight nose. An aristocrat wherever I flee. And my eyes are curious, big ones. They all say I have very fine eyes.

Sebastian entering the morning room. Guilty look at the destroyed desk. Miss Frost putting a great platter of sausages on the table encircled with mahogany. There was a tablecloth, back rashers. Bowl of milk and pile of neatly cut bread. Sugar. Plates clean and sparkling, a knife on one side, fork on the other.

Miss Frost sat down, her hand reaching and pulling at the end of her skirt in modesty and lurking sensuality. Dangerfield hesitant. Must let the boarder always make the first move towards the food.

"This is certainly very good of you, although I don't think it's really fair to let you do it, Miss Frost."

"It's nothing, really, Mr. Dangerfield. I enjoy having something to do like cooking."

"But after a hard day. I think it's asking too much."

"O no."

Miss Frost smiled with rather large, well shaped teeth. Something like my own. And no lipstick. Pleasant to look at her mouth. Sitting sedately across, passing me everything going. That platter there.

Sebastian took four sausages, leaving five. Meant only to take three but some uncontrollable instinct made me take four. And pass the bread to Miss Frost. Must show that I'm not all absorbed by the sausages. Marion perhaps was at her, telling a lot of lies about me. Miss Frost will find out for herself that I'm all right. If there were more people like Miss Frost, people with kindness and consideration. Her gray hair is most becoming.

"These sausages are delicious. I don't believe I've had them before, Miss Frost."

"I get them on Pembroke Road. A shop just past the bridge. Homemade."

"It just goes to show, doesn't it, Miss Frost, that there's no beating the homemade."

"I do agree, so much, Mr. Dangerfield."

"Well, how was work, Miss Frost?"

"It's always the same, I'm afraid. When I'm put working in the shop, I enjoy it because I see a lot of different people."

"And how is business?"

"It tapers off around this time. Early potatoes are being ordered now and I think it's a good time to plant fruit trees."

"Do you? This is fascinating."

"O, I think, Mr. Dangerfield, were you to do it for awhile, I think you would get very bored."

"So jolly interesting."

"It bores me."

"Bores?"

"A little. I'm tired of working for other people. I'd like to work for myself, Mr. Dangerfield. But it's so hard to get started."

196

"Yes, Miss Frost, things are a little difficult these days. Not what they used to be, of course."

"It's so true, Mr. Dangerfield. All sorts of people are keeping gardens these days. Yesterday I had a little man come in to me for petunia seeds. 'By goom' type. I assumed he was someone's gardener. Then I discovered he was a very wealthy man and keeps a big account with us. It's so hard to tell, these days."

"Extraordinary. Quite extraordinary."

Sebastian filled Miss Frost's cup with tea, reached for a piece of bread. Miss Frost had three sausages. Must show her I have no interest in the remaining two. Bide my time. Let her make the first move. Patience was the thing. Suppress these animal desires.

"Have those two sausages, Mr. Dangerfield, before they get cold."

"O I couldn't, Miss Frost, I've had much more than my share. Indeed. Won't you?"

"I've had a sufficiency."

"But I do insist that you have at least one of them, Miss Frost."

"No, really. Here, let me help you."

"Well. Must say, I am a little hungry. I'm usually very careful about my diet. Tell me, Miss Frost, do you like Ireland?"

Miss Frost chuckled softly. A gentle, sweet sound. She's very nice.

"Well, Mr. Dangerfield, it's my home, but I can't honestly say that I haven't thought of living elsewhere. I like it well enough. The people are good."

"I should say, the Erse are a very fine race. Now Wexford is your county. Would you say Wexford had a better class of people?"

Miss Frost gurgled tiny laughter.

"O I don't know, Mr. Dangerfield, but they are industrious."

"And a great characteristic."

"Work?"

"A very necessary thing for most people, Miss Frost. Now, Miss Frost, I don't want to be personal, but if you had your choice, what would you do in this world?"

"I guess, just to own my own business. What would you like, Mr. Dangerfield?"

"Well, Miss Frost, to be quite frank with you, I would like nothing better than to be an underwriter to Lloyd's or inherit a large fortune."

"Ha, ha, we would all like that, Mr. Dangerfield."

"Ha, ha, quite."

"But that isn't easy, ha, ha, ha."

"Hey, heh. No I'm afraid it isn't, Miss Frost. To be sure. Ha, ha."

"Ha, ha."

"Miss Frost, come out and have a drink with me?"

"Well."

"Come along now, you've had a hard day. And I think you deserve something after this extremely pleasant meal. Do you good to have a little walk. I know a very interesting house, The Three Eyes."

"But I don't want to give the wrong impression, Mr. Dangerfield—you know the way people talk. I know there's no harm in it. O it makes me so upset."

"Be all right. It's dark and rainy, won't see a soul."

"All right, then."

"O, just a little thing. I wonder, Miss Frost, could you do me just one little favor. I wonder could you let me have this week's rent, I'm a little short."

"I've already paid it to Mrs. Dangerfield."

"O I see, that's a little difficult. Now I don't want to inconvenience you any, Miss Frost. This is entirely up to you and I don't want you to feel obliged in any way. Could you let me have a pound of next week's rent in advance? Now don't feel any obligation whatever. I certainly would never dare think of asking such a thing save for the circumstances. You understand."

"No, I understand, but Mrs. Dangerfield took all next month's rent. In advance."

"Why that dirty bitch. I beg your pardon, Miss Frost. I do beg your pardon. I get so confused sometimes."

"That's all right, Mr. Dangerfield."

Miss Frost went to her bag on the window sill. She took a pound from her purse. Sebastian distracting his attention by bending, grunting, and tying his shoelace.

"Miss Frost, this is, indeed, most kind of you."

"It's nothing at all."

"I do hate so making these requests, Miss Frost, but could you ever lend me a scarf? I'm afraid the one I have is most unsatisfactory."

"Yes, certainly, do go and choose one. They are in the top left drawer of the dresser."

Sebastian in her room. There was a yellow one. Bright and soft.

"May I wear this one, Miss Frost?"

"Yes, certainly."

"Handsome. I like a bit of color. I think you will like The Three Eyes very much. Miss Frost. Ah, I feel quite refreshed. Sporting, in fact. Give me the facts, Miss Frost, and to hell with the fiction. I want the facts."

"Ha, ha."

They stepped down the little front porch. Sebastian offering his arm. The soft million drops coming down. She held his arm lightly. And through the middle class streets and in these windows there were comforts. Dry chairs. Sebastian whistled a tune.

On a back street, through vacant lots, lanes of the poor and whitewashed walls, folding roofs, slates shining everywhere up these black twisted streets. Chickens making noise.

The Three Eyes was small and warm. They went into the snug, sat on the hard, narrow bench. A ring of the buzzer. A head. Good evening, sir. And the drinks. Miss Frost had a glass of port.

"What made you come to Dublin?"

199

"To be a nurse."

"To abuse poor unfortunates."

"I gave it up."

"Why?"

"I didn't like it much and I didn't get along with the other girls. And the pay was bad."

"What did you do then?"

"I went to work for the Dublin Assurance Company, but I didn't like it there either. I went to England then. There was a man in the office whom I didn't fancy very much. We didn't get along."

"Why?"

"He thought a great deal of himself. He was my boss."

"I see."

"And I wasn't going to give him the satisfaction."

"You did right, Miss Frost. Now, tell me, Miss Frost, how old are you?"

"O, Mr. Dangerfield, I can't tell you that."

"O yes you can, Miss Frost."

"O I couldn't tell you. I just couldn't."

"Miss Frost. I'm your friend. Remember that. Friend. You can tell me anything, anything at all. Least of all, your age. Now how old are you?"

Sebastian reached over and covered Miss Frost's hand in her lap. Comfort in a moment of distress.

"O dear, Mr. Dangerfield, I'm thirty four."

"Excellent age. Best."

"How do you know?"

"Miss Frost, sometimes I feel fifty three. Seldom, but at times, I feel twenty. Like the days. Ever feel a Saturday on a Tuesday? Or a week of one Friday after another? Recently I've been seventy. But I remember thirty four as a fine age. Do you mind, Miss Frost, if I have another, quickly?"

"O, no. Do."

"Now, Miss Frost, let's get down to business. What do you want? What do you want out of life, anyway?"

"Dear me, what a question."

"Answer me, now. Truthfully, Miss Frost."

"Well, your question covers so much ground. There are a great number of things I want out of life. Of course, as I've said, my own shop."

"Ah, you want money, Miss Frost. Money is what you're after."

"I'd hardly put it that way."

"But that's what you'd like, isn't it?"

"Doesn't one work towards saving one's soul, too, Mr. Dangerfield?"

"People ingratiate with God. Think he can do something for them. O.K., Miss Frost, now what do you think of when you first get up in the morning?"

Miss Frost was twisting her glass and watching it.

"O just getting ready for work."

Miss Frost chuckled, a high throated one. And said she'd better go back because she had to be up early. Sebastian bought a Baby Powers. Whipped it into his pocket. Banged the door for the bartender for a quick one for the road. He put his hand in the small of Miss Frost's back, guiding her, my dear ship, out the door. Don't foul the rudder, darling.

Back at the house.

"Mr. Dangerfield, would you like me to make you some coffee. I bought some today."

"Miss Frost, do you know, you would make someone a very fine wife."

"O Mr. Dangerfield."

"You would."

"O, ha, ha. O."

Miss Frost into the kitchen. Sebastian in the supine chair, bringing it up a few notches. Poured himself a drink. Cruelty's not the word, Marion. I made every effort I could to start our little family. Things weren't ideal, but I was willing to make the best of them. I want to get out and enjoy things too. I'm human. But Miss Frost has been very good to me. The way she moves around that stove. The flex of her rump isn't bad and a good strong developed leg coming out of her brown boot. A heavy hand but that's all right. Heavy hands are sadness. Miss Frost has a rather good physique. Kind and youthful. See all the turns, cups and pits, fingers. Yum yum yummy. O aye, grip, fasten and feel. Go ahead. Good for you. I need help and a polite period of rest, of sleep, of peace, to eke out these few more weeks till I'm absolutely rotten rich.

"Miss Frost, let me pour you a little drink."

"Just a little."

"Do you know, Miss Frost, it's a great comfort to have you here."

The blood was gorging her head. Miss Frost turned away.

"I really mean that, Miss Frost."

"I like being here."

"I must apologize for subjecting you to all this upset."

"I don't mind."

"I'd hate you to be unhappy here."

"I'm quite happy. I really am, Mr. Dangerfield. I think this is the nicest house I've been in yet. It's so free and easy."

"It's that, Miss Frost—it's certainly that."

"I like things to be free and easy."

"I agree, a good way. Free and easy. Easy and free—it's the way things ought to be, and I like things that way, Miss Frost. None of these binding things."

"Yes, I think so too."

Miss Frost brought out the pot of coffee with a plate of biscuits. They smiled across the table.

"Things crop up all the time, don't they, Miss Frost? Unpleasant things. But we'll see better days. Every cloud, you know, lined with lead. I like you, Miss Frost."

"I like you too."

The biscuits were passed to Sebastian. He took four. Miss Frost stirring in the sugar. They preoccupied their eyes. O the eyes.

Yes eyes.
No eyes.
What things

They see.
Some say happiness
Others
Misery.
O the eyes.
O aye,
The eyes.

"Miss Frost?"

"Yes?"

"I'm going to be quite honest, as I know I can be with you, without being misunderstood."

"Yes, Mr. Dangerfield?"

"Miss Frost, may I sleep in your bedroom?"

There was a pause. Miss Frost's face was touched with a bit of redness. Her eyes gone down to the coffee. Sebastian continuing in the voice of good fellowship, a businesslike sound.

"I don't want you to misunderstand me, Miss Frost. I'll put my mattress on your floor. It's a rather peculiar thing with me. Having had so much upset I don't think I could bear to sleep alone. Would you mind awfully? I know it must seem a bit irregular, but dash it all, I may as well be honest."

"O no, Mr. Dangerfield, it isn't irregular at all. I know how you must feel. I don't mind. I understand what you mean."

"It's really very kind of you, Miss Frost. To take it like this."

"But are you sure you won't be uncomfortable? I don't mind sleeping on the floor, I'm used to it. I did a lot of it in the land army."

"Heh, heh, not a bit. The mattress is absolutely perfect. It's just that I hope I'm not imposing."

"You're not imposing, Mr. Dangerfield."

"I'm enjoying your coffee. Very good."

"I'm glad. I make it in a jug."

"Proper way."

"Yes."

"This has been a most pleasant evening for me, Miss Frost."

"I enjoyed it too."

"I'm glad you did."

"So many people look down on a woman who goes into a public house."

"Old fashioned, Miss Frost."

"I agree."

Miss Frost cleared away. Ran water. Hear the sound of cleanliness in there. Nothing like not facing grease slimed dishes of a morning. I'm in here getting my mattress. It's gray, striped, and a wet mass. Gently now, on the floor. I've got to have a blanket. Can't let Miss Frost see these dirty sheets—it wouldn't do. Let's go, through the door, get this chair out of the way before I let it have it. Give it the treatment. Like Skully's genuine antiques. Put back Miss Frost's scarf. Fold my trousers. Must have everything neat. My underwear is a little tattered. Whether to sleep naked or have the modesty of these torn undergarments? Modesty at all costs. These are the things that make the marriage happy. Meals on time, sugar, butter, and salt on the table. Socks darned and go to the drawer and find a clean shirt. Miss Frost was right in there with those dishes. No fuss. No excuses. Fine person. Am I smelling? Sniff a pit. Little musty. Can't have everything.

Get this blanket around now, cover up any sign of scruffiness. Miss Frost's room has some soul. Personality. Call it lived in. Perhaps I ought to appear asleep? No. None of these sneaky pretences. Lie here, forthright, honest and awake.

Miss Frost came into the room.

"Are you sure you're comfortable there, Mr. Dangerfield?"

"Quite sure. Surprisingly comfortable."

"I'll just get some of my things."

Miss Frost took her dressing gown from behind the door and a green, cellophane bag from the dresser. She went to the bathroom. Running water. Door shuts. I face a fateful week. Week of constant Mondays. I think I will set sail of a Friday. And I must play this game of not being seen, perfectly.

Miss Frost comes back.

"I'll turn off the light, Mr. Dangerfield. I hope you're all right there."

"Blissful. I know this is a dreadful inconvenience for you, Miss Frost. I want you to know I really appreciate it. I have till now counted my friends on a hand of amputated fingers."

"O Mr. Dangerfield."

Light went off. She stood at the foot of her bed, taking off her robe. I shouldn't be straining my eyes to see as much as I can. I wouldn't want her to notice. Got on green pajamas. From what I can see, they suit her. She's climbing up from the bottom of the bed. This thing, lust. Get away. Carnal appetite or overture to the orifice. Climb into her brain. She's settled in her bed. Limbs pushing around between the sheets. I'm careful to listen to those things. O there isn't much that I overlook. And Miss Frost, lying there as you are in your little bed and me here, prostrate, on the floor because everything is so tiny in the world. Over the edge, through gloom and whatnot, I see your two big toes sticking up under the covers. And if I lift my head a little I can see the rest of you. I'm so lonely and you're lonely too. Hearts clicking. Remember that. Just so many times and click, we go away in this roofless world.

"Miss Frost?"

"Yes?"

"May I hold your hand?"

Miss Frost moved her arm towards the voice and curved her wrist over the edge of the bed. And his fingers closed around her hand. I was a little boy and wet the bed because I thought I was out with a lot of other kids playing in a swamp and could piss anywhere. To touch Miss Frost seems safe and sad. Because I guess I pull her into my own pit. For company or the bones in her hand. Fingernails and knuckles. But I can tell she's tightening her grip. Her muscles tugging at my bones. Now I'm on my knees. And elbows on her bed. Her head trembling. Hair splayed gray and dark. Sighs of her mouth. Feel her sad hands around my back. Let me get in under these covers. Got her tongue touching my ear. Juice. Open the buttons, warm my cold chest with hers. Miss Frost. O Miss Frost.

She put up her back. And I'll pull down your pajamas. Throat of birth weeping. Kiss all the tears away. All gone. You've been lonely in the dark.

They lay side by side. Miss Frost held her hand to her brow. Sliding back into her pajamas. Goes to the bathroom.

"Miss Frost, bring me back a glass of water."

He was sipping it when she began to cry. He reached for her hand and she brought it away to her head. Holding her hands over her eyes.

"Now, now, this is no way to behave."

Miss Frost turning away.

"I shouldn't have done it."

"Now, now, it's all right."

"It isn't. O God I shouldn't have let you come in the room."

"Through charity."

"It wasn't. It was wrong. O dear—God forgive me."

"Don't take it like this."

"It's a mortal sin. And you made me, Mr. Dangerfield."

"You made yourself, Miss Frost."

"O God, I didn't. It wasn't my fault. I could never confess it. Why did you?"

"Why did you? Takes two to congress."

"Please don't make it worse."

"I'm not making it worse, Miss Frost. You're being very childish about this."

"I beg of you."

"You're saved if you say the act of contrition."

"I've got to tell it."

"God's in the room. Tell it."

"Don't say that—we could be struck dead."

206

"Relax, Miss Frost."

"I didn't want to do this. I know I didn't want to."

"Yes you did."

"I didn't, please, I didn't."

Miss Frost turned away on her side, her body choked and sobbing.

"Miss Frost, God is all merciful."

"But it's a mortal sin which I have to confess to the priest and it's adultery as well."

"Please now, Miss Frost. Take hold of yourself. This won't do any good."

"It's adultery."

"One mortal sin is the same as another."

"I'm damned. It isn't."

"Do you want me to go?"

"Don't leave me alone."

"Don't cry. God's not going to condemn you. You're a good person. God's only after people who are out and out bastards, habitual sinners. You must be sensible."

"I'll have to give your name."

"You what?"

"Your name. I'll have to tell it to the priest."

"What makes you think that? Nonsense."

"He'll ask me."

"Not at all."

"He will. And they'll send the priest to my mother."

"Ridiculous. The priest's only there to forgive your sins."

"No."

"Miss Frost, you've done this before."

"Yes."

"For Christ's sake. And they sent the priest to your mother?"

"Yes."

"And they asked the name of the man?"

"Yes."

"I can only say that it's just fantastic. And when did it happen?"

"When I was twenty."

"How?"

"A man who worked for us. They sent me to a convent in Dublin to do penance. The priest said he wouldn't give me absolution till I gave up his name. And you're a married man."

"You're afraid of the priest?"

"Yes."

"There's a special church on the quays where you can confess these things. I'll find out for you."

"God, don't. I couldn't be seen there. It's not respectable."

"Sin, Miss Frost, is never respectable. Now just relax a little and everything's going to be all right."

"I don't know what to do."

"All priests' confessionals are not the same. Ask around for a sympathetic one."

"I know them and I couldn't ask anyone about such a thing. Word would get around."

"Go to sleep now, it'll be all right in the morning."

Sebastian put his hand out to her. Few friendly pats on the shoulder. She dried her tears and blew her nose. I took a sip of water and swallowed for the quench that was in it. Miss Frost had closed her eyes. She would sleep. She had a nice little salary, nothing to worry about. She may as well get as much as she can and confess it all at once. O Lord, for all thy faults I love thee still. And will he ask you, did you wiggle? Your nates. There must be a lot of steps to heaven. And Ireland is closest of all. But they're ruining Jesus with publicity.

18

At six a.m. on Monday morning, Sebastian climbed over the body of Miss Frost, and touched his way through the dark to the bathroom. Using Miss Frost's scented soap to wash the face and around the ears and the back of the neck. Then throw the icy water generously over the head for the stimulation. Good habit of a morning. And toothpaste, brush way back there round these molars.

Tiptoe back into the room and into Miss Frost's dresser. Pull the drawer out slowly. Miss Frost sleeping soundly. Take the drawer out into the hall and borrow one of these blouses. Whoops. Drawer out too far. Have lost touch with it in the dark. What calamitous clatter.

Miss Frost was awake with a dreadful fear in her voice.

"Who's that?"

"Me."

"O Jesus, Mary and Joseph. What happened?"

"Little accident."

"O."

I think this is the first early morning conversation I've ever had with Miss Frost.

Talking through the dark.

"I wonder, Miss Frost, could I ever trouble you to borrow one of your blouses?"

There was silence. Dangerfield standing, unclothed in the darkness. He waited. Her voice a little high, touch of uncertainty.

"Of course, do."

"God bless you and keep you always."

Sebastian groping on the floor for the drawer, dragging it with a chair out of the room. Had the light been on I would have been mortified. The naked are defenceless. I think night is my best friend. And death an obstacle to overcome till the good ripe years of lust, gluttony and sloth. I have lain in my lair with blankets tacked up over strategic windows. Miss Frost has been good to me. Leaves me breakfast. But I have been put to oakie cakes. My last unpalatable resort. I'm down to my accent.

She gets all upset. And remorseful. Cloacal communion isn't the great fun it was. I comforted her with readings from this Aquinas because he says it's good for you. And I said, tenderly earwards, heads on the pillow, that from manure, lilies grow. To know the real goodness one had to be bad and of sin. What good is it to God, dear Miss Frost, for a child to be born pure, to live purely and die purely. Where was the grace in that shallow, white sterility? You don't want that stuff. No. Get down in it, down. The greatest whiteness is touched with black. The righteous were a sneaky bunch anyway. And she took this little comfort. Nude and at my side, saying, if my mother ever got wind of it, it would kill her. Even to confess on the quays, Mr. Dangerfield, would have the bishop to this very doorstep and I'd be put into the nuns. My dear Miss Frost, were we to get the bishop here, I think, I myself would join the priests.

He found a yellow shirt. For the cheerfulness. And Miss Frost would never miss one of her vests. I must have warmth. Cold as a eunuch's balls on the quays.

He dressed and went into the morning room and put a few oakie cakes in his raincoat, took down a curtain rod and stepped out into the cold, dark morning. Passing through the limp front gate, sauntering down the street, sucking in the atmosphere.

Run the curtain rod on these rungs of gates. Everything is wet and silent. White, low clouds. Some light flicking on in the houses. Here comes a milkman whistling. And I hear the roaring tram. Morning is great.

Walking down the Custom House Quay, the cobbled street filling with the rumble of carts and huge, pounding horses. Stand back and watch them go by. Taxis and hansoms collecting at the boat exit.

Dangerfield leaning against the warehouse wall across the street from the third class door. Giving final attention to his clothes, little nip at the tie and the rather fashionable long collar of Miss Frost's blouse. Good to see O'Keefe again.

The passengers coming out. Sebastian rapping his curtain rod against the building. He took out an oakie cake, crunched it, and ate. Stale fat. Dry and gluey.

Suddenly framed in the door, the half man, half beast, red bearded jaw, the same green shirt he left in, same trousers. Kit bag slung across his chest, same smileless sad face. He paused, looked at a newsboy suspiciously and bought a paper. He opened it quickly, closed it quickly, sticking it under his arm. He threw his kit bag strap higher on his shoulder with an awkward flick, and bending slightly forward, lowering his head, started to drive forward up the quay and stopped. Turning his head slowly. His eyes met those of the silent, austere spectre of Sebastian Dangerfield whose cadaveric lips, widening, showed his newly brushed teeth, as he leaned carefully against the bricks.

Dangerfield crossed the dung-covered street. Reached into his pocket and stretched forth his hand to the waiting O'Keefe.

"Kenneth, will you have an oakie cake?"

"I figured on this."

"On what, Kenneth?"

"Oakie cakes."

There was an evil laugh.

"Kenneth, aren't you glad to see me? To have me welcome you back to this green garden in the sea?"

"That depends."

"Come, my dear Kenneth, put down this animal caution. Just look. The commerce, barrels and barrels, steel girders and see these fine beasts, ready to be cut to size. A grand prosperous country."

"We'll see."

They walked by the huge boxes and stopped to let a drove

of bullocks pass across the street through the lifting, half light. The wild fearful eyes of these animals. A long line of spidery bikes, flowing along the edge of the sidewalk and the taxis and horse cabs coming up from the ship. They were cold figures passing on into this ancient, Danish city.

19

They had come to Woolworth's Café for breakfast. Sun was out. Sitting, facing one another across the white table. Bacon and eggs, tea, bread and butter. Yummy.

"Kenneth, let me hear about your travels."

"Dull."

"Did you go to a professional in Paris?"

"No. Lost my nerve at the last minute."

"I take it then—?"

"That I didn't have a smell."

"Quite. It's a pity, Kenneth. Something will have to be done for you. An arrangement made. Bring you to the Congo or something. How would you like a Pigmy?"

"Where's this seven quid?"

"Be all right, now. Don't worry about a thing. Taken care of. Just tell me, what else happened?"

"Nothing. I got nothing. Just nothing. Wrestling in the dark with this student and I gave that up because it wasn't getting me anywhere and was driving me crazy. The only thing that kept me from going completely around the bend was this fantastic correspondence with Lady Eclair."

O'Keefe quickly slitting the soft tissued white of egg. Wiping up fat with a piece of bread. They could see from this window down into the early morning stirrings of Dublin.

"It was really fantastic. I told you about the ad for a chef. I write and get this reply written in the third person, Lady Eclair would like to know if Kenneth O'Keefe is Protestant or Catholic. I wrote back that Kenneth O'Keefe is neither and will not require to be delivered to Church on Sundays. She writes back, Lady Eclair feels that Kenneth O'Keefe should have some religion because everyone needs a church for the development of their immortal soul. So I said that Kenneth O'Keefe's immortal soul is already developed there-

213

fore did not find churches useful. Next letter she says Lady Eclair would like to quote from Proverbs, 'Poverty and shame shall be to him that refuseth instruction but he that regardeth reproof shall be honoured.' I answered that Kenneth O'Keefe has already suffered much poverty and shame while a member of the Church of Rome and that 'The simple believeth every word; but the prudent man looketh well to his going.' "

"And you're hired?"

"So far. This religion business will present a problem. I'm suspicious about people interested in saving other people's souls. Where's the money?"

"I beg of you. Eke. Beg. Patience. Kenneth."

"What's in this house. Does it have a toilet?"

"Every amenity. A place for soap. Four gas burners. Wooden floors. Bit of the damp and loneliness."

"Your own kitchen?"

"Everything, Kenneth."

"And you're alone?"

"No."

"You're not alone?"

"Exactly."

"Who's living with you?"

"Not with, Kenneth. In the house. A Miss Frost. A charming young lady from Wexford. I'll have you meet her."

"Marion. Where did she go?"

"Away. Scotland. Not feeling well."

"What's the matter? She pregnant?"

"I hope not. Now I think I can see you right. Come out to the Geary with me."

"Doesn't Marion mind your being in the house alone with Miss Frost?"

"Hardly think so. Miss Frost is a very good Catholic. Quite above board. No fear, no scandal, Kenneth. A most interesting person."

"You've got money out there?"

"Just come."

214

"God damn it. You've got nothing on you?"

"I'm a little short."

"God damn it. I knew it was going to be like this. All right, I'll pay the bill. I'm just an utterly defeated bastard."

Dangerfield leaning back. Wiping the mouth. Waitresses watching them. O'Keefe led the way down the stairs. His jutting red beard. Put his hands in his pocket. Dangerfield behind him, walking curiously.

"What's the matter with you?"

"This, Kenneth, is the spider walk. I've been trying to perfect it for some time. You see, every two steps you bring the right foot across from behind and skip. Enables one to turn around without stopping and go in the opposite direction."

"What for?"

"I'm a little self-conscious about turning around these days. Mobility is what I like, Kenneth."

They were approaching the bottom of Grafton Street.

"I'm thirsty, Kenneth."

"Yeah."

"Drink of water."

"Go into a shop. They'll give you water."

"That's very complicated."

O'Keefe suspicious. Jaw clamped. Walking faster.

"Now, Kenneth, is there anything wrong with wanting a little drink of water."

O'Keefe stopped. Threw his hands in the air. Eye wide. Screaming.

"You God damn drunkard. Damn this damn country. Drink is the curse of this country. God damn it."

The crowds stepped back to make room for this shouter. Dangerfield abandoning his spider walk set off swiftly across the street towards O'Donogue's Public House. He missed the door. A great slap of body into the wall. He stood there stunned. Scratching at the bricks.

O'Keefe watching him, broke into wild laughter. The

crowd stepped back further. When shouters laugh, there's violence.

O'Keefe speaking to the crowd.

"Can't you see I'm mad? Drink is the curse of this damn country."

He followed Dangerfield who was standing, a bit twitchy inside the pub door.

"For God's sake, Kenneth, what's the matter with you? Do you want to have me spotted?"

"You bastard, you got me into a pub anyway. Boy did you look silly running into the wall."

"Well I think you're cracking up."

"I've come back to this place after putting in a half year of loneliness, not enough to eat, no sex life, nothing and this is what I have to face. No money waiting and I'm not going to buy you drink. I just can't stand it. I don't want this life anymore."

"Kenneth, you're upset. Now don't be upset. I know you've had a hard time of it and I want to see you enjoy your return."

"Shut up. Get your drink. Here. Take this. Get it but shut up. Drink, drink—go ahead."

Sorrowfully, Dangerfield took the half crown. He whispered to the man behind the bar. He came to O'Keefe with a pint of cider and a pint of stout for himself. In O'Keefe's eye, a bit of mist. Dangerfield put the pennies change down. O'Keefe swept them aside. Sebastian put them in his pocket.

"Look, Dangerfield. When someone farted in my house you could smell it in every room. At every meal there were seven pairs of hands reaching for a pile of spaghetti. Fights and yapping. Yap, yap, yap. I'm here because I want to get out of that forever and there's one thing that will get me out and that's money. I don't give a damn what you do, drink yourself to death, murder Marion, but me, I've had all I want. What have I got to show for two years over here? This sack has everything I own in the world."

"I'm only trying to be of help, Kenneth."

"Well you're not. You're sucking me down. I don't want you on my back."

"You don't mean that, Kenneth."

"I mean it. I don't care if I never see you again as long as I live. You could be dying in the gutter, I don't care. All I want is my money and you can go and drink yourself to death."

"O hard words, Kenneth."

"What the hell have I got to show for all the time I've been over here? Nothing. And it's because of people like you. The Irish are all the same wherever they go. Faces compressed into masks of suffering. Complaining and excuses. And the Irish rasping, squabbling and bickering. Hear me? I'm sick of it. I hate it. I thought you got places when you learned to be an electrician. Good steady job. Good money. Have kids. I don't want kids. I don't want to be sucked down. And listen to some priested mick saying this is the second Sunday after Pentecost, there will be a communion breakfast next Sunday, and I want to see you all put a dollar in the basket. And every time I get a chance to get out of it, something screws me."

"O you're distraught, Kenneth. Now calm. And remember poverty is sacred. But don't strain to get away. All these other things will come. Let me sing you a little song."

> All the way
> From the land
> Of Kerry
> Is a man
> From the dead
> Gone merry.
>
> This man
> Stood in the street
> And stamped his feet
> And no one heard him.

20

They arrived in the Geary. The sea is right down those streets lashing and lapping. And have to bend down to get under these clouds. O madam bend over, I want to tell you something. Out here it's like soft bread and fish things burrow and hide. I used to climb around here. Get the tiny creatures caught in these crystal cradles of rock. Like me. Until they take the fearful sun away and give me a bosom of deep.

In the post office. Of the Geary. Dangerfield approached the counter abruptly. Clicked his heels.

"I say, my good man, would you see if there is a letter for Percivil Buttermere?"

Clerk turning to the row of boxes. Dangerfield rotating on his ankles. O'Keefe standing glumly aside. An apostate. Man murmuring seeing is. Pound in the pocket is twenty in the post. There were guilty smiles.

"Have faith, Kenneth. They say they build a lot of things on that. O I wish the world had more faith."

"I've no sympathy for the grief it's causing you."

Clerk going through the butter. Pulls out a letter for a good look. Puts it back. Comes to the end. Grumbling is heard and mumbling.

"Sorry sir, no Buttermere."

"I say, doo ding dong, there must be some mistake. A mistake, I say. Or said."

O'Keefe drew his shoulders up around his head. And let them down slowly. A shift of the pack and he bent towards the door. Drove his weary self out into the street.

"I'll take another look for you, sir."

"Would you. Very urgent matter."

Clerk, nearsighted and whispering.

"There's Butcher, Buttimer—there's Buttermede."

"I say, ding dong, that may be it."

"Blotted."

"Let me see it."

Sound of ripping.

"This is it. Ding dong. Come up you numb bunch of bastards out of that hold and batten down or something."

"What, sir?"

"A sentiment."

"O."

A cat, his eyes afire. There were three five pound and broken notes. And a letter. And a moment of hesitation and instant of animal. Reading these sweet Erse words.

TA GUIG PUINT STERLING INIOCTHA AS AN NOTA SO LE N-A SHEALBHOIR AR N-A EILEAMH SAN SO I LUNDAIN.

Out into the street. Alone. Did I say that this faith was rampant? Or did I say it was just like hot tamale. Check me please. O yes, put this brown stuff in my pocket. If I can get up the street away. O'Keefe gone.

Sebastian went hurriedly to a building with an eagle over the door in which they were serving liquor.

"Good day, sir."

"Good day. Put a bottle of brandy on the bar."

"All of it, sir?"

"All."

A figure appeared. Beside Dangerfield. And an out-stretched hand. Hungry palm.

"O.K."

"Kenneth, won't you join me?"

"Just give me my money. You would have left me without a cent."

"Had to get change."

"You're a no good bastard and where's that money coming from?"

"Ye of little faith. This is going to be a great night. Have you got your coffee grinder?"

"Give me the money."

"All right, Kenneth, if you prefer. But I can only spare four."

"God damn it. Give me the four then."

"Be my guest. We'll have dinner with Miss Frost. Be nice. I think she gives, Kenneth. Might be worthwhile looking into it. Wouldn't you like a bit of that thing they do in the dark?"

"You're just a son of a bitch. You'd leave me to return to Dublin without a penny. Tomorrow I see Lady Eclair and I want nothing to screw this deal. I have to get the eleven-thirty bus to Roundwood. I'm going."

"Don't leave, for the love of God, Kenneth."

"I know you. I don't want to see life through a haze. You'll be talking with some bogman all night."

"Now, Kenneth, you're a man who speaks fluent Greek and Latin, a man of much useless knowledge, schooled in culture, who knows what Plato said to his boys, buggering them in the bushes. Where do you think this harshness is going to get you? I'm going to report you to the Legion of Mary."

"I'm going."

"Jesus, stay. I beg of you, Kenneth. Don't leave me in this time of want. Or wampum. Drink up. Motto. Drink up. Come on, Kenneth. Snap out of it. A great world this."

"Where did you get the money?"

"From across the seas."

"Yeah?"

"Absolutely."

"Sounds fishy to me."

"The name of Dangerfield has never and will never be touched with such."

"You're up to monkey business."

"These are strange times, Kenneth. Very strange. There's a world out there with people with eyes and mouths. The eyes see these things and the mouths want the things the eyes see. O but they can't have them. That's the way things are arranged. Got to have things unequal or nothing would happen. Men like yourself who want to have carnal knowledge of the female nates and boob-si-boobs and the other thing they have up there between the legs that we can't get at so easily without first twisting off the garters and whalebone. It's there, but you can't have that."

"I'll get it."

"And I hope you do. But if you get put down without it, don't be bitter, Kenneth. Those things are for a reason. Saints and things. You're a man equipped for old age. Don't waste your time on this sexual appetite. I think we are natural aristocrats of the race. Come before our time. Born to be abused by them out there with the eyes and the mouths. But the likes of me, Kenneth, get it rectally from all manner of men. The professional classes take exception and it is among this class that I would take up my place but they want to make mock of me and drive me out, rip my privates away and put them on a public pole with a sign, Dangerfield is dead. That's what they want to hear. But there's no bitterness in me. Only love. I want to show them the way and I expect only taunts and jeers. But there are the few who listen. Worth it all. I put this to you, Kenneth. Go back. Go back to this church of yours. Put down these things of making money and living in a fine big house with nice comfortable chairs and an Irish maid putting logs on the fire and bringing in the tea. Get these tweed suitings out of your mind and trousers lined with satin and put down the desires of the flesh, nipple nuttiness, nate needy, boob bothered. You don't want an M.G. and a manservant, shallowness and deceit, or lawns to the lake and garden sets where one sits thinking of more money. All I want out of this life, Kenneth, is my rightful place and for others to keep theirs. The common people back down where they belong. And if it's not too much to ask, Kenneth, how do I pass these exams?"

"Study."

"My mind's a blank."

"What the hell is the matter with you?"

"Kenneth, I'm beaten. I'll never pass. I must dine with my tutor but I can't appear wearing these frightful rags and with hunger written around the eyes."

"God damn it, in spite of everything, I love this country."

"Why Kenneth, are you off your jump completely?"

"I love it."

Dangerfield's face the color of gold, eyes, bright fires. O'Keefe hoisted himself on a stool, his pack hanging between his legs. Sebastian pouring out the brandy.

"It's good to have someone to talk to, Kenneth. I've been a bit on my own lately."

"This country can be so damn exasperating but just to be in Dublin sort of gets me all excited. I tingle in all my bones. And with nothing but four pence for a cup of coffee in Bewley's. I used to lie awake at night memorizing new French words and dreaming about coming back. If I could open up a restaurant with the money saved from this job, I'd be set."

"All you would need would be some chairs, tables, forks and lots of rancid grease."

"Yeah."

"Be very fashionable."

Dangerfield pointing east with a nervous finger.

"I'm going over there, Kenneth. Across the Irish Sea and there will be a bit of the good life. I've got plans. If one stays in the land of the crut too long it gets a bit tight around the various glands. Sun and the dance. And perhaps the song."

"Well have your song and dance, I've got to go. So long."

"Don't."

"So long."

O'Keefe turned and pushed through the door. Dangerfield counting the swinging of the hinges.

I'm a friend of all kinds. And animals too so long as they don't get rough. Some of them have to be put in the cages but o aye, they deserved it. Everything is always fair and square, anyhow. Part of the rules. Heavy breasted Mary and your foul father. Chasing you around the house, you in your

222

nightdress, he with a broom. One doesn't know what goes on in these suburban houses. Must watch for these incestuents. I have a friend in Miss Frost and Mary has faith. Must read this little note.

Dear Sebastian,

I hope this finds you all right. Please write to me and tell me. Please try to arrange to see me because I'm very lonely, and worried because my father is suspicious and threatening to write to the bank. Tell me what day I should leave for London and where I should meet you. The boys have gone to Cavan to stay on my uncle's farm.

Please think of me and write to me. I want to see you so much, and want to be in bed with you. Write, please.

Love,
MARY.

He moved out with bottle. Under the eagle. Into good air. Night and Ireland. Like licking moisture from leaves. Eating up green. And up the Geary Road. I do not trust this acute joy. Misery is my forte. O'Keefe will be caught by Lady Eclair. Be on a maid. And Eclair will beat his bottom with a Bible. Poor chef. I'd put it that there are only a few more days before I see the end.

He pushed in the front gate. A bit twisted. A light coming through the garage window from the kitchen. Must watch that. I'll just pretend I'm Egbert and check up. A few windows need attending to. The back door locked. Good thing, Miss Frost. That's the way I like to see things, everyone on their toes.

Sebastian knocked. Miss Frost's shadow twisting the key. She smiled. A little shy around the eyes, a little embarrassed around the teeth, her face atwinkle.

"Good evening, Miss Frost. A bit of softness."

"Good evening, Mr. Dangerfield, are you very wet?"

"No. Pleasant out. Nice smell."

"A friend of mine got me some sausage meat from Bray."

"Jolly good show. How are you, Miss Frost—tell me, how are you?"

"O, I'm all right. A little tired. I was in the shop today."

"On your feet?"

"Yes."

"Miss Frost, give me a kiss."

"O, Mr. Dangerfield."

Sebastian approaching in the hard kitchen light. He put the brandy on the table and reached out for her wrist. Tightening his fingers around the bone and she let go of the frying pan and it fell on the floor. Miss Frost in her gray sweater and her mouth a little uncontrolled. This evil man from Mars, hand on the flat of her back. Pressing with dignity. And whatever else happened, if we have that, we're all right. Whispering in Miss Frost's ear.

"Miss Frost, you have a lovely nape of neck. Chew your ears. Ever chew ears? O Miss Frost, chewing ears is the thing, down on the lobes. Especially the lobes. Get down on those soft things of flesh."

"O, Mr. Dangerfield, you'll bite them off."

"Tender."

"You like them that way?"

"Mixed with eyes."

"Hee, hee."

"Eyes."

"You go on."

"Miss Frost, are we going to put the sausage in that nice pan? Lash it with a bit of butter. Sizzle. O I think we're going to like this with the drink that's in it. Now would you say, Miss Frost, that there's a bit of drink to go with it?"

"Hee, hee. O please. Dear me."

"Give you a little bit of the mouth along the shoulders. You'll take this off later like a good girl, Miss Frost. Later? Yes? Smell them. The sizzle. The silly sizzle of them, Miss Frost. And do you know, Miss Frost, you're a very fine person."

"You've had a few."

"Five for the road. Never let it be said that I took to the highway or even byway without fuel for me little heart. Hear it in there. Go ahead, feel it. Here. Little feeble now until I get my fangs fastened to this meat. Meat."

"Dear me."

Sebastian released Miss Frost from his arms. Your gray sweater and their shape in there. And your hips have a nice swell. Want to press a tip of warm nose in your white cool ear. And smelling this new bread. Get the juices well around the teeth. I think, Jesus, we're just two little bread breakers. I want a big loaf. Big enough to get inside. Safety. Miss Frost, take my clothes off and put me in a big loaf of bread. A touch of gold on the crust. Float my ears and eyes. Do that, put me in there and save me. Little naked body, shrivelled with fright of the world and cock by which I'll poke my way to poverty and my tiny buttressed buttocks, fold me all up like these noiseless nomads and put me in the bread. Don't burn my balls, just brown and cozy, fat with fine crust. And take me out in the morning baked to a fine turn and put it on the table. And I'll be there inside. My little self with my lovely strange eyes looking better than ever. Then, Miss Frost. Eat me.

Dangerfield cutting the bread. A nice little pile now. I feel I'm just a crazy boat on British waters screaming what ho bastards on port, starboard and everywhere. Are you mad? Want us to founder? Or spill me into the sea? Or twist me in the rigging. Fire all the guns. We're at sea you bunch of vulgar pigs and when I tell you to fire, fire. Batten down all balls and by Jesus, any erection gets the guillotine.

"Miss Frost, I've a declaration to make. I love you."

"Mind, you'll cut yourself, Mr. Dangerfield."

"But love."

"You're just going on."

"Let me repeat. I love you."

"I don't believe it."

"I mean it, Miss Frost, and there's not many or none I can say it to. I only feel that it's better to be in this world with a few polite possessions than without. Get that meat in there. See there's a way of doing it so O'Keefe says, give the pan a bang just here and it slides nicely around. I am partial to the oil of the olive. Now have a little drink. Have you ever seen a color like it? Little sniff? Would you say there is a bit of mellowness there now, Miss Frost, would you say that?"

"It's very nice."

Miss Frost leaning against the sink, watching Sebastian carefully from glistening eyes. He was sitting on this white kitchen chair, waiting for the fry. And sticks his finger into the sausage meat and sucks the stickings down his throat.

"It's so very good, Miss Frost. Now there's another shop on the Pembroke Road that sells a meat that would put ten years on your life. Need a little garlic."

"O no, Mr. Dangerfield. Garlic?"

"Why yes, Miss Frost, garlic, of course garlic."

"But it smells."

"That's what we want, Miss Frost. We want that smell. O I'm going to see some times yet. I'm thinking seriously of buying a large new cup for the breakfast. I love breakfast. Going to be a few changes made. A lot of changes. Some big. Some small. Miss Frost, can I rely on you not to spill a bean or utter a word? Can I? Even though they take the hook to you and other Irish instruments as well, yes?"

"Yes."

"Miss Frost, this is top secret, an affair of state the like of which would finish Ireland were it ever to get out, and me as well. I'm going to London on Friday."

"You're not."

"I am."

"What will you do?"

"A few little things. General clearance. Need a little rest from tension. Few matters need clearing up, tiny grains of sand in the vaseline. Miss Frost, I like you very much. Do you know that?"

"O Mr. Dangerfield. But I don't know about all that's happened. I like you."

"Know what, Miss Frost?"

"Between us and things."

"Tell me."

"I don't know. Sometimes I feel I'm right and then I don't know what's going to become of me. In my church it's a mortal sin. God forgive me I wish it weren't true and that it was all a pack of lies. And they watch me in the shop. If it's ever found out, I think I'm going to die and with this sin I'd be doomed forever to hell."

"Have a little more, Miss Frost."

Filling her glass with brandy.

"No more than that, please."

"Tell me now."

"And a country like this has nothing for a girl like me. That I won't be able to get married until I'm too old and they want so much money and a farm and anything they can lay their hands on. That's all they ever look for is the money. You're one of the first people I've ever met for whom money doesn't mean everything."

"Well, I don't know, really, I wouldn't say that was entirely true, Miss Frost."

"This isn't a country for women."

"I would say that was true."

"And I've had horrible dreams. They frighten me. I don't think we should do it ever again. I wish I could go away. I know they are talking about me at work."

"Now Miss Frost, don't let these little things upset you. Don't let them do that."

"But it's more than that."

"Nothing is more than that."

"If someone gets word that I'm living alone with you in this house without Mrs. Dangerfield here, it would be the end of me. And they find out, they don't miss anything. They would go to the priest, and he would be down here in a minute."

"So long as there's drink, we're right for him, Miss Frost. Take it from me."

"I've seen people watching."

"When?"

"For a long time from across the street."

"Strollers."

"O spies, Mr. Dangerfield. I know."

"Now, now, a little of this sausage. Everything is going to be all right, Miss Frost. Not a thing to worry about, good days ahead. Beep beep. Days of richness."

Sebastian leaned back in his chair and looked at the eyes of Miss Frost. Short hairs growing from the sides of her head. And around your nose the flesh turns up. Something I've never noticed before. I think you are just a little girl, Miss Frost. That's what you are. You need to be held, that's all. Come let me hold you in my own little forest where the crows are crying down all the trees. And into the big doors of my house. O they're thick to keep them out. Because you don't want people, trust none of them. I think I want it in bronze for weight and looks, with good quality brass hinges. See it. Dangerfield. Big S.D. on it. Keep people like Skully away. I say, Skully, would you mind awfully getting out of the way while my man closes this good door. Clang. What relief. No one will ever know the great relief to have these people shut out. Or a walled-in garden. Walls forty feet high and I think the three-foot thickness for strength. Hundred acres of it. Boxwood mazes for me to get lost in. Monkey trees. Magnolias and odd yew. My heart is mended and splendid under the yew tree. And then there will be lots of bells. And bells are balls. All balls bells. Big ones and little ones hanging all over. Ring them. Ring them out like mad. Me the mystic maniac. Fill my wholesome little garden with sound and the child in me crawling around the garden floor while my bells ring and birds sing and all the fluttering in me dances down, filled with all the silences and I'll sit thinking in the rare light and this part of me I can hang in the trees.

"Mr. Dangerfield, why don't you believe in hell and things like that?"

228

"Hell is for poor people."

"Hee."

"Miss Frost, I think I am a man with a future. What do you think? Do you think I have a future?"

"Of course, I think you have a good future. You'll be in law."

"And the jigs and jail and incognito. All those."

"I think you would do well in almost anything, Mr. Dangerfield. I think business would especially suit you."

"I think we will get on with the meat, Miss Frost. I have a hunger on me that has me belly screaming my throat's cut."

"O Mr. Dangerfield."

"Thank God up there for codes, Miss Frost. Get down there now on your knees and thank him and for the meat as well. All down on our knees. But never hit a man when he's down. Wait to see if he tries to get up and then by God, let him have it. The sledge between the eyes. I think my unlimited faith is killing me, Miss Frost. I want to chop this house down."

"I don't believe a word you're saying."

"A little underdone. Rawness of all types is for me."

Miss Frost moving the pan, circling it over the fire. Exhaling sound of gas. At the peak hours. The despair of the fading pressure. These damn people in the gas works. No one wants to do a decent day's work anymore.

"You're so strange to be with, Mr. Dangerfield."

"You can't mean that, Miss Frost."

"You're not like other people."

"Well, geek, geek and all that. Perhaps there is some truth in what you say."

"Mr. Dangerfield, would you pass me your plate. Why do you water that little plant in the front with an eye dropper?"

"Miss Frost, you've been spying on me. On me in my secret moments."

"O I haven't. But why do you do such a funny thing?"

"I'm poisoning the plant."

"Lord save us."

"Now look at that plant out there, Miss Frost. Would you say it was much longer for this world?"

"O Mr. Dangerfield I don't know what to say. That poor plant."

"It's something in me, Miss Frost. I thought to myself why don't I slip this plant something to kill it."

"You don't mean that."

"I'm a killer."

In the air the smell of spiced meat and brandy. A soft slow whistle of wind bleeding under the doors. And in my heart a sorrow. First sorrow of the end. Of this strange week of things. Of plans and movements. Of seeing the wild beast O'Keefe. Of these uncanny bedlam moments in the streets. Everything fruiting in a cold winter week. Months of being in the bed with the bedclothes all twisted with my anxiety. The wild things that were going through my mind like storms, I'd wake up my legs spinning round in the freezing air. I need another body with me. I've tried the hot towel on the eyes and made meself some balm but with these trickly chemicals you've got to watch it. I tried mustard plaster all over me and I won't forget that blunder in a hurry or even ever. But I'm not badly off. Not complaining really. Just wouldn't mind a complete change.

Miss Frost and Sebastian Dangerfield sat in this cold dining room eating sausage meat from Bray and drinking a pot of tea. Across from one another, looking up and down to food and back to each other's face. Smiles.

Is this no longer home? I feel all my homes are behind me. Only a house here because I think I must have nearly pawned everything in it except Miss Frost. The Rock gone. The Balscaddoon. The Rock, The Doon and Trinity. And that first day there when I got off at the back gate out of the green upholstered tram. And there was the university through my apprehensive eyes. A chill wind blowing. My new suit, white shirt and black tie. I felt all dressed up for failure, but feeling important because they were looking at me. There's the porter's lodge and a parking lot and in this building I see the contortions of glass, bubbling pots and skylights poking out of the roof. I want so much to learn. To know what you do with acids and esters and make my experiments go pop at the right time like the rest of you. From the very first word you tell me I'm going to remember. On my way to my tutor. Through these playing fields, flat green and velvet. How lovely with benches where I can sit watching, reading, or anything under these old trees. I think late summer is still hanging in the sky. And by these flower beds still smelling, into this pretty square where the opulent members of college live behind granite and big windows. That's for me. I see a man filling a pail of water from a green pump. He salutes me with a wave. How can I make a good impression, tuck my tie in, smile perhaps. I hope they will see I'm eager, ardent to listen, ready to take notes for all four years. That building there must be the library because I can see the stacks and stacks. I will borrow and read. I promise. What luck has brought me here because it's so beautiful. I'm told scholars can play marbles on the dining hall steps and shoot birds in college park. Got some great rules. Perhaps some day will see me shooting with the best of them. There are little clusters of students and I can hear their beautiful voices as I go by. And I can't help but look from face to face seeking out those who will also fail. The rest of my natural life without a degree. I almost wish now some little white angels would flutter down and take me or my dread away. Across the cobbled square a bell ringing and into this building number eight. Up the foot carved stairs where I see an open door. I'll knock lightly so's not to be rude. Hands out of pockets. Do the right thing. Always wait till asked. Come in. From behind the door he's telling me to come in. How shall I do it without making noise with my heels. I said as best I could that I was Dangerfield and he said ah delighted, do come in. Piles of papers everywhere and books. Must have been like this since God. Great waves of hair on this man's handsome head, a scholar in Greek and Latin for sure. Ah

Dangerfield, I'm very glad you're here and I trust your trip across the Atlantic was pleasant. My God, this gentleman is telling me he is glad I'm here and what can I say. I can say nothing, there's no chat in me because I'm trembling. I hope it won't mean some awful thing is to happen. He's only being nice and saying, now Dangerfield, I would like you to meet Hartington, it is Hartington, isn't it? And this tall person standing in a shadow stepped out, said yes and offered me his hand. You're to attend the same classes together. I tried to say splendid, couldn't and said safely how do you do. Our tutor rustled in the papers, came out with pamphlets and said I hope you will be very happy with us here Mr. Dangerfield. And now what could I say, trapped on this casual note of friendship. I did so want them to know that I knew I would be, but it was too late, no space left to tell them I was overjoyed to silence. On that cold morning in October I came away from that old room filled with books and paper with this strange tall person walking beside me who asked softly and slowly won't you come and have coffee. I was scarcely able to say thank you I'd like to but I was smiling so pleasantly willing to please.

If there were music all the time. I can hear the tap in the bathroom. Miss Frost washing her hair. I'm finishing the brandy, I guess teetering on the edge of this chair. London a big city. I'll manage. Just let me get there, that's all. Just bring toothpaste. Pack it safely in a little bag. On the corner of Newton Avenue and Temple Road there is erected a cross to mark the end of the Pale. And I'm outside it now in more ways than one. I just hang my head forward, lick my lips because they are so dry and I see that the edge of this carpet has been destroyed by feet. My hand to my brow, and over my eyes. I've forgotten so much. Too much going on, too much confusion. I just feel numb having fertilized. A moment of fatherhood comes at the birth. Malarkey told me all about it. I think he'd like to see me fertilize more often, told me what a joy it was to have kids. Now I know. What a joy.

The bathroom basin gurgling out its water. Must be going

down the Geary Road under the street and it will pour into Scotsman's Bay. Miss Frost will be twisting water from her hair. I know she uses vinegar in the rinse. From the bathroom, the shuffle of her slippered feet across the hall. Her door banging against the green chair. Dark furniture in her dark, damp room. Used to go in there and just look. So hidden away. Unrelated room. Touch the fabrics. This house at the end of the street. Little do you know out there, you strollers and spies perhaps, how much despair and yelling for love goes on in this shrouded house.

Miss Frost standing at the door in her thick, woolly robe, her green pajamas, her red slippers. Sebastian looked up slowly.

"You're so tired, Mr. Dangerfield. You look so tired."

Sebastian smiled.

"Yes. I am."

"Let me get you some chocolate before you come to bed."

"Miss Frost."

"Yes?"

"Miss Frost, you're kind."

"No."

"Miss Frost, I'm weary. What will you do when I'm gone? I'm worried about you."

"I don't know."

"Move somewhere else?"

"I guess so."

"Leave Ireland?"

"I don't know."

"Leave."

"It's a bit of an undertaking."

"Come with me, Miss Frost."

"You don't want me."

"Now don't say that."

Sebastian fell forward on his face. Miss Frost caught him beneath the arms and half lifted this light body to his feet. She led him slowly and carefully to her bedroom. Lowering

233

him to the edge of the bed. He sat there elbows on his thighs, hands hanging from his wrists.

Dreaming out this sunset. Tacked up on a cross and looking down. A cradle of passive, mystifying sorrow. Flooded in tears. Never be too wise to cry. Or not take these things. Take them. Keep them safely. Out of them comes love.

Miss Frost stepped from the door shyly. Her head a little bent and red spreading under the flesh of her temples. There was a small spot middle way up her nose. Her lashes dark and flickering, the wandering skin around her eyes. Some lines of her hair and her age of thirty four. The vulnerable steep bottom of her skull. Never to turn around and look at our backs, or as we are walking away. But her feet stepping with red toes. The part of her that was her falling arches, the sway bent ankles which put a tender part in her eyes. For women are lonely people, lonelier with women and with men, enclosed by sunless children and the little vanishing things that go away during the years of waiting. And hearts. And how was love so round.

> If
> There's a bell
> In Dingle
> And you want to say
> How sorry you are
> I'm gone
> Ring it
> And make it go
> Ding dong.

21

Wednesday. That morning Dangerfield picked up from his front hall strewn with bills, a picture postcard of the Lakes of Killarney with an inset, a poem.

> My heart is yearning
> For that familiar scene
> Of those dear blue lakes
> In that land far and green.

Turning it over.

I am kaput. Meet me in Jury's lounge, Wednesday, seven.

Duke of SERUTAN (ret.)

Dangerfield rode the roaring tram to Dublin. At the bottom of Dawson Street he swung gingerly from the screeching instrument. Moving swiftly, face deflected to the left to look in shop windows and avoid eyes. In Brown and Nolans here, I see they have some beautiful books, so nice never have to look in them. That's the way it ought to be, saves time. Received correspondence from this fine firm. Polite. Not like the others. They say perhaps dear sir you have overlooked such a small amount or would like us to bill you yearly. Yes, yearly I told them. My, time flies.

There's a lovely smell in the door of this restaurant. Look at them in there, wealthy happy people. Some coming out. Getting into that luscious car. This elegance does my heart good. I know something else I need. With a very tricky maneuver of the feet I take this turn into this place by the back alley. Lovely girl give me a glass of malt because I cannot face those beaten in battle without some little thing to still my own restless despair.

He crossed over College Green. Glanced at the Trinity

clock. Seven five. A newsboy standing in my way. Mister give us a penny. Here's my heart, sonny. And did your mother come from Ireland too? And sonny, give me an *Evening Mail*, please. And here's a half-penny for yourself. May you never have another poor day, sir.

Sebastian entered Jury's by the side door. Seated in a far corner, half obscured by a palm leaf, sat the retired Duke. Before him on the table, a brandy glass.

"For God's sake, Kenneth."

"It's you."

"Ah Kenneth yes, I see."

"You see an utterly broken man. I'm going to drink this till I'm stinko."

"Wisest words you've ever spoken."

"I'm finished."

"Tell me what's happened."

Dangerfield settling himself comfortably in these wicker chairs, folding his hand to hear like father confessor, this red-bearded man's tale.

"I gave myself up."

"What?"

"I went to the consulate and told them to ship me back."

"Surely you're not serious, Kenneth."

"Ship sails tomorrow night. It's in Alexander Basin right now. Sick man and I'm taking his place. Lady Eclair was a dead loss. As soon as I got out there I knew it was no go. Could feel it in my bones. Too good to be true. She took one look at me and almost had a fit. And I almost went right off my rock. I just said to her give me thirty shillings and I'd get out because she was driving me nuts."

"Do relax, Kenneth. Now how did this happen?"

"She thought I was French. Never gave me a chance to get started and my foreign accent just went to pieces, I sounded as if I had just got off the boat from U.S.A. What could I do? In a situation like that there's no point in prolonging the misery. Neither of us were getting anywhere so

236

I just said give me thirty shillings for my expenses in Dublin and coming out and I'll leave. So I left, that's it."

"Cheer up now. Let's see a little smile. Every cloud, you know."

"I'm sick of people. The less I have to do with them for the rest of my life the better. I don't care if I die."

"Nonsense now. Where have you been staying?"

"And that's another thing. I'm staying with Malarkey and my Christ was that depressing. Do you know what's happened?"

"What?"

"Clocklan committed suicide."

"Jesus."

"When I left you Monday I went to Tony's to stay. I didn't sleep because I kept hearing knocks on the window, then I heard a fight on the steps. I didn't know what the hell was going on. I wanted to get a night's sleep so I'd be at my best for my interview. Now I could have been beating my brains out all night against the wall for all that mattered. God it's weird. Then about a quarter to ten we see this uniform coming down the steps. We open the door and it's a policeman and he asks does a Tony Malarkey live here. We were all going to say no just on principle when Tony screams from one of the back tunnels for his tea and the policeman says is that Mr. Malarkey? Tony comes to the door and the policeman asks him if he knew a man by the name of Percy Clocklan and Tony said remotely. Then the policeman said he had a message addressed to him at this address, to a Mr. Tony Malarkey, which was picked up by some people on Portmarnock Strand. He said the message was found in a Power's whiskey bottle which was washed up on the beach. Then the policeman reaches into his breast pocket—we're all watching the whole proceedings from behind the door—and he takes out a crumpled piece of paper and hands it to Tony. I think Tony went a little white. Then the policeman asks him if he knows anything about it and Tony said he didn't know a thing except that Clocklan left for England about a week ago and hadn't heard a thing since. The policeman asks if he were depressed before he left and Tony said he couldn't notice because he was drunk all the time and the policeman says he was just checking up and that if they got any word on anything he would let Tony know. Tony came in the door and stood there and says it's that bastard Clocklan, he jumped off the mail boat and if he thinks I'm going to waste my time claiming his body he's mad."

"Blessed Oliver intercede for us all."

"Tony didn't seem to give a damn but I felt rotten. He just went on saying that if Clocklan wanted to commit suicide why did he have to get sentimental and send him notes. The note said he was fed up and couldn't take it any more and felt rotten, it was the only way out and that he wanted to be remembered to Terry and the kids. Jesus I was really upset. Tony standing there with a cup of tea saying that if he knew Clocklan, he'd never jump off the boat before it got to Liverpool because he'd feel he didn't get his money's worth out of the trip. Honest to God I felt depressed. That's why the whole Lady Eclair affair was such a dismal failure. I thought that if such a happy-go-lucky guy like Clocklan would do himself in what hope would there be for me?"

"What's this business of being shipped back?"

"I took the bus out to Roundwood. Waited around the local pub and I was picked up. Then the interview. I don't know what happened to me. A few days ago I was all hit up about it. Conjuring up wonderful dreams of zinc table tops, pans, dishes, scullery maids. Then bang when it comes for me to do my stuff—puff—smoke. I was as nervous as a kitten. I was thinking of Clocklan floating in the Irish Sea. Then I knew it was all up. As soon as I got off the bus on the quays I went straight for the consulate. Went in and said deport me. The vice-consul was a nice guy. He phoned, found this ship and that was it. Now I'm on my way back to the States. A beaten and finished man. Malarkey thought it was wonderful. To me this is worse than death."

"Poor Percy, good heavens. I liked him."

238

"Yeah."

"Perhaps, Kenneth, with all this bad news to bear we had better have a little something."

"Yeah."

Dangerfield snapping his fingers, O'Keefe twisting his glass round and round on the table.

"Don't let it get you down, Kenneth."

"I've never felt so damn screwed in all my life. I've now commenced my last twenty four hours in the ould sod. When I went back to the Catacombs they were all congratulating me. Can you imagine that?"

"I think it's possible."

"Tony can't seem to understand."

"Perhaps he's thinking about the food you'll be eating over there."

"I'll say one thing for him. He's generous. That's one thing about the Malarkey household. Nothing's too good when you come to visit. Go in there to that cellar and they haven't got a penny but everything is neat and clean and when they invite you to eat something, even though it's potato cakes, heavy as lead, you feel you're getting a meal. As tough as this country is I hate to leave it but if I don't I'll die."

"It's a pity about Percy. He could have fixed you up in the Iveagh House."

"It's all over now anyway, and what are you going to do?"

"Kenneth, the mail boat, Friday night."

"I don't get it. Your affairs are so fouled up that I don't think you know what you're doing. What are you going to do in London?"

"Rest from the eyes. Ever notice the eyes along the street. Ever notice them? Looking for something. And in this fine cultured city it's me. Marion's in Scotland with baba. O having a fine time, great girl is Marion. Of course I'll have a chance to get down to my studies and perhaps a little ballet in the evenings."

"On what?"

"Kenneth, do you know I think you have the arse of a servant."

"Have I now. Do you know there's something just a little fishy about this business. I was talking over your affairs with Malarkey and he says that rumor has it that you're taking off and that Marion's left you, and that there's a little irregularity and carnal knowledge going on in the Geary. Also that you're socked in with a woman in Rathmines who works in the laundry in Blackrock and another one in Cabra. As Tony says it's just gossip but isn't it always true?"

"I can see your faith is so strong in Malarkey there's no point in saying anything. But I would like to point out that my life is an open book. Yes, open book."

"Dangerfield, you're not fooling me. I leave this setup tomorrow so it doesn't make a bit of difference how you screw yourself up but let me tell you one thing. Women, drink and the general chaos will ruin you and this crazy dancing in the street. I think you'll end up in the Gorman."

"Have it your own way, Kenneth."

Two glasses were placed on the table by a smiling waitress.

"Your brandy, sir."

Dangerfield with a twitch.

"Ah."

O'Keefe with a sigh.

"How much, how much?"

Waitress bowing concernedly.

"That's seven shillings please, sir."

O'Keefe with sadness.

"And here's a shilling from a poor man because I'm leaving Ireland and won't need it anymore."

Smiling a blossom of blush.

"Thank you, sir, very much. I'm sorry you're leaving Ireland."

O'Keefe looking at her.

"What do you mean sorry? You don't even know me."

Waitress intently.

"O yes I do. You used to be in here a lot last year. We all

240

remember you. You didn't have a beard then. I think it suits you."

O'Keefe astonished, leaned back in the creaking wicker chair. He smiled.

"Do you know I really appreciate that. Thanks."

The waitress reddening, walking away.

"God damn it, Dangerfield. I'm a hard son of a bitch but do you know I think I'd get down on my hands and knees and kiss a Jesuit's arse if it meant I could stay."

"I'll take up the collection if you do."

"Jesus, people are interested in you here."

"Foreigners."

"Even so, they shit on them in U.S. This morning I got up early and walked down Fitzwilliam Street. It was still dark. I heard a clip clop coming along and the milkman singing. It was lovely. Jesus, I don't want to go back."

"In the land of the big rich. The monstrous rich. Over there the quids."

"I feel every minute spent in U.S. is wasted."

"Now, now, a fine great place of opportunity for the young spirit such as yours, Kenneth. Maybe a bit of that unhappiness and people whoops out of the windows. But there are the odd moments of joy. May even solve your problem."

"If I can't solve it here I'll never do it there."

"How will you bear it being waved in your face. I don't think I'm exaggerating when I say bodies over there are beautiful."

"I can wait."

"And how's Tony?"

"Makes his kids toys all day. Gets up in the morning and yells for his tea. Then he goes out and sees his accountant and places a shilling bet. Then he gets keyed up till the horse loses. And then, as he says himself, when the horse loses I go home and pick an argument with Clocklan. When I was there I tried to get Tony interested in taking the North by force. And Tony was telling me about a time when they went over the border. Everyone going to shoot a policeman, couldn't hold them back, going to declare the North under the tricolor. They get over the border, pockets filled with homemade bombs, hand grenades and gelignite. Then they meet a policeman. There are forty of them and one policeman and he comes over and says, 'ere, 'ere, this 'ere is King's land, now behave yourselves or I'll have to lock the whole lot of ye up. They all get long faces, roll up the tricolor, put away the bombs and go into the first pub and get drunk, with the policeman with them as well. It was good. Do you know I don't think they ever want to take the North. Barney says they're the finest people on the earth. Do you know perhaps the North ought to take over the South."

"At least we'd have contraceptives then, Kenneth."

"What about these women of yours when you go to London?"

"Do you think I keep a harem, Kenneth? I lead a life of spartan self-denial. Miss Frost is one of the finest people I know, good Catholic and in every way leads a gainful respectable life."

"Malarkey says the neighbourhood is in disgrace over this affair."

"Miss Frost and I would never stoop. Or set upon one another lasciviously. Within the bounds of good taste and dignity. Furthermore I'd like to point out that Miss Frost is joining the nuns."

"You awful bastard."

"Have you ever known me to involve myself in anything not above board or on boards or anything? I say, out with it, O'Keefe. Geek. You're so starved for it, Kenneth, that you're imagining things. You think I sin. Not me."

"You're socked in there like a banana in the peel. Tony says that you give her so much that she can barely crawl to work in the mornings."

"Absolutely outrageous. Miss Frost tiptoes through the tulips."

"You think you're getting away with a lot. It's drink."

"And sure it's only the sociability that makes me drink."

"Do you know what my ambition is when I get money? To move into the Shelbourne Hotel. Strut in through the front door and tell the porter would you garage my Daimler for me please."

"No, Kenneth. Would you garage my car."

"Jesus you're right. That's it. My car. Would you garage my car. And into the Shelbourne rooms. They say it's the most beautiful bar in the world. Have Malarkey come and meet me. How do you do, Tony, how are things in the Catacombs?"

"Yes, Kenneth, you have the arse of a servant."

"You mean for riding. Built for a horse. Do you know that if it weren't for the British this place would be so many wild savages."

"I'm glad you've come to see it that way."

"The Irish feel that children are brought down upon them by the wrath of God for screwing. All you hear is that if it weren't for you kids life would be rosy and we could have a good time. But we worked and slaved ourselves to the bone to give you a little more than we had and now look at you, won't bring a penny into the house. No-good loafer wasting your time with these books when there are good jobs on the railroad."

"Geek."

In the eight o'clock sound and smell of Jury's lounge, they sat with stretched legs and toes twitching in their shoes, thawing damp bones in the centrally heated air. Priests scattered through the room, red faced, watery eyed and smoldering. Immaculate collars choking their scarlet necks, clerics in pain. With waitresses, young, black and round. Potted palms. It was not what was inside but what was outside that made what was inside so good and desirable. Because outside there is the gray wet over everything. And it came up through the shoes, soaking socks and squealing between the toes. Near here is the Bank of Ireland. So great and round and granite. Outside it a whore and a beggar.

243

"Well Kenneth it is fitting indeed that we should have the comfort of this fine room for our last day."

"That waitress, did you notice her teeth? They were white."

"Her eyes very fine too."

"Why can't I feel I could ever marry one of these girls?"

"Nothing more fashionable these days than to marry down, Kenneth."

"Be marrying one of my own, that's the trouble."

"I like your blood, darling."

"Yeah. My whole sexual life depends on the nuances of wealth. Come back from a good hard ride around the edges of the estate looking for poachers."

O'Keefe leaning back in this sudden glory, continuing with mellow aplomb.

"I pass the scullery out back and call, I say, Tessie, what's for dinner and Tessie scurries into the cook. Lady O'Keefe has already told me what's for dinner but in my little democratic way I have a banter with the scullery maids. Lady O'Keefe at one end of the table and I'm at the other and we discuss the estate and horses. I ask her what she did at the flower show and if any of our blossoms took a prize. After dinner to the library for expresso with a twist of lemon and a bottle of Hennessy. She reads me a play till ten. Goes up to her room. I wait in the library for about ten minutes and go up to my own. I notice that the door between our rooms is slightly ajar. I wait a discreet ten minutes, tiptoe over, give a delicate knock, may I come in dear? Yes dear, do. Ha."

"Eeeeeee. Kenneth, if you're ever rich it will be an anti-climax."

"By God."

On O'Keefe's head a brown dirty tweed cap. Women in this lounge looking at the two of them with their legs stretched all over the place. And they were cocking their white ears to hear that bearded man go on about such fantastic things with that awful accent of his and who is that man with his haughty ways and county voice, flicking his

244

fingers exquisitely and rolling his head back to belch laughter. So sure of themselves.

And between priests and pouting matrons were business men from Manchester who made furniture to sell to the civil servants for the sitting room and they were a little red faced, with a touch of proud overtone in their voices. They wore striped blue shirts with white stiff collars and their gent's natty suiting with white pin stripe and short coats where underneath it all were braces, red, blue, green and overlaps of wool and buttons here behind and everywhere. And men from Bradford and Leeds looking out of conservative corners of eyes. I know you are rich, in silk underwear and have finished a fine cut of meat with a small mountain of mushrooms, carrots, peas and other things.

Kenneth O'Keefe told the waitress he wanted coffee. He looked around the room to see who was watching or listening. Bent his head forward, removed his cap and scratched the back of his light brown head. Dangerfield semi-supine, his chin resting on his chest looking out broodingly at O'Keefe.

"This is our last night audience, Kenneth."

"Yup."

"After this the curtain comes down."

The business men from Bradford and Leeds who live between the brownstone buildings in sunless smoky streets, feeling and pricing cloth with darting eyes, spending long afternoons over tea and fittings for suits, with winter fogs outside their dark stone mansions. These men lean back in their chairs, pulling from their pockets silk, feathery handkerchiefs, and removing their glasses, pass the fine cloth sensuously back and forth, round and round, hard and then very softly touching the exquisite glass, holding them to the light and with rare, long fingers put them back over their eyes. In the throes of prices and bottoms dropping out of the market they are smiling, thinly but smiling, the richest men in the world.

"Kenneth, I'll walk as far as the quays with you."

"Suits me."

Kenneth O'Keefe gave a last smile to his charming waitress. They finished their coffee and stood up. The lights in the room grew brighter. Everyone stopped talking. In the silence, the two walked across the lounge. Waitresses in their black garb stood along the wall by the serving hatch. One of them nipping her head smartly in the hole and said they were going. Three more faces appeared with sparkling eyes. As they neared the door all faces were on them. All on their feet clapping. Shouting out of their mouths bravo. The lights brighter and clapping swarming up from their hands louder. The gentlemen from Bradford and Leeds cornering silk handkerchiefs in the tears in their eyes, twisting with an index finger, then blinking and watching. The priests up at last. I know they think us glorious. And uproarious. Our backs go out the swing door, pass into this street, narrows of warehouses and brokerages by day filled with the making of money and a deserted lane by night.

"When you come back, Kenneth, I'll walk naked wearing a green bowler to greet you at the boat. With a donkey cart flying green streamers and shamrocks imported from Czechoslovakia and a band of girl pipers blowing like mad. Did you know that they imported the English Sparrow into America to eat the horseshit off the streets?"

"No."

"Look into it. Got to fight, Kenneth. Must resist or go down in the pile. And perhaps there'll be a little richness for one of us soon. And when you're out there on that high sea I want you to remember to pray. Because I'll be in that city of London and London is groaning with lust. What do you think of that?"

"Nothing. I hate the place. One look out of Victoria Station was enough for me. What the hell, maybe you'll make out."

"Must fight. There are books, Kenneth, that tell us that we must. And also about the animals who gave up the ghost.

246

No fight. They put a little word at the bottom of the page to tell you something. Extinct. To be avoided."

"Here's where I leave you."

"Well, Kenneth, it's ironic. Taking leave of you in the North of Dublin. Never thought this would ever happen to us."

"Give my regards to Tony and everyone. Although I think it unlikely, I hope to see you on your arse in the Old Bailey."

"Count on it Kenneth."

"Good luck."

"Take care."

O'Keefe sauntered sadly off and disappeared down this gray dark street called Seville Place. Dangerfield walked back across Butt Bridge, a finely divided rain falling. My body has blue joints. Ireland is heaven bound with this low weather. Rub my knuckles because this climate is only for brains. Cranes and masts down the river. On Aston Quay the last buses leaving for the country. And clusters of men hunched in black overcoats sucking cigarettes, spitting and mean. With tongues of shoes hanging out like dogs' hungry mouths. I'd give anything for a drink now. Wearing this rag of despair and sorrow. Full of holes and dirty. Across my shoulders wet and cold. They say nothing lasts. It's all gray. Gray for what? Gray for rain. And pink for poodles. Colors for everything. They say, green for work. Now what is it? For Idleness? I think the black. You there below decks, run up me little black ensign. Well? For lust. What are they going to say? Red? No. Not red. I think the brown. Brown for lust. Red is for money and blue for deads.

> Take deads
> Away.
> Play music
> Please.

22

Miss Frost was lying upon her back, her head supported by two nice white pillows. There was a grayness under her eyes. Near to tears. Her hand divided over the back of her book, holding it face down on the covers. Mr. Dangerfield, arbiter of wisdom, stood erect at the bottom of her bed, concerned and loving. Looking at her eyes as they flashed sorrow and asked him to come to her for now. And they were in their little room together shut off from the rest of the house and world out there ready to axe them. How to get out of it. And Dangerfield. And Miss Frost.

"I am going to call you Lilly."

A shy smile tightened upon her lips, her eyes turning away and back and tight lips and the edge of her teeth coming to nip her mouth and her face up to face his.

"O."

"I think it's time I called you Lilly. Lilly."

"O well."

"Lilly."

"Dear me."

"Are there eats, Lilly?"

"Just some bacon and tea but take that ten shilling note, Mr. Dangerfield, and get some eggs."

"No. I couldn't."

"Do. Please. I insist."

Dangerfield to the dresser. Slipping the note in a pocket.

"Won't be a minute."

Yet I stoop to menial things. But there just hasn't been enough money. However, in the flux. Keep one's eyes wide and never know when or what might come up. Live off the environment. Take fruit from my trees. Fine shirts from counters and charge them. Ton of turf from my fuel merchant and bill me later. Take one large turkey, rat trap and rare

248

cheese, pound of Robert's best coffee and bit of salami, oh
and a quick quart of sauerkraut and would you mind frightfully putting it on my account. Air filled with certainly sir.
O it was good. Creamery butter? How many pounds sir? I
think the three. Rashers? A nice bit of back please. A ton if
you will. Picture me walking up Grafton Street. I am passing
Mitchell's Cafe and the doorway where I have always looked
carefully to see aristocratic faces poised out of necks of
flowery, sweet-smelling dresses and looked at their noses and
rather lovely nostrils, racehorses for sure and eyes sparking
with vitamins always hoping one would smile at me. And
one speaks. O Sebastian wherever have you been? What?
Not really. You mean you're hungry. Ghastly. O you're joking. Shocking. But do come and have tea with me. Of course
I'm paying. Whatever are you wearing? That thing. Yes,
that thing. My God, it's a blanket. Rakish. Only thing I can
think of. Frightfully I.A.F. I mean it's sort of R.A.F. sort of
thing. I.A.F.? Irish Air Force, of course, stupid. Do come and
have tea. O no, wear it. I like it. Suits you. Frightfully exciting. You do some rather weird things, everyone says so. And
there I am with this girl, by the window upstairs. She's paying. Me under my brown blanket. Brown for lust. Eating my
cake she bought for me. Eat one. Steal two. Eat one. Steal
another. After tea. I go to the lavatory and flush my blanket
in the toilet. I take a cardboard sign and fashion it in a stiff
collar. Use my black shoelace. Black for private means. I
return wearing this and nothing else. You might say making
an obvious gesture of indecency. But fed.

And tonight I go in and buy eggs. And Miss Frost, my
lily and Lilly, wherever will you go? I've not wanted to
cause you pain but to understand, be with you and give you
love. And we got our bodies mixed up on the bed and one
night I wore your pajamas. Green suits me I think.

"A dozen of the very finest please."

I think they are coming along very well in this shop. New
counter and glass and I notice a clean fingernail here and
there.

Sebastian hurried up the Geary Road and with two acute lefts into his cul-de-sac. Walking towards a wall. Searching on the green gate for latches. What did these neighbors do? Light on in that house. What were they doing with their bodies? Toasting in front of the last coals. Tomorrow I go bye bye. O'Keefe on the high seas. And Miss Frost, I see a peak of light coming round your curtain. Bad for security but it'll do for this last day. Only hours left. I'm coming in the house to hold your hand and spend my last night with you. I want to take you with me but I can't. Would you be willing to put your shoulder to the big wheel? Push. I'll show you how. You've been good to me like none of the others and kept me company in this last loneliness, might have gone quite mad were it not for your body and sweet smiles and breasts. Saved me. Even the little secret smells in the pits of your arms. Like bears in winter lairs. Nuzzling the short hairs.

He walked around the side of the house. Looking at the laurels. Dark round here. Get this light on. Miss Frost keeps a clean kitchen. Into her room.

"Please don't get up, Lilly, leave this to me."

"Let me. You're tired. It's no trouble at all, Mr. Dangerfield."

"On this last night, Lilly, do call me Sebastian."

"I just can't. Don't make me, but come sit down. I'll make it. You have such a long journey ahead."

"Aye. It's very good of you. May I look in your book, Lilly?"

"It's one of those awful things."

"Lilly I'm terribly chilled, that walk I think has given me a little a-choo, my nose is stuffed. I wonder could I just get into your nice warm bed here?"

"But we really shouldn't anymore."

"Just till I get my teeth into the rashers and eggs."

"You have an awful way with you, Mr. Dangerfield."

"It's your hot water bottle, I just can't keep away from it."

She left him sitting on his chair. And he took his garments

250

off. Shoes neatly beside the bed. Winds outside. Keep telling myself they are temperate, moist and warm. Spend my life huddled over a weather map. Guest in Lilly's cozy bed. Pretty name. What made me do it? Call her white and pure. Virgin. Driven snow. And I'm sneaking between these sheets, deep down after the bottle, catch it, hook it, pull it up here near my balls and wait for her. When I'm in London I think I'll join the Trinity College Dining Club. I read the soothing words which said the Dining Club exists to promote mutual intercourse and good fellowship among T.C.D. men, to provide an opportunity for renewing old friendships and keep Trinity men in touch with the life of the University. I keep telling myself that I'm one of you because I never want to lose faith. Something to hang on to. And I'll come along in the evenings and sit with you. I will be reserved and listen. To those things dear to me. I hope it's raining. And step out of my carriage, suck down a few lungs of fat fog. Wearing my Trinity tie. What a handsome tie it is. Most illustrious of all. I say, Trinity? Why yes. You? Yes. Forty-eight. Forty-six and any other year you want to name. How do you do, I'm Dangerfield. Jolly good show, this. Quite. In fact, bung, frightfully ho. Will there be chandeliers? Chicken? Sprouts? Fire? And will this be what I want? Please.

Lilly came in with tea. The long red strips across the plate and the two yolks glistening. And buttered bread. A light green napkin. She puts it down.

"Lilly."

"O you'll make me spill it."

"Just a little one. On the lips. There."

"It'll scald you if I drop it."

Just my cup of tea. You are.

"Lilly, this is very good of you. I need this, this warmth and food. I sometimes wonder if there is an island a little smaller than this one where we could go."

"It would be nice."

"Lilly, you've been packing your bags."

"Yes."

"This is all a pitiful life. I want to settle somewhere. Stay there for good. I'm sick of moving. We must have somewhere to call our own, Lilly. I think that's what we all need and stop this moving."

"My aunt said she would do with me till I got other digs.'

"What's your aunt like?"

"She has a studio out in the back of the house where she paints these models in the nude. I posed for her once and felt awful."

"Why?"

"The way she looked at me."

"Lust?"

"Yes."

"It's everywhere, Lilly. Everywhere. I don't see how it can be stopped. It'll never get you anywhere save to bed."

"O Mr. Dangerfield, you go on."

"I hate to leave you. I feel it's unfair."

"You don't have to worry about me, Mr. Dangerfield. I'll take care of myself."

"But I want to know that you're going to be all right."

"What about Mrs. Dangerfield? I know it's none of my business but I felt you were so right for one another."

"Little confusion. I don't think there was enough of the money. Mrs. Dangerfield thought I was rotten rich. I think there is a considerable fortune somewhere but it's a little tied up. But I've got plans."

"I'd like to get married."

"Be careful. Want to watch these Irishmen."

"Not one of those. I'd like an Indian."

"An American one? Like me. Did you know I'm part Mohawk? Woo hoo."

"It's been a great experience knowing you, Mr. Dangerfield, even though I don't agree with all the things you say. But inside I think you are a good person."

"Lilly."

"I mean it."

"Come here."

"But I've made an oath not to, again. Please. No."

"There is no harm."

"Just on the cheek, because I can't stop you once you get going."

"There's no harm, Lilly."

"Mind, you'll knock everything over. Don't."

"Come lay beside me then. This little kiss on your ear will never hurt. Just the one. Lilly, you're wearing perfume."

"I beg of you, Mr. Dangerfield, please don't make me feel awful."

"I want you to come and see me in London. Will you?"

"We should never see each other again. And what's to become of the house, Mr. Dangerfield?"

"I've made arrangements. Come closer now. This is our last night together. This is great tea."

"There are a lot of letters for you."

"I'll take care of those too. Now let's not bother about these things, you just get cozy in here and never mind about the rest. Everything's taken care of."

"Mr. Dangerfield do you like me even just a little."

"I like you, Lilly. You've been good to me. A comfort. Take my hand. There now. Easy. All's going to be all right. I haven't felt as good for some time."

Miss Frost in her green pajamas. I put the orange egg yolk over my bread and ate it up. I think this is near it now. As near as ever could be. Peace. Sacred silence. On the move or run, just as you wish, tomorrow. Perhaps Skully will try something a little too clever for himself and get tripped on the secret wires I'm organizing on my trail. I don't want to be caught by anybody. Nor imprisoned or put down. In England they put a rope around the neck and let you go, whoops. Just across the channel they hoist that thing, shined and sharpened and tell you lay your sylph-like thing in there. I don't know why I'm so terrified by this capital punishment because I feel I'm a gentleman and live by all the rules and regulations any of you have put down and even a special few of my very own. O watch the noose and knots

253

and knives. And these doctors too. Once you let them get in these white coats and hold you by the wrist they want to tap you on the chest. Then they want to see in the mouth. Later they put you on a table and go to the cabinet for the knife. They say they just want a peek inside.

Lilly, I never get tired of your white thirty four year old bubas, buns or beauties. Or will I ever get over how much I like to imagine them under that green pajama top. Rare that I ever make these dogmatic statements but I cannot help feeling that when other things are gone that carnal knowledge is here to stay. I guess with me it has been a case pure and simple of a little frightened man looking out and seeing all the prowling animals. I've had other women. Lilly. Kissed them in bed with me. And a girl who lives by the Bleeding Horse, another body rich with tender muscles and nuzzling in the sparkling curly hair. Take juice and comfort from my thighs. And walked and talked to her along the edges of the canal where I heard once years ago, the coach was coming up from the South laden with people and it fell from the bridge into the canal and they thought like good Irishmen and engineers they ought to float them out and opened up the sluice gates and drowned the whole lot of them. The canal is a favorite place of mine for this reason and others. And this girl too was kind to me. There is no use otherwise. Kindness. And you came into my life for this collusion, boarder bedded down with the landlord. Common sort of thing these days but different with us because we were both in need. And the little talks we had. I told you about the journey of the exposed penis. You laughed. O those things are funny now but I was fit to be tied on that Tuesday. It was your willingness and interest which bound me captive, Lilly, to your body and nice teas we've had. I can coin the odd phrase with the best of them. But I'd rather keep that part of me secret. Like the entangled laws of this church of yours. But I know a bit about law and the ones they call Canon. I even went into Brown and Nolans and got the book, stood three hours at the counter reading to the assistants' utter concern because

254

I'm sure they must have noticed that I was wearing the remnants of a chasuble under my mackintosh and these laws were so interesting. I felt I was poking through sin and limbo. Lilly I've heard you whisper when in the throes, holy mother of God, they will never forgive me. But of course they will, you succulent, tender chicken and gorgeous creature to boot.

With the light off and B.B.C. closed down for the night. Tiny sounds outside. And warnings of gales in Malin, Rockall, Shannon, Fastnet and Irish Sea. Rain beating against the window panes. Laurel leaves shaking crazily. And our green curtain swelling out and a light slicing the room. Out there on the water. I think it's my grave. The Isle of Man, Dalkey Sound and harbors of Bullock and Colimore, a hundred and twenty miles to Liverpool. Let us hold tight, Lilly. And give up this right and wrong. And you tell me, Mr. Dangerfield, if they ever hear of it and it's not as easy as that just to be forgiven because they make you confess it all and as soon as you let on to something they start asking questions was it alone and about marriage and did he? Between your legs, my child. And what other departures were there and did he do that too. Yes. He did. Lilly I will make all this suffering up to you. I am no cheap chicken myself. Corporation law and fixing treaties between nations should pull a lot of weight up there. I'll tell him, Mr. Jesus, I knew Lilly and if you knew Lilly as I know Lilly. Well. You wouldn't have minded having a bit yourself, now would you? Not at all. Jesus and I have been through a great deal together. And I tell you Lilly, he would roar with laughter and say, why my dear child you laid with the ginger man? Great. Don't worry about it. What's a piece of arse between friends so long's you both get a good chunk. Got a few of these self-centered people down there, efficient but finicky who don't get much themselves who try to put the lid on lads like Dangerfield. I know Dangerfield. His whole life. Oceans of integrity and puddles of dependability. By God, myself, as great a man as ever I did split from a rib or even make with

255

the fishes on whatever day I made them. Like him up here with me. When you're dead Danger. They say you've never been beaten in chess, dominoes or croquet or for being right when the others say you're wrong. And to use one of Dangerfield's rather amusing phrases, I'm no cheap chicken meself.

So Lilly. There you are. Come to me now. For think of it, Friday we are sundered. When I reach out for your parting white hand. On the trumpeting boat leaving for sea. Will you stand by the gas tank and wave? When I rub my chest on yours. I'm sad. Dropping away body from body. I plead the please tonight. And any mortal sin you care to commit. And do you remember the little white pan in the garage that you got one night when I came home from my overtime in the pubs and I said would you ever, Miss Frost, get it. Fill it with water and bring it to me. And I put my feet in it and you let me use your talc. And you helped dry. Me leaning a hanging head between my legs. Like they found me mornings slung over the chains in Trinity my hair touching the top of the grass. Lilly what a nice white scalp you have, not a sign of dandruff. When you held my feet. In your hands. Miss Frost you're the kindest person I know. I held you by the shoulders. That's why I do this. Because I like you. And take off your green pajama top. Just after you enjoy it, you begin to cry. Let me take your nipple. Nor am I nutty like Kenneth, but needy nevertheless. This string quartered around your waist. Pull it below your navel which is a deep one. May I button up your belly, Lilly? Did you know I have a degree? In navels. Did graduate work. Published papers. Lot of things I've done. Is there a tide of flesh rising? Why Miss Frost, you're giggling. Whatever for? You think it's funny after all? Is fucked and finished. Or because I said God was on my side or splitting his sides up there over this tender little scene. Or are you watching as if you were an eye in the ceiling? What's happening on the sheets. Catch as catch can. Don't turn away till I'm finished with your mouth. Just this last time. Sins are sticking out everywhere. Tempt me,

256

Lilly. And is this you? And your voice in my ear. Taking an oath and can't you wait till we're finished. Lilly, you can let me. No I can't let you. On this last night. I want you to but I can't let you. Now, now. I'm going to miss you and making love to me. Nothing to do but sow me ould seed Lilly. Sell my seed Lilly. In the shop. They planted the mother of the Lord and they say it didn't have anything to do with the flesh. But Lilly you turn your back to me. On this last night telling me this is what you will let me do, for I did it once before and a few times since. They learn all sorts of things on the farm watching the animals. But won't it hurt or pain? I may pretend, but I'm shocked, but on the other hand I can't help laughing at the whole silly setup. Offered me your arse. I'm touched, too. Somehow. Like July Fourth at that party in the Phoenix Park. Soft sunny summer day with people driving up in shining cars in dresses and jewels. I almost tiptoed to the door half hoping to sneak in and then they took my little card from me and read out Sebastian Balfe Dangerfield and I almost asked the man not so loud please. I faced one smile after another. I'm a little short on fellowship but I put a little squeeze into each handshake. Filet of sole. On the tables were eats the like of which I'm sure have never been seen on this isle. I shot over to one of the tables. Champagne, sir? How can they be so kind? Where can so much drink come from? Mushroom eclairs. I never said a word to anyone. Marion talking with the Earl of Kilcool. I looked a little rough shod to be mingling. After about an hour or so, however. I think I had something to say. Marines were called and someone whispering see that man is taken out at once. I was just going to scream for God's sake don't take me away from all this booze. An elderly gentleman said something as they approached me. And I was left. Later during someone's aria I crawled under the tables untying shoelaces and, I'm afraid, looking up dresses. Next day I think I read in the *Evening Mail* something about the Minister being raised to the status of an Ambassador. One thing begets another. On the one hand. And then on the other. On these white sheets

257

tangling white bodies. Turning from me Lilly as I bump these mounds. And the cool pressure. It's as they say, tight circle with nothing beyond. And my arms around your neck. Riding you. Brown for lust or bronco. I'm throwing my heart down your throat and you tear and tell me tender hearted Lilly. And the pain of it up and down my legs. And even though you are just passing the time away, say lying on your side, twisting a shoulder to get the blanket up and keep out the cold, think of me. If you look up the Liffey under a low sky in setting sun you're in heaven. My dreams of collecting the ha'pennies on the metal bridge. Miss Frost. Pure as the driven snow. White as the North Pole. And buttocks a trifle soft. And why, Lilly, did you want me to do it this way? I've tried to be a member of Christian society, for I am a Calvinist at heart, with one or two reservations of course. And I've been a bit puritanical watching out for the improperly dressed and those coarse of accent, for what else is there if one doesn't keep one's place. And we're all within a stone's throw of heaven. O happy humping ground. And even the day I took a look around the Municipal Museum of Modern Art saying to myself by jove this is a jolly good show. Yes, suggestive pictures. With the things there that are displayed in flesh tint. Is this to confound conception, Lilly? And done by all the farm folk. In zoos too. I love the Zoological Museum. Learned all about the Irish Elk with it standing just in the entrance way with antlers from one wall to the other. And stuffed fish and birds around Ireland. And an Irish Wolfhound nicely stuffed too. And upstairs a whale hanging in the middle of the room with a balcony all round where they have this thing evolution displayed with the bugs getting bigger and bigger. I prefer to feel that Big Chief up there started us with Adam and Eve.

Miss Frost's hair has its pleasures and a light green smell. A down on the back of her neck. A slim neck. I could easily choke her to death. She looks broader from the back. From the front there are those two distractions. Distance grows shorter with familiarity. I'm acquainted with the facts. Good

258

pair of shoulders built for work. Been a little dream boat of mine that if Marion drowned on the mail boat, Miss Frost would live with me and would go to work in the garden out back. Dig it all up and lace it liberally with lime and phosphates with mounds of kelp mixed with ould bones and guts laced with dead leaves all of it rotting graciously making a nice gooey compost. Visions of Miss Frost laying down the seed. Especially the spuds. Some think it a dumb vegetable. Not me. Like the lion, king of them all. I would have helped Lilly sow the potatoes although I don't like to use my hands too much. Pour on the rot now. And a little chicken dropping will do no harm. Why does food make so much money in my dreams?

"Lilly, why did you want me to do it this way?"

"O Mr. Dangerfield, it's so much less of a sin."

And
Fun
Too.

23

He was dreaming.

Choosing the blue socks and then a pair of red ones. They were made of this material nylon. Wear forever. And stand up by themselves and as they say, walk away. I'm in these narrow streets and into one shop and out of another. Here is a woman who is middle aged and plump. Plump, ripe plum. Standing behind the counter telling me she loved foreigners. And I'm filling my bag with millions of socks. And can't get them out of the shop. And they call a waste truck to take them all away. Hear a sound which puts the shudder of fear through me. I think of a rat.

His back was stiff. He stood up. His eyes tight with sleep. They don't ever let you sleep enough. And my body is so cold.

Miss Frost turned over. He went to her and kissed her cheek. Her eyes fluttered open.

"Don't touch me."

"What?"

"Don't kiss me."

"For Christ's sake, what's the matter? Are you drunk? God damn it."

"O don't carry on. You walk out of here and leave the scourge of the tongue on me."

"Now, what is it? Lilly, I say."

"You're well away."

"God damn it, what's the matter?"

"You've no worry. Off on the boat. I can't help it. They know."

"Who knows?"

"They'll be talking."

"If you're eating. Don't worry about the talk."

"That's easy."

"Now, now, let me get you a little something. Can I fry you a sausage? It's the meat, me Lill, forget ould talk, and tongues."

"Mrs. Dangerfield will have me in the courts."

"She won't have you anywhere. Do you want a sausage?"

"She will. And they'll fire me."

"Just a second, Lilly me ould love—"

"Stop."

"I'm going to brush me teeth."

"Jesus, Mary and Joseph."

"Never mind the Jesus and the Mary and Joseph. Put plea to B.O.P. Blessed Oliver Plunket. My patron. Have an in with him."

"You've had your way with me. I have to stay behind."

"Not at all. Come to London."

"That's a wild idea."

"Have to brush my teeth. Me teeth will be coming out of me—"

"Don't."

Sebastian scurried in his ragged underwear to the cold bathroom floor. Put his hand over the melted soap. It squeezed through his fingers.

"God's teeth."

Bristle brush best. Nylon wears the white stuff away until there are just stumps. Sebastian turned the tap and put his joined hands under the blisteringly cold water. Put a little touch of Miss Frost's Mum in the pits. With one of these rusty razors I'll cut the hair off my numb jaw. And put my brown corduroy trousers on for the rough traveling that may be in it and the unpredictable fly. For the honey drenched mercy of Jesus, prevent that. Never again because I couldn't bear it. What's got into Miss Frost? Me. Yes, of course. She's turning treacherous. No telling. Liable to foul the rudder of the ship. Can't trust her if she's feeling like that. Might spill the beans. Boston baked. Must keep all beans in my own little pot.

Sebastian went back into Miss Frost's bedroom. Went to

261

the dresser and picked up her tiny wrist watch, reading the time. Perhaps it would get three pounds at my broker. Mustn't. Not playing the game. Although it's a little hard to know who's on whose side.

"Lilly, I'm going to cook some sausages. Would you like some? I'll make a nice pot of tea for the both of us. Now won't that be nice? Buck you up. Yes?"

"I hate to be alive. I hate this country."

"Don't despair."

"You don't have to stay here and suffer with them wagging their tongues and they'll hear of it at home."

Sebastian walked out of the room. He put the black pan over the gas. Caught a corner of grease and melted it off on the edge. Sliding down and vanishing. Passed the knife through the connecting skin and the little sausage fell neatly, hissing in the fat. Don't know what to tell this Lilly. Could tell her that life is a matter of resistance. Been telling too many people that. I have an aesthetic. Tell Miss Frost to get one. Judge these little difficulties with it. My, look at that sausage swell. A spout of richness coming out of there that will drown the whole lot of us, aesthetics and all.

Sebastian left his pan and went to the bedroom. Miss Frost standing naked in front of the mirror and said O as he entered. Folding her arms over her breasts.

"Lilly, we know each other better than that."

"O."

"Get your toothbrush and I'll take you to London."

"I couldn't go. Everyone would know."

Sebastian went back to the kitchen. Shook the pan. Sausage shrinking and splitting, juice pumping out of its side. From now on it'll be eats for one. Must drink more tea for me nerves.

Miss Frost came into the morning room as he was biting off next to the last length of sausage. She was wearing her black skirt and gray sweater and little red hearts hanging from her ears. Heart of Jesus.

"Bread, Lilly?"

"Please."

"Butter?"

"Thank you."

"Tea?"

"Please."

"How many sugars, Lilly?"

"You think it's all cod."

"Very nearly."

"You don't know Ireland."

"I know Ireland, Lilly."

"O dear me. What am I going to do?"

"Out there in the front hall, Lilly, is the most fantastic collection of fan mail in the world. People spend many pounds writing to me. Hiring detectives to trail me round Dublin city and environs. Posting children on corners to watch me. Lilly, you see talk is the least of it."

"But you won't work. Mrs. Dangerfield told me you were missing all your classes."

"That isn't the point. Do you know, Lilly, that I arrived in this country with the largest wardrobe ever seen on these shores? Now in the hands of Mr. Gleason, my broker. A fine man but he now has practically every material thing I have ever owned and even a few I didn't. Ownership to me means nothing. All I want now is peace. Just peace. Don't want to be watched and trailed. Don't care what they say. I owe this mess to two things. Firstly my father-in-law. A lovely old gentleman, an admiral in His Majesty's fleet. And I'm a naval man myself. Well, he put me in charge of the most fantastic kind of dreamboat. Two hundred and fifty quids. The quids, Lilly. Quids. Always watch the quids, Lilly. I don't say they mean everything, but watch them. And then the doctors. They got me. One after the other. They come in to you in the white coat with that thing for hearing hearts and they put it right over my wallet. I'll take just another little sup of tea."

Miss Frost passed the tea. Red rimmed around her eyes.

Off to work. How small we make our worlds. Gather them in, tighten them up into little castles of fear. Must get out into the meadows. Miss Frost ought to go to the Gold Coast. Get in on this ground nut scheme the good British are doing. Get what she wants for sure on that coast.

"Write to me Lilly, care of American Express, Haymarket. All right?"

"I don't think we ought to write to one another."

"Cheer up."

Miss Frost carefully chewing her sausage. Sebastian reached over and pulled the little flowered blinds apart. There's the garden that's figured so prominently in my dreams. Everything wet. Rickety tool shed. I don't believe I've even had a look in there. Broker would collapse if I arrived with rakes and shovels. Explain I was finding gardening a bore. Out there. To put one's hand to the cold earth on a morning such as this would be a hardship. Too late now for seeds or sowing. Wind bending over the shrubs. Laurels make fine hedges. Across the garden I see the tops of windows and the electric light. How cold. Wonder if anyone ever tried to pawn a plant.

"Lilly, may I have a cigarette?"

Lilly took one from her little Woodbine box and handed it across.

"Now, now Lilly, cheer up."

Tears moving down her cheeks.

"O Lilly, don't."

There was a sob. Sebastian lit his cigarette. Miss Frost shaking, stuttered breath pumping out of her throat. She stood up. Sebastian stood up. She twisted away from him.

"What's the matter, Lilly?"

Miss Frost ran from the room. Banging of her bedroom door. He waited looking at the mantelpiece. Maps and a wooden statue with a cross on the belly. Going over to the desk he pulled back the top. Hanging off by the hinges. I fouled this and beat it with the poker in rage. Everything screwed. The front door slammed shut. God save us. Sebastian quickly moved into the hall and to the door. The front gate squealing in the rain. Pulling open the door. Miss Frost was running. Dear Lilly. I'll just get down these steps and watch from the gate. There's something historical about this. A nice leg on Miss Frost. What will the neighbors think. Can hear the curtains twitching. Running down the street with the tears pouring out of her head and soft rain touching her hair. There she goes round the corner. She can move all right. I'm standing here wearing her blouse.

Sebastian went slowly back into the silent house. Stopping at the door to look at the letters all over the floor. Pick them up. Twenty-three. Would you believe it. Mean, gombeen handwriting. Every one of them rotten. They couldn't help it could they. Not at all. Had to earn a living. Clichés are the only things make sense these days. I don't want to inherit the earth. All I want is my only little barn filled with hay. Perhaps Lilly got upset because I ate the biggest sausage. I can't help myself. Don't mind with tea, can always make more. And it's mostly water so I feel it's cheap. But meat. My. Blood brings out me worst. About five shillings worth of stamps on these envelopes. Companies come to me. And I'll give you each a seal on the arse. I have always felt even in the throes of indiscretion, folly, lust and lassitude that business was for me and I for it. I've even practised twiddling my thumbs and showing my teeth in the mirror so's to amuse myself in the office when I was alone. And a few naughty habits I have too. O I'd say I've got me gambits ready. Promote me, please.

Standing in the hall, letters at his side. Sebastian at rigid attention. He did an about face. And another one. I'm on guard duty. The pictures on the walls were shaking and he marched into the morning room. Went to the desk and tore off the broken top. That'll be the last squeal out of these hinges. Picking up his calling cards. Sebastian Balfe Dangerfield. Many is the door these got me through. Perhaps to leave discreetly by the back. And on this long sheet here I have a list. Debts. I owe the whole world. Even the Eskimos. But. And this is the main thing. I've kept the dignity. Dignity in debt. A handbook for those just starting out. In debt in death.

Sebastian got a shopping bag from the garage. He moved around the kitchen filling it. Delft. Tell Mr. Gleason this cutlery is heirloomic. And a tea pot and one mixing bowl. Bag breaking down the sides. Greed befouling me. Ought to tell meself the story about the men in the boat in the West who filled it with loot till they all sank. Miserable micks.

In the bathroom. He wrapped Miss Frost's soap in the oily sort of paper the Americans are great for. Can't beat us when it comes to wrapping something up. Tie this with a nice ribbon. Hanging here are Miss Frost's nylons. Dear me, I am somewhat of a thief. Poor Lilly, but do realize it's the awful plight made me take them. Thirty shillings at a good London broker. Don't want to laden myself too much, might have to move fast. Speed's essential when spotted in the street. I'll pay you back with love and interest, Lilly. And now into your bedroom. Somewhat of a mess. If only there were more time. Might make use of these curtains for a coverall. Better look under everything. Lift them up. And this little dresser cover won't come amiss for future scarves.

Sebastian back into the morning room. Through the letters. One from the landladies.

Dear Mr. Dangerfield,

We hope everything is satisfactory, however, we would like to remind you that you are considerably in arrears—

Fix that with a little note.

My dear Misses Burton,

It has become incumbent upon me to make an extended business trip to Tangier. I have taken every precaution in closing the house having had a man from Cavandish's to polish and cover all furniture except the hall stand, and a

266

man from a reputable ironmonger's to check the locks on doors and windows.

I know that you must feel a little anxious about the garden and I am sure you will be glad to know I have gotten in touch with the Department of Agriculture to take samples of the soil so that I may have it properly prepared for a spring sowing. As soon as I have their report in my hands I shall have steps taken to have the garden brought up to standard.

I realize you must feel a certain disquiet concerning the rent now outstanding, however, upon my immediate return from Morocco I shall send a draft to you through my bank and bring the rent up to date.

The weather of late has been rather unfortunate but perhaps it will make the spring an even greater pleasure. Both Mrs. Dangerfield, who is presently holidaying in Scotland, and I extend our very best regards to you both and look forward to having you to tea upon our return.

Yours sincerely,
Sebastian Balfe DANGERFIELD.

He licked the stale glue and sealed the envelope. I'll give satisfaction if only illusory. I think it might be put I've polished. Off the furniture.

Taking the rest of the letters and knocking a straight edge, Sebastian ripped them down the center and placed them reverently on a crushed newspaper in the fireplace. Matches are one of the things I still have besides my life. Bye bye letters.

He went for a last time around the house. Into Marion's bedroom. Inspect the curtains, tuck in the corners, shut out all light. There are three library books. Overdue for eternity. Wow, it's lonely here. And this baba's bedroom. Dada, mommie says you are a cad. Easy, child, don't talk to dada like that. Dada's good dada. He big, good man. Mommie says you pawned all the dishes and pram. Nonsense, child, dada big, good man. O it might be worse. Worse than that.

He closed the doors behind him. Stood in the hall to look at a picture of a man with a beard. A handsome man for sure but must leave it behind. Now I think that's it, just lock this front door.

Turning from it he heard the front gate swing. He nipped smartly into Miss Frost's room. Through the spy hole wearing a black chesterfield, white starched collar, blue striped shirt and brown tie, Egbert Skully. His hat looks a little wet. Rain dripping fore and aft. A man in black hat and black shoes. Black is for private means and I've got none. All right. All hands. Abandon ship.

From the hole Sebastian watched Skully retreat suspiciously down the steps, look up at the green tiled roof and reclimb the steps silently. Bending over, Mr. Skully brushed his sleeve across the frosted window to look in, but the frost remained. He went down the steps again, pausing to put his face close to his and Marion's room. Thank God the windows are closed. Skully will be making for the back door and a peek in the kitchen. This is dreadful. Skully, despite your predilection for gold I think you must come from the bottom of the lowest bog. If I shoot out the front door he will see me before I get to the bottom of the street. Have the police to me for sure. Must think fast and furious. Get on this mackintosh and a quick scarf for the throat. Prepare to be prepared. This is no prepared piano. Remember the letter and must make off with this package at all costs. Eeee, Skully knocking on the morning room window. Must have spotted warm grease on the plates, you scoundrel. Trying to trap me in bed. Great Jesus. Smoke from the burning letters. He's looking up at the roof. Sly gombeen smelled one of his own cheap envelopes burning. One hope left. One way out.

Sebastian checked his shoelaces. Made a last inspection of his self-addressed envelope in which were his quids. He waited. More knocks on the morning room window. He waited again. Skully trying the back door. Security measures

268

were paying off. Now was the time. All hands. Lower away.

Sebastian opened the front door, waited an instant and then with a massive heave slammed it shut. The whole house trembled. He stood absolutely still in the hall. He heard Skully's running feet coming around the house. They stopped. Then the swinging gate squealing. This was it.

Sebastian turned on his heel and into the morning room picking up his bag and closing the curtains. Skully will come back from the bottom of the block and think he's got Sebastian, shrewdest of beasts, Dangerfield, trapped. Not so, Egbert, just not so. Opening the kitchen door quietly, locking it. Take it easy heart, save your beating till later and stop jumping round my chest. Moving across the garden and lifting himself up on top of the chicken house. On top, balancing himself, the sound of breaking. The rotting wood gave way beneath his feet. He caught the top of the wall with both hands. Paper bag came apart. God's merciful teeth, me loot lost. Control. Full steam ahead. Over this wall. A loud crash of glass at his feet passed through the top of a cold frame. For Christ's sake, twisted Jesus. Looking at the back of this house for eyes. Whoa, woman looking at me from the window. What to do? Smile, by God, smile at all costs. Come through smiling. She's scared shitless. Just as well she won't be out trying to befoul me little lifeboat or taking brooms or bricks to me. Yell to her.

"I'm sorry full moon tonight. I mean I'm mad, my wife's had an accident."

He ran between the houses and across the front stingy garden and flowerbed and with a slightly miscalculated leap cleared the iron picket fence. Put the fear of God into me, picket fences and balls don't mix. He landed falling forward on his knees, and set off at a fast run down the street. Please Skully don't be waiting behind one of these bushes or walls because my heart won't stand it and the ould lungs are coming up out of me mouth. Pity to lose my well earned plunder.

269

Egbert will never suspect that this is it. He'll wait outside the
house for weeks waiting for me to slip the white flag out
between the curtains.

And

I

Won't.

24

It's said people of letters and fine conversation frequent this place and they call it a Palace. I'm keeping out of sight. In my pocket is a ticket bought from the British & Irish Steam Packet Co., Ltd. Guarantees to get this flesh of mine to a civilized shore. At eight tonight. Signed and sealed for delivery.

Sebastian lowered malt. Walked out of this public house and moved swiftly under the portico of the Bank of Ireland. If this roof ever fell, boys, not even Skully could find me. Running across the street through the front gates of Trinity. Stopping at the notice board. Never know. May be a message from God. Peek into the porter's lodge. All of them in there smiling and rubbing hands round a nice cozy fire in the grate. Wearing nice black uniforms. Ready to give any little hope or help.

"Good morning, Mr. Dangerfield."

Boys, I give you me grin of guilt and paste it on the notice board because I won't be needing it soon. And good morning full of rashers and fresh eggs from the hot chicken rumps with coffee hopping on the hearth to the sound of the meaty sausages splitting sides in the ould thing of a pan. Good morning and how are you? Student's morning. Come follow me, students. Get the noses out from between the sheets of paper and get some of this air. You don't want this security, bad for digestion. You want something better than that. Out under the trees. I am the piper. Beep beep. You up there in the garret with your arse white with sitting. Avast. Ahoy and avast. Little right rudder. Left unfashionable. I see you all up there in your windows before dawn when you think there's no one looking, extending the piss stains down the walls. They say it has seasoned the rock. It's said the Junior Dean was hit on the head with a sackful of it wrapped in the *Irish Standard*. And don't think I've forgot when you invited me to tea and we sat round the winter fire friendly and full of cake.

Dangerfield was skipping, using the rotary step. Moving along the raised concrete at the side of the library. My passion purple, my pendant pink. Trinity covered by lovely soft rain and all its smooth carpets of grass. In the doorways over there are milk bottles which I drank. Handy for hangovers. And down here is the printing house, set back from the silvery black street where they print the exams. My little tortured dreams of breaking in to see. And along this iron fence with the chain from post to post with tops of tiny spires. And the trees in the square. Branches thrown like stale hair. And the lamp posts and inside the shiny glass. Boot scrapers on the granite porches. Seagulls wheeling from the stone buildings and standing in the street screaming. No world outside. Or hearts boiled in grief. Or scheming, cruel dying eyes. Nor spades hurrying into the soil for gold. Just micks.

A professor followed by a gray cat crossed in front of him in a dressing gown. Green white pajama legs catching a rim of wet and blue feet showing from his slippers. The professor nodded, a little early for smiling. I dip my head. I see him go up the steps and down the stone hall on his lonely academic legs with the milk whine of the cat behind.

Up in the windows here I see things that make me feel that I'm a tourist. See a man with a beard behind the grease and steam-stained glass. He's pouring tea in pots or something. Give me some. Think I met him at the Student Christian Movement. Hale and hearty fellow. O I remember reading about that in the calendar. They said the Student Christian Movement is a fellowship of students who desire to understand the Christian faith and to live the Christian life. This desire is the only condition of membership. I beg you, let me belong. Met that man there. Apt to forget a lot of things. I came to the Student Christian Movement with an open heart. And mouth. And stood at the door of No. 3

272

shyly aware of salvation. A blond, curly haired young man came forward offering his hand in a strong warm greeting. Welcome to our little society, come in, let me introduce you. You're doing law? I've seen you around college. We're a very little group here. This is Miss Feen, Miss Otto, Miss Fitzdare, Miss Windsor and Mr. Hindes, Tuffy and Byrne. Now won't you let me get you some tea. Weak or strong? Weak please. In the corner a kettle on a gas ring, steaming in the evening air. A piano. Miss Fitzdare wore a soft woolen light gray frock and as she passed under my quivering nose, a winter perfume. She offered me a cream cake and asked is this your first time here? First time, yes. I thought she was lovely. While she was saying not many college people are interested, I leaned and said tenderly to her, a cordial group. We try to be. O I think you succeed admirably. I'm particularly looking forward to attending your prayer meetings. I let out my halo and she said she was so glad and are you fond of singing. The song is of course for me. Please say some more, Miss Fitzdare. We have some very fine voices in the group. And you, Miss Fitzdare, do you? With me. Sometime. Maybe. Pass under my nose again. I went out that night in the cold smells of Dublin and last streaks of light. Down Dame Street with hope and massive heart. In that little group singing me high twisted notes. Not altogether agreeing in all respects but at least warmed by their kind considerate faces, their bright eyes. I loved them so much.

He walked between the corners of the two buildings in back of the Queen's Theater. Feeling all is closed for winter. This back end and never noticed place. One night I climbed up on the bank of grass by the playing field and wept between my knees. And Saturday afternoons I came here to watch them bust each other's head chasing a ball. Just a few people lined along the edges of the field in mufflers and up-turned collars. Back here are the science buildings where they put the stuff together to go boom. And the Botany Department and pretty flowers. It must be so nice to just grow

273

plants for a degree. And the examination hall. Begging permission to live. Better than most. The Physics building where I spent a shilling to go to the Gramophone Society. Chilly but pleasant. And beyond the tennis courts the Zoology building. In there is an impressive collection of insertivora and an elephant standing in the middle of the room. I went up those steps and pressed the shiny bell for visitors and they came to usher me in to look around. And after lectures in law I came to this little museum to look at the bats. You might say I had a lot of little fancy occupations. Stuffed animals my specialty. And the sports pavilion. Played the odd game of tennis here with Jim Walsh. You didn't know that either. And the tub of cold cold water. These rugby roughs in from the pitch to plunge in bellowing. I was content to stand under the shower till I was nicely scalded.

Sebastian passed under the arch of the back gate of Trinity College. Crossed Fenian Street amid the wild manoeuvers of carts and cars. Walking with head bent, looking up now and again to chart the territory ahead. Up Merrion Street and the sun came out shining on the government buildings. Secretaries with morning hip swinging turning in the doorways. All their lips bright red. Red coats across their broad backs. Men in dark overcoats passing with red noses, red raw hands. Girls had purple ankles. I go on. Faster. Along the Lower Baggot. Quick right, lash up Pembroke and around the Square with pretty Georgian doors. I crossed Fitzwilliam Place and touched the iron fences as I went by. Till I opened a narrow gate and went down the steep steps. Knocking. No answer. Rap the S.O.S. on the window. Bring him for sure. I know Tone's a great man for the seafaring. The light goes on. Door opens and Tony Malarkey peeks out.

"Jesus, Sebastian, I had to be sure."

"And quite right. Hello Tony."

"I haven't answered the door for weeks."

"A little bit of the landlord?"

"I'm beat. How are you? Come in while I bolt it up."

Sebastian waited behind Tony watching as he closed the

door and lowered a stout board into place, jamming it tight with several wedges.

"Eeeeeee it's good, Tone. Good."

"O Jesus it's taken the youth out of me. No more just rapping, they try to break it down. I worked all night on it and had it ready in the morning. They came along with two policemen, thick peelers, couldn't make it budge. They just stand out there with their bloody papers mumbling and me just behind the door ready to send the first head through to the moon. Bad for the kids, couldn't let them out at all."

"I say, Tone, what's happened?"

"I moved everything out. Sent Terry and the kids down to the country. I'm in this tomb holding out just in case they give up trying to evict. It's good, isn't it."

Sebastian sat on the window sill. Tony leaning against the stove, grinning over his folded arms, a pair of pampooties on his crossed feet. This bare room with a single pot hanging over the stove and their voices echoing on the damp thick walls. Looking at each other. Dangerfield bent himself double. Squealed. Tony put back his head and laughed. The windows shook.

"Would you say Tone that there is no end to it? Would you say that now?"

"Jesus I would and I haven't even got a spare bullet for the gun."

"Would you say you're ready for a little bit of sleep, a nap in the 'Nevin'? Here lies the body of Tone who left only a moan. Would you say that?"

"Sebastian we're all finished. This last month has really been the worst. When things are bad you keep telling yourself they can't get worse. Then they get worse. And stay that way until you're so weary and screwed you can't even worry anymore. It gets like that. So damn bad that you have to cheer up or die. Clocklan was right, the whore. Up there selling God clouds."

"Kenneth told me."

"That was the way to do it. A bottle of Jameson and off

the mail boat. I've been reading in the papers to see if the old whore will wash up somewhere. Just like him to come up on some bathing strand next summer and frighten the life out of some poor defenseless kids."

"Do you really think he went off the boat, Tone?"

"I don't know what to think. No one's heard from the ould whore since. It wouldn't surprise me if he's off somewhere like Cardiff screwing some old hag for the few quid she's worth. O'Keefe's finally gone. It's a shame."

"On the high seas."

"A pity."

"Well, Tone, what are you going to do?"

"I haven't a whore's notion."

"Where do you sleep?"

"Come here till I show you. This will give you a laugh."

Sebastian followed him down the long passage, their voices echoing from the dark deep rooms. Sebastian stopped at the door. Malarkey went over to the wall and striking a match on the scaly stone lit a gas mantle.

"Twisted Jesus. I say Tone that's a little bit of the fantastic."

"I knew it would give you a laugh."

In this long pink room. At both ends there were huge railroad spikes driven into the wall to which were attached stout ropes suspending a gigantic hammock lined with a black overcoat.

"Tone, may the Blessed Oliver pray for us all."

Tony with a swift skillful leap landed in the center of this mammoth black cradle. He reached out his hand.

"Hand me that cord on the wall, Sebastian."

Grinning Malarkey pulled on the cord drawing himself towards the wall, releasing it to slip through his fingers. The hammock rocking gently back and forth. From the door faint animal squeaks of Dangerfield.

"Tone, if this weren't the Catacombs, if I weren't deep down here in the cats with an honest man such as yourself

276

I would say it was lies I saw but seeing is, and watching is, believing."

"I'll tell you something. I would have gone out of my mind if it weren't for this, Sebastian. It's been the saving of me. I had nowhere to sleep and just this coat and ould junk. I couldn't get a night's rest on the floor with the suburban community of rats. So with the coat a rich American gave me and this rope I found while looking for something to whip into the pawn I got to work."

Tony lifted up the coat.

"I braided this out of some old bits of string and rags. It's the good gas."

"Tony, you've got so much brains you'll never amount to a thing."

"Isn't it the way, Sebastian. Tell me, what's new?"

"I'm going to London."

"You're not?"

"Tonight's mail boat."

"What's happened?"

"It's so involved I don't know."

"That's fair enough."

"Tone, we're all going to the wall."

"They've been trying to get me out of this place for over a year and they haven't succeeded yet. It's the only satisfaction I get out of life. Just screwing this landlord. But I'll tell you Sebastian, while there's a spud left in Ireland, I won't be beat. A lot of faces will be bashed in before I'm finished."

"Them's the words, Tone."

"It's the kids. I don't know what I'll do. They've got to have a place to live. I've got to find something. Get my hands on a few quid. Just a few nicker and I could get a little farm in the Wicklows."

"Turn to gangsterism."

"Sebastian, I couldn't."

"Tone, pride has you at its mercy."

"Has me by the very ballocks."

"Tony, I think a pint would see us right."

"I think you're right for the first time since you last said that."

"Wait till I use your toilet."

"You can't."

"I say, Tone, what?"

"Jesus, I ripped the damn thing out and sold it down the quays for thirty bob."

"God's teeth."

"A fine bit of lead too, fetched eight and six."

"Will we ever see the end."

"I'm desperate."

"Now Tone, tell me. I'm professionally interested. How did you get a thing like that down to the quays?"

"In the pram. Tied a ribbon on it. Pillow and blanket."

"I think it can be said Tone that we've both pushed more than babies in the pram."

"Terry had a fit."

"How is she?"

"Fine."

"And the kids?"

"They have no idea. Everything's great. Beauty of kids. They only miss love and food."

"And while there's a potato left, eh Tone?"

"You're right."

"I think the pint now. Time for pint."

They paused at the front door. Tony fiddling with his elaborate fortifications.

"Now watch this, Sebastian."

Tony adjusted the stout board wedging it perpendicularly at the side of the door. Sebastian stepped out, watching with interest. Tony slammed the door. Inside the sound of the board slipping into place.

"For the love of the B.O.P."

"Isn't it good?"

"I wouldn't relish you as an enemy, Tone. How do you get in?"

"Now watch."

Tony opened the door to the coal cellar. Reaching carefully around the wall grinning. He held out a cord.

"This goes through the wall and you just pull it back until the board jams up against the door frame and bob's your rudd. Took a lot of fiddling."

"Someone told me Tone that you can take sixty thousand volts through one ear and out the other while singing *The West's Awake*."

"Who in Christ's name told you that? I didn't want that to get around."

"Eeeee, we're going to win. Win win win. Do you hear me out there? Win."

They set off for Lower Baggot Street. Into the house on the corner. Malarkey wearing a purple scarf with tiny yellow and green stripes tucked up carefully to hide garments that had seen better days on the back of a rich American. Dangerfield holding his female mackintosh closed with a baby's big safety pin.

"Sebastian, I hear from reliable sources that you have been getting a bit from your boarder."

"I beg your pardon, Tone."

"You shrewd whore."

"Miss Frost is joining the Carmelites."

"You mean a kip."

"I assure you, Tone, for your own peace of mind that no commerce, carnal or otherwise, has taken place between us. On the contrary, Miss Frost and I often attended Benediction together. Took the holy water on the cheeks. Of the face. Do you know she has a very fine voice. Bit of baritone but with heart. Yes, heart. Puts her heart in it. Sings from the bottom of."

"If you weren't screwing Miss Frost day and night and mostly nights, I'd give up drinking and betting for life."

"Eeeeeeeee."

Gathering pennies from the bar, they moved to another pub on the Baggot Street. Sebastian who said he felt a slight chill coming on had several double brandies.

"Do you know Sebastian I've got to get a farm as soon as I lay my hands on some quids. Only way to live. Make packs of money."

"Tone, I think we put too much faith in the farm. Get this farm and then be out there at dawn feeding pigs and some bull sneaking up for a good butt in the arse."

"You're right."

"I'll be sorry to leave, Tone."

"Not at all."

"A bit of sadness. The burial boat. But I need the change. Over the water and far away. The greenness will be gone. Strange, Tone, how you, direct descendant of the original king, take so much in your own country. Without land or spuds."

"If it weren't for me ould blood being blue I'd have sold it at the hospital long ago."

"But never mix it, Tone. Never do that. Our day will come. Just stave off the starving and a few other things and our day will come."

The holy hour of two-thirty when public houses get the big iron gates shuttered across the doors to keep the thirsty out. They went to the Green Cinema where they sat at a white table and golfed down platefuls of rashers, eggs and chips. When they came out the traffic was stopped. Heads out of the cars and honking horns. Down the street a huge hulking man lay himself down in the road and went to sleep. Some said he had drink taken. Others that he was listening to see if he could hear the pulse of the city. Sebastian danced and yelped. Newsboys in the crowd asked him what he was doing. Dog dance, sonny.

They walked down the Friday throng of Grafton Street and by the customers waiting for the cinema. Heavy skies coming over the city. Dark dark. Glow of lamps in the Grafton Cinema Cafe. My haven. Bikes flooding up towards the traffic jam which was becoming general throughout the city. The public houses filling with the huddled men wiping noses across sleeves and on chilblained knuckles. Bartenders hard at work. Serving up to the voices touched with bravado of payday, and mouths shut on Monday. And now we go down Wicklow Street because on this street there is a public house which I have always found very special. It can't be beat for the mahogany or barrels. When I go there the man is nice to me and has even asked if I went to the theatre. For once I didn't lie outright, and I said no. What do I say when I lie? I'll tell you. I say my name is a Gooseky and I'm from Westsky every Leapsky.

Dangerfield got his hand through to the man for two foaming pints of plain. They retreated to a corner. Put the pints on a shelf. Tony brought out a box of butts.

"Good God. Tone."

"I got these out of the fireplace of an American in Trinity. They throw them away big."

"Put them away. Away Tone and permit me in a moment of lavish to treat you to twenty."

Huddled over cigarettes and porter. There comes a time in the city of Dublin, when the glass tinkles. Morning despair and afternoon's passive agony fruits in a jell of joy. And leaks all over when it melts later. I look into Tone's face, which is Ireland.

"What would you do, Tone, if you ever got money. A lot of money."

"Do you want the truth?"

"I want the truth."

"First thing, I'd get a suit made. Then I'll come along to the Seven Ts and put a hundred pound note on the bar. Drink up the whole kip of ye. I'll send a hundred quid to O'Keefe and tell him to come back. May even, if I get drunk enough, put a plaque in the sidewalk on the corner of Harry and Grafton. Percy Clocklan, keeper of the kip who farted on this spot, R.I.P. Then, Sebastian, I'll start from College Green and I'll walk every inch of the way from here to Kerry getting drunk at every pub. It'll take me about a year. Then I'll arrive on Dingle Peninsula, walk out on the end of

Slea Head, beat, wet and penniless. I'll sit there and weep into the sea."

"Tone, take this."

Dangerfield placed a folded pound note in Malarkey's fist.

"Jesus, thanks Sebastian."

"So long, Tone."

"Good luck."

Shaking hands. Sebastian drained his glass. Hand in front wedging cracks between the overcoats, finding a way out into the street. He stood on the corner. Look up into the wild, dark sky. Pin the mackintosh up around the throat. Stop the sneaky drafts. And hands in the wet cold pockets. While I try to get up heat rubbing the pennies. I've got a passport. Two hours left. I've seen whores walking along this street. In there they sell the dishes. And this ironmonger's great black window. Think of the basins in there, miles of copper pipes, tubs and lawnmowers. I love it along here. I want to die in a country district with the cemetery not far away. Rural for me. Rural last ride. A casket without handles. All I ask is don't nail it too tight.

Sebastian entered the side door of the Bleeding Horse. Lowered a Power's Gold Label. A man approached in British attire speaking French. I told him my bile was green. He said you speak French. Goo goo mick mick.

Out the door. Up the street. Down the steps. Peek in the window. Knock on the door. Shuffle of her slippers. Twinge of hesitation. In there is flesh I took against mine. I licked it, pinched, pushed, tickled. O aye, her buzzuma. And when I've felt a bottom like hers I won't forget too fast or ever. I ask you heart to stop beating like the hammers of hell. Here comes her hair round the door.

"Me."

"O."

"May I come in? Please. I know me big foul man. Big beast. All that. I know. But."

"You reek with drink."

"Chris, cross my heart, like any good Romish Papist."

282

"Come in then. Sit down. No need to stand. Sit. I don't want to be used. Just like some shoe you put your foot in. Why haven't you come to see me before this?"

"I'm leaving for London on the mail boat in an hour. Cheer up."

"I won't cheer up. Not for your leather soul."

"Whoops. Wait a minute. Now I don't want you to feel like that. Please. Not the leather soul. Maybe plaster or jade."

"Why didn't you tell me before this? Your affairs were in a mess and there were some misunderstandings."

"There were. Please now. Come out and just have a drink."

"No."

"Please now."

"What do you think I am? Here day after day. Lonely. Hoping you might come. Not a word. What do you think it's like? What do you know about how a woman feels? You don't know anything about life."

"I know about life. I'm in this too."

She turned and smoothed out a pantie. Ran the iron over the lace. Folded it and laid it on the pile of neat clothes. Sebastian sat, face adjusted for listening. With elbows resting on knees. Legs split for comfort in slight despair and chin resting in the cups of his hands.

"Couldn't you have written?"

"I meant to."

"And now you just come here to tell me you're going. Just like that. Haven't you ever suffered? Or been miserable?"

"I've made mistakes. I never know when they're going to get me. I'm not heartless. If I could catch my breath. I'd make all this up to you. I don't forget when people are good to me. But when I risk getting my arse caught on a spike, get chased and beaten up, I've got to do the best I can. Start over again in London. There's a little money I'm due for across the seas. I'm not a bad person."

"Don't be such a fool."

"Ireland's been too much for me. Badgering and insult. You can come to London."

"Write me about it."

"Will you come? Jesus, come."

"Write me. That coat looks ridiculous."

"My magic cloak. A little kiss."

Kissing in the lonely basement room. Footsteps in the hall. Holding one of her softened hands. I've made peace. Go up and out. A last look. Bye.

A blast of wind and rain beating me on the back. Across the street now to get that warm lighted bus and swing inside. I see Chris closing her door. Busman's bell and hot wet air. Wipe some of this steam off the window because out there are shop fronts of toys, sides of beef and stained secret windows of public houses.

On the quays with bag-laden figures hurrying on the candy cobble stones past the gangway lights of moored ships. Seagulls fluttering white wings in the dark. Under the light of the entrance, passengers scattering good-byes between the taxis and newsboys. I buy my last *Evening Mail*. I travel East. To the more established civilizations.

"Baggage, sir?"

"None."

"Anything to declare?"

"Nothing."

Between the narrow steep rails. Ship's light bleak yellow. Along this deck the windows shielding against the sea. Nearly eight. Nearly gone. Go around to the Liffey side of the ship. Down there are the waters from Blessington. Man taking the cable to the other side. I want to see some seamanship, boys. Smartly. Making too much noise with those oarlocks. South over there is the Trinity College, the Ballsbridge, Donnybrook, Milltown, Windy Harbour and beyond. I know them all. Cold killing wind between my knees. Slant black spires of the little mountains. Within that carpet of light. All my tiny sad despairs. Like watching out of my tower. Gather my ships from the edges of the sea. Called from where they were dying. I don't want to go. But if I don't? I have nowhere to call my own again. What can I say? Tell me. What can I say? So much I would like to keep forever. Flecks of water brushed from oily laurel leaves or my steps during the silences of morning or late night. And the donkey calls. Or as I lay on my back in Ireland looking up out of the world. There was a day in summer when I walked up the mountain and stood at Kilmurry. From the bottom of the steep green fields and all the way to the Moulditch Bank, a blue trembling brim of sea, a little white. On this day there was a train coming up from Wicklow town towards Dublin. Crawling across my hand. Spread on the meadowed bottom land. The sun was shining on this train. Carrying my heart away. They send off the whistle so I almost jump out of my shoes. And it comes back from the broken houses along John Rogerson's Quay. I hear the winch. Click and growl. White wash fanning away on the water. Tenderly to midstream. By other boats and the half island of Ringsend. Is there a nest of fire and home within those windows? This ship slipping between the lighthouses of Bailey and Muglins. Man riding a bicycle on the Pigeon House Road. Howth and Dalkey. I feel the sea under me.

> I set sail
> On this crucifixion Friday
> With the stormy heavens
> Crushing the sea
> And my heart
> Twisted
> With dying.

25

Undo this safety pin. Miss Frost's blouse. This rusty pull-over. Put these on the chair. And I think cover my nudity with trusty blotched mackintosh. Walk on the rug in bare feet, dig the toes in something awful.

Opening the door, stepping out into this wide hall. A chamber maid coming around the corner. Her kindly young smile looking rather closely at my ankles.

"Would you like a bath towel, sir?"

"Well—"

I'm confused, pausing in the hall in an embarrassing condition for consideration of a towel due to possibility of foot smell and the valleys of me soiled with deposits of poverty.

"Only a minute, sir. They're nice and hot."

"Well. Hot. Yes. Is that it there?"

"The door on your right, sir."

"Well thank you."

"Not at all, sir."

The vagaries of this species. Her little hat. Flounce. Pushing open this impersonal door and switching on the light. In the far corner of the room a tub to bathe the world. So fat and far and full. Cork topped chair. Taps. Gigantic things. Just take off this waterproof garment and get a sup of the libido. A little of this ego admiration in the mirror. Now I haven't a bad build at all. Trifle swell at the waist. Odd rib showing. Flex the muscles. Good god. Must join an athletic club.

He was closing the little window, looking out in the stream of chill air to see all the windows. In this enormous city. I know there are business men here. I know it.

A knock. Of a type well delivered with the metacarpals.

"Sir?"

"One moment."

Opening the door. Naked shoulder. Please don't think me devoid of modesty. Young woman, do you know that this is risky business? I mean to say, you know, two of us and one man and one woman. Honestly, I think perhaps I wouldn't be past possessing you. Out of kindness if nothing else.

"Here you are. It's nice and big. Silly little towels wouldn't dry an ant."

"Ha, ha."

"Prewar, sir."

"Indeed, I thank you very much."

"And very welcome you are, sir."

Closing the door and taking this towel which was every bit a rather large carpet. And turning the taps and the water pouring out. Lowering into it. Sitting back in this warm balm. I have been delivered from many a tired year and cold day with walking streets ill shod, ferrying my educated soul, slipping sensibly behind barrels, walls and battlements, playing undiscovered and overdrawn at banks and everywhere.

Floating. Nothing like it. Bit of the body suspension. Last night in the ship's lane. They asked me where I was staying. Under a bush in Hyde Park. And out of the train I saw the scraggy trees. Delighted to see so many streets. Tomorrow read the personals.

Gentleman going abroad for year, wishes contact suitable person, fond of shooting, country life, to care for estate, fully staffed. Must love animals. Adequate remuneration.

More. More of same. I tell you there's lushness. And other straight figures and delicate fingers like my own. And tall lank women. Low shoed. And pink for pure. Rust for honesty. I'm a piece of old iron.

Huge bathroom warmed up. Sitting on the cork and drying carefully between the toes. Up for a last look at me in the mirror. I think the steam has made it bigger.

Enclosed in the mackintosh, stepping into comforts. Large double bed, and sink and mirror sparkling in the light. Thick flower covered comforter. And perhaps an Axminster rug, the like of which the likes of Mr Skully has never seen. The Irish do have these small pretentions. Dear Egbert, do you think I'm still behind the curtains?

Corner of the bed laid back and bare. Just let me lie down here now. I don't think I've ever been quite as nude before. Makes you think. Of others. Lilly, lately I've thought of you. Don't join the nuns.

He reached out for the phone. Buzz buzz. Click click.

"May I please speak to Mr. MacDoon."

"I'll see if he's in."

With these talking machines hear a lot of queer things. Leprechaun feet coming.

"Hello?"

"This is Dangerfield."

"Say that again."

"This is Dangerfield."

"Just once more."

"This is Dangerfield."

"Now for the mercy of our savior who has wasted his Rh negative blood for the poor likes of us, don't tell me you're in London?"

"Mac, I am. And tell me is there violence here? I abhor violence and those who wander the streets kicking the very bejesus out of the downtrodden."

"As soon as you hang up I'll tell Parnell, bare and hairy chested king of killers, to alert the underworld to let you pass safely and swiftly."

"Can you put me up?"

"Up. Exactly. I can if you want to hang by your throat from the ceiling. We supply all guests with a hook. I've got little rings in the ceiling. The room is nine by eleven and I can put up forty guests of an evening. His Majesty couldn't do any better. Of course I sleep on a bed. A little disconcerting to have so many twisting feet pointing down at you of a morning, get that trampled feeling."

"Would you say, Mac, there was a bit of the abbattoir in it?"

"I'd say that. When are we going to see you?"

"Right away. Just have to dress so as not to present a state of undress to the public."

"Do you know how to get here?"

"I'd say so Mac. But this is top secret. Not a word to anyone. Expect me in an hour."

"The red, white and blue carpet will be out. There are two huge animals out front. Put your fist in the mouth of the one on the left, nothing political in that, and pull on the tongue."

"If it bites me, Mac, I'll never forgive you."

"Bye bye."

"Beep beep."

Ah O me O my this is it. I'm just a mad stallion. With pink eyes. Wouldn't you just like to see me now. Marion, wouldn't you? I'm not bitter. O no. I'm quite calm. Completely relaxed. But when you come to me in Mayfair when things are as they ought to be, don't try to move in and think things are going to be jake again. Don't worry. The time of the faithless will come and you'll get a good boot in the arse. God I look good tonight. Color in me cheeks. My nostrils just quiver with the sensibility that does be in me. Lashings of the hot water out of this tap. This soap is fragrant. Mary, I'll wash you with it.

There were smiles in the lobby. Marble halls for sure. Out into the night life. A quiet park across the street. I like this. Walk around here. And down into the Underground. Everybody's got jewelry on. That girl has a nice gray suit. Hands bit heavy round the knuckles. But a pair of legs that must be lovely. I hope she doesn't think I'm staring at her. Because I'm really aloof. I'm just looking at your legs and wondering how they are further up. Or maybe you could even give me directions how to get to MacDoon's. These seats are comfortable. Keep my legs like this because I think my soles are going to drop off any minute. Have to use the shuffle walk from here on in. Not a time to be chased.

So many faces to look at. Up these stairs. Her legs are extraordinary. I must ask her the way. I've got to.

"I beg your pardon but could you tell me the way to Minsk House."

"Yes, certainly. Third turning on the right."

"Thank you. I hope you won't mind my telling you you have lovely legs?"

"Well no. I guess not."

"Take good care of them now. And thank you very much indeed."

"Thank you."

I haven't got the heart to involve her. A girl like that deserves a fair chance. Her teeth bit small but even and clean and I always say give me the even and clean to dirty big ones all the time. Not a bad area at all. Must say MacDoon keeps the fashion at all costs and now that I've seen a bit of this city I think I'd agree with him there. Good heavens. That must be it. Are those lions or what. I daren't put my hand in there, might never come out again. But I've got to do it. Blessed Oliver deliver me from fangs. He said pull it. Feels like something I'd rather not talk about. I don't see a thing anywhere. Perhaps Mac is a bit whoopsie doodle in there. I know he gets up to the most fantastic things. I hear something.

A door opening and closing. A shadow passing on the wall. A figure bending over a barrel. Stuffing something in, pulling something out. Somebody say something.

"I say. I say there, Mac? Is it you Mac?"

MacDoon. Small dancing figure. It is said his eyes are like the crown jewels. A sharp red beard on his chin. Leprechaun for sure. Can't speak too loudly to Mac, else he may blow away.

"Come down, come down, come down. Down Dangerfield down."

"Mac, everybody I know these days lives down. Now why is that?"

"The times, the times. And how's your hammer hanging. Step this way, Danger. Into the jaws of strife."

There was a door with a mouth around it. Lips were red and teeth white.

"Mac, this is terrifying. Will I get out undigested."

"And unmolested."

"Mac, I'm relieved to be in London."

"Sit down. I would say you had the odd bit of angst around the eyes."

"A bit of it."

"Now tell me all. I hear they have new bells in hell."

There were two nice soft chairs. A gas fire burning a blue flame on top of which was a pot of glue. On the walls were private prongs. Large ones, medium and curved and, as Mac said, one in the image and likeness of. From a little colorful box came whimpering.

"Mac, for heaven's sake what's in there?"

"Progeny."

"My."

"Now Danger I want news."

"Well I think I can say I've come a long, a rather long way. I can see it all now. It's been hard, evil and even unfair at times. Shall we look at it that way."

"Danger, I want blood."

"Now of course there's been the odd bit of blood. A bit of that. And confusion. Marion's at Withwait with Felicity."

"To interrupt for a moment, Danger. Now I always thought that you would do the right thing and take over one of the wings of Withwait Hall. It's always been the feeling in Dublin that that would be the natural course of events. We felt it would only be a matter of time before guilt drove Admiral Wilful Wilton to suicide and that old lady Wilton would be immediately sent to Harrogate to recover from the blow while you sold off the shooting rights and became the squire of Withwait. Fashion now Danger."

"Mac I agree. Death can do me lots of favors."

"And we hear old man Dangerfield isn't well."

"That's true Mac and I must say it makes me very anxious. I'm just screwed. They call me an apostate. They say I've tried to save my own rather blemished skin. Here I am reduced to accent. No hearth nor home. But being here makes me feel there's hope yet. And I'll tell you this. As badly treated as I've been I'll not forget those who gave the helping hand. Even now Tone Malarkey is down behind his battlements. I think if God ever took him into heaven he'd never get him out again. And I think he is secretly planning to win a few quid and buy cement blocks and just concrete himself in with a tunnel down to the Daids for the odd pint. He said the pumping parts of his heart are pure carborundum. Now both of us know that that's pretty hard stuff even with the current rampant scientific advance. Tone said he got the way he is eating live salmon out of the Shannon. And Tone is the only man I know who has never told a lie."

"Danger, I have to admit that what you say is true."

"What in the name of God is that, Mac?"

"He, he."

Mac lifted from a crumpled heap at the foot of his bed the head of a kangaroo. He put it over his skull and wagged it. He climbed into the rest of the body and danced around the room.

"Mac, I think it's magnificent."

"My drinking suit. And here, a little present I know you will appreciate."

Mac hands over a small brown replica of the head of Blessed Oliver.

"Mac, I don't think you'll ever know how much I need or will cherish this. The teeth are perfect. Most significant part of Oliver. Eeeeee and E for effort. Help me spread the fair name of Oliver to these ones with not an ounce of God in them."

"I made the teeth from a piano key."

"Miraculous."

"Wear it."

"I will. And now Mac I must ask us both have we got mouths."

Climbing up out through the jaws, gray trees and night. Along the empty wet streets. Huge windows there and a servant comes and pulls the curtains. A great black car glides by, tires humming on the street.

"Mac, that's good to see."

"I agree Danger."

"And I haven't seen such wealth for years. Not for years. And I need it. Need it."

"And up here Danger is the Bear Pit but first I must show you something across the street which I know you will be taken with."

MacDoon led Dangerfield over the road. They stopped in front of a fountain and a recess in the wall. There was a poem.

God
Bless
The
Poor.

"Mac, I hope it won't embarrass you if I just kneel down here and offer up a little prayer from the pavement. That's a very fine thing. If more people felt that way would we have strife? Would we? I ask you would we have strife?"

"I can only say Danger that I have been driven to designing bras the uplift of which will put a new lust into the hearts of these citizens."

The mellow lights through the frosted windows. Entering into the saloon bar with its flowers and decks of sandwiches. The polished chairs and tables. People of a class with dogs.

MacDoon brought over the two pints and laid them on the shiny table. Thirst was general.

Dangerfield leaned back in his chair, folding his legs far away under the table. He smiled.

Sitting talking of Dublin when it had been the Rome of the world. O it's little pitfalls and despairs. Of Clocklan who abandoned ship. MacDoon told of the hard demands made by woman, of how he was beginning to wish he had none at all or that it was so big as to be carried by the London Fire Brigade for use on major fires.

And these dogs. Happy hungry animals. If only I owned one. I know they foul the streets and are at times disgusting with others on various village greens. Despite indelicacy I want one. Preferably of a fine breed and pedigree to go with my own. And MacDoon I must admit you're extraordinarily handsome with fine hands and here you are tinkering in this endless city. Perhaps Mary can pose for you when you design the large sizes. And bring home the bacon to some nice airy room with a fine gas ring and rugs hanging on the walls where I can sit like a detective smoking a pipe and resting feet. I'll read books. Polish my fingernails. I don't care about the other greedy ones. I think I'll have another bath before I go bye bye to my bedi bo.

They parted at the station. Where the red trains went in went out. An Earl's Court for sure. And I ride along on these nice cars looking at everyone.

Back at the hotel crawling weary on the heavy bed. Face on the pillow, covers up over me. And cars squealing around the corners out there.

I set sail all right. Saw the lights of Holyhead. The black Liverpool. And the still birds standing up on top of that building. Cotton, meat and grain. I look down from the deck into the faces terrified of recognition. Safe only at sea. I got breakfast, a three-penny paper, and looked at all those girls in red lips and curlers. I'm alone. And took the train. The land was gray. And when I got here all the others were taking big cars and taxis everywhere and I had no one and just walked down the platform wondering what to do. I see them all greeted with kisses.

And not
One
For me.

26

Upon London Sunday, Sebastian Dangerfield went by advice of MacDoon to a place in the Bovir Road where he took a room on the top floor of this yellow Victorian house. Tiny tidy room. A soft bed covered with green ticking. In the corner by the large window an oak table, a chair and another of basket weave. Twisted electric fire in the wall and a shilling meter by the door. A basin and a bath across the hall where on a chair you can see down on the tracks and station.

Every morning a rap on the door by an Indian woman. Breakfast. Reach out and on with the electric fire. Into the clothes. Down these dark stairs. Come in where they all smile and say hello and others good morning. Cozy trimming and pots of dried flowers. Always been partial to them. I know these people are from the Commonwealth. That woman says her son has a new job. Yes, you know they decided to move him up. Madam, that's just great.

Every morning it's like this. Porridge with lashings of milk and sugar. Then the bacon and eggs. Bring them on. O I tell you. And the Indian woman bringing in the pots of tea. And every morning I go back up the stairs and look out the window while they go by in the street with little umbrellas. And that woman over there who delights in it. I know she does. Standing naked and unabashed by her window with a certain hauteur looking back at me from between the towel drying her face. Don't think I don't see you, sister. You've got a good husky body. But if I saw you in the street dressed I think perhaps you would be different with your white lace coming out at various places from your suit.

Come down the stairs and look for my name on any of the letters. Up the street and stop to look in the pit of a bombed out building where a cat prowls. Buy a paper from the woman in the newsagents. Go back and sit with legs up

on the window ledge. O I think there's going to be a sign.
Big one. And it's going to say Dangerfield Lives.

On late Monday there was the guilty letter to Mary, O me
ould tired, tried and true love, come to London and bring
fifteen pounds and I'll meet you at the station and take you
back to my little womb.

Wednesday night. Having come up frightened of the dark
on the stairs. A telegram on the bed.

ARRIVING EUSTON FRIDAY FIVE P.M. LOVE MARY

Thursday. Dangerfield up the road cutting a fine figure
and putting his hand in the animal mouth and giving a tug
on the tongue. In the steamy air MacDoon twisting a wire
to make a kangaroo tail. This man Parnell holding an end of
it with pliers. MacDoon reaches and pulls a yellow envelope
from behind a mirror. Hands it to Dangerfield.

"For you Danger, arrived this afternoon."

Sitting, Dangerfield opens the envelope with nervous
fingers. There was silence. All waiting. A frown and smack-
ing of lips.

"Mac, would you ever pour me a cup of tea with a twist
of lemon?"

"Bad news, Danger?"

"Remains to be seen. My father's dead."

"Sorry to hear that."

MacDoon hopping to the pot, pouring the tea. He swept
out a narrow of lemon into the cup with his gouging chisel.
To the bottom of the iodine tinted tea. Sebastian leaning back
in the chair. Parnell turning the wire with the pliers.
MacDoon going up in the air at the other end. Dark outside.
Watching the blue flame eating up the gas and reddening
the tiny asbestos nobs. Perhaps no time to face the future.
They say there is good in everyone. If you just give them a
chance. And a good boot in the arse.

"O.K. out out out. Everybody. Quick. To the Bear Pit.
Mac. Whiskey, whiskey."

MacDoon drops a shoe he was fitting into the foot of the kangaroo. Parnell adjusting his glasses with a certain academic flourish, clearing his throat several times. And a whimper from the little babe in the box.

"Mac will you let me some day take your son away with me for a little trip I intend to make to the Isle of Man for a rest. I'm considering having a small chapel built on the top of Snaeffell. And perhaps you'll say a little mass for me there."

"Certainly, Danger."

"Parnell, would you look up a reputable tailor in the Row for me?"

"Sure, Danger."

"Something like a prewar Humber with a luggage carrier might suit me. Would I see one of those in Mayfair, Mac? Would I?"

"For certain."

"Good. Yes. Yes. That's very good. See a lot of things. Brass name plates. They're in there. In there behind that brass. And I think I will go to live in Old Queen Street."

"Danger, do I smell richness coming into your life?"

"You might put it that way, Mac. Yes. I think you could put it that way. Would you ever say now that this room had the universal twitch. Could we say that?"

"You could say that Danger."

"I've known Mondays come on a Friday. Thursdays on Tuesdays. But Sunday is a day I can never accept. Can I put it this way? I think we all need a drink."

"Danger, Parnell and meself have been driven to agree. And now if you will all kneel down I'll give you me black blessing and sprinkle the holy juice over your young innocent heads, a fine bunch of pagans you are anyway."

"Mac, you'd say I was conceived in idolatry. Parnell here by mistake and you yourself not even at all."

"Aye."

There was a certain amount of giggling. Dangerfield squeezing into the kangaroo. Parnell attaching the wire tail.

Danger was lifted to the street. A strange crew. The kangaroo head rolling the little blobs of eyes around in the cellophane sockets. Red bearded MacDoon supporting himself with a shepherd's staff. Parnell beating an empty tin with a spoon. Procession of saints and beasts. Fourteen wild stations of the cross. Pagans.

The bar was awash. Uncontrolled pints. It was said in the pit that there had never been a night like it. Dublin brought to London. Some say the Romans were Kerry men in disguise. Talk about resting and seeing everything a little more clearly and arranging affairs. Conclusions were reached. Better with than without. And if without better here than there. Thirst.

Dangerfield sitting with the kangaroo head off looking a sight with the pregnant belly Mac had put to the animal and the little baby hanging its confused head out of the pouch. There was talk about MacDoon getting inside the little one and Dangerfield carrying him in the pouch so as to make it cheaper traveling to Soho. Tonight it was decided they must see the Soho.

People out of the pub to watch them walk down the street. Parnell beating out the death rhythm. MacDoon dancing the Bali dance to lead the way for this kangaroo.

Moving slowly along the center of the streets. Windows opening to watch this strange spectacle. MacDoon cuffing the kangaroo with his long staff. Parnell out front walking backwards up the Kensington Church Street where a girl threw a flower from a top window. To Notting Hill where they tried to close the gate and Parnell stopped it with his foot. Bayswater road. O this was wild. Dance of the idiot trinity. A bobby said 'ere 'ere now, a little quiet and they said by appointment to His Majesty the King and this giant bobby stopped the traffic so they might safely pass. MacDoon doing the leprechaun tumble. A laugh for tired England. And out with a hat which was filling with pennies. At the Marble Arch, groaning under the money and pouring it into the kangaroo's pouch so that they were only fit to be dragged on so laden down with gold and success. Maddest street circus the world has ever seen.

At the Arch they boarded a bus. A woman, touched with a long furry lapping ear, turned and saw this animal sitting behind her and screamed and all the heads on the top of the bus looking at this beast. At the Tottenham Court Road with the pouch dripping pennies they had to drag the beast out with the help of the conductor. MacDoon said there was nothing like it since the night they let all the cattle out of the markets before dawn and Dublin was aswarm with the moos of bullocks and the city came to a standstill and some have said that Dublin has never been the same since.

They walked around the Soho Square and then in the Greek Street they went into a public house.

The kangaroo was talking at the bar. It raised its voice in song.

> Tell me Britons
> How do you know
> You like it
> In the Soho ho.
>
> No joy no juice
> You pigs no use
> I want to know
> How you like it
> In the Soho ho.

There were some grunts and growls and MacDoon said now Danger these people here are good people enjoying their pints.

> Grunt and growl
> Spit and scowl
> You poor pigs
> Are just foul.

They were up. Fourteen in all moving toward the kan-

300

garoo which was singing come all ye faithful. The black brute Parnell was at them. It was on.

Parnell picking up the front man and holding him an instant above his head flung him against the advancing crowd. MacDoon rotating his staff over his head and they said get that little bastard of a helicopter and Mac neatly broke the man's nose. The kangaroo reached behind the bar and was draining a bottle of gin when a chair was lowered on his head from behind. The kangaroo fell spread-eagled to the floor. Parnell attacked from all sides with MacDoon pulling them off with the hook of the staff and beating them to the floor. The building trembling. Eight left of the fourteen, six unconscious under the trampling feet. MacDoon went down and they were kicking him and he was catching them by the ankles with the hook and tripping them to the ground. They were driving Parnell out the door and they were yelling these damn Oxford intellectuals think they can tell us we're pigs. They had Parnell out and drew the latches. They were dragging the unconscious figure of MacDoon to fling him on the street, saying we fixed that big fella, he'll not try that again. Outside a great war whoop. They turned to the door. Another war whoop and a voice yelling I'm coming through. The brown vomit-tinted door parted with a squeal of hinges and splintering wood. The door came asunder into the room. Parnell, face covered in blood, clothes in tatters, launched his ferocious counter attack and three of the remaining eight fled up the stairs crying the man is insane, call the bobbies. They were holding him off with chairs. A crowd gathering on the street. The sound of the police. A half-revived MacDoon and Parnell dragging the stricken kangaroo out the door stumbling into the street. Flinging the beast into a taxi and yelling into the terrified man's ear, away you Cockney bastard like the hounds of hell before we deliver the wrath of the Celts on your English skull.

The kangaroo groaning that it must have a drink or die. That life was not worth living without a lash of something. The taxi man was saying he would get the police if they didn't stop fighting in the back and that they better get to the hospital because they were covered in blood.

They came to a stop and hobbled into the white smells of this hospital. Crippled trinity. Down the warm halls. The nurses coming out of closets everywhere to see the spectacle of the limping kangaroo.

In the hot head he could see out of the pinhole eyes the buxom nurses and the kind nun who got the Chinese doctor. And this nun said whatever is it? Did you go to a pub with it? We did. We've never had patients like you before and you are, you know, rather beat up, but the doctor will do an especially good job on his face, a serious wound. Parnell is a fierce man. O a brute man and Mac here, by God, could lay waste a Cockney hoard in his prime were it not for the fabulous thirst of your young English maidens and even others for a sup of his Irish juice.

The hospital called another taxi and together with the Chinese doctor, compassionate nun and thirteen nurses called from their beds they stood watching the tragic trinity troop out the gate. But the kangaroo, touched with a slight madness what with being poisoned by his own wind accumulating in the animal head and other things like this shower of lovely silver dollars, shot out the door and came in the other until they were racing around the taxi in one door and out the next. The nurses' quarters alive with popping heads until these three weary wastrels set upon each other choking and collapsed and were taken away. The hospital people waving goodbye.

27

Dangerfield turned up the gas flame and rubbed his hands at three o'clock on this gray Friday afternoon. He took a bottle of gin from the pouch of the crumpled kangaroo. From the bed the stricken voice of MacDoon.

"What in God's pukka name have you got there, Danger?"

"E. Just e. Holy water. A little fast blessing for all of us. Parnell, wake up. Up I say. MacDoon for God's sake see if he's dead in there. Don't want to smell up the room with corpses."

Parnell wreathed in bandages stirs, looks out from under the covers and goes in again.

"Danger, come over here with that."

"O I had this neatly tucked away in the bedlam. Looting is part of the battle. You think now MacDoon that this is going to be a time of richness. Do you think that now. Or that from over there the motor birds are bringing me an egg. Big. Big. Nothing like that land of the big big rich."

"Danger. Listen to me. I want you to know your friends will stand by you during delivery of egg. Never let it be said I deserted in an hour of wealth."

"Mac, I think a bit of the Algeria for a breather. We destroyed the city of London in one mighty blow."

"I'd say however, there was a bit of the counter attack somewhere."

"There was that. Mac, one of these days I'm going to tell you the story of how I joined the Legion of Mary. The things of the inner struggle. Intestinal and other things. But got to spruce up. First little bit of the Parnell's peanut butter. Nothing like the nut butter. O I've had the speedy trip to the broker with the ungreased pram. I've had the pride. You wouldn't believe it Mac but at one time I wouldn't stoop to the pram greased or ungreased. Or live on woman's earnings. But through all this, the battering, shell shock, detours and even falling into the minor traps of Egbert Skully, I've come through with part of the inner man still there. Onward you crazy Christian soldiers. Just call me Major Dangerfield."

"Major bring me the bottle."

"And Mac only once. Once, mind you, have I ever had the ignominy. I'll take all the rest but not the igno."

"Danger, let nothing more be said to spoil or foul the beauty you have released into this room. Give us the bottle."

"Parnell. Up out of the covers. I've a request to make. Would you ever now have a clean shirt for my urgent appointment at five which demands I present myself without stains of blood or battle."

"A shirt in my closet there I wore in the nick."

"The very thing."

"Behind the door. The only dignified thing I possess these days."

"O handsome shirt. The cut is everything. Some day, Parnell, we must hear more of this nick. B. Berry maintains three years in the Borstal good as four at Harrow. What have these British prisons?"

"Ten years lose some of the advantages."

"Inclined to believe that a bit long even for the Ph. D. O I say, rather fine shirt this. How do I look? I think it suits me. Now a little something for under the pits. Must have something for the pits. Must be no odor of body."

"Danger go out in the hall and slip in the second door on the left. Landlady's bedroom. Might be a little something for the pits."

Dangerfield returns.

"Very nice. I've always been partial to the fragrance as opposed to the unfragrant."

MacDoon propped and prostrate on the bed.

"Danger do I see a woman of blackberry stained lips, raven hair and haughty teeth? Do I?"

"Gentlemen, in due time. In due time there will be an announcement."

He stepped out in the cold twilight along this road with the triangular park. Nice room Parnell has in this pleasant street. Now any one of these houses would do for me. Mary wash the windows and sweep out the path and make me ould porridge of a morning. Import sausages from the Pembroke Road in the Dub. She's stuck by me. Trusted me. And if there's one thing it's faith. I'd even suffer the igno for faith. And whatever else, I've got to see her right. I know they think me hard because I've not shed the tears over the death. But I'm not. There's just nothing I can do. Well Marion. Now you know but you were too fast. That's the trouble with people, too fast. Don't wait, see you down and think you're going to stay there, might even use the heel on you. But what ho, as I've said, no bitterness in me. Nothing like that in my heart any more. Marion will find out soon enough. Little note to the solicitor and perhaps we will see a little investment here and there. Small and conservative at first.

Down into the Underground. Standing on the platform with a few afternoon people going somewhere. The glassy, smooth train parks neatly. Stepping in and gliding away. I am told whatever else I do in this fantastic Underground, to stay off the Circle Line.

He walked along the windy tunnels. Up and out into this vast station. Throngs. Where is she? I'm late. Track seven. Watch for an Irish face. I couldn't have forgotten what she looks like. Spot me anywhere because I look Victorian from behind. Must greet her with gladness.

In a black coat she came shyly down the platform bent with a large leather bag, biting her lips.

"Hello, Mary."

"Hello, I thought you might not come."

"Not a bit. By God you've lost weight. Have you been ill?"

"I'm all right. I wasn't well for a while."

"Give me the bag. Good Christ what have you got in it? Rocks?"

"I brought some things to cook with and some plates. And part of a sewing machine. I hope you don't mind?"

"Excellent. Not a bit. We'll check it. I think those are the things we want these days. Now we go over here and take care of this."

Dangerfield led her out of the station. And turned her around to see the building. Take a tour by Danger. See up there and the big pillars. That's architecture.

"Now what do you think of that Mary? What about that?"

"I don't know what to say. I suppose it's nice."

"It's the size Mary, the size. And who paid for it. But we'll go along here now and find a nice restaurant."

"I brought twenty pounds."

"Wow."

Into the warm room with tables along the wall. Dangerfield told the boy to bring a little something from the château and a chicken and cheroot too.

"Isn't this expensive, Sebastian?"

"He, eeeeee."

"Why do you laugh?"

"Because the word expensive is no longer in my vocabulary. No longer in use. I think I can safely say that."

"Why?"

"Later on, Mary. Later on for that."

"Well tell me what you've been doing. You look thin. And nothing of mine fits me and I've had to alter this old black dress. I got so worried when I was ill because you didn't write."

"Give me your hand, Mary."

"This is a nice place. I'm glad to be shut of Dublin."

"Lot say that."

"When I got ill and told him I wasn't going to jump for him anymore he was soon up out of his bed."

"What did he say about London?"

"Said he'd have the Guarda. But I told him to go to the devil and if he put another finger to me that I'd have the Guarda."

"What did he say?"

"He'd get the priest to me. I was fed up. I told him his own soul was covered with lies. And that the boys were well away not to have to listen to him again. He's had his own way for long enough. Told me he was an old man and didn't have long to go and that I shouldn't leave him alone. And I said you want me to stay now. Me who has been out with men. Then he said his heart was ticking its last and to call the priest for him before I left the house."

"O I wouldn't be too hard now. Poor man. Perhaps the only little comfort he's after is to poison the Pope."

"I'm glad he's had to suffer. And to be shut of it all. The Tolka was the only thing I enjoyed anymore. To walk across Phoenix Park to Chapleizod and Lucan Road. And go into Sarsfield. It's so lovely along there by the river in the trees. I used to think of you there. Don't laugh, I really did."

The smell of wine and sweet chicken meat. The waiter bringing sprouts and baked potatoes. Whee. Were it not for my tram rides through sleep when I got off at the stops called despair and had to get up out of the cozy bed to make myself a cup of milk and honey and sat on the wobbly kitchen chair. O that thing called food. Or as Malarkey used to say, Jesus, Sebastian if I ever had money I'd have all my friends to a place of mine in the country where we would sit to a table an Irish mile long with our fists greasy with the lashings of beef and turkey and our women coming from the fire groaning under the weight of the wild berries and plover plucked from the sky, and beat bulls' heads for sport and pick up a whole field and flip it over on its back for planting and Jesus, cover it with a foot thick of chicken shit and rotting kelp and then lash it with ten tons of peaches black decay. O have you ever heard of oats. Or spuds fit to put heathen desires in ye for the rest of your life. Mary leave some chicken for me.

Over there sit three secretaries. And two bald men. I think

I like this. Healthier than the pub. O I may give up the pub. And just keep the cheroot, slippers and sewing machine.

"Mary, will you excuse me while I make a phone call?"

"Yes."

Now Landlady, me dear Mrs. Ritzincheck, be big hearted. Put down foul caution and reserve that these limes tell you is playing a sunny wicket.

"Hello, Mrs. Ritzincheck?"

"Yes."

"Mrs. Ritzincheck this is Mr. Dangerfield. I'm in a rather difficult position. My fiancée has just arrived in London. Of course I know this is rather an abrupt and perhaps unusual request but I know you will understand and I wonder would you mind awfully if I were to share my room with her. She's a very fine girl."

"Well, Mr. Dangerfield, it's against the rules of the house. I'll have every gentleman requesting to have a lady in his room overnight. I'm sorry."

"Now, now. I know it's asking a bit much but I thought I'd be honest with you since you've been so straightforward with me. But I assure you everything will be conducted with the utmost decorum and perhaps you could explain. My wife, you know. Well, it's only a few weeks till the day. We do so want to be together. And we've been so cut off and she's come all the way from Ireland. And Mrs. Ritzincheck I'd never dare make such a request if I didn't feel you were a woman of sensibility and experience."

"Well, Mr. Dangerfield you certainly have a way of putting it and if there's no disturbance and mind you, if it's a different woman every night there will be no more of it."

"You don't know how grateful I am to you Mrs. Ritzincheck. You have no idea."

"I have an idea all right."

"That's excellent. Thanks again. We'll be arriving in a short while."

Dangerfield austerely at the pay booth saying indeed I will when they said I hope you will come again sir. And he pivoted exquisitely to usher Mary out before him. Taxi sweeping up. Mary holding his hand as they went for the bag, looking out the window in the crowded streets. Bury me on neutral soil. Perhaps in Austria with simplicity and subdued colors and faces. With my children around me. I want my last moments to have some dignity. Mary sit right up close. Don't be scared of me because I'm all right.

Mrs. Ritzincheck smiled at the door and wiped her hands in her apron. I always say be straightforward when you can.

Up the stairs and finally in this little room. Mary sat down on the bed. Sebastian laid the bag on the floor.

"Well Mary here we are."

"I like it. It's nice to see from such a height. I like London, everything is so exciting. So many interesting looking people."

"There's that."

"And so many strange ones you would never see in Dublin. All the blacks and those Egyptian fellows. Some of them are terrible good looking and they've got such white teeth."

"Mary show me this sewing machine."

"Kiss me."

"The machine, Mary. The machine."

"Kiss me."

Mary upon him with arms and legs. Back to the bed. Down. Please. You know how I feel about direct assault. What a tongue. All I wanted to do was take a look at the machine.

Outside it's night. And they're all pulling the curtains across. And going to sit in their chairs. Mary at least let me up to take a quick plunge in the bath.

"I want to have it together, Sebastian."

"But we mustn't set a carnal example for the other guests."

In the tub she said the water was terrible and no lather and it looked all gray and dirty and you'd think she didn't have a wash in a tinker's age. She smiled up out of the tub.

Pulling him down for another kiss. Dangerfield's feet slipping on the soapy floor. Watch it for Christ's sake, I'm falling. A roar of water over the side. Mrs. Ritzincheck will think we're up here at it hammer and tongs, hanging from the chandeliers and divers bathroom fittings. And that causes jealousy. Everybody will be wanting it.

"You look a sight, Sebastian."

"We've got to go easy, Mary."

"Take off your clothes, I want to see what you look like."

"Mary, please."

"You've got no chest."

"Wait a minute. Just look at this. There. See?"

"It's so funny."

"I beg your pardon."

"But you're thin."

"Now Mary look from behind. Give you some idea of the breadth of me shoulders. I'm deceptive."

"I'll admit you're broad."

"But you've got a chest there, Mary."

"But you mustn't look, I know they're too big."

"Not a bit."

"But they're smaller than they were."

Dangerfield stepping into the tub. Must control myself. Keep it down. Mary will stop at nothing. Somebody come break down the door and catch us at it in the tub.

"Sebastian, you're queer looking when I see you like this in the light."

"Don't grab, I'll get drowned."

"Isn't it an awful death?"

"O I don't know, Mary. Out there on the waves with the ships at sea."

"Rub me with the soap."

"Melons, Mary."

"Don't say that. Take me to the sea."

"We'll go and live by the sea."

"And I'll go naked on the beach."

"What ho, Mary. We'll see that."

"I read about these French painters. Awful men, they were drawing without clothes and it must be nice to be able to pose for them."

"Mary there's a change come over you."

" I know."

"I like you, Mary."

"Do you mean it?"

"Yes. Bit of a rub here, Mary."

"Your back is a sight."

"A scrubbing with your fair hand it needs. Haven't known such peace for years."

"I'm glad, and glad to kiss your back and pull your hair. I used to pull my little brothers' hair in the tub when they were carrying on. You have nice soft hair. Sort of silky almost. It's more beautiful to be a man isn't it?"

"I'm sure I don't know the answer to that, Mary."

"I've got some lace and frills to wear for you."

Standing on the linoleum in water slop. Little dark haired Mary pinning up behind her head a swath of wide black curls and rolling a towel around her. And face in full blush. She stopped and wiped up the puddles. Out that window and down on the tracks, the Underground trains sliding in and out. Long gray platforms. And skipping across the gloomy hall and get a little of the electric fire. Mary's dancing feet.

"It's cold. Does anyone ever be in the hall?"

"London, Mary. Never worry about that. See everything here."

"I guess they do."

Sebastian stretched out on the green ticking watching naked Mary brushing her long hair.

"A nice body, Mary."

"Do you like me?"

"Massed army of all the saints couldn't keep me away."

"You're awful. I'll tell you something if you promise not to laugh. Do you promise?"

"For God's sake, Mary, out with it. Out. Don't keep it from me whatever it is. I've got to know."

"You might think I was queer."

"Out. Not a bit."

"I used to practise being naked in my room in front of the mirror so I wouldn't mind when I was with you in London. And I'd make believe you were watching me and I'd stand around like this. You don't think I'm crazy?"

"No."

"Have you seen a lot of women?"

"Wouldn't say a lot."

"And what were they like?"

"Naked."

"No. Tell me. How do I compare with them?"

"A fine figure."

"And would they stand up in front of you?"

"Sometimes."

"How did they stand in front of you?"

"I can't remember."

"Would they go around like models showing off their best points or anything?"

"Jesus, Mary."

"Would they?"

"In a way."

"You don't think I'm too forward. I thought you were queer when you said all those funny things to me at the party but when I thought them over on my walks and got used to them I didn't think they were queer anymore. I used to think of you in the Botanical Gardens. In that big house with all those trees and vines and it was just like a jungle. And where they have the lilies floating in the big tank. They're so strange. I felt I just wanted to jump in. But I get the feeling there would be things on the bottom to bite my feet. I'd just do it for a lark if the man wasn't watching."

Mary sits on the edge of the bed. I lean back here watching. You've got big ones. Use them as a pillow. I am the hot ticket to eternity riding the melted rails in all directions. To Kerry and Caherciveen. For a dollar I'll do the bull dance and you know how I am when I do that. O.K. you ones with the

312

dollar, line up there and watch this, those from Cincinatti, Ohio can come up to the front.

"Sebastian, it's so nice and warm and cozy to feel your body and I thought you'd never be at the station. I thought I was just dreaming that I had ever met you. All the days I had to waste in that damn house and we could have been like this. Do you think I'm curvy?"

"You're my little circle."

"Squeeze me harder."

"Call me gorilla."

"Gorilla."

"Give my chest a few good beats now. Whoops. Not in such good shape as I thought."

"Just love me. And I want children because you'll love them. And I could get a job. I won a prize for acting once. I want to rub them all over your chest. Isn't that what men like?"

"Love it."

"And I used to think I could feed you with them. Would you feed off me?"

"Good God, Mary."

"O I can't tell you."

"Tell me. I'm only joking. I'll feed off you."

"I guess it's because you're thin. I want it something awful. Is that awful? And that night I wanted it so much."

"It can be hard to get at times."

"But you'll give me as much as I want."

"Do the very best I can, Mary."

"I read you can sit up on it."

"There's that all right."

"And get it from the back."

"And that too."

"I'm so excited."

Perhaps there is even someone somewhere getting it from all sides. Round Mary. I may be just a bit younger than Christ when they tacked him up but they've had me outstretched a few times already. And Mary you've got me

313

pinned right here on the bed. With your lust. Stuck on it. And twisting with your eyes full of black fire. MacDoon forging relics for the Holy Church of Rome. And others dressed as priests in the North of Dublin, patting cherub faces and blessing these children coming out of the school gates and then whispering an indecent proposal to the escorting nun. What is it that makes my heart die? Is it all my little Dangerfields popping out of wombs all over the globe? I'll go back to Ireland with my pockets filled with gold. Break in Skully's windows with lumps of it. And Malarkey can put a train in his tunnel down to the pub. Mary how is it? It's grand and feels so good and will we always stay together? Please. And you'll never go out with others or do it to them and I'd keep house and cook for you and make shirts and darn socks and make you happy. And Mary, what of other men? There are no other men because my heart has gone out to you. And if you don't laugh I'll tell you what I think. I won't laugh. I think it's a fine instrument that God made for the poor likes of us to enjoy.

28

On Sunday morning, holding Mary's black gloved hand, they turned into Earl's Court Station. Lovers warmed and wrapped with smiles and looks and little words whispered in the ears. And I am newly shaved and laced with stinging lotion because Mary you say you like so much to rub your cheek against mine.

Ushering her in the train. When you cross those legs like that Mary it makes me gulp. I see you've done a bit of the plucking around the eyebrows of which I don't approve.

They came up from the Underground at Victoria. Where a few bright faces went by. And then along the Buckingham Palace Road and Semley Place and into this red brick church. Through the green curtains to the music and gold.

People scattered over the floor touching foreheads to the ground. I smell the smoke. And there's song. Come out of those altar doors with the balm and blessing and touch me. And put some on Mary too. And when I go to my last bed I want you all to wear this gold raiment, and put lots of balm on the coffin.

"How do you like it, Mary?"

"It's wonderful. All the music. Makes me feel all strange inside. It makes me feel I want to go back to the room. Will we?"

"Jesus, have you no reverence in you at all."

"I know it's awful. I can't help it. But how long does it go on, when does it end?"

"Goes on all morning. See they come and go."

"It's strange. What are they?"

"Russians."

"I wish I were a Russian. It's so exciting."

"It's that."

"And the men with beards. Would you grow a beard Sebastian?"

"I'm a little conservative."

"I always wanted to marry a man with a beard."

"Come up now and we'll get a bit of this frankincense."

And they went up to the little group for blessing. Danger-field put a fistful of change as offering. The motor birds are coming with lots more from across the seas. And I want to be loved for my money.

With church bells ringing, they came out and went into a white-walled cafeteria for tea.

"You know, Sebastian, how they have all these things here. Churches of all kinds and the trains running all over under the city and you'd think that the way they were doing with us in Ireland that they wouldn't have time to build all this."

"British find time to do a lot of things, Mary."

"Will we go right back to the room after this tea?"

"Mary, really. Just a little walk in the park first. Breather."

"I want to try those other ways you said there were."

Sitting facing one another. Hunched Mary gleaming at him over the cakes. Mary you're the very devil for it. But I must have a stroll in the park. Catch my breath. O I know you think I'm able for it night and day with lights off and on but it can wear out like everything else. Just let's take this quiet walk, go up Bond Street so's I can get an idea of the things I'll be needing from now on. And may even have to see the odd disguise because some friends get very close when there is largess.

They got on the bus to the park. Those enormous gates with cars streaming through. And there's Rotten Row be-tween the trees. Horses galloping by. Must give them awful big arses, pounding and prancing up and down. I feel all sin starts in the park. Like marriage begins in the dark. And ends with the lights on.

"Mary, we'll walk to the round pond."

"What's that?"

"Where they sail boats."

"And then will we go back?"

"Why do you want it so much, Mary?"

"I don't know why. I just feel like it. I even felt like it before I ever had it. Sometimes even when I was kneeling praying at a Legion of Mary meeting."

"A fine organization."

"Don't be such a liar. You don't think it's a fine organization. Isn't that a short way out of the park?"

"We're both Legion members, Mary. I'll have you know I'm in good standing as well. Young girls like you just after cock with not a trace of religion left."

"The Legion can go to the devil."

"All right, Mary, if you want to be like that, but let me say this much. If it weren't for the Legion in Ireland, everybody would be fucked to death. Archbishops as well. And every nun pregnant."

"You don't want to take me back to the room."

"Not a bit. I'm just a little sensitive about the Legion, that's all. There's a bit of good in everything. Everything's good. Everything. I can see by your eyes you don't believe me. All right. Taxi. Straight back to the room. Straight back."

Mary pulled across the curtains. I can see them outlined. Says she likes to wear tight things. Every time I take off my trousers you give a gasp.

And they stayed in the room till Monday. Passionate Mary. And there on Tuesday. Mary relentless, regardless. But on Wednesday with a gray dreariness general over the city and sprinkle of cold rain, he was called to the telephone to hear MacDoon say there was mail of an official-looking kind. And kissing Mary between the open door and Mary I think you're as hard as nails. And I guess I've been driving you constantly with my hammer. But don't cry if I'm gone too long or grieve. Go to your sewing machine and whirr out a little tune. Put in some yellow thread and make me a flag to wave.

Down the four flights of green carpeted stairs. And at a quick pace, up the street. I've got a nice little niche up there with Mary. She can't get enough. And I can't say I'm capable of much more. Got to ask the Doon for advice. They say if you don't give them enough they go looking elsewhere. Send me apples from New England and a few spices from the East as well. Keep me supplied with juice. O.K. MacDoon what have you got for me? I'm a little drained with Mary after so much. And I can remember times in the days of my youth, spent tinkering with buttons, straps and pins, twisting, pulling and breaking, trying to get it. Now I wouldn't be up to it. Just take it off, darlin'. This is surfeit for sure. A man who reveled in saucy escapades and perversion until it brought about his death at ninety-seven. Mary can be petulant. Didn't like the look in her eye when I asked her to hand me my socks from the back of the chair. Sign of rebellion. Might get to be the hard woman after awhile. Got to watch it. And keeps her own things in her own drawer and her own towel. A bit scruffy anyway. Had me by the wrists when she was on top with that look, see if you can get out of this one. I've got a few things up my sleeve to deal with that nonsense. She didn't like it much when I slipped my arm around her leg and gave it the Egyptian twist until she was biting her lip and almost cried.

"Mac, for God's sake where is it?"

"O I've got it, Danger. Now quiet your poor suffering soul and Jesus give me a minute to tell you a little story. Now once there was a man in Ireland walking along a country road and he met two little girls whom he asked to come and play with him. He said it was just a naughty little game and he would give them a bag of chocolates. And so the little girls played the game and he gave them the bag. When the man was gone they opened it and it was filled with stones."

"Stop. Stop. Give us it for Christ's sake. Where's the letter, the letter?"

"Now take a seat. May be your last in poverty. And the

318

only way to enjoy richery is to remember paupery days. Reports, Danger, are coming in that you haven't been out of the bed since she arrived and I'll tell you straight to your face that it's a disgrace that a good Christian such as yourself would indulge in such lasciviousness as to keep you indoors for three days."

"Mac, I'm beside myself. My heart can't take this type of treatment."

"I've only one request to make. That I give it to you on my silver platter."

"Give it to me on any fucking thing. Serve it with your prick if you like but give it to me."

"Ah here we are. Here we are Danger, on me own silver platter dating back to the time of the Geeks who were Gooks from Gaul."

A finger parting the envelope. Unfolding this bond paper. The law. At the end, eyes riveted on this:

—a sum held in trust to provide an income not to exceed six thousand dollars per annum which income is to commence upon your attaining the age of forty-seven at which time—

You'll find me prostrate and completely mad.

Mac swilling hot water in his little brown teapot. Said it was a special kind of tea he was using from Shaba Gompa.

> All I want
> Is one break
> Which is not
> My neck.

29

Christmas. Lying here on my back listening to carol singers in the street. Two weeks ago today I woke up in this room and Mary was gone. Left a note on the little table and said she loved me anyway and only hoped I didn't mean all the things I said to her.

And Mac had said he met her on the street and talked to her and she was asking for me and how was I and did I eat enough and why did I have to behave like that when she was willing to help. Mac said she got a part in a play. And a job posing. Outsizes in underwear.

I've not enjoyed this desperation. But I've never once said I'll give up. Mrs. Ritzincheck says she must have the rent. O I know she's just a little anxious and doesn't really mean it.

If I wet this towel here I can put it over my eyes and I'll feel much better. Don't worry, don't despair, save hair. Heave to, head into the wind, sails aback and I'll ride this out even though most decks are awash and I'm taking water amidships.

On my plate this morning I found just an extra rasher and even another egg and Mrs. Ritzincheck said I was a very interesting person to talk to. She's a fine looking woman about forty. Not past it for sure. But please don't take advantage of me.

And last week I went to the National Gallery in Trafalgar Square where they say these pictures are priceless. I sat on a comfy chair and had a little nap. And went for walks till my shoes gave out. But Mac said he had a pair in the kangaroo feet and would I trade mine. And now me shoes are hopping around the Abbey Theatre.

And this is the afternoon before the birth of Christ. Good will towards men. How about a few quid as well? I'm thin and worn but not yet up to selling me body to the medical colleges or landlady either. Mac told me there was a party tonight with pucks of food and drink. Each time I subtract twenty-seven from forty-seven it leaves twenty. Well I've waited before. That's what they all say now. That's what Mary said, that waiting would get me nowhere. At least Mac was sensible enough to take me around to the museums to let me see all the engines and machines and the boat models. And even this big pendulum they have to show the world's rotating. I could have told them that. And after he took me to Chelsea and bought a bottle of wine to have with the roast beef and salad rolls and I said to him, Mac, I can look back over my life now and see certain things. And would you say, Mac, that marriage put me down. But I was in love, her straight blonde hair like a Swede and perhaps her slim light limbs drove me to the altar with maybe an odd push from the in-laws.

Mac and I just sat there in that cultivated pub and I said I wasn't being sentimental but I had to tell him what it was like over there. How the leaves crackled and the bright moons. New England air rich and clear. Women good enough to eat. Ripe summer tans and arses which wagged, wow. But Mac, for display purposes only. Keep off the grass. And don't you see how it could drive me down on my knees weeping? And I thought I'd go back and settle in the Hudson Valley or along the Housatonic in Connecticut. But no. I'm the month of October. Facing winter forever. And I can't go back.

Then Mac said, easy Danger. No tears. Now come along and we'll take a radio taxi for a thrill.

We went to a strange suburb and in a door and up stairs and Mac said meet Alphonse, so I said how do you do. Then I had to take a piss and he said use the sink and I remembered how Englishmen piss in the sinks of France and even their own and I felt well that's all right for the English and no doubt they taught the poor Irish the same only they could never get to France due to the cost and language, so I said if

321

you don't mind I'll use the bowl. And we discussed the wages of sin and agreed they were high. After this little meeting I picked up a flowerpot and threw it through a bank window. Mac was gone in a flash and said I was unstable.

Next day on the Earl's Court Road I had drink taken and they said, rather unkindly, that I was seen running down the center of the street swinging an umbrella and that I attacked poor MacDoon who only asked that I desist. They said I belabored him severely about the ankles and Mac told me I was incorrigible and a ruffian, which, of course, was quite true. They took me away in a wagon and put me in a room with bars. And I've never been treated so well before. A bobbie's wife baked a cake for me and I beat them all in chess and they all said I was a most amusing type of chap and if they were all like me, why a bobbie's life would be a paradise it would. They said I would have to pay a visit to the American Embassy.

So I went. Wearing a Cossack hat. And I think I caused a stir. Someone asked me was I a spy and they brought me to a man sitting behind a desk cleaning his fingernails. He looked at me and said nothing. Then he brought out a file stuffed with papers. He went through them shaking his head up and down. He asked me could I remember my serial number in the navy. I said I only knew it was high. He said that's bad. I got worried and said it was low. He said that's worse. Then he leaned over towards me and said how do I know you're not an impostor. Buddy, I wish I were. He got on the phone. He looked through the papers, and said you've obviously spent some time in the British Isles and I said in Ireland and Great Britain because Malarkey insists on things like that and he said it's all the same to us bud. I watched him while he said Miss Beef check on case A48353, and then he said he was a very busy man but looking through this file of yours Mr. Dangerfield which is the longest and most complicated I've ever seen, I can see you've had a few scrapes here and there, owe money but there's no sign of your being disloyal to the United States. I thought we would both laugh

322

together but I only got a chance to show my teeth. And I thought before I leave here the least I can do is to take advantage of a good toilet. And I went down stairs a bit shaky on my feet due to the interrogation and through this door and the fact that there was a woman with her back to me combing her hair didn't disturb me in the least. So I went into one of the booths and did my little bit. Stole the box of toilet paper, but the seat unfortunately was well attached. I'm sure it would have given my broker a fit. But it's an indication of the times we live in. When I came out of the booth there were screams the like of which I haven't heard since Bedlam and a woman come right up to me and yelled, get out, right into my face. Whereupon I slapped her for her crass vulgarity. Someone must have pulled the fire alarm because a bell began to ring. I just said to myself, Blessed Oliver, I'll see you raised to sainthood if you get me out of this one and I'll even pay for the candles I lit before you in Drogheda but get me out of this. Fingers were pointed at me. They said there he is. There was nothing left but to abandon ship and I made a dash for it. I got ten feet when an obvious football player tried a tackle and were it not for another college boy coming the other way I would have been finished but they met head on. I spidered away up the stairs. Howls of virgins on all sides. With only one girl hanging on to a remnant of me mackintosh and I knew I could at least forsake this strand and ripped it loose. I went out the door like a shot with the marine guard coming to attention.

Yes, out there they are singing. O little town of Bethlehem. And Mary left me thirty shillings and a towel. They say, throw in the towel.

I must get up off this bed. Mac says the party will cheer me up. A little wash first. Down trousers. God it's getting thin and worn, old before its time. Pubic hair going gray. I hear in the New World they have dyes and permanents. Some, they say, even have it dekinked but you can't pay much attention to such rumors. Anything for sensation. I see a few Christmas decorations in that window over there.

Think I'll pin something on my curtain and have a little Christmas all of my own.

This hall cold and black. Lights down there in the station make me feel so pitiful. People with red toys. I know the pubs are jammed. I know they are jammed. And in the Dublin right now I could be hanging on to the rim of a round. Sucking it back free, not noticed for the festivities afoot. Close up my little cell and put the key safely away and find my way down these stairs and out.

Hesitating in front of the house. Looking up at the window. The singers have gone up the road and there's that woman coming out of her house with tightly rolled umbrella which she is hitting on the pavement. I think just trying to attract my attention. Ought to go up and say, look here it's Christmas and let's you and I be merry together. If you don't mind, get out of my way. But, madam, I've watched you undress every evening, doesn't that mean something to you? Nothing but that you're a frightful peeping tom. Madam I resent the inference. Get out of my way you tramp. O aye. The buses are bright and cheery and laden. I know the pubs are jammed.

Dangerfield crossed over Earl's Court Road and stood in front of an antique shop, rubbing his shoes on the back of his trousers. Put his hand into his pocket, took it out and held an open palm to the sky. Turning to watch the traffic in its Christmas Eve swarm. A taxi drawing to a screeching halt.

The door of the taxi slams. Dangerfield turning away. And turning back suddenly. A man. With a cane squeezed under his arm, handing the taxi money and turning with a grin. I'm mad. Absolutely out of my mind or body or is this a street in heaven or are we all riding a fast road to hell? Or am I seeing an impostor or bogus bugger?

And with a wider grin. White gloved. Do I know anyone anymore who wears white gloves? Or this ebony cane. But it's this round face flowering angelically about a bud of pearly teeth and a roar of laughter right in my own. Get away, Percy Clocklan. Get away. The dirty ould madness coming upon me. Get away.

Into the speechless face of Dangerfield.

"Why you sneaky whore, Dangerfield, why didn't you tell me you were in London? For Jesus sake are you on your way to the grave?"

"Percy, if it's you, I can only say I might well be and I need a drink."

"I was going to ask if you had a mouth at all."

"I've got a mouth, Percy. But you've given me a terrible fright."

Percy Clocklan pointed with his black cane up the sidewalk to a lighted window. There was singing inside. Come ye merry gentlemen. And they came. Into the bar and surrounded by song. Two brandies.

"May I have a cigarette, Percy?"

"Anything. Anything you want. Keep the change, keep the change."

"Percy, I take all this on faith. Although from the taste of this brandy I'd say I was in a saloon bar at the Christmas. But allow me to point out that up till a minute ago you were dead."

"O the whores believed me."

"Malarkey was the only one with reservations. Said you wouldn't miss getting your money's worth out of the journey. All others were believers. But Jesus I'm very happy to see you alive and prosperous looking."

"Prosperous looking? I am prosperous. O they believed me. I finished off a bottle of Irish and thought it would be a shame to waste it. So I put the note in. I knew ould Malarkey would deny he ever knew me. And Jesus what about yourself?"

"Percy, I'm down. Things seem to get worse by the day. But I'll manage. Where were you going?"

"Going to pay a surprise visit to Mac's for this party when I saw you standing out there on the pavement as if you had no home. I couldn't believe my eyes. I frightened the life out

325

of the driver. You look a disgrace. What are you wearing at all? Bloody ould sacks and newspapers."

"Haven't seen my tailor for some time, Percy."

"Well you'll bloody well see him with me. I'll have you made one of the finest suits in England."

"Percy, tell me. Where did this prosperity come from?"

"Never mind where it came from. Never mind that. But I worked me ould fingers to the bone and got into a good thing. Now I'm making bags of money. Rolling it in. I left Ireland and I told myself I was going to make money and have plenty to drink and fuck. I've even bought meself a Rolls."

"Surely you're joking."

"Joking, me tit. I'll take you for a ride in it."

"This is too much for me, Percy. Christmas, the little boy Jesus and the cold Bethlehem all at once. I'm finished."

Clocklan reaching into his pocket, withdrawing a black wallet.

"This is the only thing I've left, that I arrived in England with, and I stole it from ould Tony's jacket in the kitchen with him in the back screaming for a cup of tea."

"Magnificent."

"The dirty eegit himself made it."

"A fine piece of work."

"If he'd get his ould carcass out of the pubs he'd be away."

Clocklan took five five-pound notes and handed them to Dangerfield.

"Percy, you don't know what this means."

"I know what it means and fair enough. But you never crowed over buying a drink or whined on like the rest of them. Bunch of pigs, the whole lot of them sitting on their arses whining. Whining for their mothers. And me relatives who wouldn't give me a smell of soup or a dirty ould shilling want to see me now because I'm pissing pure gold. And the rest of them talking their mountains of crap."

"Percy, I'm very grateful."

"Don't be grateful to me. Drink up. Drink up. Don't be

wasting the pub's time. And get rid of those dirty ould cigarettes and we'll get some good cigars. What's the matter with you at all, Sebastian? Where are your grand ways and silver tongue?"

"Turned to lead."

"Fetches a good price. And those rags. Jesus, get out of them. Better in the buff than them ould dirty things you're wearing. Drink up and we'll get you a decent shave and haircut."

"This is very good of you, Percy."

"Put the bloody drink in you and take what you can get while it's free and don't be asking me questions about money or the prices. Bloody Clocklan owns London. Own the kip. Me Rolls is so long it gets stuck in the traffic."

"What's it like inside? Just tell me that, Percy. That's all I want to know and then I can go to my reward."

"Have to wear a life preserver for fear of drowning in the softness."

"More. More. Eeeeee."

"And a compass so's not to get lost inside."

"Great."

And they went across the street to a barber who wrapped Dangerfield in towels and covered his face with puffy cream and drew a razor across his fair cheek. Then the vibro machine. In the corner, Clocklan engaged a Jap in conversation. A few little clips at the back of the neck and a bit of smell juice sprinkled all over. A bit of powder for the face, sir? A bit, please. And I think we've done an excellent job with the singe, sir? O aye, excellent. We are shipshape now, aren't we, sir? I'd say ready to put to sea.

Anchors
Aweigh.

30

Arriving at MacDoon's. Hello, hello, hello. Mac standing with open arms. Receiving. In this limbo. For the repose of pawned souls. And Clocklan how did you get so rich. Woman's earnings? Or fly by night or hundred to win. Come in all of you.

"Tell us Percy."

"I pay me taxes to the King and me an Irish blue blood talking with the likes of you. Before I'm finished I'll have me own militia to keep you shanty Irish out of my way. And Dangerfield, get out of them ould dirty rags. Get out. And put something decent on your back. Here's me address. Take a taxi to me house and don't be pawning me things and put on one of me suits so you won't be making us all look like tramps the sacred night before the birth of the greatest Irishman of them all. Sure, he wasn't a Jew."

Dangerfield on the Brompton Road, hand raised and a taxi pulls up. To Tooting Bec. They say it's great for mental hospitals. And across the Thames. French letters floating out to sea. Ought to auction them off in Dublin. Natives would go wild over them. Tell them they're waterproof socks and can hang them on the line to dry. Mary doesn't like them to get in the way. And now she's on the stage exposed to the grossest type of immorality.

Through all these strange suburban streets. Over there is a clock tower like a crazy moon. And up to this bell which glows in the dark. The face of a young girl saying Mr. Clocklan phoned to tell me you were coming and to show you to his room. Through this dark drab house. Canes galore and hats. Young woman, you're from Ireland. And you're Mr. Dangerfield. O Mr. Clocklan has told me a great deal about you. But I don't believe all he says about Ireland, I've never seen any of the things he tells happen. O they happen all right.

Following her up the dark stairs. A strange painting of mountains on the wall. In the bedroom a pink bed and desk covered with newspapers and a picture of a wild face. And she says Mr. Clocklan is a great collector of art but they don't mean a thing to me. And she says I like to know what I'm looking at. And would you know what this was if I showed it to you?

Dangerfield took a black speckled tweed from the closet. And I look so well with this first white shirt since when. And put on this nice green tie. Socks and shoes. Cane out of the hall. And a bit of paper in this hat to make it sit just right. Bye bye now, you're a sweet girl. It was a pleasure to meet you, sir.

Down the brown stone steps and this transformation must make the taxi man confused. Pardon my saying so sir, but you don't look like the man who went in. I'm not except for my underwear. Quickly back to the city now. And I think straight to Trafalgar Square for a look at the tree.

And look at the bright lights. O it's good to see. I've come out of many a sunless room. And Piccadilly. Driver. Can you hear me? Go round the circus. O I feel part of it now, the smiles and singing. Look at them out there. I can't get enough. And I've got to have more. I know the pubs are jammed.

This car sped in and out the streets. By tall office buildings and I picked out the little lanes and said driver down there fast to see if there's madness or breaches of morality in dark doorways. And see that door there. Stop and come in for the brandy that's in it. And now I'll go and phone them from that fancy phone booth.

"Is this you, Mac?"

"It's not Cromwell nor his mother. A letter here for you."

"Destroy it."

"From O'Keefe."

"Thank God."

"What's keeping you Danger? From reports you are laced with quids and as I've many times told you—I will not desert you now. And further in the matter of money there are lots of Americans with us tonight and I'm sure they will be glad to meet a brother in a foreign land."

"Good. I need that. Earth erupting golden udders. Clocklan's one who's seen me right."

"I've just wired the Pope to canonize him the instant his heart misses a beat. And, Danger, I bought you a kidney, a fine beef one and stuck it with garlic. Now will you get your mouth over here so's I won't have to be giving it to the likes of these other hungering creatures. They stand looking over my shoulder at the blood. I'm frying it with my best bacon fat and as you know, the fat is hard to come by. I think we have discussed that?"

"O aye, we came to the conclusion that fat was hard to come by and in particular, bacon or fat of pig. Mac, I love this life. My hands are beautiful white and exquisite to boot. I'm taking close note of my performance in front of these rich as opposed to the many poor I've known in me time. And I feel at home. And I've something to tell you in strict confidence so spread it everywhere. I know that my reedemer liveth."

"Danger, I'm really touched. I knew beneath that cold, hard exterior there beat within you a Christian heart. And I've another thing to tell you and perhaps a shock. Mary's coming tonight, and she's got a film contract."

"You're not serious."

"Jesus is my judge. She's a good looking girl, Danger. Wouldn't be past a little carnal knowledge of her meself. I think she likes you."

"I'm fond of her."

"I think you might well consider the reconciliation. With you behind her Danger, you'd both be in the films and it's the general opinion here that you'd cut a fine figure on the screen."

"I draw the line there. Now my kidney. This is very good of you, Mac. Now would you wait till you hear me coming down the steps and then plunge it toward the pan and just before it touches, turn it over and then put it on my plate?"

"Am I to assume, Danger, that you are out for blood?"

"For blood. Bye bye."

"Bye."

The walls are panelled here. And the people rich. The lyrical quality of money is strange. I better look to my fly because women are staring at me. Mary an actress. Dreadful. Pity. I've got to do something about it. I'm to blame, may have even put the idea into her dark head. If she goes to fat they'll fire her. I believe she'll screw her way to stardom. Pole by pole. Like others do to marriage. And some to poverty, fewer to riches, less for love and of course there are those who do it for a dirty old thrill. Thank God there are still some who give it up for life. Now driver, fast to the Minsk House, scene of the reincarnation.

The room was jammed. Just enough space for a foot in the door but I drove through to the smell of my cooking kidney. They wanted to look at me and I showed them, and even got up on the table for the slow dance of the moo cow.

"Percy, it's a strange house you keep in Tooting Bec and a lovely maid."

"Keep your dirty fingers away from me help. And me bloody cane. Will you look at him with me bloody cane? Keep them. And give me part of the kidney."

"Percy, you're welcome to whatever I possess in this world."

"Don't come the hound and give me the bloody kidney."

Mac with smiles brought forth the rare organ and it was set upon wildly. Dangerfield withdrew from this savagery with a raised eyebrow. Mac handed him the letter over the heads. What's the news? Look at my white cuffs. Look. And this tweed is some tweed. Clocklan said something like eighty-four shillings a yard.

Dear Hoodlum,

This ship had no ballast and we were tossed like peanuts all the way to Bermuda which for me was curtains. But the ship's crew were damn good skins and gave me enough money to get to New York grimy and broke. Now let me tell you just one thing; if you have ever entertained the idea of coming back here, no matter what your condition there, I have one word of advice. Don't. I turned on my accent full blast when I got to Boston but found little encouragement from friends. Another thing. I went out with a Radcliffe girl to see if I could finally carve out a normal sex life. My efforts met with blowing and no throwing which makes me think I need to see the coo coo doctor.

What about you? And that woman who worked in the laundry and the other one, the boarder? And tell me, how do you manage to get so much ass? What's the secret and what am I doing wrong? I'm going mad. As much as blowing is classically significant, I don't find it a substitute for the real thing and to complicate matters, I don't even know what the real thing is. Every day I walk down Brattle Street hoping some old lady will break her leg getting into her car and with my European aplomb I'll rush to her assistance and she'll say, my dear boy, aren't you sweet, won't you come and have tea with me when I get out of the hospital. But no one has so much as even tripped so far. I saw Constance Kelly too. Her face is covered with pimples. I went up to her and turned on my accent and she laughed right in my face. Jesus, I'm homesick for the ould sod. I even broke down and wept in Harvard Square with Constance and do you think she held my hand and stroked my brow? She just turned on her heel and ran.

Do me a favor. See if there are any jobs open for lavatory attendants in London and I'll come back. But in closing I want you to remember this, that this is America and we out-produce, out-sell, out-manufacture, out-fight and out-screw the rest of the world but the latter is elusive.

God bless,
Kenneth O'KEEFE
(*Absentee Duke of Serutan*)

Easy now, Kenneth. This is the way you do it. Just walk up to them and pinch them right in the arse. Ah what tender meat, baby. But if all else fails. Remember, in France they have the guillotine. Cut it off altogether. And Mac, I'm sure, would send you a false one if you ever needed it again. I spot a blonde head over there with gold spangles.

And I hear hymns. Away in a manger. Taxis collecting outside. Follow the leader. Out this hall and through the mouth behind this blonde girl. I can smell her. We're all here together, rabbit stew and dumplings.

On the street, Dangerfield approached by this shining girl.

"Excuse me, you're Mr. Dangerfield, aren't you?"

"Yes."

"Mr. MacDoon tells me you're an American. Is that right?"

"Yes."

"Well I'm an American and I'd like to go in your taxi. I think Americans ought to stick together. What are you doing over here?"

"I'm—"

"That's swell. I came here for Christmas. England's so rustic. And this taxi is quaint. Meet my friend, Osgood."

"How do you do."

"His name's Osgood Swinton Hunderington. Isn't that nice?"

"Excellent."

"Let's all ride together. My name's Dorothy Cabot. I've got a middle name, Spendergold."

"Mine's spice."

"Ha ha. Gee I'm glad we're going to ride together."

Three of them in the taxi. Past the packs of choir boys and

mothers lugging red toys. Mary with a film contract. No one can tell me about the law of contracts. And Mary I'm going to have a word with you. Running wild in London and perhaps you've put your picture up on one of those public notice boards for gentlemen to take your measurements. And I'd say they were partial to the big ones. Pumpkins. Like one I saw when Mac went into a shop to buy a tin of Australian corn beef. And that was when Mac told me about designing the brassiere. About the uplift and to get them to point out a little. To preserve the supple look and a certain degree of bounce. We agreed the bounce was extremely important in separating the real from the false. And Mary I'd say yours were nothing but the truth. And this Dorothy here has two tiny pearls hanging from her ears. Her hair a soft curve round the back of her head. And Mac I'd suggest that Dorothy here had the pear shape which you said was rare and in demand. I'll move over a little and take a look through the open coat. Just as I thought, the strapless kind. And Dorothy you've got a pretty jewel on your pale winter breast. And hairless hands. Mine are cool and joined. I've not often been a man for light hair, preferring the black, the deep, the West. But you're rich and I prefer that. But from the poor the lilies grow and roses too. I'm a fair flower.

Osgood turns to Dangerfield.

"And do you like living here, Mr. Dangerfield?"

"Very much. I think it might be said I love England."

"Well, that is a compliment you know. I hope Dorothy will come to like England as much as you do."

"But I think it's swell already."

"I'm trying to show Dorothy some places of particular interest. Perhaps you would know of something Mr. Dangerfield. I thought I got off to a rather good start in having her meet a celebrity like Mr. MacDoon. He is delightful isn't he."

"Perfectly."

"But, of course, I am, you know, a little shocked by some of his things. Gives one a bit of start the first time you know.

334

The Irish have such vitality and wit. And I do think wit is essential."

"But Osgood, he's just wonderful. I just love that little red beard of his. So cute. He'd just slay them at Goucher. He's so virile and mature."

"Where are you from in the States Miss Cabot?"

"Call me Dot. New York, but I've outgrown it. But Mommie and Daddy live upstate. We've got a house in Cornwall here but I've never been yet."

"Dot has told me a great deal about New York, Mr. Dangerfield, it sounds a most amazing place. Must be frightening living in such tall buildings."

"O nothing. Mommie and Daddy's apartment is right on the very top of one and it's just wonderful. Looks right over the river and I just love throwing rose petals down."

"Miss Cabot, or rather Dot, did you know that in New York one is not allowed to throw dead animals into public waters, or to seive, agitate or expose ashes, coal, dry sand, hair, feathers, or other substances likely to be blown about by the wind or to transport manure or like substance through the streets, unless covered so as to prevent spilling, or to throw garbage, butcher's offal, blood refuse or stinking animal into the street, or to permit any human being to use a water closet as a sleeping place. Guilty of a misdemeanor."

"Gee, I didn't know that. I never thought about that."

"I say, are you trying to be funny, Mr. Dangerfield?"

"I'm weary and fearful for future and must get a laugh."

"I don't quite understand."

"Knaves and thieves. I'm tired of drivel. Cads and benefactors and knaves. I'm tired. Let me get away."

"What are you driving at sir?"

"I can't bear any more of it. I think I am going to faint. Faint and fade. Driver stop."

"Yes, driver, do stop."

The taxi came to a halt. Dangerfield stumbling to the sidewalk. Dorothy said I mustn't leave. But the taxi pulled into the traffic again and went away. And leaning against the

335

wall of a bank. Need a bank for support. Eeeeee. Only a certain amount one can stand. Banks. I must see banks. I'm for the banks and they for me and I've got to get to the financial district of London or go crazy. Sometimes too, I think I would like to be an assistant in a pox shop but not now. Tonight I've got to see the banks.

Inside another dark taxi streaking down this Fleet Street and ahead the dome of St. Paul's. Everything dark, closed and empty down here. Along Cheapside to the Royal Exchange. This is the cheapside but I know there is wealth. Wealth alive. And all these high windows. Inside there are counters and books and ledgers collecting dust over the holidays. Driver, down that street. I see a light. Star of Bethlehem. Not a soul here save money. Let me out right here and I'll go up this alley for a pot of brandy.

Along a tiled hall into an enormous room. All men and no women. Pale faces. I know these people must work in the banks and here they are laughing and carrying on with back slapping and jokes. And there's a man at the end of the bar with a walking stick who looks the spitting image of O'Keefe. All these people so polite and contented. Boy, what a night. Holy infant so tender. And a pint of mild. Must call the party. I'll fix Mary.

Dangerfield walks along the street bound by walls big and black. On the corner, phone booths, red, bright and warm. A wind blows and whistles around the door.

"Hello?"

"May I please speak to Mr. MacDoon, the royal celt. And tell him to come quickly for I weep for home, the clatter of fangs and the green, greedy mouths. Tell him that."

"By all means, sir, do hold on."

"I am holding. I've held on to everything until I've just a vestige of dignity left. And that was a fig leaf. Hear me? Fig leaf. I'll hold on. Who knows what this is? Anyone know?"

"What for the love of the little Lord Jesus are you saying, Danger? Are you drunk? What happened? These people said you went mad in the taxi, said you were fainting."

336

"They were mean to me. Mean, Mac. I'm disappointed in the rich. Lost faith."

"Where are you?"

"In the center of the financial world."

"Now Danger, can I even credit you with knowing what night this is?"

"Tomorrow is the saviour and my Christ I'll be glad to see him."

"Now where are you?"

"Haven't I just told you I'm in the middle of the financial world? Haven't I just told you that? I want you to come down here and see for yourself, Mac. Streets are empty and as they say, not a soul. And I want you to know how it feels to be here. You understand, Mac? And there's a street called Cheapside. Now Cheapside."

"Now Danger, would you ever shut your hole for a second. Mary is here. And Danger, a lovelier girl never moved where whores fear to tread."

"Mac stop telling me lies. You're a great one for the lies to a poor unfortunate like me who has drink taken and's confused and upset over recent richness. I won't believe because seeing is and I feel the hoax is in it to get me in the clutches of the party."

"Now Danger, the general feeling here is that you're mad. And I think the nervous tension caused by quids has you afoul. But the American girl thought you were fascinating. Never met anyone like you before and she's worried lest you're molested in the streets. But Mr. Hunderington claims you were rude. Mr. Hunderington is Lord Squeak, heir to several pig sties in Kent. He says you were insulting, however. Percy turned on him and said he'd push his face in the caviar if he heard another word against you. I think we are keeping the British in their place tonight. This party is in your honor."

"Are things, then, coming to a head, Mac?"

"To a head, Danger. The size of a mountain."

"Sound the tune of reconciliation to Mary. So's I can give her the chastising of her life."

"I'll have the horsewhip ready. Now kneel down in that booth while I give ye me special yule blessing. Get down in that booth. I know you're standing, you dirty ould cheat. Get down. For Jesus, what are you doing, ripping the phone out? Repeat after me, the Lord is my shepherd as I am one of his sheared sheep."

"The Lord is my shepherd as I am one of his sheared sheep."

"Now get over here fast and I'll pave the way right into Mary's womb for ye. And you might consider this American girl. She says you're exciting."

"Mac, I've decided that I'm a titillator for sure. I'll be there. I insist upon the carpet."

He waited by the road, wet, shiny and black. A taxi roaring by. Wave it down. To the Red Lion Square. Fast.

Dangerfield steps out in front of a Georgian house. Not a sign of lights or sin or anything. Up the stone steps. And pound this knocker. Good piece of brass.

The large green door swings open and a great din. Take my hat and cane. Lovely staircase, wide and winding. Announcing me. Sebastian Balfe Dangerfield.

MacDoon hurrying over and the sound of Percy Clocklan's laughter. Gay chandeliers. I tell you I see old masters on the walls and tables squealing with repast.

"This way Danger, she's waiting in the library. You're looking well. She's expecting the rags and not the riches. And I'll have a bottle of champagne sent in to cool off your hot hearts. If things don't go well I'll serve up the Yank to you, she's panting and can't wait to tell you how wonderful you are."

"Mac, thanks from the bottom of. The banks have put a fervor in me."

The rugs were deep. A room vast and dreary. Mary's black hair over the top of the chair. Turning the pages of a magazine.

338

"How are you, Mary?"

"I thought your friend Mac was codding me that you would come."

"In the flesh. I hear that you've been posing?"

"What of it?"

"I don't like it."

"Well it's none of your business. I suppose you've forgotten what you said to me that night. You called me a whore. Told me to fuck myself and go to hell."

"Look here, Mary. I'm a little weak. I'm not up to it. That kind of talk will make me have a relapse. You look lovely tonight."

"O it's soft talk."

"It's the truth."

"And are all the other things you called me the truth too? Am I to forget those?"

"For the moment. This is the eve."

"I guess you're holy now."

"Not holy, but I've taken the eve into consideration."

"Why didn't you arrange to see me or something?"

"Needed a little time to think things over. I feel much better now. Don't I look better?"

"You may have fine clothes but you've got bags under your eyes. And there was a fuss here over what you said to that American girl in the taxi. I'm inclined to think you were rude. Exactly as you were with me."

"Cut it out. I'm not going to stand for this kind of talk. For the infant Jesus will you stop it."

"No."

"Well god damn it, another word out of you and I'll bat you in the bloody face and fix this damn film contract as well."

"You're the one who ought to shut up and get a wallop in the face. I don't want to have anything to do with the films but I thought if I could get some money I could help us. I'd do anything to help and you talk to me like this. Well bugger you, you damn bastard. I can tell you off too."

339

Sebastian's arm whistled through the air. The flat of his palm cracked against the side of her face and Mary sat stunned. He slapped her again.

"I'm going to kick the living shit out of you. Do you hear me?"

Her arms raised to ward off the blows. Mary and chair fell backwards. Dangerfield tripping over a table on top of her.

"You won't do anything to me. You can hit and hit me and I don't care. I don't care what you do but you're a bastard and will always be a bastard, always and always."

There was a silence catching breaths and a discreet knock on the door. The door opening tentatively.

"Pardon me sir, but shall I leave the champagne here?"

"Do, please."

The door closing quietly. Sound of pumping chests. Sebastian gripping her tightly by the wrists to hold the flailing nails down. Ribbons of sting. Mary glaring into his eyes. Her white wrists and fingers. She is a slimmer soft thing, where she was so fat, so strong. O slim and soft for sure.

"Get up."

"No."

"I said get up."

"No."

"Get up or I swear to Christ I'll drive your face through the floor. When I tell you to get up, get up."

"Your dirty bastard. I still say bugger you and I'll do what I want"

Mary slung back on her straight arms. White legs and knees. Pathos of her pins. I can't go on when all I really want is your white bare legs scissored around my throat, crushing out fond gasps. And I'm standing on a deep rug with books for a setting. And assault with the weapon of the flat hand.

"Up or I'll use the boot."

"I love you and look how you've treated me."

"Up or the boot."

"Why are you like this?"

"Now sit down. You're going to get off this damn stage and out of these films."

"Why shouldn't I try. I wanted to make some money because you said you wouldn't want me otherwise. You told me you'd push me out the window, tied my towel in knots and soaked my underwear in the basin and now I've got a chance to make something of myself and you don't like it either."

"I don't like the stage in any form. It's rot. I don't like it. You're coming back with me tonight."

"That's for me to say."

"Now, Mary, come back quietly with me. And tomorrow we'll go out together. Save this bottle of champagne for the morning. After the rasher and roll. Leave the stage and forget the films and we'll live in some quiet place."

"It isn't that I like it either with everyone trying to go to bed with me, men and women alike. But how can I be sure you're not going to turn on me again. I won't come back with you tonight. But I'll tell you where I live and you can come and see me in the morning. Have you ever thought of me living alone and queer men calling me up on the phone and following me through the streets? Did that occur to you?"

"There's been a special place for you in my thoughts, Mary. Very special place. Took me awhile to get over the shock. And I feel a little better now. Ready to go out in the world again. But there's been the special place for you. Am I forgiven?"

"I'll see. Take me away from this party, and take me home."

"Transgression. Been guilty of the transgression. You look lovelier than I've ever seen you before. And there's something I must tell Clocklan before we go. Pack up this champagne."

In the drawing room there were the punch bowls and tables laden with lobster. Pretty blonde worried about me. See her breasts right through that dress. MacDoon in a cluster of virgins, wand ready to bless, forgive or fertilize.

341

And Clocklan with a nurse for sure again. Always with nurses. Always with blonde hair. His maid has black and I guess he thrives on variety. And over there are some elderly ones with diamonds on their chests in lieu of the other things. Sometimes have a yen to get one of them in the bed. Old age no object. Logs in the fire. I don't believe in Christmas. A fraud. I know it's a fraud. No one noticing me. Take care of that for sure.

Sebastian sucking in his breath and roaring.

"Christmas is a fraud."

Noise echoing away and smiles crossing the faces of MacDoon and Clocklan for they knew that this was honesty night for sure. Mary waiting inside the door of the library for the worst.

"Christmas is a fraud. This room is filled with knaves and thieves. Jesus was a Celt and Judas was British."

There were grumbles shall I stop him, will we have him thrown out? Clocklan spoke up, if any man here so much as touches the fair hair of Dangerfield I will remove his jaw.

"Thank you, Percy. Now as you all know, Christmas is a fraud. Jesus was a mick and Judas a lime. I am king beast. A big muscular Yank. Hear that? I know you would all like to beat me up. O there are a lot of them would like to do that. But tonight I was in the Lombard Street to get the feel of investment. Now I have it from good sources that some of you own pig sties and I must confess that the rearing of pigs to me is extremely distasteful except at the breakfast table when it is tasteful. But I know you people have bacon hidden in your attics and beef and hides in the cellar and the best of clarets and brandies. But I'm a man for bedlam. What about bedlam? Do you ever relish the broken dish or twisted chandelier? I'm taking my host's champagne home for the morning away from you horse lovers. Bye bye now. I know you have bacon in the attic and beef and hides in the cellar."

Clocklan roaring with laughter and a tall man, the host, beaming with pleasure. O perhaps you can't beat these British after all, because they not only have it both ways but all ways. And there's no beating that ever. And Percy I have just to whisper in your ear.

"Come closer, Percy. Listen. One night I was walking behind a lovely young girl with long golden hair and my heart beating with desire. She turned around and I saw her face. She was an old toothless hag."

"Jesus, Sebastian, here's another fiver."

"Percy, I'll use it to buy meself a set of silk undergarments."

And as Dangerfield was coolly leaving the party, the butler came running after him bearing brandy and bacon. A bottle and a side. How can you beat them?

"Mary, isn't this good of him?"

"You're a terrible man."

"They've left me holding the bag. Thank you."

"Not at all, sir. The master was charmed by your little speech."

"Eee."

"I have a taxi for you, sir. I liked that very much, about Judas being British. Ha, it's very good. Merry fraud, sir."

"O. Aye."

"You're a terrible man, Sebastian."

"Merry fraud."

Entering the taxi. And standing at the door, MacDoon next to Clocklan. MacDoon eating an eclair. Clocklan's hand engages with a haunch of nurse. His other with a cigar. And from the windows I see some of the elderly and the face of that blonde American girl. I think she must be crying. Are they all weeping in there? O taxi man, away, away, away like a devil shooting between the stars. And don't be making stops for traffic either.

Mary you're beside me now. And I want to ride on the train to Dublin, along the cliffs and through the tunnels to Bray. When it's raining. You've got tiny ears. And I'll take you to live in a house out Tooting Bec way with Clocklan's quids near by for quick reference. I'll buy a little mower to take outside to the lawn and give it a fast trim every Friday.

343

not much of a lawn because I don't want to overdo this exercise. Ten by ten. We'll have a small sitting room with plants one of which will be a rubber plant. And during tea on gray afternoons I want you to read me stories of adventure.

"Why aren't you like this more often, cuddly and cozy and things?"

"I've just been thinking of a little house for us."

"And babies?"

"O aye."

"You'll give me a baby? I'd like to have one."

"I'm not father proud but that's one of the things I know I can do, Mary. I'm your man."

"And we'll make one tomorrow on Christmas Day?"

"It's Christmas now, Mary."

"No. I want you to come to me. I've got a grill. And four eggs too. And we can have the champagne and brandy after."

"I'm a shit, Mary."

"No you're not."

"Touch of meanness in me."

"I've got a present for you."

"I've nothing for you."

"You've got what I want."

"Mary, really."

"And we'll have a baby."

"Aye."

"And you won't tie my towel in knots again?"

"No knots ever again."

"You look lovely in your suit and your hat and cane. That American girl was after you too, wasn't she?"

"Just wanted a brother in a foreign land. When you're Yank, Mary, only other Yanks are friends."

"She didn't mean anything she said. She was just after your dong. But it's mine."

"For sure, Mary."

Crossing Earl's Court and down the West Cromwell Road. Up over the bridge and the wasteland of train tracks. Out there in the buildings I see dim lights on. Old brains slumbering. And on the roofs the chimney pots are awful twisted things. One of them with a fan squeaks in the Bovir Road. O for God's sake let me feel your pretty little breast, Mary. Let me feel it. Let me touch it. Saint Anthony guide. My hand. You're an awful man, Sebastian but you'll not get me hot. I know your tricks.

"Tell me what my present is, Mary."

"I bought you a pair of woolly slippers."

"Lovely, what color?"

"Brown so they won't show the dirt."

"I'll wear them tomorrow."

"And I've got new underwear and perfume called Jungle Desire and you'll think I'm an animal or something."

"I'll bring me drums, Mary."

A kiss goodbye. And back to the Bovir Road and up the stairs. Where I always feel I'm going to get a bust in the head from some prowler. Violence is forever on my mind. Get the key in this damned evasive hole. I'll run the hot water for a cheap sense of warmth and cheer the room a bit with some steam. A shilling in the meter for sure. Little comforts, little joys. Pull back the bedspread, expose the sheets. And tuck my pillow up and lay me quietly there, ready for the white sky.

31

Night wakes up. Hear the wind is blowing hard. My bed has been so warm. Shut my window, curtains trembling. My dream was all lament. But the white thin skins of new pota-toes washed up in the clay and marrows big as zeppelins hiding in the leaves and tips of willow trees. I was wearing boots in a frog pond. At the end there was a horde coming across the fields with hooks so I swam away to sea.

Rub the chill out of my hands, slap them for heat. I think a sup of my electric fire would be very cordial. Right, ripe, ready, quick like that. Hurry up the hot water to me in the pipes before I pull them out of the house altogether. To wash my face is a great relief and my teeth too. I'll not wear this underwear but get into my suit nude. When I die I want to decompose in a barrel of porter and have it served in all the pubs in Dublin. I wonder would they know it was me?

It's good to be up in the early morning, dressed and off on a journey walking. Did you say I tied your towel in knots, Mary? Did you say that? Is it true? Tell me. Is it? That they bring children down upon us by the wrath of God. For fucking.

Coming down the stairs guiding on the smooth banister, stopping in the hall to smell breakfast. Opening the door and coming out into the fierce wind where there is a weak sun in the sky. Turning up this road, a long empty gray. It's cold around my throat. I think I'm weary of my terrifying heart. But not let the cold get to it now because I must keep it hot for hours yet. Now this bridge. Curving up over the trains and their tracks. The grass down there is black. From here I can see that massive roof. And Mary, I'm on my way. I never thought I would see elegance again, like the fit crack of my cane on this bridge. Sure it was good of Percy to see me right. How are you now, Mary? Still in the bed? Or up over me

346

rashers? Toast too. Hot bowls of tea. This warehouse badly needing repair. I must stop and look through these busted grimy windows and see what is being stored away. The sun is weak, Mary. The city suffering from emptiness. Can they really all be in the houses? In there is Christmas and fire and the kids having a time with tinny toys. This is the strangest part of London being not one thing and certainly not another.

He was walking down the slope side of the bridge past this broken building, a straight dark figure and stranger. Come here till I tell you. Where is the sea high and the winds soft and moist and warm, sometimes stained with sun, with peace so wild for wishing where all is told and telling. On a winter night I heard horses on a country road, beating sparks out of the stones. I knew they were running away and would be crossing the fields where the pounding would come up into my ears. And I said they are running out to death which is with some soul and their eyes are mad and teeth out.

> God's mercy
> On the wild
> Ginger Man.